THE
THIRD
CLAW
OF GOD

AN ANDREA CORT NOVEL

ADAM-TROY CASTRO

An Imprint of HarperCollinsPublishers

This is a work of fiction. Names, characters, places, and incidents are products of the author's imagination or are used fictitiously and are not to be construed as real. Any resemblance to actual events, locales, organizations, or persons, living or dead, is entirely coincidental.

EOS
An Imprint of HarperCollins*Publishers*
10 East 53rd Street
New York, New York 10022-5299

Copyright © 2009 by Adam-Troy Castro
Cover art by Chris McGrath
ISBN 978-0-06-144373-2
www.eosbooks.com

First Eos paperback printing: March 2009

HarperCollins® and Eos® are registered trademarks of HarperCollins Publishers.

Printed in the U.S.A.

10 9 8 7 6 5 4 3 2 1

RESOUNDING ACCLAIM FOR
ADAM-TROY CASTRO'S
FIRST ANDREA CORT NOVEL,
EMISSARIES FROM THE DEAD

"T ...."
.... ein

"_E................_ .... _of_
_th_ .... A
cl.. yer

"W..._is-_
_sa_ ...._na-_
tio ...._of_
da ....o-
ne

...._us_

"A .... th
sci .... ly
co ....els
of

...._ly_

"Ad .... re
thr .... itt

By Adam-Troy Castro

The Andrea Cort Novels
EMISSARIES FROM THE DEAD
THE THIRD CLAW OF GOD

For the Ellison Nine,
who had an adventure of their very own
aboard another elevator entirely

ACKNOWLEDGMENTS

With each book I write, I ask the same pressing question. To wit: does anybody, anywhere, ever read this page if they don't have some pressing reason to expect their own names to appear? And how can casual readers know that I'm not making stuff up? Seriously, would you even have any reason to suspect that I was pulling names out of my nether regions were I to testify to the sterling example of one Gordon Mung, who lent me money, cleaned my clothes, spent six months on a cot in his garage so I could move into his bedroom and sleep beside his wife for that period, and who generally proved such a model of generosity, courage and moral rectitude that I despair at the very thought of ever living up to his standard? I gotta tell you, Gordon's an absolute saint. You want him as best friend.

That said, this book would not exist if not for my lovely wife, Judi. I must also thank Brad Aiken and my webmaster Dina Pearlman, who tolerated tuckerizations; Michael Burstein, Jack McDevitt, Jerry Oltion, Joey Green, and Rob Sawyer; the various members of the South Florida Science Fiction Society writing workshop, including Chris Negelein, Wade Brown, George Peterson, Dave Dunn, the aforementioned Brad Aiken, Cliff Dunbar, Ben Burgis, and Melinda Galy, who read and critiqued the MS in progress; good guys Stanley Schmidt, Scott Edelman, Johnny Atomic and Harlan Ellison, for other forms of support; agent extraordinaire Joshua Bilmes and editor extraordinaire Diana Gill. There are also the various regulars of my newsgroup on *www.sff.net*, who provide distraction on a daily basis. If there are any names I left out, blame the Unseen Demons. —A-TC

THE CAST

Not all of these people appear onstage in the pages that follow; in fact, many of them don't. But all are mentioned at least once. They are all given equal status here to avoid giving away the identities of any who might make unexpected entrances. To further inhibit spoilage, one is a fraud with no relevance to anything that happens in this novel, even in passing. You may assume that this personage was off somewhere, minding his or her own business or solving some other crime among the idle rich, while Andrea did her thing.

ANDREA CORT AND ASSOCIATES

ARTIS BRINGEN: Andrea Cort's long-time Dip Corps superior, no longer her boss but still a handy information source; back home at the wheelworld New London.

ANDREA CORT: Infamous child war criminal, now all grown up; Prosecutor-at-Large for the Diplomatic Corps of the Hom.Sap Confederacy, and secret defector to the alliance of software intelligences known as the AIsource, now honored guest of Hans Bettelhine.

BERNARD CORT: Andrea's father. (Deceased.)

VERONICA CORT: Andrea's mother. (Deceased.)

OSCIN PORRINYARD: Andrea's bodyguard and lover, the male half of a cylinked pair, sharing the same enhanced mind and personality.

SKYE PORRINYARD: Andrea's bodyguard and lover, the female half; like Oscin, is not to be considered a separate person but rather a separate avatar of the same composite intelligence.

The Two Known AIsource Factions

AISOURCE: Conglomeration of software intelligences, originating from several ancient civilizations predating the dawn of Mankind; secret employers of Andrea Cort and her companions, Oscin and Skye Porrinyard; tired of their immortal existence, they're seeking their own mass extinction, and have hired Andrea Cort to help them tie the noose.

UNSEEN DEMONS: Otherwise known as the rogue intelligences; the minority faction among the AIsource collective that wants to live, and is willing to commit any number of crimes to avoid the march to extinction; responsible, in some as-yet unspecified manner, for the outbreak of madness on the planet Bocai that led to the deaths of Andrea Cort's family.

Known Members of the Bettelhine Family

CAROLE (BETTELHINE): Estranged wife of Philip Bettelhine.

CONRAD (BETTELHINE): Younger brother of Kurt Bettelhine. (Deceased.)

HANS BETTELHINE: Current patriarch of the Bettelhine Munitions Corporation.

JASON BETTELHINE: Son of Hans Bettelhine; full brother to Jelaine, half brother to Philip.

JELAINE BETTELHINE: Daughter of Hans Bettelhine; full sister to Jason, half sister to Philip.

KURT BETTELHINE: Father of Hans Bettelhine. (Deceased.)

LILLIAN JANE BETTELHINE: Sister of Hans Bettelhine. (Deceased.)

MAGNUS BETTELHINE: Younger brother of Hans Bettelhine.

MELINDA BETTELHINE: Bettelhine cousin. (Unknown lineage and current status.)

PHILIP BETTELHINE: Son of Hans Bettelhine; half brother to Jason and Jelaine.

KNOWN BETTELHINE CORPORATION EMPLOYEES

MONDAY BROWN: Personal aide to Hans Bettelhine.

ERIK DESCANSEN: Bettelhine employee; fiancé to Colette Wilson.

JOY (LAST NAME UNKNOWN): Bettelhine employee; "best friend."

DINA PEARLMAN: Bettelhine employee; wife to Farley.

FARLEY PEARLMAN: Bettelhine employee; husband to Dina.

ANTREC PESCZIUWICZ: Security Chief of Layabout, the orbital terminal of Xana's space elevator.

VERNON WETHERS: Personal aide to Philip Bettelhine.

THE CREW OF THE BETTELHINE ROYAL CARRIAGE

LOYAL JECK: Steward aboard the Bettelhine Royal Carriage.

ARTURO MENDEZ: Chief Steward aboard the Bettelhine Royal Carriage.

PAAKTH-DOY: Human woman raised by alien race, the

Riirgaans; currently temporary steward aboard the Bettelhine Royal Carriage.

COLETTE WILSON: Bartender aboard the Bettelhine Royal Carriage.

KNOWN CRIMINALS

PETER MAGRISON: "The Beast Magrison," infamous terrorist, wanted for crimes against humanity.

VEYS NAAIAA: Bocaian assassin.

KARL NIMMITZ: Retired thief; current husband of Dejah Shapiro.

SHAARPAS THARR: Bocaian assassin.

ERNST VOSSOFF: Multiple convictions; ex-husband of Dejah Shapiro.

MISCELLANEOUS

BARD DAIKEN: Debt Arbitration Specialist, Dip Corps, missing in action.

JANE ELLERY: Determined amateur.

HARILLE (last name unknown): Homeless runaway.

THE KHAAJIIR: Bocaian scholar; personal guest of Hans Bettelhine.

NEKI ROM: Bursteeni tourist.

DEJAH SHAPIRO: Long-time enemy of the Bettelhines; tycoon with vast fortune based on sound investments and habitat construction; personal guest of Hans Bettelhine; wife to Karl Nimmitz.

THE
THIRD
CLAW
OF GOD

PROLOGUE

ater, much later, after I died, I tried to remember why.

There was all the death and pain I'd come from: neighbors turned to savages, tearing their one-time friends to pieces with bare hands and bared teeth. I'd seen my mother murdered, seen my friends torn apart; seen my own hands red and glistening from the lifeblood of a sentient I'd loved as much as my own father. I'd been eight then, but however many years I placed between myself and those horrors, however many steps I took toward a redemption I was not sure I deserved, that long night had always remained with me, and was always an eloquent argument in favor of the worst anybody could ever decide to do to me.

But that was not why I'd died.

It was cold where I was. My throat burned, but not with thirst. It felt raw, like I'd swallowed fire. It was agony, but I welcomed it, because it was the only part of me that felt anything except the vague impression that I deserved much worse. I'd done so many bad things. I'd killed in anger. I'd sold my loyalty to forces inimical to humanity. I'd shown my true face to the only person since my parents who had ever cared for me, revealing before one of my love's two beautiful faces a potential for cruelty that had transformed everything s/he felt for me to pity and revulsion.

But even that was not why I'd died. It was why I'd deserved to die.

I remembered a corpse stewing in blood and worse, a monster even more terrible than myself telling me she'd seen in me a kindred spirit, another mind so damaged by the forces that had twisted it beyond recognition that it was left with no other choice but murder.

But even those were not the reasons I'd died. Those were just the things I'd seen in the hours before death.

How had I died?

I remembered drifting in airless space, high above a beautiful blue-green world. I was in a space suit, but my heart was pounding and my breath was arriving in ragged gasps. I'd seen several people die tonight, but they were behind me; now I was alone but for the hundreds of guns leveled against me on all sides, and a course that could either carry me deeper into the vacuum or down into the fiery embrace of reentry. I'd screamed and received no answer; begged and received no pity.

There was no possibility of rescue. Orders had been given, and they were orders that could not be questioned or defied.

A stabbing pain in my chest, followed by another and another, and my air exploded outward. My blood crystallized and boiled, even as I watched, drifting away like scarlet, smoky confetti. My throat and my lungs burned. I tried to scream but there was no air to scream with, nobody to scream for.

That's how and where and when I died.

But I could not remember why . . .

1

ASSASSINS

Hans Bettelhine may have been an infamous merchant of death, whose munitions empire was even now fueling slaughter on a hundred human worlds, but I had to be fair: it was for precisely that reason that I wouldn't blame him for today's attempt on my life.

Bettelhine would not have invited me all the way to his home system just to have a couple of incompetent assassins ambush me in his spaceport. Had he wanted me dead all that badly he knew my address, and could have nuked it on a whim or, given the preference for a more surgical strike, sent semi-intelligent flechette drones into New London to hunt me down and vivisect me in my sleep. Juje alone knew that he was supposed to have done stuff like that before.

Still, there was no denying that his headquarters world, Xana, set an entirely new record for the shortest interval between my arrival at a place I've never been and the very first attempt on my life there.

I'm talking about minutes. Minutes.

It happened before I took my first step onto its planetary

soil, even before Bettelhine should have known that my transport had arrived at its main orbital terminal, Layabout.

The Porrinyards and I were walking through the concourse off Layabout's main docking facilities, an array of liquor stores, restaurants, boutiques, gift shops, and even brothel booths where bored execs waiting for their passages offworld could spend a few minutes being brought to multiple orgasms by pulsed sonics. Strolling to the elevator dock, where we'd been assured a berth on the private car normally reserved for Bettelhine use, I counted four sentient species, not counting human beings, among the travelers waiting for their ride to the planetary surface or for their transports to other systems. There was at least one I didn't recognize, who to my eyes looked a little like a terrestrial donkey—after that donkey had been burned with a blowtorch and then explosively decompressed. All of this would have provided more than enough distraction, after all those weeks in Intersleep, were I not also arguing politics with the Porrinyards, an exercise that amounts to being outnumbered even when only one of them is talking.

A pair of striking physical paragons, one male and one female, each with wise eyes, kind smiles, and stubbly silvery hair, Oscin and Skye Porrinyard have one supersized composite mind between them and often champion ridiculous points just to twist me into rhetorical knots.

The first of the assassins stood up the second that Oscin and I came into view at the far end of the concourse, but there was still no reason to believe that his aimless stroll away from the seats and into the area of greatest foot traffic was intended to end with me bleeding my life out onto the cold permaplastic of the terminal floor. He was even easy to mistake as human. Bocaians made many of the same evolutionary choices as human beings. You wouldn't ever mistake a member of one race for the other on close examination, but their basic outlines are almost identical, the most prominent difference when clothed being the bumpy Bocaian ear and the oversized Bocaian eyes. Any Bocaian dedicated to killing me, as most Bocaians are, can therefore get well within striking distance before being recognized for what he is.

This one began to pick up speed as Oscin and I passed by, still lost in our ridiculous argument. His path paralleled ours, but there was still no obvious reason to think that suspicious in a bustling place like Layabout.

Even as he stuck his hand into his jacket pocket and retrieved a featureless disk backed with a metallic loop designed to bind it to the palm of his hand, there was no reason to suspect him of murderous intent.

Not even as he came up from behind and reached for the back of my neck.

Traveling by myself, I would have been dead.

But that's why I always have one Porrinyard walk ten paces behind me in public.

Oscin said, "Oh, dear."

By the time I turned to question him he had already pivoted on his heels and seized the Bocaian by the forearm.

Oscin wasn't the one who'd seen the Bocaian's approach. Skye had. But he was privy to everything she was privy to, and so he was ready the instant she was.

She caught up a second later, her smaller hands seizing the Bocaian farther down his arm. Her grip and Oscin's was enough to halt the Bocaian's lunge before the disk came anywhere near my skin.

All of this happened before I completed my turn.

Next to the Porrinyards I'm a turtle on neural dampeners.

The first I actually saw of the fight, when my pivot was completed, was Oscin and Skye using the Bocaian's own struggles to force him to his knees.

Then I heard a familiar cold voice in my head. *Counselor: Five o'clock.*

I whirled again and caught a glimpse of another hate-filled Bocaian face, as its owner charged me from the opposite side of the walkway.

This one was older and taller than the first: a full head taller than I, with a reach that put me at a disadvantage. He must have been watching his friend's attempt from cover before using the confusion caused by the first charge to initiate his own.

I didn't see a weapon. But I didn't have a weapon, either. My satchel had several interesting items that only somebody with Diplomatic credentials can get through customs, but I didn't have the time or the space to access anything that could possibly be of use now.

That was all right.

There was a bulkhead some ten paces behind me.

I grabbed the second Bocaian by his shoulders and spun, adding my own momentum to his. We ran the last meter or so together. I tripped him at the point of no return. There was a very satisfying crunch as he hit the bulkhead face-first. Before he could fall, and possibly rise again, I drove my knee into the small of his back, a place every bit as vulnerable on a Bocaian as it is on a human being.

He managed to turn and wrap his arms around my legs, as much to support himself as to maintain hold of his hated enemy. A keening moan, halfway to a howl, exploded from him, carrying with it a level of pain he might have borne his entire life. I shoved him away. He fell back and curled into a ball, his low moan continuing. Bocaians do not have tear ducts and do not cry as human beings do, but that sound transcended species. I knew. I'd made sounds very much like it myself, on the world that had given me both life and reputation. On Bocai.

I asked him, "What's your name?"

He coughed out a word, along with a pair of tooth fragments.

It was not one I knew. "Are you alone?"

He gasped, and then something happened to his eyes: they strobed, bright enough to leave purple afterimages on my retinas. By the time I blinked away the blindness, his expression had gone blank.

Crap.

There were microteemers behind his eyelids. The flash, triggered by him or some confederate I couldn't see, was a packed visual impulse capable of overloading his brain with a single preprogrammed image, intense enough to occupy every neural function but the autonomic. Yelling at him, or shaking him, or trying to wake him up in any way would do no good. He'd be catatonic for days.

I'd been teemed a few times myself, most recently as one of dozens put down by New London police, when I'd chosen the wrong moment to try to get to the other side of a political demonstration turned riot. The next thing I knew it was five days later and my head was cottony from clearing away the fractals.

I looked for the Porrinyards and was not surprised to see that the Bocaian they'd disarmed and cuffed had also gone limp. I didn't bother asking if they were all right. Of course they were all right. They were the Porrinyards. "Did that bastard just teem himself?"

"Yes," they said in perfect unison. "And wet himself too. I'm going to need a washroom."

"What was that weapon?"

"Something interesting. I suggest that wait until after we're debriefed by Security."

I scanned the concourse and, behind all the startled human faces and sometimes unreadable alien ones, saw a dozen armed security officers running toward us. Even from a distance I could tell that they were armed with all the usual weapons approved for orbital environments including widespread teem emitters of their very own. A half dozen minicams, insectile in both size and maneuverability, already circled us, assessing the situation and transmitting it to the tactical forces still too far away to risk taking out the innocent in the crossfire.

Given the calibre of the materiel the Bettelhine Munitions Corporation willingly sold to the festering offworld conflicts that were the Family's chief clientele, there was no way of telling what obscenities they reserved for use on their own territory.

Even if teemers were the extent of it, I did not want to spend the next few days wearing a vacant look at my face while drones fed me and wiped my ass. Nor did I want to see whatever all-consuming image they'd chosen to imprint upon my consciousness. Given a choice, security forces rarely shackle your mind to anything pleasant.

I fell to my knees, placed my hands against the back of my head, and allowed the guards to surround me. The Porrinyards did the same.

So far I wasn't enjoying Xana very much at all.

Reading my expression, the Porrinyards counseled, "You know what they say, Andrea. Never judge a world by its spaceport . . ."

My full name is Andrea Cort.

My official job title, following a recent surprise promotion that my superiors in the Dip Corps had nothing to do with, is Prosecutor-at-Large, Judge Advocate's Office, Diplomatic Corps, Hom.Sap Confederacy.

It's a good thing I don't always have to say that whole thing with teemers pointed at my head. I might stumble somewhere around the sixth or seventh syllable.

The Prosecutor-at-Large part means that nobody, up to and including the President of the Confederacy, ever tells me where to go. I make my own agenda, enjoying an access known only to internal heads of state.

The promotion came as a great surprise to an upper management that had, up to that point, considered me the most disposable of all their fully owned commodities.

Back home in New London, the corridors of power still boiled with speculation over what strings I'd pulled to finagle myself such independence.

The truth was that the orders, issued to them and as far as they knew from among them, were in fact excellent forgeries provided by another civilization entirely. They were creations of the ancient software intelligences known as the AIsource, who had enlisted my help in their civil war with their own internal enemies, known to the AIsource as the Rogue Intelligences and to myself, for personal reasons, as Unseen Demons.

My secret defection amounted to exchanging one set of masters for another, but I'd not yet worked out just what my increased autonomy within Hom.Sap circles was going to cost. The ground beneath my feet was still less than solid. But my credentials were, and they mollified the local cannon fodder and swept us past the third and second levels of management to the office of Layabout's Chief of Intelligence, one Colonel Antresc Pescziuwicz.

Pescziuwicz affected a shaved head, monocle, and a mustache of sufficient bushiness to render both upper and lower lips a matter of conjecture. His office was a construct of polished dark wood and ancient edged weapons displayed complete with the flags of the nations that had used them to spill entrails onto battlefield earth. It was the kind of display only an asshole, a historian, or a warrior could have felt at home in; not that those had ever been, or now were, incompatible subsets.

By the time the witnesses confirmed that we'd acted in self-defense, the colonel's mustache bristles were foaming. He dismissed the guards and stared at me through eyes that roundly damned me for bringing such a nightmare into his working day. "You know, I'm not all that fond of Confederate types. I consider you a bunch of arrogant, self-righteous, and impotent frauds."

I refused to be baited. "It's not the most inaccurate assessment I've ever heard."

He continued: "Under normal circumstances I'd lock the three of you up on general principles and damn the diplomatic shitstorm. But I see that you're an honored guest and that I'm obliged to extend you every possible courtesy."

"I must say, you're doing an excellent job so far."

A grunt. "I can't interrogate those wogs we're holding, because my teem specialists say that they'll both be drooling and incontinent for a week. But I have you. Is there any reason they'd be so all-fired anxious to paint a target on your back?"

I came within one firing neuron of telling him to just go look it up, but the Porrinyards had been working on improving my own basic courtesy. "Their race considers me a war criminal."

He didn't blink. "Do they have a case?"

There was no point in being shy. "When I was eight years old, Mercantile, my family lived in an experimental utopian community with Bocaians as neighbors."

His eyebrows knit. "And what was the bloody point of that?"

"That the two races could live together in peace."

"Was there ever war between humans and Bocaians?"

"No."

"Even any serious disputes?"

"No."

"Then why would anybody think that an argument worth making?"

I coughed. "I never said it was a *radical* Utopian community."

The truth, as far as I know it, was simply that my parents and their friends liked Bocaians, and considered them a fine people to live with. Until I was eight, I believed the same thing. Still do, for what that's worth, even if I'm now under a death sentence there.

He asked, "So what happened?"

It took a while to tell, but this was the sense of it. After years of living together in peace, sharing each others' possessions, and helping to raise each others' children, the Bocaians and human beings of our little community had gone after one another without any discernable provocation, tearing each other to pieces with weapons that included their bare hands and bared teeth. Most reasonable authorities believe the mass insanity to have been some kind of environmental influence, and explain me in particular by saying that I was too young to exercise restraint when nobody else was. But the incident's become a political issue among some of the alien races who would use it to attack human interests. Bocaians, in particular, seized on a famous news holo taken of the evacuees, which focused on me as a traumatized little girl covered with blood, and elected me the symbolic face of the atrocity.

They were not happy when I turned up, many years later, working for the Dip Corps.

I concluded the story with, "There's a bounty on my head."

Pescziuwicz ran his fingertip along his mustache. "How much?"

"I don't know. I haven't checked the exchange rates lately."

"I have," the Porrinyards said.

Of course they had. "Going up or down?"

"Up," they said.

I gave them an irritated look.

They grinned identical grins. "We're not tempted."

Pescziuwicz winced at them. "Do me a favor, you two? I don't care what kind of unnatural procedure you had, to make you talk at the same time like that, but please take turns. For as long as you're in my office. You're driving me crazy."

"As you wish," Skye said alone.

Pescziuwicz fiddled with some virtual interface visible only to him and called up a holo of the Bocaian I'd taken down. "First pair of these wogs I've ever seen on this station."

"They don't like to travel," I said.

"Stay-at-home types, huh?"

"Not just stay-at-home, but stay-by-themselves. They have little interest in interspecies diplomacy. Most never even learn to speak Mercantile. The ones we lived with were considered peculiar for wanting to settle alongside human beings, and even they had trouble learning a tongue other than their own. The race doesn't retain the ability to learn additional languages much past puberty, and are pretty bad at learning offworld languages at any age. If you ever get around to interrogating these two, you might need to find yourself a translator."

"Annnnh, that's going to be a headache." He tented his fingertips. "But the point is, these two weren't just random tourists just passing through this station who saw the famous war criminal by chance and decided, on the spur of the moment, to take advantage of this once-in-a-lifetime coincidence and do the patriotic thing."

"I would assume not."

"They were waiting for you."

"Looks that way."

He let the moment linger. "I don't like you, Counselor."

I shrugged. "I don't particularly care."

He glanced at the disk the Porrinyards had taken off the first Bocaian, which was now floating in a levitation field, safe from any clumsy hands capable of accidentally activating it. "Got any idea what this is?"

Oscin spoke alone. "It's called a" (insert noise that sounded like a pair of Tchi suffering from joint digestive disturbance). "Mercantile translation: Claw of God. It's a K'cenhowten weapon invented almost sixteen millennia ago. The oppressive theocracy in power at the time used it for the ceremonial execution of heretics. I wouldn't have recognized it myself, were it not for a short tour of duty to our embassy at a K'cenhowten holding where one was kept on display. Prior to this I would have assumed no working models existed outside of museums and private collections."

For some reason the Porrinyards assigned the punchline to Skye. "They're very valuable."

"That's good to hear," I said. "The day I'm successfully assassinated, I don't want anybody to say I cost pennies."

Skye said, "Little chance of that here. There were never more than a hundred Claws of God in existence. There are supposed to be less than twenty still extant. I suppose we'll need to contact the experts and get the precise numbers, to see if we can trace this one's provenance."

"Is that even necessary?" Pescziuwicz asked. "It's just a machine, like any other machine. My bosses could figure out the basic specs in half an hour. What's to stop anybody from building one today?"

Oscin took over. "In practical terms, nothing. But determining the authenticity of this one seems a natural first step."

"Why?"

"If a genuine antiquity, it's worth considerably more than the bounty on Counselor's head. The sponsors of these assassins would be losing money on the deal. If a contemporary artifact, then somebody's gone to an equal amount of trouble duplicating an obscure weapon for, we can assume, symbolic reasons. Either way, determining its age would help us determine what the assassins were thinking . . . or what kind of resources their employers, if any, brought to the table."

Under the circumstances, I knew I'd regret asking the next question. "What would it have done to me?"

Skye's softer voice matched Oscin's measured cadence. "Once activated in close quarters, it produces an intense localized harmonic capable of liquefying an enemy's organs without disturbing the skin. Your brain would have remained functional over the next four minutes or so, or however long it took your entire digestive system to seep out your bladder and anus."

This was nasty even by the standards of our present hosts. Bettelhine factories had produced poisons and bombs and energy weapons capable of sterilizing entire planetary hemispheres, but the Claw was horror on a smaller scale, nasty even to the employees of an enterprise whose products had so often set new standards of genocidal efficiency. The Claw did not sound like something they would have built. It was too . . . intimate.

The room fell silent long enough for me and Pescziuwicz to enjoy all the appetizing sights and sounds conjured by our respective imaginations.

I said, "It does sound like an efficient way to lose weight."

Pescziuwicz's head swiveled. "Am I supposed to be amused?"

"No, sir."

"Let me count the reasons I'm not." Pescziuwicz ticked off points on his fingertips. "First, a Dip Corps priority transport arrives at my station without any advance word. Which is fine; the Big Man has his fingers in a lot of pies, and he's under no obligation to keep me apprised of everything. It's just one of the many things that keeps my job interesting. But second, the dignitary aboard turns out to carry her own personal set of concentric red circles tattooed on her back. That's a little bit less than fine. Not that drawing moral judgments is within my job description, but I would have liked to know that there could be safety concerns aboard my station. Still, I'll let that one pass. I'll also overlook this pair of mynah birds you have working for you; I don't even wanna know what their story is. We get to third. You're an honored guest, which means this little errand of yours is bigger than I even wanna think about, and nobody ever got around to tell me that it came with her own personal security issue. Fourth. These suckers who *don't travel* were here *waiting for you, at the precise time of your arrival,* armed with some obscure K'cenhowten gizmo from *sixteen thousand years ago,* a weapon that's *almost impossible to obtain,* a weapon that even if new indicates that somebody's gone fanatic somewhere. That's so far from *Fine* that it leaves *Fine* back home with the goldfish, because any reasonable respect for the logistics of this particular assassination attempt assures that the not-inconsiderable process of getting all of those pieces into position had to be well under way by the time you three even boarded your transport back on New London. Put that all together, in one portable package with a pretty red bow, and I can only note that we've just seen a security breach of pretty fucking historical proportions."

I remained calm. "Yes, but whose?"

"What's that supposed to mean?"

"My Dip Corps liaison, Artis Bringen, passed Mr. Bettelhine's invitation on to me within an hour of receiving it himself. My associates and I departed New London within twelve hours of that. We've spent most of the months since then in bluegel, with our drive set to full acceleration. Any conspiracy against my life originating from a security breach at New London, or from anywhere else outside this system, would have had to find out about my itinerary, made its own travel arrangements, depart, and then somehow beat me here in time to spring the trap with Claw of God in hand, an accomplishment that depends on so many nested miracles that we can assume the security breach, and the provision of that Claw, took place here, at some point between Mr. Bettelhine's decision to invite me and that invitation being sent to my associates back home."

That shut him down. "That's it? Good night and good luck?"

"I'm afraid it has to be, sir. My companions and I are here for a specific purpose, involving the interests of your employer, Hans Bettelhine. We have traveled a great distance to be here, at his personal request, and we need to hurry down to Xana and begin addressing his issues right away. We do not have the time, or the resources, to devote full attention to the investigation into this matter. But your own duties do include working with Bettelhine and Confederate law enforcement to gather data on the activities of individuals who would engage in criminal activity aboard this station. So we might as well get out of your way so you can get started."

Pescziuwicz's mouth opened, then closed, then opened, then closed. He appealed to Oscin. "Is she always like this?"

"No," Oscin mourned. "She's being concise today."

Pescziuwicz might have exploded then, were it not for the interruption: a signal, unseen and unheard by us that nevertheless commanded his full attention as he warned us to silence with a single index finger, held upright. His Adam's apple bobbed up and down, reflecting his own subvocalized responses. His manner grew heated, then disbelieving. He glanced at me, then closed his eyes, substantial tension visible in the throb of his temple and the set of his jaw. "That was the boss. The big boss."

Hans Bettelhine. Might as well say *Genghis Khan* or *Vlad Dracul* or *Adolf Hitler* or *Peter Magrison*. Any characterization of myself as a monster had him as instant rebuttal: *You think I'm bad? Look at him.* "Yes."

"It's his planet. His laws. I can't help it if he wants you released into his custody."

"But," I provided.

He folded his arms. "A cautionary tale. A few years ago, your corps sent an unfortunate young man named Bard Daiken to appeal the terms of a debt incurred by a world we don't need to talk about right now. The member of the Bettelhine Inner Family handling the negotiation is a reasonable man and had no problem negotiating an equitable settlement, but Daiken imagined himself a ball of fire and wanted total debt forgiveness. He wanted to do even better than the terms his superiors had set for him, better in fact than the terms any self-respecting person could be expected to accept. Even then, Mr. Daiken was safe. An agreement could have been reached, eventually, but Daiken exerted certain pressures on Mr. Bettelhine's negotiators that Mr. Bettelhine considered criminal."

"Were they criminal, Mr. Pescziuwicz?"

"Just asking the question proves you miss the point. Xana may do business with the Confederacy, but we've never been a member world. This is an independent fiefdom, a kingdom unto itself. The Bettelhine Family determines what is criminal here, and it determines how to prosecute those who think they can challenge their law." He shifted position in his chair and went on. "Ninety-nine point nine nine whatever nine percent of the time, this is not a problem, for us or for our visitors. But then we run into that fraction of one percent, usually in the person of arrogant visiting dignitaries who think they can do or say anything and still trust in their own diplomatic immunity to protect them. I've had enough exposure to your personality to warn you that attitude alone didn't help Daiken."

Even asking the next question was a sign of weakness,

but I could afford it. "What did you do? Torture him? Kill him?"

Pescziuwicz showed teeth. "Local fashions go in and out of style. But if you ask me, what happened to him was worse than both those options— This was a warning, Counselor. Not a threat. I hope you have a productive stay."

Not a *nice* stay, I noted. I nodded and rose to my feet, aware without looking that the Porrinyards had also risen behind me, reading my mood with an accuracy that could not have been improved even if my mind had become a third, wired into theirs. Then I hesitated. "You need to issue an alert. There's a third assassin still at large."

His spine turned to iron. "Oh, really."

"Yes, sir. I don't know if he's still on Layabout, but if you move quickly and shut down the elevators, you might be able to catch him before he escapes."

"Did you see this individual? Or are you just guessing?"

Behind me, the Porrinyards moaned as one, either forgetting or ignoring Pescziuwicz's distaste for simultaneous speech. "Please. Don't ever accuse her of guessing."

I merely turned my trademark chill a couple of degrees colder. "I never guess."

Pescziuwicz was not impressed. "Go ahead."

"Equipping two conspirators with one handheld weapon amounts to the waste of a perfectly good assassin. Under normal circumstances, one would expect the other to carry something of equivalent lethality. Empty hands suggest a certain imbecilic quality of planning that I would not credit to anybody capable of obtaining this Claw of God thing."

He regarded me with a certain wary respect. "Agreed."

"Even assuming for some reason that they could only obtain one weapon of that kind, why would the assassin without the exotic weapon be without *any* kind of weapon? By any measurement, it's just poor planning."

Pescziuwicz's smile, now broad enough to escape the cover of his mustache, was much easier to read as pure appreciation. "What are we missing, Counselor?"

"The safest course is to assume that they planned better than we believe, that there were weapons on both sides of that concourse, and that the other one was no longer available by the time I showed up. We must further assume that it became unavailable only a short time before my arrival, as there had not been enough time to replace it. My guess? He'd needed to get rid of it in a hurry. And there are a couple of possible explanations for this, chief among them the fear on his part that he'd somehow revealed himself to your Security forces and therefore needed to discard the evidence. But since none of your security people have reported giving these two any special attention, we're forced to another explanation.

"That's where the third assassin comes in.

"Imagine a spotter, not involved in the planned attack. The only possible reason one of these two would put a weapon in his hands, and leave himself empty-handed, would be the sudden appearance of a target they hadn't expected to see, somebody they wanted dead even more than they wanted me dead, somebody this third party needed to start chasing.

"I suspect that you're running out of time to save whomever he wants to kill."

Silence filled the air between us.

I saw Pescziuwicz trying to find some flaw in my reasoning, and perceived the moment of resignation when he knew that he could not. His throat muscles moved as he commenced subvocalizing again.

The corridor outside his office began to shake with the sound of pounding feet.

2

ROYAL CARRIAGE

The Security shutdown of Layabout inconvenienced thousands of travelers that day, a number of whom complained at great length while Pescziuwicz tasked all the men and machines at his command to finding my hypothetical third assassin.

There were additional baggage inspections, random passengers pulled out of line for special interrogation, even one or two body-cavity searches of travelers who'd asked that indignant question, "Do you know who I am?"

(*Yes, we know who you are. You're somebody not nearly as important as you think you are. We will now demonstrate this you in terms that will calibrate your self-image to its proper level, once and for all. Please bend over. This will hurt.*)

Since four elevator cars had already departed Layabout for the planetary surface between the attempt on my life and the precautionary shutdown of the station, additional security was called to the dirtside terminal, Anchor Point, and ordered to take all passengers into custody upon their arrival. This measure would lead to the temporary detention of hundreds more, most of whom were going to be irate indeed when they discovered that their respective positions among Bettelhine's work force and clientele were not sufficient to declare them above suspicion.

The third assassin, if there was one, remained absent. Pescziuwicz connected the two Bocaians we knew about to the *Grace*, a passenger liner of Bursteeni registry that had arrived at Layabout only ten hours before I did. But he'd failed to evidence any special interactions between the Bocaians and other passengers. Nor had they interacted, in any special way, with anybody except for a couple of food vendors, in the hours they'd waited for me.

We knew the names on their travel documents. The Porrinyards had saved me from Veys Naaiaa, and I'd taken down one Shaarpas Tharr. Even with their every move in the terminal recorded by security monitors, it would likely take months to collate their movements to those of every other civilian passing through at the same time. By then the potential suspect pool, both potential assassin and potential target, would be distributed across the length and breadth of Xana's two habitable continents, as well as occupying berths on more than a dozen vessels headed for destinations throughout civilized space.

None of the searches turned up any more Claws of God, or any more Bocaians. Travelers passing through Layabout at the time did include races from Humanity to Tchi, Bursteeni, Riirgaan, K'cenhowten, Cid, and Mundt, only some of those who might have harbored high moral dudgeon over a crime committed against the relatively obscure Bocaians. Special attention was paid to K'cenhowten, whose race had provided the exotic weapon, and the Bursteeni, since it was one of their vessels responsible for carrying the two acknowledged assassins here. But even that felt like a formality undertaken for due diligence and no other reason. Pescziuwicz wasn't about to prove anything in the minimal time his people had to clear and release hundreds of travelers and almost as many station employees.

At one point during the two hours it took Pescziuwicz to surrender to the increasing pressure from the surface and release us as the first group of travelers cleared for transport, I broke down and asked, *You wouldn't be in the mood to just break down and tell me, would you?*

The AIsource interface in my head didn't always respond to direct questions, but was voluble today. *We're sorry, Andrea. Your usefulness to us is limited if we hand-walk you through every dangerous situation. Just warning you about the attack from behind was controversial enough among our kind. Those handling your case debated it at length and with considerable rancor over a period equivalent to several years to our perception before deciding to err on the side of good employee relations.*

Since their thought processes were more or less instantaneous, on human terms, that controversy may have occupied as much as a fraction of a second, real time. *Is it safe to assume that I'm not done with this business?*

We can neither confirm nor deny.

Can you at least tell me whether the Unseen Demons are involved?

They are always nearby, much as we are always nearby. But of their input into the current business, the present rules of engagement prohibit the release of that information. We can neither confirm nor deny.

Once again, my part in the war between the AIsource majority and the so-called Unseen Demons felt too capricious for any facile comparisons to a pawn in a game of chess. *You're the ones who urged me to accept this bullshit invitation. What can you tell me?*

A moment's hesitation. I knew it was meaningless, given their computation speed, but such pauses seemed to be built into their communication paradigm, indicating for my benefit those moments when my questions had required special consideration. *Your next few days will be very difficult.*

How?

You will soon find yourself faced with the most contradictory impulses of sentient behavior: treason in the name of loyalty, betrayal in the name of love, tyranny in the name of freedom, corruption in the hearts of those who believe themselves driven by the purest motives. This assassination attempt should be taken as no more than a side issue, but we can warn you that it will not be the last you experience before we are done with this business. Nor will it be the last development that involves you, personally. Some of us feel we should fear for your capacity to absorb trauma. We hope you'll survive the shock.

Thanks a lot.

I was really looking forward to fulfilling the terms of my contract with them, which happened to be finding a way to put all of them, AIsource and Unseen Demon alike, out of their immortal misery.

This was the essential nature of the war between the two factions. The AIsource had lost all interest in life and wanted to die. The Unseen Demons among their collective wanted no part of their planned mass suicide. I'd joined the AIsource side because the Unseen Demons had admitted causing the massacre at Bocai. I still didn't know what subtle switch they'd pulled or what advantage they thought they'd gained in doing such a terrible thing to us. But I wanted both sides gone and humanity freed from their machinations.

I wanted it so much that I'd come here, to this place run by merchants of death.

I hytexed my liaison Artis Bringen for information about the missing Bard Daiken, and was just finishing that when Pescziuwicz returned, looking like a man whose birthday party had ended with too many tears and not enough cake.

"Your hypothetical third assassin hasn't materialized. Nor have any additional Claws of God. We're left with hundreds of angry travelers and no reason to suspect a deeper conspiracy."

"You're missing something."

"Maybe. But if so, it's something I haven't found by turning this entire station into a transportation bottleneck that's going to play hell with our arrival and departure schedules for days. You'll forgive me if I refrain from trying to make that '*weeks.*' It's gonna take another couple of hours before anybody gets out of here as it is."

I nodded. "I understand, sir. Just as I hope you'll understand that I'm stating hard truth, not giving you a hard time, when I point out that this matter will likely end some time very soon with one of those Claws of God being used on its intended victim, and the blame falling back on you for not doubling or tripling your investigation time."

The tightening of his jaw muscles confirmed that this possibility had already been weighing on him. "My career will just have to survive it. In the meantime, the Boss has ordered me to make sure that the three of you get wherever you're going."

"Thank you."

"By that he meant *down to Xana.* But he left that unspoken, so I have room to ask you if that's what you really want. I won't stop you from returning to your transport and heading back home, or to any other out-system destination, if that's what it takes to get you out of danger." He hesitated. "Your business aside, that happens to be what I recommend. Nobody's personal security can protect you from an assassin who doesn't mind giving up his own life, or the lives of innocents, in the attempt."

It was well-meaning advice. Too bad I couldn't follow it. "We didn't travel this far just to leave without finding out what Mr. Bettelhine wants from me."

He nodded. "I know. Your escort should arrive in a moment."

He subvocalized again, admitting to his office four of his security men and a fifth individual impossible to mistake for one of them. He was a man in his mid-thirties, with shiny black hair, a twig of a mustache, and big brown eyes that so dominated the rest of his face that they might not have changed proportion since his last stages in utero. His own uniform included among its many jarring elements fringed epaulets, a red-ribbon sash bisecting his ramrod-straight posture from right shoulder to left hip, and shoes so polished that they qualified as an additional light source. One look at him and I knew he had to be a servant of some kind. Only rich assholes would force employees to wear anything that ridiculous.

"This is Arturo Mendez," Pescziuwicz said. "He's the Head Steward aboard the Royal Carriage. He'll see that you're comfortable."

The Porrinyards were as dumbfounded as I'd ever seen them.

I said, "The *what*?"

We had been promised a ride in Bettelhine's private elevator car. We hadn't known that there was anything royal about it.

But the Royal Carriage, its local nickname, was just that. One of a matched pair held in dry dock at the two endpoints of the cable linking Layabout to Anchor Point, the terminus on the planetary surface, it was installed on the cable only when members of the Bettelhine Family, or other passengers deemed of equivalent importance, needed shuttle rides up and down. As such, it was a vivid illustration of the kind of luxury wealthy people believe they deserve, and the rest of us either envy or view with jaw-dropping embarrassment.

The elegant obsequiousness we received from Arturo

Mendez (the perfect servant, in that any actual personality he might have possessed seemed completely subsumed by the formality his job required) should have provided us with our first indication of the excessiveness we were in for. Then the outer doors, embossed with the raptors of the Bettelhine Family crest, irised open, revealing the rich auburn grain of the local woods that lined the bulkheads, and the glittery gold fixtures that adorned the trim. The overhead light fixtures were hugged by jovial cherubs. A pillar at the center of the room bore a reservoir of bubbling seawater and a glittery, silver fish that stunned me by its astounding facial resemblance to an elderly human being, complete with fleshy nose and sunken blue eyes. As its lips popped open and closed in conjunction with the gills behind the jowls, it looked like it intended to complain or say something unbearably wise. It had a family resemblance to the Bettelhines. I wondered for whom it was bioengineered to flatter, and answered my own question: some Bettelhine patriarch, of course. It was not a form of immortality I would have wanted.

There were no free-fall issues. As with Layabout itself, the interior was equipped with Specific Gravity systems, maintaining a pleasant .8 gee that wouldn't budge one fraction of a percentage point whether the craft was in ascent, descent, or dry dock. The sofas and lounges were ornately carved antiques of the sort that might have seen service on more worlds than I had, without a fraction of the wear. The ceiling glittered with jewels the size of my fists. The observation window, made of some material that refused to take a fingerprint even when I flattened my sweaty palm against the "glass," covered the entire exterior wall of the shared lounge and the one suite assigned to us, and offered a panoramic view of the planet below, including a wedge of daylight blessed by more green than most worlds inhabited by human beings have historically managed to keep.

Arturo led us to one of the four suites on our level, which

included a bed large enough to welcome not only the Porrinyards and myself but also any other half dozen sentients
we might have elected to invite. (There was, he said, another
suite level, less luxurious than this one, giving the car sleeping accommodations for thirty.)

After a dazzling tour of the other wonders we'd been provided in our quarters, he led us back into the central parlor
with that discomfiting fish and showed us a bar stocked with
the finest liqueurs of a hundred worlds and the most popu-
lar narcotics of a hundred more. An actual, real-paper book
set into its own recess on the bar, bound in something that
felt organic, turned out to be a menu of available delicacies
longer than some encyclopedias.

"Please make yourselves comfortable," Arturo said as the
Porrinyards and I collapsed in grateful heaps. "I'm afraid it
will be another hour or more before all the other passengers
are reboarded, and we're ready to depart."

"There are other passengers?"

"Yes. Two of Mr. Bettelhine's children, three Bettelhine
employees, and a pair of personal guests. I believe more may
be coming, but you'll have to ask the Bettelhines about that
when they arrive."

"They weren't the target of assassination attempts today.
Why aren't they here with us already?"

"They expected to be, Counselor. The Bettelhine youngsters and their personal guest rode up from the surface with
the express purpose of greeting you, and several others
boarded at various times while we awaited your arrival.
Then the unpleasantness occurred, and all of those notables
needed to be evacuated offstation for security reasons. Now
that Layabout's docking facilities are opening again, they
can return to the station and rejoin us for the descent to Xana
proper."

Interesting. I was not just some peon summoned to await
the pleasure of the Great Man, but a personage of sufficient

importance to deserve an escort by his offspring. "Can you tell me how long they were waiting for me?"

"The youngsters? About twenty hours, if you only count all their time in dry dock, thirty if you include their hours of ascent."

I moaned. "Flights to and from the ground would be faster."

"The Bettelhines limit ground-to-space traffic for security and environmental reasons. In any event, the other guests all arrived by various transports in the past day or so, the tardiest among them joining the party some five hours before your arrival. I'm afraid that there may have been some unkind words about your own late arrival, words that grew more heated as the unfortunate crisis required their own evacuation, but I assure you that neither of the Bettelhine youngsters held this against you in the slightest."

"That's a relief," the Porrinyards said.

I ignored them. "Who was that last passenger?"

"That would be the gentleman, Monday Brown."

The name meant nothing to me. What did was the timeline. The Bursteeni ship carrying the two Bocaian assassins had docked at Layabout ten hours before my own arrival. This Brown person hadn't checked aboard the Royal Carriage until some five hours later, meaning that he'd possessed ample opportunity to meet with the Bocaians while they were waiting for me. Following that, he'd been an evacuee offstation for the entire duration of Pescziuwicz's security sweep. In the absence of any other intelligence about him, I already found myself worrying about Claws of God in his luggage. "And aside from him? Was anybody other than him aboard the carriage for less than eight hours?"

"Not that I am aware of, ma'am. I can investigate, if you'd like—"

"Never mind. That'll be all for now."

Had Arturo clicked his heels, I might have been forced

to kill him. Instead, he merely bowed, an act that simply argued for a light wounding. He didn't stick around long enough to receive either punishment, but made his descent to the lower levels using the spiral staircase at the other end of the parlor.

I stood up, folded my arms, and wondered, not for the first or even twentieth time, just what Hans Bettelhine wanted with me. Up until now the closest I'd ever come to dealing with the Family on any substantial basis was a few interviews with distant cousins representing the corporation's interests in remote outposts, and so far removed from the wealth and power of the Bettelhine Inner Family that they must have felt like human skin cells connected to the organism but superfluous and unconnected to the beat of its huge, cavernous heart.

But this was the belly of the beast . . .

Behind me, the Porrinyards said, "Andrea?"

I didn't turn. "What?"

"You're obsessing again."

I still didn't turn. "This is going to be a bad one, love."

"I would not be surprised. On this corrupt world, with these corrupt people, it could not be anything less. But that's just an additional reason to face our trials properly refreshed."

There was something familiar about their shared tone, something that made me turn.

They were cuddled together on a nearby love seat, Skye resting her head on Oscin's shoulder and playing, idly, with the fingers of his right hand. She peered at me from beneath half-closed lids, a special look of hers she'd always used to communicate her boldest invitations. Oscin faced me head-on, his smile so slight that only a curlicue wrinkle at the edge of his lips distinguished it from the one he wore at his moments of greatest concentration.

Their shared mind meant that they both found me amusing in the same, exact way, but the subtle differences between her smile and his seemed to express complementary attitudes that arrived at the same place by coincidence alone. It was a pose, but one they must have practiced with great care.

"The main problem with focus," they said together, "is losing your peripheral vision."

I felt foolish. "For Juje's sake, love, somebody just tried to kill me!"

Their fingertips traced each other like old friends searching for changes in familiar faces. "True. And it was a catastrophically incompetent attempt, wasn't it?"

"So?"

"So why not celebrate?"

"Because there's another assassin out there!"

They tsked. "That deduction, brilliant as I found it, remains unproved. It's entirely based on the premise that the actions of sentients dedicated to mad and murderous causes can be trusted to make some kind of consistent internal sense: an idea easily debunked by any look at the history of mad and murderous causes. Tonight, in these spectacular accommodations, I don't even see a reason to let it ruin our mood. The operative phrase in this place should be, *We've hit the big time.*"

They patted the couch cushions in unison.

As always, when the Porrinyards surprised me by seizing the initiative, my cheeks burned. "Now?"

"Your path is a difficult one, Andrea. You'll never have a perfect moment, unless you stop from time to time to make one. I see no hypocrisy in suggesting a little wine, a little music, and some time putting that big bed in our suite to some fine recreational use. After all, our next venue might not be even remotely as nice."

I remembered my first glimpse of them. They'd been as beautiful as anybody I'd ever seen. Sometimes, faced with pressing problems, I forget. Sometimes they take the time to remind me.

Oscin's smile became broad and challenging, while Skye's became more sly, implying secrets that she and I could find some way to hide from him. This was a transparent fraud, as Skye could no sooner keep secrets from Oscin than I could decide, on a whim, to keep secrets from the right half of my brain. But the pretense had its intended effect. The two of them—dammit, the one of them—had mastered all the skills they needed on me.

"There's a shower in there," Skye said. "Big enough for three."

"Water," said Oscin. "Not sonics."

Skye: "I noticed a handy menu of expensive topical euphorics."

Oscin: "Some I've tried and some I've always wanted to try."

"Together," suggested Skye, "and in combination."

Oscin said: "We have plenty of time."

And then the two of them, together, rising as one: "Why not?"

There was no point in further resistance.

"God damn it," I said, and went to them, lowering my head against the cleft formed by the place where their shoulders met.

I think I came within a heartbeat of calm, before I felt the sudden tension in their postures. "Andrea," they said.

I took a step back and glanced at their faces. Both wore looks equal parts astonishment, alarm, and anger. Oscin was staring over the top of my head at something behind me; Skye had seized my forearm with a grip that prevented me from turning around right away. I gave her a questioning look. She nodded, then gave my arm an extra squeeze, just strong enough to approach but not cross the threshold of pain.

This could only be a warning to be careful how I reacted when I turned around and saw what they saw.

I nodded to let her know that I understood.

She loosened her grip on my arm.

I turned around and did not overreact at all.

"Son of a *bitch*."

3

THE KHAAJIIR

The Bocaian licked the edges of his lipless mouth. "Andrea Cort. I hope I may take that as an expression of surprise, and not as an appraisal of my character."

Bocaians don't suffer the same problems with worn-out skin elasticity that causes wrinkles in untreated humans of advanced years, and therefore don't need regular rejuvenation to remain smooth-faced until their advanced dotage. But I had an experienced eye and had no trouble spotting the signs betraying this one's extreme antiquity, from the paler cast to his skin, to the bent posture that betrayed the traditional complaints of any upright spine suffering from too many years spent arguing with gravity. He rested much of his weight on a staff, taller than himself, that seemed to have been carved from a glassy transparent wood I had seen many times in my childhood; it had been polished to a high sheen, and reflected the overhead lights in a manner that made it look almost as bejeweled as the garish furnishings around us. He wore a loose-fitting hooded tunic with a ruffled ankle-length hem, and a gold medallion bearing a shiny embossed symbol of some kind. There was no ROM disk affixed to the center of his high, hairless forehead: a rarity for the few Bocaians who travel, given that the absence testified to unassisted fluency in Mercantile and the other common languages.

Damned if he didn't seem to be smiling. Bocaian evolution hadn't produced that expression as a way to communicate warmth or amusement, but they knew what it meant to human beings, and could simulate the look when they wanted to. He could just as easily be showing teeth for the other traditional reason. I certainly didn't like the looks of that staff. Deadly as a Claw of God could be, I wasn't any more enthused about the prospect of going down to an old-fashioned blow to the skull.

A pair of well-dressed human beings, in their late teens or early twenties, stood behind him.

From the young man's resemblance to the famous Hans Bettelhine, I assumed him to be one of the Bettelhine "youngsters" Arturo Mendez had mentioned. He had a chiseled jaw and an aristocratic nose and a physique so slight it bordered on the unhealthy. I wondered if he'd been ill, or if this was some local affectation I didn't know about, akin to the one that had once required the royalty of Ancient China on old Earth to grow their toenails and fingernails to a length designed to render them utterly dependent on their servants for everything from feeding themselves to basic hygiene. His attempt at a reassuring smile held back just enough to establish he'd known enough suffering to take a few degrees of warmth off any happiness he'd ever know. You expect to see looks like that on the faces of the poor. When on the rich, it usually evidenced a past that included failed attempts at self-destruction.

The young woman was a different story. She resembled the princess of so many fairy tales, her skin porcelain, her shoulder-length hair a shade of gold that rendered the mere metal a gaudy pretender. She wore a loose ankle-length silver gown, just translucent enough to accentuate the difference between its comfy shapelessness and the shape of the curves underneath. She didn't look like she'd ever suffered at all, though her concerned glance at the young man I assumed to be her brother suggested that she had been touched, in some way, by whatever had happened to him. There was a story here, one that might reward a closer look.

But not now.

Not with a Bocaian in the room.

I said, "Stay right where you are."

The Bocaian cocked his head. "Forever? That would be tiring."

"I have as much time as you do, sir."

The haggard young man stepped away from the Bocaian and held both his hands out palm-first, in a placating gesture. "Counselor Cort? I'm Jason Bettelhine. This is my sister, Jelaine. I believe we can straighten this out, if you'll just calm down and let us explain."

I laid on the chill. "This is calm, sir, and an explanation is exactly what I was about to demand. Your Mr. Pescziuwicz just turned Layabout upside down looking for Bocaians. He said that the two who attacked me were the only ones he'd ever seen. Now you waltz in here with another. Was your Mr. Pescziuwicz lying or incompetent?"

"Please," Jelaine Bettelhine said, her voice so soft that only breeding and immense personal will could account for the way it commanded the room. "Can we at least sit down while we discuss this? The Khaajiir hasn't been well. He shouldn't be forced to stand for too long."

I hadn't taken my eyes off the Bocaian, but I assessed him again with this claim in mind, and took special note of his tight grip on that staff. He rested as much weight on that as on his own two legs. This didn't remove him from consideration as a special threat; I'd known a petty criminal, once, who could barely walk but whose arms were deadly weapons. But neither could I see any pressing reason for the Bettelhines to drag me all the way to their world, if all they wanted was to place me in the same room with such an unlikely assassin. "Very well."

The Bettelines escorted the Khaajiir to the nearest sofa, which was rich enough and plush enough to make me feel somewhat safer, as even the most able-bodied human being might have had to struggle for a few seconds to escape from its decadent comforts. The cushions beneath him whooshed with escaping air when he surrendered to local gravity. He rested the staff itself against his knees with a comfort that suggested years since the last time he'd allowed himself to be parted from it.

The Bettelhines saw to his well-being with a solicitousness surprising for royalty of any kind, then parted to settle in a pair of high-backed easy chairs bracketing his sofa. Their attitudes as they sat were so complementary that they might have been rehearsed for my benefit. Jelaine leaned back, tucked her long legs underneath her, and allowed the chair to envelop her like a protective parent, the ripples and folds of her gown bunching up around like additional pillows. She held a warm half-smile, beneath understanding eyes. Jason sat, too, his eyes imploring even as they bled pain from past traumas.

Only when they were seated did I relax and take an easy chair opposite the Khaajiir. The Porrinyards, following their own instincts, remained standing at either side of me, alert for any betrayal.

Jason did not urge them to sit. "Your friends are a linked pair?"

"Yes."

"I knew a linked pair once. Two women, working on a project for one of my many uncles. They used to visit the Central Estate quite a bit. I had a serious crush on them, when I was twelve."

I radiated chill. "I'm so delighted for you."

Jelaine curled her delicate pink lips in the tiniest of all possible amused smiles.

Jason fluttered his hands in wry surrender. "We expected this to be difficult, Counselor. Even before today's unfortunate incident, we knew you'd be upset by the Khaajiir's presence. Given the circumstances, we've asked the other guests to remain in the shuttle, while we make sure you're okay with this."

"They can wait. Right now I want you to finish explaining how your crack security chief, Mr. Pescziuwicz, could miss the presence of another Bocaian aboard this station."

"Pescziuwicz is good at his job," Jason said. "But he operates under certain limitations he may not have made clear to you. He only knows about registered travelers passing through Layabout. He doesn't receive information about those who bypass Layabout using Family visas."

" 'Family visas,' " I repeated.

"The Inner Family enjoys a full exemption from all local travel restrictions. For instance, down on the surface, we're the only ones allowed personal intercontinental aircraft. It makes for a cleaner sky. Within this system, only Inner Family members, their guests, or employees bearing the Inner Family crest are allowed to take direct flights to and from Xana without using Layabout. And when this carriage is docked, we can transfer from it, to our own orbital shuttle and back, without ever passing through the terminal."

"Without going through customs?"

"It's our planet," he reminded me. "Our customs."

"That must be convenient. Institutionalized smuggling."

Jason winced. "Please, Counselor. It's not smuggling if it breaks no laws, and we break no laws if we make the laws and have the power to give ourselves exemptions. Besides, it's not like we don't police ourselves at all. We had an out-of-control cousin once. She was caught bringing in narcotics on my family's no-no list. My father downgraded her status in the Family and banished her for life. The same thing happened to our aunt Lillian, for political reasons. There was another uncle, a few generations ago, who broke more serious laws and was handed over to the local legal system. He did prison time. This is all part of the local historical record."

"You're still able to come and go without official notice."

"Exactly," Jason said. "And I agree, that would be *wrong* if this world wasn't, in addition to being the home of millions, also private property and the headquarters of a major interstellar corporation. Is it your position, Counselor, that families aren't allowed to keep secrets on their own ground? That heads of State, and the leaders of major corporations, aren't required to keep some of their activities out of the public eye, just to protect their own proprietary business?"

"That does sounds a lot like talk I've heard about other 'family' businesses."

"Criminal families, Counselor. I understand you probably think the description applies to us as well, but I'll let that pass so we can move on to the main point, which is that the Khaajiir, here, is a personal guest of my father, traveling under the Family exemption. He's never been through local customs, and never set foot on Layabout. Pescziuwicz wouldn't have had any reason to suspect his presence aboard the carriage."

I still wasn't sure I bought his defense of a planetary policy that rendered the Bettelhines above the law on a world where their actions affected the daily lives of millions, but he was right: it was time to move on. "You had to have heard about the two Bocaians involved in the attempt on my life. Why didn't you tell Pescziuwicz about the Khaajiir, then, just to make sure he had all the facts?"

"Nobody's supposed to know about the Khaajiir except the people in this carriage, my father, and a few associates of my father. And now, you. And your associates—associate, if you prefer." For just a moment, parsing the plural, he seemed frazzled, and I empathized with him; it sometimes amazed me, how many simple sentences became labyrinths when they referred to linked pairs like the Porrinyards. After a moment, he recovered and said, "The bottom line, Counselor, is that his presence here is entirely peaceful, his intentions toward you entirely benign."

"But still," I said, my voice still radiating chill, "not entirely unrelated to what happened in the concourse."

Jason didn't flinch. "No. Probably not."

On either side of me, the Porrinyards coughed. "I'm afraid you're a little ahead of me, Andrea."

I may have been answering the Porrinyards, but I kept my eyes focused on Jason Bettelhine. "It's simple. That cute little theory I spat out in Pescziuwicz's office? The one about secondary targets? I had it upside down and backward. Those thugs weren't lying in wait for me. Just as I said, there was no way for anybody originating on Bocai to find out our travel plans and beat us here, with or without any ridiculous ancient weapon in hand. But a security breach could have alerted them to the Khaajiir's presence on Xana months ago. They would have had plenty of time to put their pieces in play. Even to get their hands on at least one Claw of God, possibly more, before they came."

Jason now sported a half-smile identical to the one that had been stamped on his sister's face since the beginning of the conversation. "That was, of course, before you showed up."

"Exactly." I found myself grimacing with equal wry amusement. "I may be the only woman ever born who could travel to another solar system on the spur of the moment, arrive unannounced, and by sheer luck stroll right into the line of fire of an assassination team waiting for somebody else who just by coincidence happens to hate her even more."

The Porrinyards emitted identical exasperated sighs. "You have a gift."

I turned my attention to the Khaajiir, who had been watching the entire exchange with rapt fascination. "As for you, sir, the Claws of God have no special significance in my life, and as far as I know no special significance to anybody but the K'cenhowten, but their presence in the hands of your fellow Bocaians might make a great deal more sense in this context once you tell me *who the hell you are*."

The Khaajiir shifted, his long, bony fingers lightly spinning his staff in place. "You live up to your reputation, Andrea Cort. You are a most impressive human being."

"I get that a lot. Again, *who are you*?"

He glanced at each of the Bettelhines in turn, receiving a nod from Jason and an encouraging smile from the long-silent Jelaine. Then he sighed, placed the staff across his knees, and said, "I'm just a poor academic, you would say 'Professor,' adept in a number of fields that would include history and the discipline your own people call 'comparative religion.'"

That told me nothing. "I've never heard this honorific, *Khaajiir*."

He seemed amused by my shaky pronunciation. "It almost sounds like it could be Bocaian, doesn't it? But it didn't originate on my world at all. It's actually an ancient K'cenhowten title, dating back to the days of their Enlightenment, and referring to the spiritual leaders of the movement that helped to lift their people out of the dark age responsible for originating the barbaric method of execution you almost suffered today. I was so passionate when discussing that particular period in offworld history that some of my students named me that in jest, in part as a pun on my real family name, Kassasir. I gratified my students by liking it, as I like most multilanguage puns, and I've worn it for so long that I'm afraid it's stuck. You may consider it an old man's affectation, nothing more."

"I'll stick with Khaajiir," I said. "Might as well stick with whatever everybody else calls you."

"Coming from you, it would mean everything to me."

It was the first moment of warmth, feigned or otherwise, that I'd received from any Bocaian since the massacre, but I was too intent on following this trail to acknowledge it. "And the assassins used the Claw of God because, used against you, it would represent the renewed ascendance of the forces the historical Khaajiirs—"

"The plural is *Khaajiirel*," he said.

"—were able to overcome. So. All right. I understand symbolism, even if it's demented and stupid fanatical symbolism. But you still haven't explained a damn thing. You haven't told me *who you are* and what your *business* is and what you're doing *here* and *why* a Bocaian hit team would be here trying to kill you."

That was met by silence.

Of the three of them, the Khaajiir seemed the first tempted to break down and tell me, but Jason Bettelhine broke in, his tone regretful but firm. "I'm afraid that much of that is tied up with the reason you're here, and my father wanted that information to wait until he could brief you himself."

I turned back to him. "Your father's agenda was set before we knew assassins were involved."

"He has his reasons, Counselor. I promise you that they're compelling ones. In the meantime, be satisfied with my assurance that the Khaajiir means you no harm."

"Oh, I can see that. But since we've established that there are people who wish him harm, and that those people also wish me harm, I'll be in the line of fire for as long as we're breathing the same air. Were this Confederate territory, I'd stick around just because protecting him was part of my job. But this is your planet, and your problem. I need a reason I shouldn't just turn around and go back to New London right now."

Jelaine Bettelhine spoke in a voice so soft that she might have been a young mother, urging a cranky infant to sleep. "Please don't."

"I need a better reason than *please*."

"My brother has given you his word of honor. So has the Khaajiir. I now give you mine. There's a good reason for all of this, one more important than you can possibly guess. You *need to stay*."

The Confederacy includes a number of worlds ruled by royalty, of one kind or another. I'd been to a number, the most recent an industrial hell under a runaway CO_2 hothouse atmosphere, where the most venerated figure was supposed to be a direct descendant of an antiquated terrestrial line known as the House of Windsor, ceremonial figures of little real power in a country best known for establishing an empire that had collapsed under its own weight. She'd been, in the most precise medical terms, an obese, insensate, limbless idiot, dependent on constant care from a servant class who considered themselves honored for the privilege. She'd been the worst of a bad lot. Whenever I encountered royalty, most struck me as fussy oafs raised from birth to confuse their whims with the common good. Precious few struck me as intelligent, and fewer still struck me as noble.

But whatever that final, overused adjective means, Jelaine Bettelhine had it. The conviction in her voice was rich with compassion, understanding, and the sense that she knew more than I'd ever known or ever would know. It was impossible, even for a congenital cynic like myself, to hear that voice, sense that poise, and not want to believe in her.

That was a dangerous weapon she had. But her veneer of sincerity meant nothing. The primary requirement of a good liar is believing in the fiction, even if only for the few seconds it took to tell it.

I licked my lips. "I'll need a quick look at that staff. Just to be sure."

The Khaajiir said, "Certainly," and extended the tip toward me.

I took it from him, and felt an unexpected pang when my fingers touched it for the first time. I'd been familiar with this wood, during my childhood on his world. A number of my Bocaian neighbors had possessed art objects made of the same material. I'd had a little carved *bhakha*, a cute, big-eyed local animal more appealing to look at than the real thing had been when I'd had the opportunity to play with one. (The toxic little mucker bit me.) The woodgrain on my carving had been so light and so smooth, that it was almost as friction free as half-melted ice, one good reason why even the richest Bocaians had never been stupid enough to use it for flooring. As a little girl I'd loved touching it anyway. The inanimate carving had possessed an uncanny illusion of life, mostly thanks to the material's talent for retaining heat, which had often made it feel a few degrees warmer than the surrounding air.

The staff was just as slippery, which made it an odd choice as spare limb for a sentient of failing strength. What mishap would result if the Khaajiir lost his grip? But further investigation revealed an invisible circular band, about three-quarters of the way up, that exerted the same pull toward the palm of my hand that a magnet has on iron filings. Gripping the staff there, I could not let it go unless I made myself let it go.

Nice trick. Some kind of imbedded tech, invisible despite the staff's total transparency. It might contain an entire battalion of nanoweaponry that I'd never be able to detect outside a lab, and I'm useless in a lab. My AIsource masters could probably catalogue everything, if they ever deigned to tell me. But I could see nothing. There were no openings, no hidden compartments, no obvious uses other than as a walking stick.

I didn't want to trust it. But I had no cause to suspect it. "It's fine workmanship."

"Thank you," he said.

I extended the staff back toward him, handle side first.

He took it by the adhesive band, and once again rested it across his knees. The simulated smile and look of genial warmth never left him. "Do you know, Counselor, that your name is a very ironic one?"

"How's that?"

"Cort, in Mercantile, sounds the same as *Court*, in the antiquated Hom.Sap language known as English. A *Court* is a room where legal hearings are held, and thus a splendidly appropriate name for a legal professional like you. Nor is that all. Have your partners here ever informed you of the secret significance of their individual names, Oscin and Skye?"

It had never occurred to me to wonder. "No."

"*Oscin* and *Skye* are both members of a pantheon of minor Gods worshipped by a cult on the arboreal colony of Farjanif, from whence I presume they hail. The names of the deities, simultaneously siblings and lovers if my knowledge of the mythology serves, are English puns as well, as they're near homonyms for that language's words designating *Ocean* and *Sky*. Splendid appellations for a pair with such an, ah, elemental union, wouldn't you say?"

I glanced at the Porrinyards, one at a time. They both avoided eye contact with me. Interesting. They'd known and never told me.

"*Porrinyards* is also a significant appelation," he said. "It comes from an extinct dialect known as Hectaish, with some roots in the ancient-Earth romance languages, and it means *multiple births*. There is a possible secondary meaning if you look up antiquated patronymics among the Cid—"

"Sir," I said.

The Khaajiir did not seem affronted. "Excuse me. I told

you I liked multilingual puns. Start me up and I'll go for hours. But Bocaian and your own Hom.Sap Mercantile are both such inadequate languages for wordplay that I leap at the opportunity to dip into others whenever possible. It's one of the few pleasures I can still afford at my advanced age. I do hope that making your acquaintance will be another."

Maybe he meant it. Stranger things had happened.

"It's been a long, hard day," Jason Bettelhine said. "We're running late, and we haven't even begun our descent. We also just received word of another late arrival, one of my brothers, who'll be docking with us in about twenty minutes. Plus we have the other guests to get situated. It's a night-mare. So why don't you three—you two, whatever—repair to your suite, get some rest, make use of the facilities, and meet everybody for dinner three hours after we embark? We'll make introductions, get better acquainted, and perhaps answer some more of your questions then. Is that fair?"

Once upon a time, not too long ago, I'd made a policy of never dining with other human beings. I still didn't like to accept invitations from anybody but the Porrinyards, but they'd loosened me up quite a bit. I could tolerate it for busi-ness. "I suppose it will have to be."

Jelaine Bettelhine's eyes twinkled. "I promise, Counselor, we'll be friends before this journey is done. We have more in common that you can possibly know."

Swell.

I got that a lot, too, and it had never been good news.

Somehow, the things I have in common with people who like to say so are always their worst qualities.

We returned to our suite, feeling less secure than ever despite surroundings so plush that I could have fallen face-first anywhere and not received a bruise upon hitting the floor. I hadn't noticed, on my first tour through these rooms, but the luxury here extended to the quality of the air.

It was not just fresh, free of that tinned quality you find in some orbital environments, but downright bracing, thanks to what may have been an increased percentage of pure oxygen and what may have been some other stimulant, jacking my metabolism in ways that might do a lot to lessen the crash that always followed Intersleep by about twenty-four hours. I tried to build up a nice load of resentment over this and failed, a serious lapse for me given that the Porrinyards say they can track my grudges in geographical strata.

Maybe I was mellowing, after all. And maybe not all the euphorics in this decadent conveyance were topical and stored in jars. The Bettelhines already seemed willing to go to extreme lengths to keep their guests happy. Maybe their efforts extended to technological means. Subaural suggestives in the hum of the air compressors? Subclinical teem-flashes in the lighting?

Paranoid? Sure. But I'd never, not even once in my life, been too paranoid, only not paranoid enough. And this was a family that had earned its obscene fortune by developing newer and more brilliant ways to kill great numbers of people.

But any difficulty I was having maintaining a mad-on could also be a mere reaction to the sheer luxury around me. The Porrinyards, who had thrived in some of the most hostile environments known to mankind, had already demonstrated their own susceptibility to the comforts this place offered. If I was brutally honest to myself I had to admit that I was having some of the same feelings.

I wondered, not for the first time, just how the obscenely wealthy ever managed to develop thick skin, with everything in their environments so carefully designed to cushion their painless ride through life.

I also wondered just why I sensed something worse in the background of the young heir, Jason.

I stood at the transparent curving wall of the suite, looking down on the bright green landscape now greeting the first hours of daylight. "I confess, love, I didn't read up on this place as well as I should have. Do you know which land-mass we're looking at?"

"There are three," the Porrinyards said. "Ice, a frozen one nobody ever goes to, Asgard, the one that belongs to the Family, and Midgard, the one inhabited by their inner circle of employees."

"That's what I heard. But which one is that, below us?"

"Think about it."

I did, then felt stupid. "Of course. The Bettelhines would never sully their own continent with anything as landscape-defiling as an orbital elevator."

"Asgard is more like a nature preserve, I understand. Be-tween the estates, the support staff, and the environmental stewards, its entire full-time population is less than eighteen thousand people. I think they use, actually use, less than one percent of the available land, though they make much of the territory available for scenic and recreational purposes. Not that Midgard is all that spoiled a place to live, either. Three million people, total, from coast to coast, most of them in a tiny handful of cities. If mankind had kept the homeworld that pristine, we never would have left."

And all of those people worked for the Bettelhines, either directly or for the infrastructure that made those cities active, breathing communities. With that much space to deal with, that many natural resources to support themselves, even before regular cash infusions from the family trade allowed the importation of anything they preferred not to manufac-ture locally, the local standard of living went beyond privi-lege. The poorest of the poor, around here, must have lived in conditions that matched the upper middle class anywhere else. "I wonder how many worlds were reduced to industrial hells, or smoking ruins, so the Bettelhines can afford to live like this."

"I could look it up and give you a precise figure," the Porrinyards said, "but I don't think any one of us is in the mood for that much higher math."

I turned away from the window, and saw them, curled on the huge bed in attitudes that suggested a pair of human parentheses just waiting for me to take my place between them, as the phrase being singled out for special emphasis. Neither had disrobed. They had no need to hurry me along. There was no urging in either set of eyes, just a certain confident patience.

Oscin spoke alone. "They're dancing around something."

"Maybe they're trying to recruit me."

"That seems likely." Skye rolled over on her back, faced the infinite spaces of a ceiling that, though only a meter or so above our heads, was designed to look as vast and the skies of heaven. "I would not put it past them; they've bought out Dip Corps contracts before. We knew a fellow, back on One One One, who sold himself to the Bettelhines as a high-altitude specialist. But if they offered you a position, would it be anything you'd want to do? Anything that would leave you room for your mission for the AIsource?"

Oscin added, "And would you want to contribute to any enterprise that has caused so much human suffering on so many worlds?"

"The AIsource can't be accused of having clean hands, either."

"True. But the AIsource prize you as an implacable enemy. They appreciate you wanting them dead; they would be delighted if you found the means. The Bettelhines, on the other hand, only want to prosper, and would only hire you for some reason that advanced their own fortunes. That's not you, Andrea. It's never been you."

Comments like that always make me uncomfortable, as if being seen as some kind of moral paragon driven by principle amounts to a guarantee that I'd someday prove a disappointment. "From the hints they dropped, they expect me to embrace whatever they have to say."

"The Bettelhines didn't get where they are by being bad salesmen, even when all they were selling was death. Whatever they want of you, they will make it sound like the greatest offer you ever had."

"Present company excluded," I said.

The Porrinyards grinned together. "Quite right."

"What do you make of these two in particular?"

Oscin said, "You did notice that Jason did almost all the talking, and that Jelaine came in only when it was time to seal the deal."

"Of course. Do you think she's in charge of, well, whatever this is?"

They spoke together again. "My perception of that will depend entirely on how much Hans Bettelhine involves himself. But no. To the extent these two are active players, I think both siblings are in charge, and that each is as formidable as the other. I think Jason's the face of this business. Whatever hurt him—and I know the way you think, so don't be surprised, I agree that something has hurt him—may even be the motivating force, in some manner. But I also think Jelaine's behind her brother, backing up his moves, and picking up the slack whenever his own considerable resources prove insufficient. I think she is, if you allow the phrase, *the will* that drives his determination. Does that make sense to you?"

It was much what I'd been thinking, and I usually trusted their shared perceptions over my own when it came to questions of human behavior. But right now their assurances failed to satisfy. I didn't know what it was, but something about the young Bettelhines reeked of illicit secrets.

Incest? Maybe. As I'd already noted, the Bettelhines were nothing if not royals on their own ground, and the one immutable element of life as a royal is the way it relegates every other human being to the level of social inferior. No doubt their family kept this in mind, and that the local social season was in large part an exercise in providing these two, and their approximately one dozen siblings, with potential mates of appropriate station. But that would not be enough to prevent all possible infatuations among siblings segregated to a family estate. It certainly fit the bond I'd sensed between them, in those few minutes we'd spent together. But so would any number of sibling conspiracies, such as being of like age and the closest of confidantes when they were raised.

Still, it was odd that my instincts had gone directly to that.

I sensed *something* between them.

"Andrea?"

I felt a jerk, a brief moment of subaural vibration, and then movement. The Carriage had disengaged from Layabout. The view through the transparent wall looked exactly the same as before, as was only reasonable given our measured rate of descent; we couldn't even see Layabout, as it was now in our blind spot, somewhere above us. But any chance we'd had of backing away from the Bettelhine plans for us, and returning to New London, without further involvement were now in the past.

We were committed.

4

PORRINYARDS

Life with the Porrinyards had its counterintuitive aspects.

They meshed so well that it was easy to forget that they'd ever been anything else. But they'd begun their lives as two people, lovers with a tempestuous relationship who had found that, as much as they needed each other, they could not coexist as individuals. They'd seen cylinking as the one way they could have a future together.

Was this the utter failure or the ultimate triumph of romantic love?

Answer: Yes.

And also: No.

The damnable thing was that both answers were equally accurate.

The shared being they were now was neither the boy who'd owned the body now occupied by Oscin or the girl who'd owned the body now occupied by Skye.

Even the names they used now were illusory, referring to the bodies alone, and necessary for convenience in describing their separate actions. They talked of the original people, now gone, with the same kind of affectionate pity that most human beings reserve for the disabled and deprived, sometimes expressing amazement that either one of them had survived long enough to reach the day when they'd walked into a branch office of AIsource Medical and asked to be rendered composite.

They'd once told me that the biggest surprise of their new life was being able to look back on the experiences they'd shared and compare the memories from a global perspective. They were stunned by how many things vital to the boy had been dull to the girl, how many things the girl prized about herself the boy had considered stupid and vain. The girl had secretly seen the boy as weak and the boy had considered the girl too judgmental. As singlets, the two of them had spent at least half of their time together lying to each other. Their love, while genuine, had been tainted with all the resentments native to the constant rivalry for dominance that always comes from the proximity of any creature whose wants and needs and whims could never precisely synch.

"Knowing what I know now," the Porrinyards told me, early in our relationship, "it's amazing to me that any singlets tolerate each other for more than five days."

That hit me especially hard, since five days had been about as long as I'd ever managed to hold on to any lover before them.

Sex after their union had been, in some ways, many times better than it had ever been before, since their shared consciousness could feel the physiological responses of both bodies, and each body was capable of instant reaction to the needs of the other. For more then a year after their transformation, they'd amused themselves doing it in every position their limber physiques could achieve. They still did, whenever I wasn't available. I wasn't the first to note that, directed at linked pairs, "go fuck yourself" was not an obscenity, but a reasonable suggestion. (They sometimes thanked those who flung those words in anger with a sweet appreciation that drove those hostile people crazy.) Still, sex with each other amounted to masturbation. They still had only one soul, which could get lonely, and that soul required an other, one capable of seeing them as a single person and not as a pair.

The first counterintuitive thing about being that other is that I never felt excluded, ever. I felt outnumbered from time to time, but it was a wry kind of irritation, identical to what I would have felt in the presence of anybody capable of out-thinking me. But there was no real sense of being the odd woman out in a crowd. They were just the other person, and the best kind of other person for any lasting relationship: the kind who was just a little bit more than I could handle.

The second counterintuitive thing about the Porrinyards had to do with their eagerness for me to undergo the procedure myself, and join them as a third.

I wanted that myself. It was impossible to be with them and not want what they had. But it was also impossible to want that without fearing what would come with it. Forget the reluctance people have just paying lip service to the commitment it takes to stay with another person forever. Imagine how much more difficult it is to take that step knowing that once you do, the person you're committing to will no longer be the same person you care about now. Imagine that you won't be yourself, either. Imagine that you'll exist in the same skin, without any secrets of your own. Imagine looking back on the person you are now, and the person you love now, from the judgmental perspective of someone who isn't really either one of you.

That was the future we faced. We wanted to link. We hoped we would, someday. But if we ever did, it would be the end of me and the end of the gestalt they were now. Andrea Cort and the Porrinyards would both be gone, replaced by a new entity who had a lot in common with us but who was, for all intents and purposes, someone else, someone who might not even like us. Someone we might not want to be.

Someone who, on top of everything else, would be alone again, and once again driven to find love. With the domestic circumstances even more complicated.

Was my resistance to becoming their Third the ultimate failure or the ultimate triumph of romantic love?

Answer: Yes.

And also: No.

Again, both answers were equally accurate.

For a full year now I hadn't had the slightest idea what to do.

And some women think they have a dilemma because their men keep leaving the toilet seat up.

There's another paradox, difficult for people outside our relationship to comprehend, something we took advantage of now: the convenience of multitasking.

The Porrinyards don't always need to do everything in unison. One can sleep while the other eats. One can interrogate a suspect while the other pursues a different line of inquiry worlds away. One can play while the other works. They both get the benefit of every experience, real-time, but they don't need to collaborate on every activity at every second to accomplish that. Two heads mean being able to concentrate on two things at one time, without compromising either.

To wit:

The Porrinyards had emerged from stasis so horny they could hardly bear it. They usually did. It may have had to do with the energy spike that always follows any space traveler's release from bluegel, but they had lust to burn, and they had wanted nothing more since our arrival at Layabout but to get me someplace private and rip my clothes off.

The long delays since our arrival, from the sudden terror of the assassination attempt to the long hours of tedium in Pescziuwicz's protective custody, had brought them all the way from simmer to boil.

I felt the same way. But we had work to do, background to acquire if we were to face our next meeting with the Bettelhines prepared, and very little time to accomplish that as well as scratch our mutual overwhelming itch.

But if even a single-skull can make love while distracted, imagine how much easier it is for somebody with that much more shared mindspace to play around with.

While we were soaping each other in the shower, which as advertised offered real water as warm as liquid fire and enough water pressure to strum our skin like stringed instruments; while Oscin's tongue explored my lips and Skye's nimble hands spread the euphorics on my ass; while I closed my eyes, lost track of which Porrinyard was doing what and forgot to care; while I wept for my own cowardice in not joining their link and moments later found my cheeks strain from smiling; while I gasped from her touch and threw my hands around his shoulders, there was no single moment when I caught either one of them absent. But each one of them was present, and concentrating on the act alone, only about sixty percent of the time. The remaining forty percent of the time, at least one of them was paused, that half of their shared consciousness tapping their shared hytex link for more background on some of the questions we'd been handed.

That protocol to absorb information at a hundred thousand words per second, shifting back and forth between Oscin and Skye, didn't prevent either one of them from enjoying the our interlude, or from perceiving it sans interruption. Oscin could be knee-deep in the history of the K'cenhowten religious wars, giving it his full attention, and still feel every individual sensation Skye felt as I knelt before her. He wasn't being short-changed at all, nor was she when his body was needed. As long as one was present, both were.

Is it better when neither one's driving blind at any point? For them it is. Twice as much viewpoint to enjoy, at every moment. I like to tell them it's better for me, too, but the truth is that I don't often catch them at it. There have been times when only one of them was physically present, the other absent because of one errand or another, and I could have sworn that I felt the other there, not just in spirit but in physical form. I once made love to Oscin and felt Skye touching me, even though she was three thousand kilometers away at the time. And there was no point in asking them how I could feel her there, when their only response would be an amused, "Well, she was." Of course she'd been. But from the point of a poor, broken single-skull: *What the hell?*

On the other hand, I didn't understand how starship propulsion worked either, and that hadn't stopped me from zipping back and forth across civilized space for half my life. As long as we get where we want to go, who cares how it works?

When we were done, I rested my head on Oscin's shoulders, allowing him to carry me to the bed while Skye dabbed my back with a towel large enough to sop up a continent. He placed me on the bed, accepted another kiss, and lay on his side facing me, while Skye spooned me, her skin still steaming from the shower.

We'd be days coming down from this glow.

I tried and failed to replace my exhausted grin with a look of determined concentration. "So what have you got?"

Skye massaged my shoulder blades. "The Khaajiir."

The K'cenhowten were squat, neckless things with an affinity for shallow water and a phenotype that would have resembled the terrestrial turtle, if turtles walked on their hind legs and had shells covered with spikes. From appearance alone you would expect them to be warlike, and they did like to pick fights, though their definition of picking a fight was so leisurely that you could swallow their provocations for centuries on end before realizing that they wanted you to shoot back. They'd once owned over a thousand worlds, and still called what they had an empire, but the incursion of races with speed settings above interminable now limited them to less than two hundred, none of which anybody else wanted.

I'd dealt with the K'cenhowten a few times in diplomatic settings and had always found them dull and irritable. They've never been among my favorite sentient races, if I could be said to have any, but I'd mark them as more congenial than the Tchi and a lot less explosive than human beings. That's because they don't change their minds easily. There's a saying in the Dip Corps. Point a K'cenhowten in any given direction, give him a reason to walk, leave for a few hours, and chances are that when you come back he'll still be lumbering toward the horizon when you get back.

Alas, that went for bad directions, too, and whenever they wandered into one of the historical morasses that afflict all sentient races from time to time, they didn't retreat but rather kept moving until it was well over their heads.

In the case of their dark age, it was a period of religious tyranny as vile as the Spanish Inquisition or Third Jihad of old Earth, or the Scouring of Deyasinq only a few centuries back. Skye didn't claim to understand the theology involved, except to say that it resembled the same old crap. More to the point, it gripped the K'cenhowten for centuries. Entire generations lived knowing that if denounced for any reason, including insufficient piety, they could be brought to the dungeons of the church and treated to the fruits of the clergy's endless ingenuity for inflicting pain. Some involved starvation, a process that given the slow K'cenhowten metabolism could take up to two years. Others involved the removal of the exoskeleton and the application of caustics to the digestive organs.

But the most feared was the Claw of God, no caress for human beings but especially terrifying to members of a race that counted on their shells to protect them. It was one thing for a K'cenhowten to be pierced by a weapon capable of penetrating his shell. But the Claw was worse. The Claw was a way of telling nonbelievers: *Your shell is nothing to us. We don't even need to damage it to get to the meat of you.*

It was hard to believe that a regime that demented could fall after holding their power for that long, but it did, after a rebellion that ripped the ruling party from its throne. A countertyranny that lasted a century or so subjected many of the descendants of that first reign of terror to much the same treatment, for equally trivial reasons. Then the Khaaji-irel, a word related to the K'cenhowten word for *agriculture*, arrived. There appeared to have been no single, messianic leader, just a determined consensus among many individuals capable of saying no when they believed enough was enough. They stopped the cycle, restoring K'cenhowten politics to something approaching sanity, within a mere generation.

Sixteen thousand years later, enter our Professor Kassasir, a Bocaian academic of impeccable credentials known for his works in fields that corresponded to history, mathematics, exohistory, exoneurology, and exopsychology. Those latter specialties, devoted to the wiring and function of alien minds, were of sufficient disinterest to most Bocaians that his achievements in those fields had earned him little more than footnoted obscurity. But that was before his fascination with K'cenhowten's reign of terror, a lurid subject that had brought him a low level of celebrity when his paper on the subject earned him more offworld attention than he'd ever received among his own people.

That had changed things for him. He'd been the local boy

who made good. He'd spent most of his time, in lectures, trying to explain how the Khaajiirel, who he called the "splendid miracle," could have halted the fevered momentum of all the bloody history that came before them.

Then he'd done something that had led his university to fire him for cause.

And some time after that, he'd left Bocai, leaving no forwarding address.

"That's all very interesting," I said, my tone establishing that it was not, "but what are the Bettelhines doing with him?"

The three of us were still in bed, the Porrinyards bracketing me on both sides, the remaining moisture from the shower prickling as it dried on our bare skin. Skye had stopped rubbing my shoulder, and now rested her hand on my hip. I could only damn the dinner invitation. We'd have to get ready before too long.

"I don't know," the Porrinyards said. "It could be anything. I know that rich people sometimes adopt artists like pets. There's no reason to believe the Bettelhines wouldn't do the same thing for obscure utopian alien academics."

"Jason called the Khaajiir's presence a sensitive corporate secret."

"True. But there's sensitive and there's sensitive. The Bettelhines could be underwriting his historical research out of noblesse oblige, keeping his presence classified until they have something sufficiently glorious to merit a public unveiling. Or they could have found some practical application to some discovery he made in one of his other disciplines, something big enough to make them want to make him a personal guest. Right now we don't have enough data to know."

Flailing for a pattern, knowing it useless, I ventured, "We have those assassins."

"True. And what do they prove, at this point?"

I hated to admit it, but the answer was Nothing. Even if we could confirm that they'd been his target, we still didn't know whether their reason for wanting him dead had anything to do with any work he might have been doing for Bettelhine. "We have me. We know it has something to do with me."

"We know it looks that way, because the Bettelhines have made such a point of withholding the information until we can connect with their father. But maybe he just considers it too sensitive to be left to the kids. And maybe he just wants you to tolerate a few hours in the Khaajiir's presence until he can you get you dirtside, separate the two of you, and tell you why he really called you here. Again, we don't have enough data. And you shouldn't need us to tell you that."

No, I shouldn't. I was, after all, the one talented at solving puzzles. "So what else have you got?"

Oscin surprised me by sitting up and staring at the blackness on the other side of the suite's transparent wall. "Jason Bettelhine."

The disappearance of Jason Bettelhine for much of his childhood had been a major story throughout the Confederacy, if one I'd ignored because of my own level of disinterest in what amounted to a celebrity scandal.

The mystery had received special coverage here on Xana. I had to expect that. He was, after all, one of the heirs to the Inner Family birthright, famous from the day he was born. Still, most of the particulars had remained vague, with the Bettelhines keeping most of the investigation away from the media's hands.

About all that came out, aside from the usual conflicting rumors and empty speculation, was that there'd been no particular reason to suspect kidnapping, a claim that by process of elimination established that Jason had left his home and his great expectations of his own volition. This seemed an extraordinary step for a boy who'd been all of thirteen. Maybe he'd been an unhappy kid and maybe he'd just been a romantic one, his head addled with dreams of offworld adventure.

For five years there'd been no more word, his fate just a perennial question, mentioned anew on his birthdays and on every anniversary of his departure. Then came the thunderbolt of an announcement. Jason was alive and well and on his way back. There was no information on what he'd been doing, or why he'd decided to return at that particular moment, even if it had in fact been his own idea. If the Bettelhines knew, they'd kept that proprietary as well.

The hytex provided access to an old holo of Jason arriving at Layabout alone, looking even more drawn and haggard than he looked now. His father, Hans, greeted him with an embrace, genuine tears running down the older man's face. It was an oddly public reunion, given that the Bettelhines never had to use Layabout if they didn't want to, but the Porrinyards didn't know whether to find anything suspicious about that. The public venue may have been nothing more than an acknowledgment, by Hans, that the boy's absence and unknown plight had been mourned by his world's general public as well.

Following that, the two of them had taken the Royal Carriage, either this car or the other one, back down to the surface, and Jason had disappeared from sight for almost two years, his doings explained away by regular Bettelhine updates to the effect that he was "recovering" or "getting to know his family again."

Sixteen months after his return, Jason was guest of honor at a ball held at the main Bettelhine estate. From precedent established by the practice among prior Bettelhine offspring, and the sheer number of articles about all the beautiful and bright-eyed young ladies from both continents who'd been invited to meet Jason at the affair, the occasion had amounted to a cattle call for consorts of high social standing, with Jason expected to determine in the few minutes he would have to dance and converse with those few that caught his eye whether there were any he considered of special interest. Local news sources around Xana identified this girl and that girl as the one they expected Jason to call again, but the absence of any further gossip implied that no Cinderellas ever received any followup visits from this particular prince.

The Porrinyards wondered if Jason might be hiding homosexual preferences, since there were worlds stupid enough to make that a secret worth hiding, but a few seconds of paging through Xana's social register confirmed that several previous past cattle calls of this type had catered to Bettelhine offspring intent on meeting candidates of their own gender. As long as there were always new generations capable of carrying on the Family name and running the Family business, the Bettelhines didn't give a damn how the parts interfaced.

No, it was just as likely that Jason was a true neuter. Or that he might be as close to Jelaine as I'd supposed. Or that his demons were still tormenting him one way or another.

In any event, Jason had started to travel again, this time with Family approval. He made a few public appearances on Xana before moving on to other systems in Jelaine's company, traveling alongside Jelaine and other Family members to worlds that included Tchius, Vlhan, and my own home, New London.

That trip had taken another year.

Then they'd returned, and Jason had disappeared from sight for a few months before surprising everybody by appearing beside his father at executive functions.

Jelaine had also been present at a number of those, as quietly radiant as she had been during our own brief meeting, but the same was true of several other Bettelhine siblings. She'd also been romantically linked to a number of eligible bachelors during that time, even if none of them had lasted long enough to become more than dalliances. But she was still young.

Her reserve, like Jason's, might mean something. And it might not.

Oscin sat on the edge of the bed, brooding. Skye, lying on her side beside me, looked just as disturbed. Something about Jason Bettelhine's story bothered them, in ways deeper than the ones that bothered this limited single-skull.

I had to ask. "What are you thinking?"

"I'm not sure."

"Try."

They hesitated. "It's just a feeling. Not even anything I can define."

"Try."

The Porrinyards always know how to express themselves. It's a gift that comes with being your own committee. But now, for the first time I could remember, they needed to grope for their answer, before producing a tone more halting than any I'd ever heard from them. "His life . . . has much in common with the broken singlets who became Oscin and Skye. A boy like that, living like royalty, but determined to flee his gilded cage—he's either running to something, or away from something."

The words hung in the air for a moment, before Skye finished alone. "Leaving our homeworld was a . . . difficult decision for us. But our singlets knew that we could never go back. He returned under his own power. What did he want?"

"His inheritance," I guessed. "His family. His home. A place to feel safe again."

"Maybe." The answer seemed to acknowledge all of those possibilities without believing any of them. "And maybe he had just figured out whatever he wanted to figure out, and needed the Bettelhine resources to accomplish whatever came next. . . ."

5

THE BIG LIE

The chime alerting us to the dinner party in the parlor was as affected as everything else in the Bettelhine Royal Carriage. It was a sylvan tinkle, the kind of sound that could only have been tolerated by people who frown with fey disdain whenever reminded of their social obligations. Maybe I was reading too much into it. Maybe the moment I'd found myself thinking I'd had enough of the Bettelhine lifestyle came when the Porrinyards and I rose from the bed and found ourselves transfixed by an amenity that began with our old linens rolling into the bulkhead, continued with mechanisms in the bedframe unscrolling their replacement, and ended with puffs of mist wrapping everything in a nice, rueful emphasis on *nice,* floral scent to keep things embossed with perfection until our return.

I moaned. "Oh, come *on*!"

The Porrinyards grinned. "Must make it convenient for any murderer who wants to dispose of forensic evidence."

I remembered the Claw of God and did not think the comment funny. "Must."

It didn't take us long to get ready. I don't own any formal

clothing. But my usual severe black suit would do, as would the Porrinyards' matching white, especially if they wore the buttonless slipon jackets they donned whenever they wished to stress their status as a matching set. I don't wear makeup either, though both Porrinyards have been known to, depending on local custom. There was little to be done with our hair either, thanks to their skull bristle and my own longstanding habit of keeping mine short with but a single, defiant shoulder-length lock along my right cheek. This might or might not be acceptable by Xana's standards, but to hell with the other attendees if they thought otherwise. We weren't here to dazzle anybody.

We emerged to find the parlor inhabited by assorted Bettelhines and associates already deep in the tiresome mill-around-and-chat that always makes me want to leap off the nearest balcony.

I caught a glimpse of a tall, elegant redhead in a silvery gown that left much of her back bare, disappearing through the doorway into one of the suites. Her movements looked familiar, but I didn't see enough to place her.

I saw a nervous couple in their late fifties, the man all high sweaty forehead bald but for a spiral spit curl, the woman beaming with a desperate contact-high that did not translate to leaving the protection of the alcove where she and her husband huddled like frightened cats. When her eyes met mine she looked away in a hurry, as if afraid that even that moment of contact would be seen as impudent.

Jason Bettelhine was across the room, in discussion with two men I didn't recognize, both dressed in black suits of identical design. The taller of the two glanced our way, revealing Bettelhine features beneath a helmet of premature silver. Probably the brother Jason had mentioned. Unlike Jason, he was not smiling. The third man was balding, shiny-faced, shorter than either Bettelhine and pale in ways that went beyond mere complexion. He could stay in the sun and tan himself to a crisp, and he'd still be pale beneath the skin, all the way to the bones. He glanced my way too, and nodded in recognition.

Jelaine Bettelhine was closer to us, sipping something vaporous as she chatted with the Khaajiir and a tall thin man whose face was all sharp lines. She'd changed gowns and put her hair up into a fractal swirl of the sort designed to reveal new flourishes and embellishments with every casual flip of her head. It would have looked fussy or pretentious on anybody else, but she wore it like a jeweled crown. I've never given a flying crap about hairstyles and I still envied her ability to pull it off, let alone her ability to put it together in the three hours since I'd last seen her. It was, I supposed, one of the inherited skills of royalty; certainly, I certainly knew few women who would have attempted that gown, a silvery bejeweled monstrosity that seemed determined to compete with the overhead lights for luminosity. She happened to spot us as we left the suite, and flashed a smile rich with either genuine warmth or a simulation too cunning to be distinguished from the real thing. "Counselor. You look radiant."

I had two conflicting thoughts, the first being *bullshit* and the second an amazed, mortifying *I do?* Against my will, the latter won out, and I felt a flush come to my cheeks. "Thank you."

"Nonsense. It's the simple truth." She turned to the Porrinyards. "And you too, dears. I'm afraid I don't know the proper etiquette for addressing linked pairs, and therefore don't know whether to say handsome or pretty, let alone when to refer to both of you and when to address you as individuals, but if you show me some indulgence I promise to learn. I look forward to setting aside any awkwardness I might have in favor of friendship."

There wasn't a single awkward, or less than charming, cell in her body. Damned if the Porrinyards, who could normally give as good as they got, weren't blushing too. "You're doing fine. I like your hair."

"Thank you. I know you've already been introduced to the Khaajiir," she said, a reference the Bocaian academic acknowledged with a nod, "but I believe this is your first encounter with one of my father's closest associates, Mr. Monday Brown."

The man with the sharp face blinked at me. His smile, unlike Jelaine's, never reached his eyes. He might have been determining the profit potential in selling the Porrinyards and me for component parts. "Counselor. How have you enjoyed your visit so far?"

I couldn't believe he'd said that. "It's been a little overpopulated with assassins."

His teeth were very small and very white. "I spoke with Antresc just a few minutes ago. He told me that both criminals remain unresponsive. But as his people were able to remove the microteemers implanted in their tear ducts, there's little chance of them waking up and continuing to evade interrogation with further flashes."

"That's progress. I don't suppose he's found their confederate?"

"No, I'm afraid not. Nor has he been able to trace their travels any farther back than their embarkation on the Bursteeni homeworld. But he's a good man. I'm certain that the second the teeming wears off, he'll be able to get the answers from them in short order."

The Khaajiir shifted his weight against his staff, the strain manifesting as a tremor in his upper arms. "And how will he do that, sir? Torture?"

"This is a civilized world, sir."

"Alas," the Khaajiir replied, "the definition of that word has always been fluid. We both know of worlds where civilization meant that slow torture only took place in soundproofed rooms. We also know, unfortunately, just what species of commerce provided our dear hosts with their riches, and therefore just what agonizing capabilities this society must be equipped to exercise at times of crisis." He then seemed to remember his hostess. "No offense, dear."

"None taken," said Jelaine. "It happens to be a legitimate concern."

"Still," the Khaajiir continued, returning his attention to Brown, "if the preferences of the apparent target have any weight here, I would prefer to make sure that any questioning remained in the realm of the humane."

Brown's face flickered with something that was not politic and was not friendly. "What about Counselor Cort? She was a target too."

My smile met Brown's irritation head on. "I'm afraid I'm not quite so principled about the treatment of people who have tried to kill me. But I see no reason to oppose the Khaajiir here."

Brown might have shown more resentment toward the Khaajiir and myself had we spoken for ourselves alone, but Jelaine had indicated agreement, too, and that changed everything. "If you wish. I'll arrange for the two of you to speak with Mr. Pescziuwicz, so you can share your concerns."

"Please," the Khaajiir said.

As Brown wandered off, trailing an invisible cloud of resentment behind him, Jelaine's expression turned pitying, like someone observing a wounded bird. "I must apologize for Monday. He's never charming, but he's at his best in my father's presence. Any place other than with my father is, shall we say, not his habitat."

I asked, "That doesn't extend to being with you or Jason?"

"Oh, we can give him orders, if that's what you mean. Father's made it clear to him that any directives coming from us are to be considered as coming from him. But there are always about three hundred relatives within the Inner

Family, with all the politics and personal competition that implies. Aides like Monday learn to back the ones they work for, clinging to them with a sort of determined possessiveness that leaves very little leeway for loyalty to any of the others. It's a lot, I suppose, like having a pet. From their personal point of view, *they* own *you*. Monday's a rather extreme example of that syndrome. My father's his entire world."

"He doesn't have a family? Or friends?"

"No, he maintains quarters in my father's house, and except for trips like this remains at my father's beck and call from the moment my father gets up in the morning to the moment my father goes to sleep at night, taking time off only when he's ordered to."

The Khaajiir shifted his weight against his staff. "It's true. I've seen that happen. Monday takes it like he's being punished."

"That's pretty sad. Has he always been that way?"

"At least as long as he's been working for my father."

"What about you?" I asked her. "Do you and Jason have people like that working for you?"

"Oh, please. Subservience on his scale makes us uncomfortable. We can't escape it, not entirely, but we prefer our loyalties earned, not imposed. So we hire out of the staff pool, as needed." She smiled. "In any event, Andrea, is everything in your suite is to your liking?"

"I'll feel more comfortable when I find out what this is all *about*."

She placed a hand on my shoulder. "Perhaps this doesn't all have to wait for my father. I'd love to be able to move past the 'necessary business' part of this relationship and proceed to what I hope shall be a warmer connection, maybe even one with that earned loyalty I talked about. Let us get you a drink first, and we'll have a private chat. If the others will excuse us . . . ?"

The Porrinyards took the Khaajiir with them, professing deep fascination with the sudden end of K'cenhowten's great Dark Age.

Jelaine escorted me to the bar, which was being tended by a petite young woman with a fresh face, scarlet hair composed of artificial fibers wired to strobe with bars of orange light, and eyes like cut emeralds—which is to say, not just possessed of green irises but actually faceted, and translucent, sans any obvious whites. I'd seen stranger body-mod combinations, but could not help wondering to what degree it affected her vision. Introducing herself as Colette Wilson, and declaring herself honored to serve me, the young lady with the bejeweled eyes and the neon hair flashed the kind of smile that confirmed the opportunity to pour drinks for me a sensation somewhere between the best sex she'd ever had and direct electrical stimulation to the pleasure center of her brain.

I didn't want anything in particular, but bowed to Colette's superior knowledge of the stock, and asked for something sweet but light, intoxicating without any euphoric or hallucinogenic aftereffects. Whatever it was also turned out to be electric blue, in a tall glass. It was sweet, as I'd requested, but one sip and I felt tingles in my fingers and toes. Light, my ass. I was going to have to nurse it.

By the time Jelaine led me to a quiet spot beside the tank with the Bettelhine fish, the scattering of guests had changed configuration. The nervous couple was still hiding in the alcove, but were now talking to the redhead in the gown, whose face I could still not see. Oscin and the Khaajir had moved to a set of plush couches so the frail Bocaian could sit; he was holding forth on something which made Oscin nod with unfeigned fascination. Skye had left them to join Jason Bettelhine and his companions, her very presence seeming to lift the mood on that side of the room. The Bettelhine brothers grinned at her, delighted by whatever witty thing she'd just said. Even the pale man with them seemed impressed. I was equally certain that her bon mot had been brilliant and that the men would have reacted with just as much glee to something banal. There's a reason why I defer to the Porrinyards on matters requiring interaction with other human beings. They're as good at being liked as I am at not.

Jelaine saw me watching Skye. "Fascinating. The way you use them."

I stiffened. "I'm sure I don't know what you're talking about."

"Please, Counselor. I'm not belittling your friends—or friend, if you prefer the singular. How troublesome, referring to them can be! I can see that they're not just assistants to you. But you're using them as a resource right now, aren't you? You're using their shared perspective to gather as much intelligence as possible." She sipped her own drink, a golden concoction in a flute. "Forgive me my sense of wonder. They're the first linked pair I've ever met."

Cylinked pairs may be rare, since the AIsource procedure that creates them is illegal on most human worlds, but I found a Bettelhine's protestations of sheltered naïveté hard to believe. "Jason told me he had a crush on a pair of cylinked women who worked for an uncle. He said they visited the main estate on a regular basis."

She placed a placatory hand on my wrist. "Yes, I know. I was there when he told you, remember? But you won't find a contradiction here. I do know who he's talking about, but I was a very naïve young girl at the time and thought they were just close in the usual way young ladies can be close. I'm afraid I never watched them at length and never registered how they functioned as a unit. I never even heard them speak at the same time, the way your lovely Oscin and Skye do. Is it really so terrible for me to be dazzled, a little? Even a little envious?"

"No," I said, watching Skye chuckle as the Bettelhine men glanced my way. I supposed I'd become a subject of conversation. "I suppose not."

"How did you ever meet them?"

I almost launched into a summary of my posting to the cylinder world known as One One One, but stopped myself and appraised Jelaine anew. "You know, you're very good."

She went wide-eyed. "At what?"

"The way you pulled me aside with hints of explanation, delayed me with a drink, and now change the subject to something safe. The way you give the impression you've opened up without telling me a damn thing. The way you take a wary and unpleasant person who has no intention of making friends and make her relax in her presence. Whatever else you are, you're a born politician. But I'm not fooled, and I'm losing my patience. *What is this all about?*"

Her secretive smile never wavered. Only her eyes reacted, and then with a twinkle of affection. "I was told you could be difficult, Andrea. I was also told that you're well worth the effort. I do want to be friends."

I almost demanded to know who the hell told her that, since the Porrinyards were pretty much the only people I knew capable of tolerating me without being ordered to. But it would have meant changing the subject again. "The explanation. Please."

She sighed, betraying not irritation but a deep, pervading sadness that might have been about me and might have been about something else. For a moment I could see the same shadow of terrible suffering I'd spotted on Jason's face. "You may have guessed at least part of this already, but you're here, at least in part, for what might loosely be termed a job interview."

"No shit."

"Not at all. My father has a specific position in mind, and believes that he can offer you terms capable of luring you away from your current employers."

She had to mean the Corps, as she couldn't have known about my association with the AIsource. "No."

She raised an eyebrow. "We know that you're not happy with the way the Corps has treated you. It can't be home."

"It isn't. In fact, I hate the bastards. But neither am I eager to sell my loyalty to an organization I've always considered evil for a little more money and a slightly fancier job title."

"I appreciate that, Andrea, but there are factors here that you can't possibly guess. It wouldn't be a *little* more money. Or a *slightly* fancier job title. And *evil* is only a function of how the power's used. Frankly, I believe that my father will be able to make the case that your loyalty's a commodity better invested with us at this critical point in your history than with any of those self-righteous slavemasters at New London."

She seemed so sure. But then, a sense of entitlement, of being able to collect people, would just naturally go along with being a Bettelhine. "I'm still not hearing any answers."

She sighed. "My father really does deserve the pleasure of telling you the whole thing. He's done so much to arrange this, and it will mean so much to him. But perhaps I can save him some time covering the background."

"Anything," I said.

"Well, let's start with this. Have you ever experienced a turning point? One of those moments so profound that it not only changed your life after that moment, but also how you interpreted everything you'd seen and done beforehand?"

I thought of the day I'd lost my family on Bocai, of my mission to the world known as Catarkhus, and of the way the Porrinyards had looked at me after the second time they'd saved my life in just about as many days. "Yes."

"Well, as it happens, the fortunes of the Bettelhine Family have experienced such a historic moment, one that's likely to alter the way we conduct business and how we relate to the rest of human civilization."

"Would this be Jason's disappearance?"

The guess did not surprise her. "Would it surprise you to hear that his absence almost destroyed us?"

"No."

"You're alone, then. I know what people say about us. They look at all the damage we've done, at the blood spilled because of us, and declare us soulless monsters profiting off human lives. I'd wager half my share in the family fortune that you've said something like it yourself, certainly before you got here and absolutely since you've arrived. Am I right?"

I decided not to insult her with empty denials. "Your money would be safe."

"We're used to that. But sometimes, when we suffer a family trauma, outsiders don't even give us credit for the ability to feel for our own. They question our tears and attribute our grief to public relations. It's different when you're in the middle of it. It almost tore us apart."

"I understand."

"No, Andrea, with all due respect, and more affection than you could possibly know, I don't think you do. A missing child is supposed to be horrible for any family, and I'm certain it is, but I think a big family with a small mob of children, like ours, feels it more. The suffering, the fear for him, the sense of loss, is not subdivided, as you'd suppose, but multiplied. We all reflected each other's heartbreak and uncertainty, and we all felt more hopeless in the face of it. But that may have been a good thing, in the long run. We may have been the first generation of my family in many years to not grow up feeling invulnerable."

"What about you?"

"I'm not arrogant enough to say that it was worse for me than for any of the others, but I became a shadow of myself. Jason and I were about the same age, and up until that day he'd always been my closest friend among all my brothers and sisters."

The hubbub of soft music and surrounding conversation seemed as far away as New London. For the moment, at least, there was no one in the room but us. "Why did he leave?"

"In part, idealism; in part foolish rebellion. He thought he'd return home a conquering hero. I was such a starry-eyed little idiot that I believed him, and even wished him luck when he left. To my eternal shame, I even helped him slip away."

"That must have gone over well."

"Nobody knew until long after he got back. And by then, the damage was done. Have you ever heard of a cylinder world known as Deriflys?"

The word sounded elegant, the way she uttered it horrific. I found part of me not wanting to know. But I'd opened this door, so I just shook my head.

"There are places where the machinery of civilization carves out a habitat for people to live, only to abandon them when the people who pay the bills either go bankrupt or decide to move elsewhere. Deriflys was one of the all-time worst."

"What happened?"

"It was supposed to be a travel and manufacturing hub, with plenty of work, but the backers disappeared and left two million human beings stranded there with no way to evacuate. No human or alien government anywhere in civilized space considered the looming catastrophe their problem. The local economy crashed. Legitimate shipping went elsewhere. More and more, the only vessels interested in stopping at Deriflys became those run by criminal enterprises intent on profiting from the misery of those left behind. Drugs and weapons flooded the place, gangs took over, and the residents who did manage to book passage off-world found themselves delivered against their wills to lives worse than the ones they'd left. Everybody who stayed had to live with the chaos. There were a few well-fed leaders and absolute wretchedness on every level below them. The inhabitants were left starving, desperate, filthy, and clawing at each other for every gram of food, breath of air, and square centimeter of space. In short, life there became a daily litany of atrocities, and an exercise in how low you were willing to sink, how cheaply you were willing to sell yourself, in order to survive." She told the story as if she'd lived it herself. She dabbed at her eyes with a soft linen. "This, Counselor, is the place where my beautiful brother Jason, my best friend, spent five years while we didn't know whether he was alive or dead."

It wasn't the only such story I'd heard. Civilized space was dotted with worlds that had made themselves hells, sometimes out of sheer suicidal neglect, other times by turning on each other with the very same weapons responsible for providing the ancestors of Jason Bettelhine with the wealth he'd forsaken when he went wandering, bright-eyed but blind, through a hostile universe. There was no reason I should have felt sympathy for him, given who he was, but he'd been a child, much like another whose innocence had ended with brutality and blood. It took me several seconds to muster words. "Why didn't he tell somebody who he was, and promise a big reward to the first ship that sent him home?"

Once again, her smile crossed the border into the pity she'd shown for Monday Brown. "Surely a woman as wise as yourself knows the answer to that."

It had come to me as soon as I'd asked the question. Of course, he couldn't have. The kind of people capable of clawing their way to the top of a world falling apart would have seen a Bettelhine heir as a commodity more valuable than any mere ransom could be. There were entire civilizations ravaged by his family trade that would have given half their treasuries just to have him handed over for execution, others that would have loved to have him chained to a wall and tortured a different way every day for the rest of his natural life. Still others would have pointed a gun at his head and advised the Bettelhines that he would remain alive for only as long as the family made regular payments. In none of those cases would any thought be given to actually returning him. Hard as it would have been to accept, Jason would have been far safer as a ragged little corridor rat, or as the plaything of powers greater than himself, than he ever could have been as the long-lost Bettelhine son, expecting a comfortable ride back to the luxurious estate he'd forsaken in favor of the adventure gone bad.

But there was another factor, even more terrible, that loomed above all of those nightmares like a massive weight set to crush everything beneath it to insignificance. Exactly how long could a naïve, pampered boy live in hell before survival meant doing something that he could never bring back to his family? How long before the only possible conclusion for him would be that he'd ruined himself, and belonged nowhere but where he was?

I said, "How did he get out?"

"He's not willing to share that at this time. But I can say that when he got home it was almost another additional year before he was willing to accept the family's joy at seeing him again. The boy we'd known had been . . . broken."

I glanced at the confident young man enjoying his conversation with Skye. "He seems fine now. As do you."

"Thank you. You don't know what it cost us, by which I mean, the two of us. We help each other carry the weight. It's one reason we remain so close now."

"And—excuse me—all this helps explain why I'm here, how?"

Jelaine spread her hands. "A changed man can change his family, and what his family stands for. Even, I daresay, how far the web of family extends. We want to reflect that with our policies, Andrea, and we believe that you can help us realize that ambition. We believe that you're uniquely suited to help guide us into that future. But the rest is for my father to say. I can see we're out of time anyway."

I heard another sylvan tinkle, like the one that had summoned the Porrinyards and me from our suite. It was followed by a gentle mechanical hum, somewhere above me. I followed the sound to its point of origin and saw a formal dinner table, draped with a golden embroidered cloth and equipped with twelve settings, descending from an invisible recess in the ceiling, sans wires. The table itself had no legs, just the dining surface, which found its natural level at the altitude appropriate for diners. Just as it settled into place, twelve chairs, including eleven built for the human posterior and one designed for the bonier Bocaian rump, came into view, lowering themselves through the illusory solidity of the ceiling, and settled into their positions. Atop the table, gleaming silver holders anchored a pair of scarlet candles, burning fore and aft, their reflections dancing on each of the bejeweled table settings. Each place had a printed name card, tented behind the plate, establishing the prearranged seating order.

Across the room, the middle-aged couple went *aaaaah* and just barely resisted clapping their hands. I stifled the same impulse I'd obeyed at the suite when confronted with the bed that had made itself. I did not exclaim, *Oh, come ON!* But I thought it. I may have liked one Bettelhine at least, more than I'd imagined I was going to, but I hated what seemed to be a family habit of doing everything as if it had to be accompanied by a flourish of trumpets.

Somewhere, Arturo Mendez said, "Dinner is served."

* * *

To me the common dinner party is as alien an environment as an ocean of liquid mercury, or an ice field on a frozen moon.

But some things can't be helped.

We took our seats, and I got to meet the other members of the party.

It turned out that I did know the dazzling redhead seated opposite me ("Counselor Cort! How wonderful! I heard that you were here!"), but that was no great accomplishment on my part. Everybody knew her. Her name was Dejah Shapiro, and she was the famous mistress of a personal empire as star-spanning as the one commanded by the Bettelhines, much of it based on the sale of high-end orbital habitats for markets throughout human space. It was said that she'd built more worlds than a year's output of the Bettelhine factories could have blown up. It was also said that, despite her youthful appearance, she'd lived longer than any human being now alive. We'd spent a week working together, about ten years ago, when she'd been engaged to double the size of an expanding New London, and I'd been the young Dip Corps attorney assigned to ease her through the permits. She'd claimed to like me, at the time, even though I'd done everything within my power to discourage it.

When the Porrinyards were introduced to her as my assistants, she sized them up and brightened at once. "Oh, wow. Counselor, you haven't."

The Porrinyards, seated at opposite ends of the long table, but enjoying themselves a little too much, said, "Surprising, isn't it?"

"Not now that I think about it. It *would* take more than one person, acting in concert, to break past Andrea's defenses."

Dejah's latest marriage, to a low-end petty thief named Karl Nimmitz, had been the stuff of tabloid journalism, impossible to escape even if, like myself, that was the kind of news you tried to. But he wasn't here. I wondered why. Had they fought? Broken up? Or were there just some pets you didn't take out in polite company? I rejected those questions as irrelevant to the moment at hand and asked a polite, deceptively casual, "And is this your first trip down to Xana?"

Dejah gave me a look of total understanding, which in her case gave the impression that she could map every stray neuron that decided to fire in my brain. "In fact, yes. I'm afraid that relations between myself and our hosts have not always been as cordial as they've been tonight."

The other Bettlehine brother emitted a laugh that sounded more like a bark. "Let's not understate the case, Dejah. The proper word, before today, has always been *enemies*. There have been times when you wouldn't have dared come here without an armada."

"Well, yes," she said, with a genteel tip of her goblet. "But I hope this marks the start of a more congenial relationship."

He matched her toast. "As do I."

Best wishes like that make the air between them seem full of broken glass.

His name was Philip Bettelhine, and he was introduced to me as the half brother of Jason and Jelaine, born a decade before them to one of their father's previous wives. The Bettelhine genes remained dominant, of course, and he had the same strong jaw, the same piercingly intelligent eyes. But his complexion was darker, a polished mahogany where theirs was a milk-fed pink. His gray hair was the color and consistency of lamb's wool and had been trimmed to meet his forehead in a jagged line like a sawtooth, suggesting either the points of a crown or the teeth of a shark, I didn't know which. As a man he seemed wearier and less prone to politic smiles than either of his younger siblings, more bent by whatever responsibilities marked his own contribution to the Bettelhine enterprises.

Tonight he sat at Jason's right hand and murmured soft comments toward his younger brother whenever conversation lagged. Only Skye, sitting to his immediate left, managed to establish that he was capable of smiling with actual mirth, rather than just sublimated tension. At least one of her comments made him glance my way with genuine amusement. I burned to know what the joke was, but would have forgone that for some understanding of whatever was going on between him and his brother.

Sometime during the salad—orange, crunchy spheres that I probed with little appetite, and much dismay, and which Jelaine leaned over to describe as a "delicious, tangy" spore native to Xana's frozen continent—Philip turned my way and uttered the only words he'd directed toward me since our terse introduction at the meal's onset. "Excuse me, Counselor? Jason and I were talking about this new job title of yours? Prosecutor-at-Large?"

I dabbed at my lips with a napkin, having rearranged the spheres in my bowl without quite managing to consume any of them. "What about it, Mr. Bettelhine?"

"It's downright unprecedented, as far as I know. In fact, from what I know about the Dip Corps leadership, it flies in the face of any of their policies maintaining command oversight over agents in the field."

I'm notorious for preferring food mixed in vats to those grown on planets, but I tasted one of the spheres anyway, just to look unconcerned. It was as tangy as advertised, even if I wasn't sure about the delicious part. "That's correct. It does."

"Forgive me, Counselor, but how you got yourself declared so independent has got to be the very best story at this table."

"You're right," I said. "It is. But I'm not telling it."

Philip surprised me by letting the subject go. But I still caught him sneaking glances at me afterward. After the first few, I knew one thing as well as I knew the litany of Bettelhine crimes against humanity: he didn't know why I was here any more than I did. He just knew the level of importance his father and siblings had placed on my presence, and being out of the loop bothered him.

The Khaajiir did not speak much—a change from his behavior before dinner, when he'd been visibly chatty—but when he did open his mouth, he was charming and kind, if more hesitant and formal than he'd been before. He kept his staff threaded between the seat and the left armrest of his chair, and touched it often, if afraid to go without it for so much a single moment.

The pale man sitting to Skye's immediate left, the same one who had been so charmed by her before the meal, was Vernon Wethers, another dedicated aide like Monday Brown, except working for Philip Bettelhine instead of Hans. For the few moments I spoke to him he said, in a voice reluctant to break into any other conversation, that he'd been working beside Philip for fifteen years, and valued the chance to see so many high-level projects from the perspective of management. He couldn't give me any details, of course, those projects being classified, but he assured me that it was exciting work. Sitting between two extraordinarily beautiful women (Skye and Dejah), facing another (Jelaine), and dealing with a fourth who at the very least did not deserve to be buried beneath the nearest rock (myself), seemed to unman him. He stammered, and faced his food, and, at the one point when Skye's shoulder brushed against his, recoiled as if burned. The one thing I would later remember him saying, in response to Mrs. Pearlman's gushing praise of the food, was, "I'm glad you like it. But I'm afraid I have no sense of taste, myself."

"I'm sorry to hear that," said Dejah.

He shrugged. "It would be a distraction from my work."

I didn't ask Vernon if he had a family. There seemed little point.

The Pearlmans, Dina and Farley, seemed to have the simplest story. They were introduced to me as a pair of middle managers from Temet, a village based around a tiny research facility on an island off the coast of Midgard. Fourth-generation residents of Xana, they claimed not to have met any Inner Family Bettelhines before. Given their dullness, I would have been surprised if they often ventured out of their own neighborhood, let alone made it offworld. But they'd exceeded their latest project quotas, and been chosen out of all the coworkers on their pay level, to enjoy a celebratory evening with the big bosses, during this luxurious elevator ride from orbit. It was no wonder they turned pale every time any of these rich and powerful rulers of their world spoke to them spoke to them for five minutes. They were people who had lived their lives in a dark box, blinded when they found themselves beneath the light of the midday sun.

Over the next course, some fishy delicacy from Xana's southern sea that the Pearlmans devoured with gusto and that I quit with after only a few bites, I heard Dina questioning Oscin. "I've always wondered, one thing about this Dip Corps. Is that the same thing as the Diplomatic Corps?"

"Yes," Oscin said.

She struggled for a precedent. "Like Hom.Sap is the same thing as *Homo Sapiens.*"

"Yes," he said again.

There was a pause, then she wondered, "Who decides that kind of thing?"

Several seats down, Skye reddened and covered her mouth. But there was no sign of a grin on Oscin's face. "There's a committee."

Monday Brown, who had been absent since his abrupt departure at the end of our conversation before dinner, returned to us a few minutes after the fish course, taking his seat with the lack of self-consciousness that must have come from years of having to interrupt or delay his meals for important business. He nodded at Jelaine, and at the Khaajiir, who immediately clutched his staff as if expecting to be summoned somewhere. "I'm sorry for the delay. I had a few other things to take care of, in addition to contacting Mr. Pescziuwicz, and even then it took a few minutes to reach him, after all the, ah, damage today's incident did to his schedule. He wants the Khaajiir to know that he's invited to join the interrogation, once the suspects are capable of being interrogated. He also suggests that you're likely to find the procedure not only beyond reproach, but also far too boring to sit through."

Jason raised an eyebrow. "Sounds just like the bastard."

The Khaajiir chuckled. "I just might surprise him and take him up on that. The ruffians might be sufficiently surprised to see me up close that they'll blurt out the confession he wants."

Brown turned to me next. "As for you, Counselor, he says he has no new information at this time, but asked you to contact him anyway."

I blinked. "Right away?"

"He said, at your leisure. Colette at the bar will help you if you'd like."

I made my apologies and left the table, therefore rescuing myself from the course Mendez was then serving, something gray and semiliquid that Dina Pearlman had already pronounced spectacular, but which, if it had an organic origin, I did not want to know about. I wondered, not for the first time, about the courage of the unknown historical figures responsible for trying certain foods for the first time.

Colette, whose fibrous hair now strobed streaks of light resembling comets, and who regarded contacting Mr. Pescziuwicz for me as yet another unparalleled highlight of her working day, told me she'd pipe the call to the hytex node in my suite.

The chime alerting me of the connection sounded the second I closed the door behind me. "Cort here. Talk to me."

His holographic image shimmered into existence, a meter away. As per the Bettelhine policy of providing their guests with the finest, it had none of the static or fuzzy signal that plague hytex projections elsewhere. It wasn't even translucent. The only way I knew it was not his actual head, floating there, was common sense and the absence of any blood hemorrhaging from the cutoff beneath his chin. "Counselor, this is Antrecz Pescziuwicz. Enjoying the ride?"

The projection followed me as I plopped into one of the suite's easy chairs. "I'm a little dumbfounded, to tell the truth. Mostly by these two guests, the Pearlmans. Do your bosses always take such excessive pleasure in awing the plebes?"

He smirked. "We're all plebes to them, Counselor. Except, maybe, I see that Shapiro woman's name on the passenger manifest. Must be odd for the Family to have a personal guest with the same number of decimal places in her ledger."

"There were some comments passed at dinner to the effect that your bosses and this particular bigwig have a bumpy past. Would you happen to know anything about that?"

"Sorry. Never came up in the course of my daily workday."

Which was not, quite, the same thing as saying he didn't know. I bit my lip. "Have you been told there's another Bocaian aboard?"

"Yeah. Mr. Brown told me a few minutes ago. I tanned his eardrums for withholding until he told me the bosses were behind it. He also said I'm not authorized to know this mucker's name or what his business is, so you should refrain from telling me."

I said, "Is that a sneaky way of asking me to leak it?"

He rolled his eyes. "No, Counselor, it's a *straightforward* way of telling you *not to tell me*. When the bosses say I'm not authorized to know something, they mean I'm not authorized to know it, not that I should rush right out and contrive to find myself an accommodating big mouth. Honestly, I *don't want to know*." He took on the look of a man fighting a little battle with himself, before he surrendered with a grudging, "But I guess it wouldn't be out of line to point out that being extra careful is always a fine idea when breaking bread with a representative of a civilization that wants you burned at the stake."

"Covered. Is that why you wanted me to call?"

"No." He hesitated again, like a high diver gathering up his nerve before that first step off a clip. "The thing is, I've spent the last few hours trying to draw some lines between you and our perpetrators, and I've run into some . . . problems."

"Like what kind of problems?"

"Like there's a lot about your personal history that doesn't make any sense."

"Old news. I've spent my whole life wrestling with the parts that don't make sense. The massacre on Bocai, for one."

He grimaced with impatience as he waved that away. "Naaah, I'm not talking about that. See, there's a difference between something we don't have enough information to understand, like what happened on Bocai, and something we take for granted that just plain refuses to add up. This thing I'm talking about? Doesn't add up at all. Maybe you can help."

I had not been impressed by his job performance so far, or by his lack of curiosity over the Khaajiir, so I didn't expect much. "Shoot."

Another pause, as he searched for the right approach. "Look, Counselor, I wouldn't have worried about it if there wasn't so much out there about how smart you are. You got a wicked reputation for solving problems by asking the right questions. There's one report, here, one of the ones that made it as far as the media, about how your bosses sent you someplace owned by the Tchi, to defend one of your diplomats accused of killing one of theirs. You went to your very first meeting with the prosecution and within five minutes of hearing what evidence they had showed them why they had to have the wrong guy. I mean, you knew right away. The entire embassy staff worked on the case for four months, and you show up and poke a hole in the whole thing before you can warm the chair with your butt. So between that and what you did in my office, I know from the very start, that you're not stupid. So either there's a factor here I'm not getting, or one you're not getting. Maybe you're so close to this thing, having lived with it for so long, that you never even bothered to question it."

I pointed out, "I don't even know what you're talking about yet."

"I know," he said, his eyes rich with apology. "Let me put this in perspective, all right? One day when you're a kid, your people and some Bocaians they live with go crazy and start cutting on each other. You survive that mess and get labeled a war criminal at eight years old. The rest of your surviving neighbors get shipped off to Juje knows where, maybe some kind of institution. I don't know, maybe they're out, maybe not. But you, the Dip Corps takes you in, gives you an education, and once you grow up decides that you're cured of whatever it was that ailed you. They figure it's safe to let you go out and earn a living, as long as you're working for them and that way protected by diplomatic immunity, because if you're not somebody's gonna snatch you and send you back to the people who want your head on a pike. I mean, no offense, but is that pretty much the situation?"

I still didn't have the slightest idea where this was heading. "Yes."

"So you spend the next few years zipping from system to system, as a Dip Corps counsel. And you make a name for yourself in legal circles, but you're always having to deal with political crap because of all the parties who want you stuffed in a sack and handed over to the Bocaians. That also right?"

"Is there a question at the end of all this?"

That's when he opened the trap door beneath my feet, left me realizing how much of my life had been based on a lie. "How come anybody even knows you're a war criminal?"

Several seconds passed before I felt my heart beat again. "Come again?"

"What," he said, "you think you looked exactly the same at twenty that you did at eight? I mean, the Dip Corps could have changed your name, your skin pigment, your nose, maybe your hair color, and a couple of other cosmetic things about you, given you a new ID file and a false history, and nobody but your bosses would have known that you were the same kid."

There was a sound building in the room. It was between my ears and it was burning at the pit of my stomach and it was crumbling the bones in my spine to powder. It was the sound of cracks forming in every assumption I'd ever made, and of the entire superstructure of all the further assumptions that followed them beginning to list, and then to sway, and then to fall. I felt the room turn red at the edges, and did not want Pescziuwicz to continue, because now that he'd taken me this far I didn't need his help to travel the rest of the way.

But he went on, every word out of his mouth a fresh spike driven into the base of my brain. "Instead, they put you to work as Andrea Cort, child war criminal grown up, and willingly ate all the seven hundred flavors of crap they had to swallow because of the propaganda weapon they had just handed all the alien governments who wanted to paint humanity as a bunch of homicidal bastards who let their own get away with murder."

I closed my eyes, desperate to shut him out, hating the way his voice insisted on making itself heard through the pounding of my heart.

He asked, "Why would they put themselves through that?"

Stop, I thought.

"Why would they put you through that?"

Please stop.

"And why would you let them?"

My eyes rolled into my head, and the darkness flickering at the corners of the room swallowed me whole.

6

FULL STOP

There was a place I had been many times.

It was a place without edges. It glowed with a soft blue light, eliminating any possibility of shadow. Anybody entering this place existed in free fall. But for the presence of an atmosphere, and sufficient heat to maintain life, it might have been the universe itself before the Big Bang arrived to litter everything with dust and debris and the molecular ancestors of stupid people and bureaucrats.

I tumbled in the center of that void, still wearing the black suit I'd worn to dinner on the Bettelhine Royal Carriage, my exposed hands appearing cyanotic from the blue tinge of the only available illumination.

I'd first encountered this place as a genuine physical location, on the space station One One One: a chamber the AIsource had built, with the specific purpose of awing the human beings who came to them with questions and petitions. Any human entering this room had to float in what felt like infinite emptiness while trying to pretend that human concerns had any relevance to the intangible, unimaginably powerful minds who lived here.

By the time I'd left One One One I'd proven the place a sheer exercise in psychological gamesmanship, or public relations if you prefer, much like a similar place of power used by the title character in an ancient novel called *The Wizard of Oz*, first described to me by Oscin Porrinyard on the day I was invited into the AIsource equivalent.

Since leaving One One One, with a direct line to the software intelligences now a permanent feature of my head, I'd also found myself equipped with a virtual doorway to that place, accessible whenever parleys between us required more than a few terse exchanges.

I had never been comfortable there. I know some people like free fall, and even see it as a fine location for energetic sex, but for me it activates the height sensitivity that, while much improved thanks to my exposure on One One One, will always remain an instinctive part of my personality. It's also an AIsource place, which lowers it yet another notch on my tally of locations that inspire comfort. And yes, I know that the AIsource are everywhere and that they're no less present on New London, or Xana, or the average dead asteroid than they are in this simulation they built, but I've never required my gut reactions to win trophies for consistency. There was no way I'd ever be able to relax in a place inhabited by sentients who had been pursuing their own agendas long before the first African hominid discovered the entertainment value of a rock thrown at an unpleasant neighbor's head.

It became even less comfortable when, at some point several months after beginning my regular visits to the place, I'd grown frustrated with conversations consisting of me shouting at a faceless 360-degree sky and demanded the privilege of eye contact. They'd obliged, with the amusement native to any superior being indulging the whims of a half-wit pet, and provided a face for me to talk to.

I often wished I'd left well enough alone.

I wished it again, now, as their avatar appeared, first as a dark spot in the distance, and then, as it approached, resolving into the form of a face designed as a compromise between a generic, asexual, panracial human being, and a number of the other, more humanoid races known to me. The creature had the all-black eyes of a Riirgaan, the high forehead and white-tufted crown of hair that marks a Tchi, the puffy cheeks of the stereotypical Bursteeni, and ears that, while human in shape, possessed the mottled bumps Bocaians have instead of familiar human folds.

Don't even get me started on the voice and accent. It was a more democratic mix of those and maybe twenty other species I know about, the combination perched on the edge of incurably annoying without ever entering the realm of incomprehensibility. *Hello again, Andrea.*

"You bastards, you should have told me!"

The avatar's lips pursed. *Our primary interest has always been in the workings of your mind, and that, sadly, includes your own substantial investment in the standard human capacity for self-deception.*

I wanted to punch that smug face in the nose, but I'd learned from long experience that it was as intangible as everything else here. However wide my swing, it would just fall short, the image appearing to hover just a centimeter or so outside my reach. "Was it all just manipulation? Was everything the Dip Corps put me through just another way of controlling me?"

Nor is it up to us to explain every single unanswered question. However, there's no harm in pointing out the implications that will certainly occur to you once you're calm enough for reflection. For instance, the Dip Corps has indeed profited by shackling you with the belief that you had no alternatives but a lifetime spent in their service. You are, after all, a valuable resource. But how could your superiors have known, before you spent a single day as their representative, that you would prove quite as re-markable as you have been? On what basis would they assume that history would prove you worth retaining in-definitely, even if that meant limiting your options by forc-ing you to live with your horrific reputation intact?

I didn't need the absence of discernable direction to feel adrift. "I . . . don't know."

Does it not follow that they found you valuable even before you worked for them so much as a single day?

"M-maybe they . . . maybe they could tell—"

The AIsource avatar was firm. *You are not the center of the universe, Andrea. You are more important than you guess, even now, but as you would no doubt realize on your own, were we to wait for you to do so, any conspira-cies that have been around you since unformed childhood must have had less to do with manipulating you than using you as a tool to manipulate others.*

"Who? The Unseen Demons?"

Again, Andrea: you are not the center of the universe. Our Rogue Intelligences would have taken notice of you, at that point, but only insofar as we did: as a potential future resource, and even then only as one of a potential many. Even if the people controlling your fate, back then, had possessed any knowledge of the war between us and the Rogue Intelligences, or if you prefer your own melo-dramatic term the Unseen Demons, nobody would have seen you as the lever capable of manipulating such a his-toric conflict. You were just a child, with few implications outside your own species.

I flailed for meaning. "B-but the massacre—"

Please, the AIsource sniffed, using a scornful tone they might have picked up from me. *Dispense with any self-aggrandizing theories you might have about the madness that swallowed your community on Bocai having anything to do with a hidden plot, on either our part or the part of our ancestral enemies, intended only to forge you, via the trauma you experienced, into anybody's special weapon. They are grandiose and ridiculous.*

To my horror, I realized that part of me had been nursing ideas very much like that. In a desperate attempt to salvage some self-respect, I stammered, "B-but you always called the Unseen Demons responsible—"

They were. They did cause what happened. But their machinations were not about you. You are not one of your kind's preordained myth figures, not a Chosen One beset by evil forces intent on preventing the fulfillment of ancient prophecies. We've always seen you as special, but not as that special. Any importance you have is either by our leave, or still just potential at this time.

"Then tell me what you're talking about!" I cried. "Tell me why what the Dip Corps would have to gain by making sure I remained infamous!"

That would amount to answering your questions for you. And as we have said, we have little interest in telling you where to go, what to say, and how to react, at any given moment. We have only pointed out implications that you would soon come to realize for yourself. We may provide additional guidance from time to time, as we did when we suggested this journey very much worth taking, but the ultimate responsibility for your own life remains your own.

I crossed my arms and turned away in a huff. It was a futile move. As is only natural in a friction-free environment, the sudden move became an unwilling pirouette, returning that impossible, smug face to stage center. "Have I told you today how much I hate you?"

Was that a smile, forming at the corner of the AIsource avatar's lips? *Yes.*

I didn't believe it. The sons of bitches were mocking me. I found myself hating them more than ever before. "When

I do put you out of your misery, I'm going to make sure it hurts."

The sideways grin expanded. *Noted. Meanwhile, you need to hurry up and absorb this information. Because we come now to the other reason we urged you to accept Hans Bettelhine's invitation.*

I could only repeat something I'd said to them many times. "Go to hell."

As you know, this is our fondest dream. But we are not the species that faces damnation today.

The silence that followed felt like a death knell for everything I'd ever known. "What?"

The avatar did everything but smack its lips with satisfaction, now that it had gotten my undivided attention. *You are fast approaching one of your history's turning points, a moment with tremendous implications, a moment that will directly and indirectly affect the lives of millions. Entire intelligent species, including your own, will be faced with extinction if subsequent events fail to play out as they must; and though, as we have said, any importance you have is only by our leave, we have placed you in a position where your decisions will help to determine the shape of that future.*

My chest burned. "And you won't tell me what to do?"

You are dispensable. Your species is dispensable. We have no interest in the outcome. As always, we take what we need from the process itself.

A legendary murderer once said that he wished the world had but one throat, and he the blade sharp enough to cut it. At the moment, I would have sacrificed humanity, the future, everything, for a single knife capable of piercing the AIsource's collective heart. "Give me *something!* Anything!"

The avatar grinned its widest grin yet, but there was no mirth in it. If anything, I detected a deep, soul-withering sadness, natural in the face of an intelligence that envied the oblivion with which it had just threatened Mankind.

Within the hour, one of your number will be murdered.

"Counselor? Do you hear me?"

Weight returned to the world. I was still sitting in my suite aboard the Bettelhine Royal Carriage. The Antresc Pescziuwicz projection was still facing me from an arm's length, an unwitting parody of the stranger avatar who had just underlined the destruction of my life's foundations. From the concern in his eyes, I'd been unresponsive for the last few seconds. Thank the software shitheads for small favors; by controlling the speed of our interface, they'd prevented it from being long minutes. Not that I cared about inconveniencing Pescziuwicz; I just didn't want him to mistake what had just happened to me to catatonia or, worse, a humiliating faint.

"Counselor?" he prodded.

"I'm fine," I told him. "I just don't have anything to say about that."

"What am I missing?"

"Me, telling you *just now* that I have nothing to say. I have to end this conversation now. Terminate connection."

His image blinked out in mid-protest.

I leaned forward, buried my face in my hands, and tried not to think of all the years I'd spent fearing a sudden knock on my door, a public snatch by extraterrestrial bounty hunters, a negative decision in some Confederate extradition court, the slow death of a trial before some interspecies court of law. I tried not to think of all the years I'd lived with a noose around my neck, about how that had all been a lie, and how the AIsource had just robbed me of even the chance to think any of it mattered.

There was a crystal statue on the table beside the chair

where I sat. I don't know what it was supposed to represent. It was like a vertical length of knotted string, rendered in fine cut glass and tinted a shade of purple that reflected every light source in the suite. It was beautiful, in its way, and typical of objects like it, in that it brought art into the room without also delivering any context or meaning. I found myself hating it. The rage boiled over. I grabbed it and hurled it, with all the strength I could muster, against the opposite wall. I don't know what it was made of, but it didn't so much shatter as disintegrate, the shards becoming bright, flaming comets that vanished before hitting anything else.

Typical. I couldn't even get any goddamned satisfaction out of that.

I wanted nothing more than to barricade myself in the bathroom and scream until the mood went away out of sheer exhaustion, but that was not an option. So I stood up and, pounding heart and all, stormed from the room, knowing I was far too angry to be with people right now but hoping for an opportunity to lacerate somebody with my tongue, before death intruded and I had to be *Counselor* Andrea Cort again.

An explosion of merriment from the table on the other end of the parlor, aftermath of some unknown witticism, greeted me as I stormed from the suite, in no mood to share the joke. I made unwilling eye contact with Oscin, who I caught in mid-laugh. He was too good to let his smile falter when he read my expression, but he did register that something was wrong.

I looked away and went to the bar, where that silly quiff Colette persisted in sparkling with hateful enthusiasm. The bands of light continued to strobe across her scarlet hair in waves, changing color with each passage in a pattern that I now recognized as linked to soft background music behind her. "Did your conference go well, ma'am?"

"I'm not your ma'am. I need another of those blue drinks you gave me before."

Her smile was bright, white, and in my face. "That particular liqueur is for before dinner, Counselor. Would you prefer me to recommend—"

"No, I don't want you to recommend. I want what I had before."

The customer's always right, even if her tone of voice is pure poison. Her friendliness not wavering a centimeter, Colette reached under the bar and produced the blue stuff, filling another glass to the rim. I took it from her and swallowed it in one gulp, feeling it hit my system with the force of a body check to the gut. I'd only managed a sip or two of the previous one. Another like this and I wouldn't know if my insides were solid, liquid, or a gas. Maybe I could drink enough to achieve the same effect as a Claw of God; it would certainly make a great name for a novelty cocktail.

"Can I help you with anything else?" she asked.

I repressed a burp. "No."

"Thank you, then," she said. "It's been a pleasure serving you."

And that was just one polite gesture too many. "What's so goddamned pleasurable about it? I was a surly bitch to you, just now. Isn't a little part of you tempted to tell me to take a hop?"

She infuriated me with an amused chuckle. "You're not the only stressed VIP I've served, Counselor. If I have to deal with any of you at a bad time, I consider it as much an honor as sharing in your happiest celebrations."

"But what do you get out of kowtowing to these people that's so orgasmic you can't wipe that pixie grin off your face?"

The pixie grin didn't waver, but it didn't seem forced either; the warmth and the grace never left her eyes. Damned if she didn't seem sincere. "I take pleasure in being good at my job."

"Then be good at it and shut up. Pour me another one."

She obliged, with another smile and thank you and another twinkle of those relentlessly cheerful eyes. Were I in a good mood I might have liked her. But in a bad mood her perkiness was an affront. Nobody had the right to feel that good when I felt this bad.

I almost gulped the freshened drink as well, but hesitated to wait out a warning rumble in my belly. That's when Skye, who had left the table to come after me, placed a gentle hand on my wrist and murmured, "What's wrong?"

"Nothing," I said. "Everything." And then the need to release anger, my frustration with being unable to take it out on Colette, the specific knowledge that so much of what I'd taken for granted was wrong, and the weight that had just been placed on my shoulders, collided with my resentment toward anybody inconsiderate enough to disturb how I felt right now. It wrapped itself up in every paranoid thought I'd ever had about the Porrinyards and their own relationship with the AIsource and how it predated my own, and how the AIsource had even prepared them for their relationship with me. I looked at Skye and saw the face of the AIsource avatar superimposed over her own. Here was someone I could be mad at. "Have you been lying to me all this time?"

She flinched, but answered without raising her voice. "No."

"What about withholding the truth? Have you been doing that?"

"Andrea, what's this—"

I kept my voice very low and very calm. "Just answer the question. Is there anything you've refrained from telling me?"

"Damn straight there is," Skye said.

The direct answer shut me up at once. I glanced across the room to see what Oscin was doing, and found him in close conversation with the Pearlmans. There was nothing in his expression or manner to betray the confrontation he was also involved in, over on our side of the room. Nor did any of the other diners, with the possible exception of a curious Dejah Shapiro, seem to realize that anything was amiss. Either we were hiding this well, or they were blind.

I realized I was afraid of whatever Skye was about to say.

She took my blue drink and downed it in one gulp, a showy gesture that could have meant nothing or everything. It could have meant nothing because while alcohol, and other mood-altering substances, had the usual physical effects on their individual bodies, their gestalt was capable of compensating for that with relative ease, by simply putting more pressure on the sobriety of the body and mind that remained.

But when she put the empty glass down, her eyes were calm. "I'm your lover, not your property. You have access to my heart and my body and my mind, but you don't own every last piece of me on demand, and never have. You want that, become our Third. You want to remain separate, that's fine too, but guess what? Secrets are what living in your own skull *means*."

I was not quite ready to discard my anger. "Yes, but . . ."

"I've given you more than I've ever given any other singlet. But there are things about Skye's past, and Oscin's past, and about my past as a linked pair, that I've never felt comfortable about sharing with anybody. There are times when other people share confidences with me that are none of your business. There are other times when I realize things on my own that are also none of your business. And there are times, like now, when you've been difficult to deal with and I need a secret piece of myself to rant and rave in, before I come back and show you patience and smiles rather than give you the fight you think you want. These are the things I withhold from you, Andrea. And these are the things you're going to have to get used to not having if we're to continue loving each other."

I opened my mouth, came up with nothing, and found myself needing to address a certain burning sensation in my eyes.

Skye gave me a squeeze on the shoulder. "Apology accepted."

"Love, I—"

"Again: apology accepted. No need dwelling on it. I'll jump your bones with special enthusiasm later. But what brought this on, anyway? Something Pescziuwicz said?"

I muttered a curse, and dabbed at my eye with the napkin Colette had provided with my drink. "No. Our bosses."

"Our Dip Corps bosses or our other bosses?"

"Our other bosses."

She turned wary. "I should have known. Ten minutes fighting that conversational rip current would make anybody cranky."

"Tell me about it."

"If it's any consolation, the Pearlmans have spent the last ten minutes dominating the conversation with cute stories about their pets and office politics, and they're still going even as we speak. Poor Jelaine's eyes are crossing."

Small talk. I've never been good at it, either making or enduring, but I sometimes envy those who have the capacity. "Just tell me. Yes or no. No details. Is there anything you've felt the need to withhold about this trip?"

Only somebody as close to them as myself would have noticed the hesitation. "Yes. Just an epiphany about a couple of these people that you might have missed. Nothing important at this time. What about you? Did our employers give you anything I should know?"

I rubbed my forehead. "Hints. Augurs. Dire warnings of imminent doom. Assurance that I have an inflated sense of my own importance. Fresh responsibilities that directly contradict that reality check. The entire fate of humanity at stake. Revelations that change everything I ever thought I knew."

Skye nodded. "The usual, then."

"Most pressing right now: advance warning that some-body in this room is about to be murdered."

Nothing in Skye's expression changed. There was no fear, no obvious alert. But something ineffable altered within her, something that would remain hidden to everybody but myself.

We were both thinking the same thing. The AIsource were nothing if not precise, and they hadn't said a damn thing about a murder attempt. They'd said a murder. It was going to happen even if I moved heaven and Earth to stop it.

And what, precisely, could I do to stop it anyway? Warn everybody, citing a hidden source I could not divulge? The second the murder took place anyway, the Bettelhines would demand to know where I'd gotten the information. The blocks in my head would keep me from explaining my special relationship with the AIsource, I'd look like I was re-fusing to answer, and the Porrinyards and I would find our-selves in a Bettelhine prison before the corpse had a chance to cool.

The most we could do was keep our eyes open and hope we could make a difference to whatever was coming.

I turned to Colette and did something that has always been very difficult, almost impossible, for me. "I'm sorry. I was a pig."

The bartender's eyes were as bright as the shimmery arcs flowing down the side of her head in sine waves. "Don't worry, Counselor. I didn't notice."

For some reason I felt diminished by that.

We returned to the table just after Arturo Mendez set down the main course, a pastry leaking a mixture of something red that I supposed to be meat, and a sauce that resembled molten gold. Greenery of some species I didn't recognize framed that concoction in a delicate spiral that turned orange at the interior vanishing point. Our arrival co-incided with several of the diners, including Dejah Shapiro and Dina Pearlman, declaring it the unseen chef's greatest accomplishment yet. Though Oscin had taken a few bites himself, and seemed likely to survive, I regarded it with a marked lack of enthusiasm. It wasn't just my lifelong pref-erence for synthesized foods, unconnected with all the messy organic factors I associate with planets. But the blue liqueur had deadened any appetite I might have been able to summon.

Monday Brown asked, "How did it go, Counselor? Was Mr. Pescziuwicz able to answer all your questions?"

I picked at the thing with a fork. "Precious few, sir, but he assures me he's still working on it."

"He will," Philip Bettelhine said. "The man has the work ethic of a machine. We're lucky to have him."

Dejah sipped her wine. "Yes, but is he lucky to be had by you?"

"He can already afford a luxurious retirement, if that's what you mean."

"But only on Xana," she pointed out.

"Yes, well, that goes without saying. We can't have him flitting off to some competitor, or unfriendly govern-ment, and spilling everything he knows about our security systems. He knew that when he took the job. But Xana's a big world, with a fine variety of climates and communities for somebody in his position. He can have everything he wants."

"Except freedom," Dejah said.

That annoyed him. "What's freedom, though? Put any animal in a cage larger than its natural range, feed it well, make sure that all its needs are met, and it may never en-counter, or recognize, the walls that keep it hemmed in. Put a man on a garden planet with unlimited opportunities for recreation, for companionship, and for his choice of lifestyles, and why would he ever long for faraway systems that can't possibly offer him any more?"

"Human beings are not animals," Dejah said.

"I know I have everything I want here," Farley Pearlman volunteered, a shy glance at the Bettelhines establishing to his satisfaction that he had not spoken out of turn. "We have the same deal, you know. We have to, with all the sensitive projects we've worked on."

"As do I," Monday Brown said.

Vernon Wethers raised his hand. "Me too. I don't mind."

Farley Pearlman said, "Temet's weather is *perfect*, most of the year. Why would I want to suck bluegel for half a year in Intersleep, just to visit somewhere that's not going to be any better?"

Dina Pearlman said, "My best friend, Joy? She was part of a trade delegation to New London once. She said the food there was *poison*, and the people—"

Jason Bettelhine coughed once, seizing the conversation without having to raise his voice a single decibel. "In the first case, the counselor and her companions hail from New London. I assume they'd have something to say about the 'poison' food."

Dina glanced at me, her eyes stricken less with the awareness that she'd just insulted the Porrinyards and myself than with the knowledge she'd done it before the local equivalent of royalty. "Oh, I'm sorry, dear, I didn't mean—"

Jason rode out her apology before she could find a way to make it worse than the original offense. "In the second place, I believe I know as much about cages, and leaving comfortable places to travel through distant ones, as anybody here."

A cloud passed over Philip's features. "Yes. And just look how well that worked out for you."

Farley, assuming that humor, exploded with forced laughter that trailed off into silence as he registered that he was the only one treating the line as funny.

The Khaajiir put aside his own entree (which, as per the usual Bocaian preference, had been seared to a blackened crisp) long enough to clutch his staff and assure him, "Don't worry, sir. Laughing in the face of irony is just one of life's perks."

"Much of what my brother says is true," Jason told us. "Much of what you see on distant worlds is formed by the same physical laws that form our sights here. The erosion that carves rocks into sand here just makes more sand that aside from a few differences in color and texture looks like the sand back home. The cold that turns frozen water into glaciers here just makes more glaciers that carve the landscape the same way glaciers are carved here. Gravity and weather patterns and everything that decides what natural places look like all work according to the same consistent set of laws that allows for variety but ensures that any wonder you see, anywhere you go, can only be a variation on something you've seen where you came from. The same thing goes for other sentient species, other civilizations. They're different, sometimes startlingly different, but also all the same. I don't know what Mr. Pescziuwicz wants from his future, or how he defines freedom, but as long as all you want is a variety of backdrops, or comfortable places to lie your head, you can get that without ever leaving your homeworld. You can even have as much 'freedom' as you can handle, as long as the folks who run the place aren't intent on taking it from you."

Farley Pearlman, who was desperate to atone for his previous faux pas, ventured, "Th-then . . . what were you looking for . . . when you—"

"The one thing distant places can give you, when you once again turn your eyes to home."

The Khaajiir and I spoke in unison. "Perspective."

We glanced at each other. The Khaajiir seemed gratified, even proud of me in a way.

I turned to Oscin and then to Skye. "So that's what that feels like."

Jason raised his glass. "You've got it, Counselor. You can't determine the shape of an object, or a society, by examining it from only one side. You have to walk around it, look down on it from a height, even—as I did—bury yourself in the dirt, to see it from ground level. It's the only way to see what something is, before you—"

That's when someone, or something, moaned.

It came from all around us: a screech of metallic agony my mind insisted on interpreting as the sound made by an enraged giant peeling back the wrought-iron bars of its cage. The floor started vibrating. The floating table tilted twenty degrees, spilling drinks and plates onto the laps of all the guests on my side. Bubbles rose in the tank containing the Bettelhine fish. Monday Brown fell out of his chair. Vernon Wethers fell next. The scenic windows went black as metallic shutters slid from the exterior housings and blocked Xana from view. I heard screams, gasps of pain, and Philip Bettelhine commanding us not to panic.

I tried to get up at the wrong moment, and a final lurch sent me airborne. I had time to scream a single *"Shiiiiiiit!"* before I hit the floor, taking all the impact on my left hip.

And then, as the story goes, some idiot turned out the lights . . .

7

THE FIRST DEATH

The power outage lasted only a couple of seconds, but neared absolute, the one real source of light during that interval being a flashing red glow that tinted the darkness rather than dispelling it. For a moment I imagined that glow to be an emergency indicator light, somewhere around the wide curve of the bar. I was correct about it coming from behind the bar, but wouldn't realize until long after the lights came back on that the source was Colette's ridiculous strobing hair.

While it remained dark, but after the tremors tapered off, Skye found me. "Are you all right, Andrea? Please say you're all right!"

"I'm fine," I said, with a tremor that rendered that assertion a lie. "You?"

"Skye's fine. Oscin slammed his chin against the table on his way down, and it hurts like hell. He's got a cut there. He's with Mr. Pearlman now, and thinks—"

The lights returned.

I sat up, regretting it at once as pain flared all along my left side. My involuntary moan of pain was louder than I prefer my complaints to sound. Skye stepped over me and positioned herself under my arm on that side, ready to support me if I wanted to stand up, a notion that for the moment failed to tempt me at all.

Most of our fine dinner was now a halo of debris beneath the tilted table. We didn't seem to have lost any people yet. Philip Bettelhine was on his hands and knees, wringing something moist from between his fingers. Vernon Wethers knelt beside him, unhurt but waiting for Bettelhine to tell him what to do. Dejah Shapiro comforted the sobbing Dina Pearlman. Monday Brown was facedown but stirring. Oscin, bleeding from a nasty diagonal cut across his chin, was helping Farley Pearlman to his feet. Jelaine Bettelhine was already at the shaken Khaajiir's side. His staff was nowhere to be seen. I made eye contact with Jelaine and saw her register that I was hurt too. Jason, who had fallen not far from Philip, managed to stand, revealing an ugly gash across his forehead that had already painted the lower half of his face red with blood. Though his eyes were just narrow, glistening slits, he still lurched around the side of the table to collect the Khaajiir's staff from where it had come to rest, avoiding all other debris as he went.

The Khaajiir, who had already struck me as frail, had not weathered the jolt well. He looked paler than he had been, and more confused. He asked for his staff, in Bocaian. Jelaine, answering in the same language, said she'd get it for him in a moment.

Colette appeared behind the bar, smeared blood staining her upper and lower lips. She wiped it off with the back of her hand, and widened her bejeweled eyes when she saw the scarlet staining her wrist, but remained at her post anyway, no doubt as much out of shock as duty.

I didn't see Arturo Mendez at all. Maybe he was down in the galley.

Farley Pearlman gasped. "What the hell was that?"

"That," the Porrinyards said, "felt like a full emergency stop."

Philip Bettelhine rubbed his face. "That's what it was. Is everybody all right?"

The Porrinyards said, "The two of me have accounted for everybody but Mr. Mendez and any other workers you might have belowdecks. I don't see anything but bruises and lacerations up here."

Philip Bettelhine scanned the room for the lowest-level employee on hand, and found Colette. "Hey, sweetie, why don't you rush to the galley and check on everybody? Get back with a head count as soon as you can."

Colette nodded, ran around the bar, and disappeared down the spiral staircase to the lower levels.

Farley Pearlman pulled free of Oscin so he could tend to his sobbing wife. He fired off a question as he ran, debris crunching beneath his shoes. "So what would cause a full emergency stop?"

"This one?" Philip asked. "I don't know."

Dejah Shapiro, relinquishing Dina to Farley's care, snapped, "The man's not asking what it is. He's asking what it could be."

Across the room, Jason and Jelaine Bettelhine were helping the shaken but still ambulatory Khaajiir to one of the overstuffed easy chairs. Jason had the staff tucked under his right arm, and made sure to hand it to the grateful Khaajiir after he and his sister lowered the elderly sentient to his seat. At the same time he shouted out an explanation to the rest of us. "If it ever looks like one car's going to overtake another on the same cable, traffic control override stops the one coming up from behind."

"What's your cutoff?" Dejah asked.

"I never worried about it, before. It's generous. Three hundred kilometers, I think."

"Three hundred's right," Philip said.

The Khaajiir clutched his staff as if it represented the only solid object in the entire universe. "That's how you stop if you have three hundred kilometers to slow down?"

Jason patted the eminent Bocaian on his wrist. "Considering how fast we're descending, three hundred's not all that much. But this was worse. This felt like a code red, or worse."

"All right," I said. "So what's a code red?"

He left Jelaine behind to look after the Khaajiir, and, ignoring his own injuries, rushed over to help Skye with me. It showed grit I never would have expected from a Bettelhine, given his own oozing head wound. "Three hundred kilometers offers ample time for a gentle deceleration. If that first brake fails for some reason, there are secondaries and tertiaries set to go off at fifty-kilometer intervals after that, each also calibrated for a gentle stop. It's only if all previous systems fail that the system goes code red at fifty K before collision. That's pretty rough, too, but still not as bad as what we just felt. I think we just experienced a manual override from the control center in the ground station at Anchor Point."

"Not Layabout?" The Porrinyards asked. "But Anchor Point?"

"Could have been either. There's certainly maintenance performed at both ends. But my grandfather, who commissioned the upgrade on the elevator we used before this one, judged dirtside emergency cutoff less vulnerable than the orbital equivalent."

"Not bad thinking," the Porrinyards said. "Unless he was stupid enough to build your ground station on a fault line, or something like that."

"He wasn't. The point is, I've experienced at least a dozens of minor emergency stops, riding up and down over the years, and never felt any even a fraction as bad as this one. Whatever went wrong this time, the danger must have been pretty imminent."

By now Jason was leaning over me, his eyelids trembling as he struggled to see me through a curtain of blood.

Skye grabbed him by the wrist. "You need to sit down, sir. You need medical attention."

Philip, who was more dazed than he would have liked to let on, only registered his brother's injuries now that I mentioned them. He took a step forward. "Yes, Jason, you'd better—"

Jason flashed a grim smile as he freed his hand from Skye's grip. "I appreciate the concern, people, but I've been wounded worse than this, in places where I had to keep moving and had no access to immediate medical care. It performs wonders for your focus."

"I'm not impressed with your experiences or your focus!" Philip snapped at him. "Let her help you!"

I seized the same bloody wrist he'd just freed from Skye, and said, "He has a point, sir. And I have another one. I'm not concerned with your focus so much as your blindness."

His lip curled. "I take it that you don't mean the blood in my eyes."

"You've forgotten that all departures from Layabout were delayed for hours following the attempt on my life, and that this car was the first to leave once traffic was cleared. Unless there's another car stopped somewhere ahead of us, there shouldn't have been any danger of us catching up with anybody."

"I know," Jason said, as Skye began tamping his forehead with a cloth napkin. He lowered his voice. "Best possible scenario: major software crash. Worst possible scenario: something wrong with the cable."

Across the room, Philip said, "I'm sure it's a software error. Give it a couple more seconds and the oversights will fix the problem. Not that I won't make sure somebody swings, down at Anchor Point—"

I already knew from the AIsource that we'd have a fatality soon, and was in no mood to worry about the delicate psyches of cringing hysterics. So I didn't lower my voice, but rather raised it, speaking to the room. "Sirs. There was an assassination attempt today. I won't believe this routine until somebody connected with security says it's routine."

Dina Pearlman emitted a soft wail and clutched at her husband tighter.

Philip looked annoyed. "I'm not saying it's routine. I think the last time we had a code red—and then as a drill—was eight years ago. But I'm not ready to give in to paranoia just yet."

"Paranoia's why I've lived to this age, Mr. Bettelhine. I refuse to believe this stop unconnected with what happened earlier today."

Oscin came around the table, carrying another cloth napkin he'd soaked with water from a carafe that miraculously retained some of its contents. He handed it to Jason, who murmured thanks and started cleaning the blood from his eyes.

I glanced at Jelaine. Monday Brown and Vernon Wethers had joined her in ministering to the Khaajiir. Monday murmured something that received a nod from Jelaine. Wethers asked the Khaajiir a question, receiving, of all things, a laugh in reply.

Wethers remained pale, a state I attributed less to the catastrophe we'd been through than to the proximity of a beautiful woman. I could *see* him stammering in Jelaine's presence. He turned a shade paler when Jelaine placed her hand on the back of his.

Philip Bettelhine rested his arms on the edge of the tilted tabletop, tilting it further and forcing a fork and spoon that had somehow survived up until now to tumble off and join the general chaos on the floor. He almost fell himself, but his reputed enemy Dejah Shapiro came up from behind and steadied him. I read the look he gave her as sincere surprise.

"Thank you," he told her, before turning his attention back to me. "Believe me, Counselor. I share your concerns. I'm pretty anxious for some explanations, myself. But by now there must be a dozen alarms blaring at both Layabout and Anchor Point. Any attempt by us to pull the emergency workers off their repairs to deal with our fears is just going to slow them down. I'm sure that Mr. Pescziuwicz, or his equivalent on the ground, will be getting in touch with us as soon as there's news to report."

Colette came back up the spiral staircase, her steps hesitant but her emerald eyes bright. Thank Juje for small favors, she'd deactivated the system controlling the displays generated by her hair and now wore a single consistent shade, even it was close to purple. "Everybody downstairs is okay, sir. Arturo got a little banged up, but Paakth-Doy's working on him, and says they'll all be around to help with the injured in just about five minutes."

I asked, "How many people are we talking about, total?"

"Downstairs? Just Arturo, Paakth-Doy, and, Mr. Jeck."

"That few? For a party like this?"

Philip Bettelhine started working his way through the minefield around the table. "We don't need any more. The food's prepared dirtside by the finest chefs in my family's employ and stored here in inert form. The galley's just the place where it gets reconstituted. And why is that even an issue, this very moment? I saw the way you picked at your meal. Are you going to tell me your palate could tell the difference?"

It hadn't, and I didn't even know if it was an issue or not. Right now, it was just raw data of unknown pertinence. Meanwhile, the AIsource had told me that the murder would take place "within the hour." How much time had I wasted since that warning? "I just want to make sure we don't lose track of anybody, if things get close."

Another wipe from the napkin and Jason blinked again,

his eyes round and red-rimmed but once again, resentfully, open. "Philip? We should have heard from Mr. Pescziuwicz, or his equivalent, by now. We better take the initiative."

"I agree," Jelaine said.

Colette had returned to the controls behind the bar. "I'm sorry, sir. But I'm already ahead of you. And no luck. The hytex link's down. We can't reach them and they can't reach us."

I tried to reach the AIsource and found similar silence.

Dina Pearlman cried, "They might not know if we're alive or dead!"

Philip Bettelhine looked like he wanted to strangle her. "I doubt that. Their instruments would be able to tell, even from a distance, if the carriage is still retaining atmosphere. Even if we weren't, they'd proceed from the assumption that there might be people in airtight compartments, using our emergency tanks."

"And then?" she insisted.

"And then, assuming they could not get us moving again, they'd send a rescue and repair craft, a Stanley, down the line to attend to whatever's wrong. Those are high-speed ascenders and descenders, faster by far than anything we clear for civilian traffic. We'd have help here in no more than ninety minutes, on the outside."

"And what if we don't have that long?" Dina demanded.

I said, "That happens to be a good question, sir. This car has already been evacuated once, today. Do we still have that option?"

His urge to strangulate seemed to have risen to a low boil. "This car can be evacuated when it's docked at Layabout and has one airlock linked to an orbital shuttle. Those connections have been terminated, so we're not attached to anything right now but the cable. You want to go outside and climb up and down the maintenance ladders on the side of this thing, go ahead; we have the suits on board, and it's perfectly safe as long as we're not moving. But it won't get you anywhere worth going, and might get you killed if there's more damage or if we start moving again."

Dina insisted, "But why do we need to wait for that, what did you call it, the Stanley thing? Why can't they just send a shuttle and fly us out?"

"Because it's not worth trying. As long as the line's intact, we'd rather not have any spacecraft zipping around during an emergency, when high-speed climbers and descenders are always available and can manuever into safe docking positions almost as quickly."

She persisted, "But if it can't get to us in time—"

"Mrs. Pearlman, this is not some struggling *Confederate* world, where all the infrastructure was put together by low-bid contractors and falls apart the second somebody breathes on it. This is Xana, the headquarters world of the Bettelhine Corporation. The people dealing with this will all be at the very top of their respective professions. Whatever the challenges, they'll *deal with it*."

"Of course," Jason Bettelhine murmured, in words meant only for my ears, "that only leads to a new worst-case scenario. Maybe the same thing that stopped us also took out Layabout . . ."

That was a cheery thought. I'd never pictured the kind of terrible things that could happen to an elevator in transit, if the cable was cut at either the orbital or dirtside termini. I supposed we'd all know if we initiated free-fall reentry, and it started getting hot in here. Or, worse, if debris opened us to space, leaving us staring through protruded eyes at a world we would not reach except as cinders and scattered particulates of bone.

Something around here smelled like an overflowing toilet. Maybe a line had ruptured. Maybe one of the systems was leaking ammonia or some other waste gas. Maybe somebody had just plain shit his pants.

"That's good," the Porrinyards said, leaving me with the impression that they'd gone insane. With their next words, I realized they were referring to Jason's condition, though only Oscin was working on him. "Keep your head back. It's just a surface wound, but forehead injuries always bleed a lot. You'd best keep it out of your eyes, to avoid burning— Mr. Bettelhine, is there more than one first aid kit on board?"

"Yes," Philip and Jason said in unison. "Downstairs."

There was a moment's sheepish silence, which Jason and Jelaine broke by also speaking in unison: "So that's what that feels like."

"I feel left out," Dejah said.

"So do I," the Porrinyards said. "I'm beginning to see why everybody always complains when I do it . . ."

The smell got worse. Jelaine went to the bar to fetch Dina Pearlman a cup of water. The Khaajiir sat by himself, his staff resting across the armrests of his chair, his exhaustion more palpable with every moment. Philip Bettelhine stopped by his chair to ask him if he needed any emergency medical assistance, and received a weak chuckle in response.

There remained no word from Layabout.

My link to the AIsource remained silent as well.

Arturo Mendez and the two remaining members of the crew came upstairs, carrying the promised pair of first aid kits. There was a dark-eyed, smooth-faced, character-deprived young man who introduced himself as Loyal Jeck, and a petite, raven-haired, almond-eyed young woman who bowed before identifying herself as the one with the strange name, Paakth-Doy. Paakth-Doy gave first priority to Jason Bettelhine's head wound, the tip of her nanite pen falling out of focus as each individual member of the microscopic fleet received its programming.

I watched for a few seconds as the bloodstains on Jason's forehead dissipated, ransacked for the supplemental mass the machines needed to repair his gash. Paakth-Doy handled the pen with the casual efficiency of a woman trained in its use, neither lingering too long at any one spot nor rushing past the less damaged places in her haste to assault the more severe. "You're good."

Her voice was whisper-soft. Her accent stressed *r*'s and added a trilling nasal vibrato to her vowels. She seemed to filter almost every word through a nose that had no room for it. "Thank you."

"Are you qualified for genuine medical emergencies?"

She frowned. But, then, that seemed to be her default facial expression, much like the whisper was her default volume. She hadn't smiled, or shown any other emotion since introducing herself. "I am not qualified for internal medicine. But we have cryofoam tanks downstairs. If it comes to life-or-death emergency we can put anybody still living in stasis long enough to get the body to the AIsource Medical crèche at Anchor Point."

AIsource Medical was the most lucrative of the many services my true employers contributed to interspecies economy, automated health care of such effectiveness and efficiency that they enjoyed a near monopoly on all such services, among those who could afford it. Even before I went to work for them, they'd saved my life more than once. It was no surprise that the Bettelhines had them on retainer. "What kind of coverage does Xana have? Is it for everybody, or does anybody have to make do with human doctors?"

"No. Mr. Bettelhine has made AIsource Medical available to all residents and visitors on Xana."

That must have cost a fortune all by itself. "Have you stabilized patients before?"

The gash on Jason's forehead was now no more than a

white line, hard to discern even against his pale skin. Paakth-Doy said, "Once, when I lived in another system, I served as chief steward on a commuter car that suffered a blowout due to collision with a fragment of orbital debris. One passenger suffered a head wound too serious to be treated on-site. We had to gel her for later treatment dirtside. She survived with no loss of cognitive function."

"And you were trained in first aid before this or after this?"

"After," Paakth-Doy said, her eyes still impassive. "I was determined to prepare myself, if ever faced with an emergency again."

"What's your official classification?"

"Medic, First Grade."

That represented two solid years of intense training all by itself. She wasn't as qualified as a genuine human doctor, but then you only found that dying breed in substantial numbers in places that, unlike Xana, couldn't afford AIsource Medical fees.

Still, something about Paakth-Doy bothered me, some kind of fundamental disconnect between our situation and her demeanor.

Her presence should have made me feel safer. I'd been hoping for a way to circumvent the prophecy of imminent murder, if I was lucky enough to get to any victim with life still left in her, and a qualified Medic with cryofoam on hand was exactly what I needed to accomplish that. But the hour deadline had passed, I still hadn't spotted anything resembling a murder victim, and the chances of the AIsource lying about an imminent murder, or simply being wrong about it, were not within the realm of possibility. So somebody here had been murdered, even if they were still walking and talking and not yet, actually, dead.

To me, that spelled poison or some other doom that gave the victim time to linger.

Like a Claw of God, maybe.

And the thought made me look at Paakth-Doy again.

She asked, "What about you, Counselor? Are you well enough to stand?"

My side still gave me a twinge of pain with every deep breath. "I'm all right. You should take care of the other bleeders first."

Jason's smile showed genuine warmth. "Nice, heroic stance, Counselor. But: bullshit. You're as entitled to medical care as the rest of us."

"I'm not bleeding," I said.

"Not externally," he said.

"I tell you I'm fine."

"You may go to the end of the line," Paakth-Doy said. "If you can stand."

Fair enough. I squeezed Skye's forearm, and Oscin ran over to grab my other elbow. The pair of them supported me as I rose to my feet, grimacing past the pain of movement. It hurt like hell. I remained standing after the Porrinyards let me go. The bruise along my side was going to be stellar, but I'd functioned with much worse. "See? I'm fine."

Paakth-Doy's mouth hung open as she worked on Oscin's chin next, the tip of her tongue pressed against her tiny, spotless lower teeth. I watched for several seconds, narrowing my reason for unease down to something having to do with her blank expression. It was setting off alarm bells, but I still did not know why.

Dina and Farley Pearlman huddled together on one of the couches, the husband whispering words of comfort to the wife. Vernon Wethers and Monday Brown treated themselves to some amber liquid from behind the bar. Dejah Shapiro, who had slipped away without me noticing, emerged after some unknown errand from the suite I now assumed to be hers. The Khaajiir slumped in exhaustion, his left hand still clutching the staff, his right curled into a claw against the armrest.

I felt a wave of black nausea, and again found myself unable to identify the precise shape of something horrible lurking at the edges of my consciousness. Again, Paakth-Doy had something to do with it. When she left Oscin and came to work on my bruised hip I said, "Excuse me. Young lady. Please forgive me for asking . . . You were not raised by human beings, were you?"

She didn't look at me, her full attention absorbed by the gray clouds swirling at the tip of the nanite pen. "No. I was an orphan raised by Riirgaans. I never met another human being until I was twelve years old, Mercantile."

That was similar to my own upbringing, in a way; I'd had plenty of humans around, but was just as close to the neighborhood Bocaians. "That's—excuse me—why you show no facial expression, right?"

"Correct. The Riirgaans have no facial muscles. I never lacked for love, of a Riirgaan kind, but was never exposed to human expressions and thus never learned any until it was too late to pick up the skill. I am aware that some people find my appearance forbidding, but I assure you I'm quite congenial if you get to know me. Is that what you wanted to know, ma'am?"

"Not yet," I said.

Philip Bettelhine moaned. "Counselor, can't you see she's—"

I held out my hand, in the universal gesture for stop. Something about my urgency succeeded in shutting him up, and even making him back up a step, as I said, "Please, Doy. I know these questions are very personal. But this is important. I've also noticed that you're a mouth-breather, which I assume goes along with the somewhat nasal quality of your voice. Am I correct in my assumption that at some time during your life with your Riirgaans you had surgery on your nasal passages, to cut off your sense of smell and further your ability to adapt to life among your adopted species?"

Paakth-Doy spared me a glance that could have been anything from annoyance to encouragement. "Yes. The Riirgaans have no sense of smell. As a human girl, growing up in one of their families, I sometimes reacted at times when it was . . . inappropriate for me to react. I assure you, I was given a choice. The surgery was voluntary. Even now, I'm much happier, without—"

And now I knew why Paakth-Doy's open mouth had bothered me so much. The rest of us were just people, enduring a stench we had written off as the expected taint in the atmosphere of any enclosed habitat that had just suffered serious damage.

But Paakth-Doy hadn't reacted to the odor at all.

Had she been able to identify odors, she might not have devoted all her attention to the minor injuries of a few pampered passengers whose wounds were overt enough to be seen from a distance.

A medical professional like her would have been trained to recognize the smells given off by things like, for instance, perforated bowels.

And she would have followed that stench, that telltale scent of biological disaster, to its source.

I yelled and lurched across the room, not hearing the cries of people like Philip Bettelhine and Dina Pearlman who must have thought I'd gone mad, and the sudden alarm on the faces of the Porrinyards, who knew that I'd only react like this in the presence of death.

When I reached the Khaajiir I seized his shoulders and yanked him forward, revealing in the process that his slump had been more than exhaustion and that his stare had been more than shock.

The gases trapped by his body billowed upward, and I

got a faceful, thick enough and rich enough that it was more like being splashed with a liquid than being hit with anything as intangible as air. The chair, designed for comfort, sloping downward from the natural resting place of a seated person's knees, was now centimeters deep in a lumpy black stew composed of equal parts Bocaian blood, Bocaian shit, Bocaian urine, Bocaian bile, and dense but colorful swirls I could only assume to be the liquefied remnants of Bocaian organs. A thin mist rose from the awful mélange, the last of the Khaajiir's internal heat, steaming as it collided with the cooler air of the parlor.

A black disk I recognized as a K'cenhowten Claw of God clung, unsupported, between his shoulder blades.

I heard gasps on all sides: coming from those who'd known the Khaajiir and considered him a friend, those who only considered him important and were now horrified that he was gone, those appalled by the sheer ugliness of the sight, those who sensed from this death that there would soon be more, even the gasps of those who did not yet understand what had happened and could only feel dread without understanding of the horror that had seized everybody else.

As for me?

All the uncertainty over why I was here, all the strain of dealing with the masters of a corporate empire, all the pressure of being owned outright by beings whose intentions toward me were shaky at best, all the shock of being targeted for death myself, all the horror of learning that a key assumption of my past had been a lie all along, and all the terror of the additional weight of the fresh challenge the AIsource had placed on my back, all went away, subsumed by something larger, something I had been carrying with me for most of the life.

For the first time since my arrival at Layabout, I was at home.

I knew why I was here and I knew what I was meant to do.

At the first moment of relative silence, I said it. "Someone in this room is a murderer."

I had to give Philip Bettelhine credit. He gave as good as he got.

He croaked, "You mean, somebody *other* than you?"

8

POST-MORTEM

There was another flurry of yells, with the Pearlmans and the stewards demanding to know what Philip had meant by that, Jason trying to tell them that it didn't matter right now, Jelaine telling everybody to talk one at a time, and the Porrinyards trying to calm them all down so we could move on.

Dejah Shapiro seized control, by slamming her palm against the bar just once, the impact a thunderclap. She waited for the chaos to collapse in the face of the order she had demanded, then spoke with repressed fury. "Yes. For those of you who didn't already know, Counselor Cort and the Bocaian people have had a violent prior history. Yes, the story's a long and unpleasant one and is not new intelligence to myself, or to our hosts. Yes, if you want details, I assume you'll hear them real soon. But this is *not the moment*." She stared down every face in the room, before glancing at me. "Andrea? You were saying?"

Any of the Bettelhines would have made an appropriate target for my next words, but Philip seemed to be my opposition here, so I went for him. "Sir. We need to organize a full investigation."

He looked like a man who had just bitten into something foul. "Now?"

"Well, you can wait until we don't have a murder victim, but that would make no sense."

He spared another nauseated glance at the Khaajiir. "Don't we have more pressing concerns right now? Like survival?"

"None," I said, "within our current powers to address."

"Yes." Philip admitted. "But whoever did this . . . horrible thing . . . is stuck in here like the rest of us."

"And damn you," Jason muttered. "Whoever you are."

Jelaine didn't offer that much restraint. "Oh, he's damned all right. "The Khaajiir was our friend. He was a personal guest of our father. His blood is *our* blood. *Whoever did this* . . . will never be able to run far enough."

I took their personal grief as very much beside the point, and answered Philip. "The corollary, sir, is that we're stuck in here with him. Or *them*."

His eyes narrowed. "Just how many killers do you think there are?"

"I have no idea, sir. But the possibility of more than one is worth considering, given that Mr. Pescziuwicz already has two in custody up at Layabout, and the existence of a conspiracy always suggests an unknown number of collaborators."

"You still don't have any reason to believe that's true here."

"Nor do I have any reason to rule it out. I once heard of a famous murder case, aboard another stranded vessel, where it was essentially every passenger on board. Right now we don't know anything except that we all remain in danger until we know who's guilty and who's not."

Philip gave me a disgusted look. "Yes, but of all the people in this room, you're the only one known to have murdered Bocaians before. Why should we trust you?"

"Sir. I don't consider myself above suspicion. I may know I'm innocent, and have faith that my associates are innocent, but I also know that I'm not about to persuade you of either proposition until I demonstrate to your satisfaction just who committed the crime. Similarly, I know that your family has killed any number of people over the years, even if the preponderance of those victims were slaughtered by proxy via the weapons you design, mass-produce, and sell. You're all part of that enterprise yourselves, and so neither you, nor your employees, all the way down to the stewards, escape suspicion, either as the Khaajiir's principal murderer or as fellow conspirators. Even the sole person here unaffiliated with either the Bettelhine organization, or myself—that would be Mrs. Shapiro—is a suspect. As you established earlier, she's been an enemy of your family for years, and we all know she has financial resources that equal your own, and thus provide her with more than enough influence to arrange this. So we're all under suspicion, and can cease taking that fact personally. The fact remains that, right now, we're all the prisoners of somebody who can not only smuggle a deadly weapon on board, but also has the capacity to isolate us by arranging the complete communications shutdown after this so-called emergency stop."

He licked his lips. "You can't know those was arranged too."

I raised my voice to a near shout. "Show of hands! Who within the sound of my voice is confident that the emergency stop, the loss of communications, and the murder of the Khaajiir all have nothing to do with one another?" Silence. "Don't be shy, people! If you believe that, stand up for it!"

The silence, broken only by scattered sobs from Dina Pearlman, persisted.

Jelaine murmured something inaudible to Dejah, who whispered something back. Skye, who was beside them, twitched her lips in appreciation. Something to ask her about, when I had a chance.

"There's something else that needs to be established," I said, turning away from Philip and sweeping my gaze from one set of frightened eyes to another. "We have not yet confirmed that help is coming. If it is coming, we don't know how long it will take to get here. We don't know if the people at Layabout or at Anchor Point have any bigger problems to deal with. We don't know whether the damage already done to this cabin poses any additional threat to our lives. We don't know if the killer, or killers, is satisfied with the one corpse or if there are any remaining targets. And finally, we don't know whether the answers to any of these questions will wait until help can arrive and take over the investigation . . . or whether we must race the clock if we hope to get out of here alive. The only thing we *know* is that we've been left with no other immediate possibility of helping ourselves. *This is something we can do.*"

Philip coughed. "And . . . I suppose . . . you want to run the investigation, yes?"

"Please, sir. I know I have no jurisdiction here. I don't mean to overstep my bounds. Were your man Mr. Pescziuwicz or some other authority you trusted available, I'd shut up and defer to him. But who in this room, aside from my associates and myself, has had experience running criminal investigations? You?"

To my surprise, Dejah Shapiro raised her hand. "Ummm . . . I've had to do it, several times."

There was silence as I gaped at her, my precious momentum derailed. I was not alone in that, either; just about everybody forgot our current predicament long enough to gather from her expression that she was entirely serious.

Of all of us, it was Jelaine who ventured, "Really?"

"Really." For a moment Dejah just looked tired, less like a woman who had spent much of her life cocooned by extreme wealth than one who had known more than her share of struggle and heartbreak. It aged her, but only for a moment, and then the vitality came rushing back in. "Some of you already know that I once found myself saddled with a sociopathic ferret of a husband, one Ernst Vossoff, whose messes needed to be cleaned up on a regular basis. There were occasions, in places cut off from my usual resources, where . . . well, where I was the only one available to connect the dots." She turned to me. "Just providing a footnote, Counselor. I'm not claiming my experience adds up to anything as distinguished as my own."

"Appreciated," I said. "Maybe it will prove helpful anyway."

Philip glanced at his brother and sister, neither of whom had raised any objections to me taking command of the situation. They just met his gaze, giving him nothing. After a moment, he ventured, "Since you do admit you're a suspect, how do you suggest we work this, so we can trust each other?"

Oscin stood beside the Khaajiir's body, awaiting further instructions. Skye was still with Dejah and Jelaine. Neither had spoken a word, or made a move to interrupt the confrontation between Philip and me since the moment Dejah silenced the party. But I didn't need to know them as well as I did to know that their shared mind was racing.

I said, "I'll need to step aside, for a moment, and confer with my associates. I'll leave one here and take the other. But even the two of us who walk away will still be in sight every second. Watch us and make sure of it. In the meantime, *nobody leaves this room.*"

I left it up to the Porrinyards to decide which one joined me. The volunteer turned out to be Oscin. He accompanied me to the other side of the capsized dinner table, at one point steadying my arm as I stepped over the place where an upended bowl oozed yellow cream into a carpet already spotted with damp. We didn't stop until we were up against the bulkhead, until recently a scenic view of Xana, now a claustrophobic closeup of emergency shutters, shutting out everything else in the universe.

My left shoe made a noise as it pulled free of something sticky. "What a mess."

Oscin kept his voice low. "Which one are you talking about?"

"The whole thing, of course. The murder. The politics. Even the family relationships, here. You did pick up that Philip's the odd man out in this particular collection of Bettelhine siblings?"

He nodded. "It's all over their body language, and the way they speak to one another. And you saw that he's not happy about that?"

I spared a look at Philip, who had stepped aside with Jason and Jelaine, the three of them already engaged in intense conversation. Philip looked angry, Jason upset but placatory. Jelaine stood between them, watching both their faces, not participating for the moment but very much prepared to step in, as either peacemaker or manipulator. "I won't say they hate him, or that he hates them, but there's definitely some powerful tension going on. I wouldn't be surprised to hear that it goes back years. Maybe even before Jason's disappearance."

Oscin followed my gaze. "Oscin the single had the same kind of strained relationship with his older brother. They didn't want to fight, but by the time they reached their teens, they always approached each other with excessive delicacy, rather than risk tugging at some emotional tripwire and setting off the explosion neither wanted. As a result, nothing ever got said. This feels . . . something like that."

"Maybe Philip never forgave Jason for going away."

"Maybe," Oscin said. "Maybe it has to do with wherever he went."

"We've been given an explanation for that." I left out the drama and, over the next few minutes, summarized the story Jelaine had told me before dinner, concluding with: "It could all be bullshit, of course. Have you ever heard of this place, this Deriflys?"

"No," he admitted. "But if the story's true, and Jason did have to live like an animal to survive, it could very easily explain why Philip would resent him for it. He's the type who would consider it a stain on the family honor, or something— more so if Jason was a favorite who remained a favorite even after he came back, sullied but forgiven. A jealous sibling, of the kind who always obeyed the rules without question, and always lived up to everything his parents expected, might even come to hate the one who involved the family in scandal but was still granted the rewards of a favorite son."

He went distant for a moment, perhaps weighing the information we had, perhaps giving his full attention to whatever Skye was hearing. Then he said, "What about the AIsource? Have you attempted to contact them again?"

"On and off since we stopped. They're not answering. I'm not even getting the buzz I get when they're receiving but not in the mood to acknowledge. Either they're cut off by whatever's shut down all the Bettelhine hytex links, or they're determined for us to handle this ourselves."

"I suspected as much," he said. "It's a pain in the ass, though. I can deal with being trapped here, but it would be nice to know what's going on outside, if help is coming or not."

"It's coming. With Bettelhines aboard, it's coming. But the silence so far gives me the impression it's going to be a long wait. Something's interfering."

He nodded without surprise. "Unseen Demons?"

"I don't know. Could be. Not enough data to know." Once upon a time I'd had the habit of nibbling my fingernails at moments of intense concentration. My fingers had looked raw much of the time, but it had been something to do, some way to postpone speaking while I chose the right thought of the many possibilities clamoring for my attention. Sometimes, like now, I missed it. "There's something else I want to ask about. Earlier, as Skye, you told me you'd picked up an implication you didn't consider any of my business."

"That was before this became a murder investigation and it became important data. Do you need me to tell you now?"

"No," I said. "I've already figured out what you must have been talking about. I think I'd already sensed it for a while, but it wasn't until after the emergency stop that I went back over everything else I'd been seeing and knew for sure. You can rest your conscience and consider this secret spilled without your help."

His relief was palpable. "Should we let on that we know?"

"We might as well pretend that we're still out of the loop, watch what happens, and reserve the big reveal in case we find ourselves needing to spring it during questioning."

"Good plan. What else?"

"Jelaine and Dejah exchanged some words during my confrontation with Philip. Skye was present. What did they say?"

He surprised me by breaking into a rueful grin. "It's not important, but you should know. It was right after you made Philip back down. Jelaine said, 'Wow.' And Dejah said, 'That's my girl.'"

I don't know what I'd expected. Certainly not a whispered confidence between two conspirators cackling that their evil machinations were all proceeding according to plan. But the answer sandbagged me. It was a moment before I could answer. "Really?"

"Really. I keep saying, Andrea: You should stop being so surprised when people are impressed by you. The universe is not entirely populated by enemies."

I looked at the Khaajiir, still slumped in his chair, his eyes still open and seeming to pass judgment on everything within his field of vision. The accusatory expression seemed new. Before he'd died, he'd seemed gentle, wise, saddened, and at most amused my understandable distrust. I realized again that he'd been the first Bocaian to treat me with civility since that long-distant day when I'd joined in the madness of my family of neighbors, and wanted nothing more than Bocaian blood. For the first time since I'd discovered his death I felt the loss become personal. How great a gulf had this sentient crossed, to stand in the same room with me and profess that he did not want me dead? Was it lesser, or greater, than the gulf he'd crossed in the last minutes of his life? Worst of all was a thought so terrible that it made my stomach lurch with a nausea I had not felt from the mere discovery of the murder: had he died blaming his death on the monster child Andrea Cort, who he had so foolishly approached without fear?

Damn you, whoever you are, for making me think that.

The Porrinyards were correct. The universe was not entirely populated by enemies. But they were still thick on the ground, and the Khaajiir's unknown assassin had just become one of mine.

I didn't know whether the carriage would start moving by itself or, if not, whether the rescue craft, the Stanleys or whatever Philip had said they were called, would reach us in minutes or hours or days. But I made a vow right then. If there was anything I could do to help it, I would not leave this place before I had a chance to spit in the murderer's face.

I rubbed the corner of my eye with my thumb. "I . . . ah . . . don't suppose anybody's said anything incriminating, the last few minutes."

Oscin had the grace not to recognize a moment of uncertainty when he saw one, "Farley Pearlman claims to have had some problems breathing. He's sure the air's going bad, but everybody else thinks it's just fear and the stench coming off what's left of the Khaajiir. I believe we may have to move everybody into one of the suites, for humanitarian reasons. That tableau over there is really more than people unaccustomed to crime scenes should ever be expected to take."

I considered that. "They're going to have to wait. Nobody except us, and whomever we're questioning, goes in or out of any of the other rooms until we can check them out ourselves and eliminate the possibility of evidence tampering. If they have any trouble dealing with the smell, we'll put them on an oxygen unit."

"That won't compensate for the evidence of their own eyes. The body's sickening."

"I know. But if we're very, very lucky, it will bother the killer too."

Oscin and I returned to the bar area, where the others stood, watching our return with varying mixtures of hope and fear. By the time we got there the Pearlmans were huddled together, breathing into cloth napkins. The somber but dry-eyed Colette remained behind the bar, where she'd been joined by Arturo Mendez, Loyal Jeck, and Paakth-Doy. Dejah Shapiro and the three Bettelhines all stood at the opposite end of the bar, all managing to look defiant and glum at the same time, if that was possible. Vernon Wethers and Monday Brown stood apart from them, the first with his hands clasped behind his back, the other with hands clasped in front. I don't believe either one intended to be a parody or an editorial response to the other, it just worked out that way. As for Skye, she'd moved to the easy chair where the corpse of the Khaajiir sat, still leaking black ooze into the cushions.

Jason said, "So, Andrea, have you come up with anything?"

Damned if he didn't seem to be showing genuine affection for me. Couldn't have that, not now. "First things first, sir. Out of my own intimidation by the circles where I now find myself traveling, and my confused uncertainty over your father's purpose in inviting me here, I've been allowing the members of your family to get away with calling me by my first name. That assumes a familiarity you have not earned. I don't know if we'll ever be cordial enough to merit such liberties, but until I find out who among you killed the poor Khaajiir I must insist that everybody except my traveling companions return to calling me Counselor. It'll remind us all where we stand. Are we agreed on that?"

Jason's nod had the ghost of a smile in it.

Philip's eyes bugged a little at my effrontery. He might have objected, but his siblings appeared, if anything, even more pleased by me, and that bothered him more.

Jelaine flashed a shell-shocked grin. "Whatever you say. Counselor."

I didn't know what was going on here, but sooner or later, I'd have to teach those two that I was not a pet performing tricks for their amusement. But not now. "Second. In a few minutes I'm going to start questioning you, one or two at a time. I will need to do this away from the others, to make sure that everybody speaks freely and without contamination by other testimony. You may nominate one person, preferably one of the stewards we know to have been belowdecks during the emergency stop, to monitor those interviews and ensure that we do not do anything to obstruct or alter the results of the investigation. That person will remain sequestered with us unless he, or she, finds reason to object to our activities. One of the Porrinyards will also stay with me throughout, while the other stays with you, serving the same purpose as the person you have designated to watch me. While I'm doing this I must insist that you refrain from discussing your testimony with one another. The reasons for this should be obvious, but just in case any of you decide to defy this request, my associate will be monitoring you to detect any signs of collusion in the meantime. Are we agreed on that?"

There was even less enthusiasm for this, but everybody mumbled and nodded and allowed as how it was all right, they guessed, the sole exception being Dejah, who actually raised her glass in approval.

According to the Porrinyards, she'd called me *"her girl,"* earlier, assuming ownership based on the few short weeks we'd worked together a few years ago. That rankled. Sooner or later I might have to teach her that I did not belong to her any more than I belonged to Jason and Jelaine Bettelhine.

"Third," I said.

This was the part that never worked. The first thing any investigator learns is that everybody lies, even if they don't have to, even if their lies are innocent, even if their lies have nothing to do with the crime. There were always things people were ashamed of, things they thought harmless to hide, things that interest the investigator not at all but that, when hidden, hide the truth behind a thicket of false leads. It was useless to even try to prevent that with a mere warning. But I had to try. "I haven't been shy about my lifelong assessment of the Bettelhine Corporation. I think it's a criminal enterprise, run by blood-soaked dynasty with a bottomless capacity for evil. I have no illusions over my own ability to bring you down. I'm just one woman with problems of her own. But right now I'm not interested in bringing you down. I'm interested in solving this one crime, and only this one crime. The time may come when you may find yourself faced with a choice between answering my questions and concealing other crimes filed under the category 'Corporate Secrets.' When that time comes, if you lie and I catch you in a lie, it will only give me more reason to consider you responsible for the Khaajiir's death. If you tell the truth . . . well, I give you my word that nothing you tell me today will ever leave Xana."

Philip's voice was a soft vessel releasing its venom in drips. "Except if you think it's relevant to your case."

I showed teeth. "That's the point, sir. I'm in your jurisdiction, not mine. Whatever happens, I won't be involved in the prosecution except, if you wish, as a witness. The best I can do once I identify the culprit is present my evidence to you and let you pass it on to whatever passes for Bettelhine justice, even if that killer ultimately turns out to be a Bettelhine and the worst he gets is a scolding from Father."

"Now wait just one minute," he began.

I held up a finger. "Honestly, Mr. Bettelhine. I don't give a damn. What happens to our unknown culprit is up to you. Either way, there's absolutely no reason for my superiors to ever hear of it. My only interest in asking any question that leads to finding out who did this terrible thing is that it furthers all of our chances of ever getting off this vessel alive."

"You still don't have the right to demand access to corporate secrets—"

Jelaine cleared her throat. It was a gentle sound, less an interruption than the mere suggestion of one, but it had enough power to summon the attention of everybody in the room. "I think I can guarantee that Counselor Cort won't abuse the situation."

"In God's name," he demanded. *"How?"*

"She's Father's guest. His *honored* guest."

Once upon a time, Philip had been a child, throwing tantrums and stamping his foot when he did not get his way. I don't know how well the elder Bettelhines disciplined their kids, so there was no way of telling whether his foot-stamping phase ended when he was two, ten, or thirty, but the contortions that twisted his face now established to my satisfaction what he must have looked like when he did it. "You're still risking the family's future on an outsider."

"Exactly," Jason told him. "And that's what Father would want."

The tenor of the room changed with those words. It was still thick with fear over our situation, shock over the death of the Khaajiir, and uncertainty over which one of us had turned the evening into an exercise in murder . . . but there was something else now: wonder. It was most visible in the eyes of the Pearlmans, who for the most of the evening could not have considered me anything more but some low-prestige offworld bureaucrat, and had now seen me not only seize control of the crisis but also get declared the personal project of Hans Bettelhine himself. They didn't know whether to bow to me or run from me.

In Dejah Shapiro's case it seemed more like fascination. She could not have expected a moment like this in my future the last time we'd met, and now that she'd witnessed one here she just fingered her chin, titled her head, and contemplated me as if hoping furious thought would bring me into the proper focus.

I remained on the wrong foot with Monday Brown. He looked like he was irritated by my very existence. Philip looked like he wanted to hit me. And I could not read Vernon Weathers at all.

I had no idea what I could have done in my life to merit loyalty from Bettelhines. Any Bettelhines. If indeed loyalty was what this was.

But if it gave me an advantage, right now, this was not the proper moment to question it.

Or as one of my teachers once said: *When you're in over your head, swim.*

"Good," I said. "Now that we've got that settled, I think there are two things we need to do. First, we need to confirm that nobody here's hiding another Claw of God, or weapon of similar lethality, on his person. Oscin will stay here while you divest yourselves of everything you're carrying, while Skye and I take the time to examine the Khaajiir's body. Have you decided who gets to monitor us while we work?"

All eyes turned to the stewards, Arturo, Colette, Loyal Jeck, and Paakth-Doy.

The truth, as I'd known when I'd gone through the motions of allowing the Bettelhines to choose between those four, was that only two seemed safe to allow near the investigation: Jeck and Paakth-Doy, the only ones I couldn't personally place within a meter of the Khaajiir at any point during the night.

In the end, it was Jason who made the choice I'd wanted them to make. "Doy?"

Paakth-Doy glanced at her co-workers, then stepped forward, with a shyness I hadn't seen from her before.

"It will be my honor," she said.

The sounds of protest and offended dignity from the crowd over by the bar provided steady background music as Skye, Paakth-Doy, and I stood before the plush easy chair and regarded the wreckage of a sentient being.

The Khaajiir sat with his feet planted on the floor, and the rest of him swallowed by a chair that would have engulfed a being twice his girth. The chair was so large that his spine failed to rest flush against the backrest, but rather leaned on it, in a position a living biped might have considered too uncomfortable to endure for long. He'd rested his staff across the two armrests, crossing in front of his now-sunken abdomen like the safety bar in a child's high chair. His left palm, painted black by the goo that less than an hour before had been solid and functioning aside him, pinned the staff to the armrest on that side, both holding it in place and marking it with the stain of his death. A shiny crust had formed where his fingertips soaked the plush fabric. His right arm pinned the other end of the staff to the armrest on the other side, but more of his hand extended over it. Sometime in his last few minutes his fingertips had convulsed in some way, scratching at the fabric on that side to produce a series of three jagged lines, all identical: each consisting of three diagonals, leaning left and then right and then left again to produce zigzags. His unmoving fingertip still rested at the base of the zigzag farthest from the right. Enduring the stench, I leaned in close and saw a wisp of fiber from the chair lodged beneath that fingertip, fluttering in some unseen air current.

"Note this," I told Skye.

"Noted," she said.

The Khaajiir's features had gone slack, free of the contorted trauma that sometimes remains on the faces of those who perish by violent means. His eyes were closed, his lips curled in an expression that looked like a smile but was probably just the expression they assumed at rest. A thin trickle of saliva, without any visible blood content, had trickled from the corner of his mouth. The only sign that his fate had been anything but a natural one was a single bloodstain, the size of a fingertip, on the tip of his nose.

I remembered the funeral of an elderly Bocaian neighbor who had died in his sleep when I was seven, about a year before so many others met deaths that had been much worse. All my Bocaian neighbors, and all of my human ones as well, had filed past the platform where the deceased lay in state, and whispered the same respectful phrase, Bocaian for *Walk in Light, Where We Must Follow*. I hadn't thought of that for longer than I now wanted to contemplate, but the words came to my lips again now. I spoke them under my breath, shook my head as I realized what I'd just done, and said, "That was the first Bocaian phrase I've spoken in decades."

Skye hovered close, protectively. "You said a few words earlier tonight."

"Really? I don't remember."

"It is to be expected," Paakth-Doy clucked. "I know at that times of stress I revert to my first tongue, Riirgaani."

I'd been around far too many dead bodies in my professional life, and had learned to face the cooling collections of meat as abstractions, more problems to be solved than truncated lives to be mourned. But being around another dead Bocaian, after all these years, was tearing the scabs off old wounds. For a few seconds I found myself eight years old again. I sniffed, rubbed my eyes with the back of my hand, and, unable to come up with any more relevant comments, murmured, "It must have been agony."

"I would not want to die in such a way," Paakth-Doy said.

"It's not what you think," Skye told us. "Based on my readings, when I worked with the species, the K'cenhowten were never torturers in the way you and I understand the term."

"How so?"

"Torture means something else to the K'cenhowten. Their sense of pain is not acute by human standards. They know when horrific things are being done to their bodies, and they feel all the dismay you and I might expect when they see their persons ravaged, but there's always been a certain upper limit to the agony they can feel, and it's well within their ability to function. It's a built-in limit that prevents them from being incapacitated by agony, and relieves them of our human tendency to faint or convulse or, for prisoners experiencing extended torture, mind-destroying shock."

"That's one hell of a survival mechanism," I said. "But would it work with a Claw of God?"

"Especially with a Claw of God," Skye said. "K'cenhowten's age of darkness did feature several methods of execution unbearable by human standards, but the Claw itself fries most of the body's internal pain receptors the same way it fries the rest of the organs. The point of the torture was not inflicting pain, but rather horror. Its victims were positioned in front of mirrors and forced to watch everything that made their lives possible drain from them, despite exoskeletons that remained intact. For a K'cenhowten, wrapped in its impervious shell, this would have upset their very perceptions of the world."

Paakth-Doy shuddered. "I'd imagined . . . agony."

"And you imagined correctly, Doy, but not the right kind. Imagine that you were a human prisoner in medieval times, slowly roasted over an open flame after first being provided a drug that incapacitated your ability to feel any pain whatsoever. Imagine you were able to watch your skin turn black, your fatty tissues bubble and run like water. Imagine that your agony was not great enough to drown out every other thought, or to give you the blessed escape of unconsciousness. Imagine instead having to dwell on what was happening to you, and its terrible permanence, at whatever length your captors decide it should last. Is that better? Or worse?"

I cut off Skye's gruesome recitation. "Still, you're talking about a K'cenhowten's nervous system. Would the Claw of God affect a Bocaian or a human being the same way?"

"It could if calibrated," Skye said. "What's more, the device is designed to locate the heart and lungs—or, with minor adjustments, their alien equivalent—and shield them from the full effects of the pulse. The blow to those organs remains fatal, all by itself, but it's the kind of fatal that would take several hours to kill. Meanwhile, they continue to feed the victim's brain for several minutes, even as the rest of him turns to soup."

Paakth-Doy had turned green. "You are saying that he might not have been aware of the terrible thing happening to him."

"I'm saying that if he failed to notice the blood, he might have interpreted what he was feeling as fatigue."

I rubbed my chin. "Meaning that we cannot use his participation in conversations to isolate the moment the Claw was used on him. Anything he said, after being moved to this chair, could have been said after he was already dying."

Skye said, "He might have been dying even earlier, though that would have been cutting it very close for the killer, given how soon after the attack the Khaajiir would have started to . . . leak."

I nodded, the ugliness of the crime scene receding as its value as evidence moved to the forefront. Signaling for silence from the other two, and sparing a quick look at the crowd over by the bar, which seemed to be enduring the search about as well as could be expected, though the Pearlmans in particular were eyeing their own small pile of valuables with the glumness of people who suspected that their own paltry wealth an embarrassment in the eyes of the people who owned their very world. There was no point in calling to Oscin to ask how things were going. If he found anything of importance, Skye would alert me.

So I folded my arms before my chest and circled the chair, examining it from all angles, sometimes leaning in close to appraise the scene from a fresh angle. As a place to obscure the fate of a sentient about to die from exsanguination, the chair could not have been better. Had the Khaajiir been sitting on one of the couches, the blood pooling beneath him would not have been hidden by raised armrests at either side.

As he grew weak, he might have collapsed to one side, and drawn the attention of others who would have been able to isolate those who had been near him at the moment of the crime. Had he been sitting on one of the hard chairs beside the dinner table, the blood mixture would have spilled over the sides and formed a spreading puddle on the floor by his feet, where it could have been spotted by Mendez, Colette, or any diner who left the table for as long as thirty seconds.

This chair, though? The seat tilted backward, forming a perfect reservoir for the accumulation of liquids. The cushions had absorbed some, too, slowing discovery of the murder even longer. The armrests, propping him up at either side, made him remain upright and thus seem healthy, if only dozing. In short, moving him here, before or after applying the Claw, virtually ensured that we would not be able to notice anything wrong for several minutes.

But was that a sad happenstance, or a deliberate strategy on the part of the killer? If the latter, it had been Jason and Jelaine who had moved him here, and Jelaine who had stayed with him for several minutes. That made them prime suspects.

On the other hand, Jason and Jelaine had enjoyed access to the Khaajiir for some time. Had they wanted him dead for some reason, they would not have needed to wait until they could commit the crime within a room filled with distinguished dinner guests.

Monday Brown and Vernon Wethers had also checked on him. Colette had been in and out of the room several times, and Dejah Shapiro had passed right by the Khaajiir on her way to doing something in her own suite. I hadn't seen the Pearlmans approach him after the emergency stop, but either of them could have clapped the Claw of God against the Khaajiir's back when the lights went out. Anybody upstairs during the crime could have been the killer, and anybody downstairs could have provided material aid.

All it would have taken was decisive action during a single moment when everybody else was distracted.

And that's all it would take again if the assassin was not finished, and I was right to expect a third Claw of God . . .

I was still considering the foul implications of that when the people over at the bar started shouting.

9

MAGRISON'S WOMAN

■scin had found an octagonal chip, about the size of pinky fingernail, and so well integrated with the skin it was imbedded in that it was impossible to discern a seam where flesh ended and metal began. I knew, without examining it further, that it would be only a few molecules thick, that it would resist any attempt to remove it, and that the thousands of infinitesmal filaments extruded on its subdermal side would be threaded throughout the wearer's nervous system, forming a braid of sorts that would culminate in a seething terminus somewhere in the meat of the brain. Worse, though, was the pattern of raised dots, at its center, forming a letter that to my eyes had always resembled a pair of serpents swallowing each other whole. The letter, corresponding to the sharpest of the three consonants Mercantile devotes to the *M* sound, did not belong to the Mercantile alphabet at all, but rather to another, famous only as the birthplace of a destroyer not seen in civilized space for almost thirty years.

The mere sight was enough to make my ears throb with trapped blood. I released the forearm bearing the hateful artifact, turned my back on the glaring figure it belonged to, and confronted the three Bettelhines, now huddled together in whitening silence. "Did you know about this?"

Jason Bettelhine shook his head.

Jelaine had paled in a manner that suggested blood loss on the scale of the Khaajiir's. "I swear to you, Counselor. I had no idea."

Philip said nothing. But I noticed that Monday Brown had moved a little closer to him, like a mother cat attempting to comfort a kitten crying after a great fall.

My fury colored my vision, like a red curtain turning everything behind it the color of blood. "You did know, didn't you? *Didn't you*?"

Philip Bettelhine's mouth had become a horizontal slash as white as a bloodless wound. "I would watch your tone of voice, Counselor. You're on our ground."

"To hell with my tone of voice! Answer my question!"

He rolled his eyes. "I knew. So did Father, if you're wondering. And my grandfather before him."

"And you had no problem with that?"

"Historical precedent. Whenever any great war ends, the victors imprison some of its leaders, execute others, release a few more, and recruit the remainder to serve their own cause. Your own Dip Corps employs some intelligence assets guilty of crimes as vile as anything this poor woman ever did. Hell, look at yourself. Are you in any position to complain about any system that puts war criminals to work?"

I trembled with fury. "*We* don't have any of Magrison's people working for us. We *hunt* Magrison's people."

His pitying look only threw fuel on the fire. "That's naïve, Counselor. Your Confederacy has several of Magrison's people on the payroll. If you want, I'll provide you with a list."

The wearer of the chip, Dina Pearlman, met my gaze with

a cold, defiant look of her own, her eyes transformed from the red weeping springs they had been a few minutes before to dry, reptilian marbles absent not only of fear but any human warmth. It was impossible to reconcile that look, and its dangerous intelligence with the vapid, fluttery idiot she had been pretending to be only a few moments before.

Her husband, by contrast, had deflated utterly, the cheerful confidence he'd projected replaced now with resignation and, yes, relief. There was no surprise in his eyes, just like there was no fear. He mostly looked like he just wanted to sit down.

I jerked a thumb his way. "What about him?"

"Farley? He's who he's supposed to be. A third-generation corporate citizen. He married her the day she entered our employ."

The Porrinyards noted: "That sounds like a marriage of convenience."

The woman known as Dina Pearlman expelled one brutal, explosive laugh. "Of inconvenience is more like it. The man's useless to grown women. If I told you what age he prefers—not just single digits, but *low* single digits—you'd all forget your civilized scruples and kick him to death right now."

"Possibly," the Porrinyards said. "You might have to wait your turn."

Farley Pearlman just hung his head, waiting for it to be over, so much a puppet of forces beyond his control that he had nothing to do or say once those strings were cut.

Dejah Shapiro placed her drink back on the bar and dabbed her lips with a napkin. "You know, Philip, every time I dare hope that your family can achieve some kind of collective redemption, new evidence wipes my face in the cold, ugly reality. I'm honestly sorry I came."

"You're a fine one to talk," Philip said, his own voice just as controlled.

"Really?" she asked. "What have I done?"

"You're married to a criminal, for starters!"

Dejah's smile communicated disappointment that his best shot had been so pathetically feeble. "I've been married to a couple of different criminals, in my time. Indeed, I've already mentioned Ernst. Which one are you referring to right now?"

"That moron you left at home!"

"Oh, Karl." She picked up her drink, treated herself to another drink, savored the taste, put the glass down, and replied, "You're absolutely right. My current husband, whom I love with all my heart, has a criminal record. That's common knowledge. He's also of subaverage intelligence. That's a verifiable medical fact. He was led astray by people with will greater than his own. What's your excuse?"

For a tenth of a second or so I thought Philip was going to hurl himself at her throat. Dejah must have thought so, too, because she turned toward him, her expression calm but her chin outthrust, her arms free, and her posture transformed into a warrior's.

Before anything could happen, the Porrinyards stepped between Philip and Dejah, positioning themselves back to back with a calm efficiency that placed any possibility of the confrontation turning violent in the distant past. They spoke, as they'd moved, as one.

"Andrea? I believe you have the subject of your first interview . . ."

There was another tiresome pissing match with Philip over whether I'd be permitted to speak with Mrs. Pearlman alone, or whether I'd have to bring Monday Brown and Vernon Wethers along, as Bettelhine counsel. I might have argued longer about the idiocy of suggesting that she even needed counsel when interviewed on the home soil of a power that had no interest in prosecuting her for past crimes, but I was eager to get past the preliminaries and into a room with a monster who, unlike myself, had committed her crimes as an adult. I let Brown come along.

The five of us (Paakth-Doy, Brown, Wethers, Skye, and me), escorted Mrs. Pearlman into my suite, taking seats around the outer room in what, without consultation, turned out to be a perfect circle with the defiant Mrs. Pearlman at dead center. She appropriated an ottoman for her own use and perched there with legs crossed, as comfortable in her interrogation as she would have been making arrangements for a formal party.

Most people who wore her current expression were dealing with unwanted infestations of insect life in their homes. "I didn't kill the Bocaian. And I didn't send those other idiot Bocaians after the bitch counselor. I'm not that stupid."

"Exactly how stupid you are," I told her, in a voice that reeked of loathing, "is yet to be determined."

"Hans Bettelhine doesn't think so," Mrs. Pearlman sniffed. "He compensates me very well for my intelligence. If you knew the amount that gets put into my retirement fund, every year, just for sharing the fruit of that intelligence, you'd likely kill yourself. Of course, Andrea, I've read in your file that getting you to attempt suicide isn't all that difficult, considering it's been—how many? Five or six incidents over the years? So that's not saying much."

I found myself missing the old Mrs. Pearlman, the abrasive but essentially innocent one that had never really existed. "What's your real name?"

She looked bored. "I've been called Dina Pearlman for as long as I wore the name before it, so you might as well use that one."

"For the moment," I agreed, aware that I didn't want to get bogged down in this one point, and that consulting the Confederate Intelligence files on known associates of the man responsible for that chip would likely uncover her identity later. "How did you become involved with the man known to the authorities as Peter Magrison?"

"He recruited me in my youth." She made it sound like some ancient epoch, as far removed from our own as the Cretaceous.

I asked, "Where was this?"

"On my homeworld. Ottomos. I was a student of nanopsychology, enrolled in a school known as Pastharkanak University, in a small town called Vivakiosy. Of course, I'm certain these names mean nothing to you. Would you like to know the names of my idiot professors, as well as the address of my dormitory?"

"Maybe later. How did Magrison approach you?"

For a moment her eyes went soft, seeing not the hostile faces around her, but whatever passed for blessed memory in a soul lost to darkness. "People only know him from the usual image, in the few holos that exist: that blurry, sneering face, half obscured by shadow, half washed-out by excessive light, with those knit black eyebrows and the eyes like bottomless pits. I think the powers-that-be have nicer images, in their archives, but publicize that one because it's so easy to sell as the face of evil. In truth, he wasn't like that at all. He had a gentle smile, the face of a saint, and the voice of a healer. Less than five minutes after he found me, sitting under a tree eating lunch between classes, I knew that I'd go anywhere with him, and do anything for him."

"Must have been one hell of a five minutes," Skye said.

"It was less than that. Maybe one question. I was hytexing my assignments for the next class period, and he walked right up, passing through the projection, and asked me: *'Do you honestly think they'll let you make a difference?'* I don't know how he knew. But it was something I'd been asking myself all semester. Nanopsych had such potential, such possibilities for changing the way people *thought* and *dreamed* and *interacted* with one another, that nobody before him had thought of asking the tough questions. He —"

I waved away the rest of it. "Why would he pick you?"

"He said later that he'd been sitting in the back monitoring classes, looking for a mind capable of following where he needed to lead. It may even be true. I don't know. I just know that I don't remember seeing him, at all, until that moment."

"You went with him," I said. "Did it ever occur to you that he might have been controlling you against your will?"

"Oh, I knew that right way. He had a subteemer aimed at my pleasure center, and he gave me a happy jolt every time I considered what he was saying, a negative jolt every time I doubted him. Of course, it was very tiring for him, keeping such a close eye on me for days on end, but he was able to manage until we met up with his people and he was able to install the automated system." She indicated the octagonal chip on her wrist. "But the truth is, it wasn't even all that necessary by then. I'd seen the brilliance of his ideas. I believed in him the way earlier generations believed in God. His dreams were my dreams, his ambitions my ambitions. I lived to realize his vision of Mankind's future."

The Porrinyards grimaced in disgust. "Soul-rape."

"Love," Mrs. Pearlman shot back. *"Passion."*

I said, "He made you feel that way."

"The finest gift he could have given me."

Skye said, "The girl he found on that university campus might not have thought so."

"She was a vapid little *idiot*."

Yes, I thought. A vapid little idiot capable of thinking for herself, and acting for•herself, and of some concern for human beings other than the one who had replaced whatever value system she might have had with one designed to serve his own purposes.

I found myself remembering the night of madness that had overtaken my family and neighbors on Bocai. We'd lived in peace until the moment when, with no warning, we'd all found ourselves wanting to kill each other. Then we became other people. Could Magrison's means of mind control be the same weapon the Unseen Demons had used on us?

Could it be associated with the upcoming extinctions the AIsource had spoken of?

Skye was asking Mrs. Pearlman, "Did he ever take physical advantage of you?"

Mrs. Pearlman's eyes darkened. "You're mocking me. You know his philosophy. He hated to be touched. He thought all human beings are deprived of their true potential by the animalistic drives that force us to crave the approval of others. He wanted to free us from that. As far as sex was concerned, there was only one thing he liked, and he refused to render it pleasurable for me; the defilement and degradation his lovers experienced was very much the central point."

Vernon Wethers, whose prissiness had already impressed me during dinner, went a little green at this; he murmured an excuse-me and rushed to the bathroom, his cheeks ballooning.

Mrs. Pearlman watched him go, with defiant pleasure at his discomfort. Then her eyes softened again, and her voice became breathless, even giddy. "Want more? Sometimes, when I was good, when I'd solved a problem or furthered his plans in some other fashion, he'd send as much joy as my heart could stand, directly into my brain, and stay with me for hours while I felt touched by God. Once he even went on a trip for six weeks, and as a special treat left the transmitter on maximum while he was gone. He had to leave people behind to keep me fed and watered and clean and turn me so I wouldn't get bedsores. It felt like hundreds of years. When he came back and turned it off, I would have done anything to be touched like that again. Anything. I wept. I even begged him to do the thing he liked. I told him he could befoul me as much as he wanted if he'd just leave me in that place again, even if only for another five minutes. One time, he—"

Monday Brown interrupted. "Counselor! Isn't this enough, already?"

Much as I hated to admit it, the man was right. The psychological destruction of one young woman, and her transformation into a creature capable of furthering the nihilistic ambitions of the terrorist history knew as the Beast Magrison, did exert a sick fascination, especially given its resemblance to what my people had endured on Bocai, but it had little to do with the reason we were here. I took a deep breath, glanced at the now-weeping Paakth-Doy, felt a moment of sympathy for her that made me hope she did not turn out to be the Khaajiir's murderer, and pressed on. "What was your personal contribution to the development of Magrison's Fugue?"

"For five years I worked on the team that developed the strain. It was not easy, you know. Anywhere people can afford AIsource Medical they also have nanites, screening out all biological infestations, whether natural or artificial. The developers had to make a sheath capable of interacting with those defenses and turning them into allies. I was one of those refining the actual symptoms, taking out everything that damaged cognitive function and enhancing only those elements that caused pain at the sight and sound of other human beings." She beamed. "When the chaos started on the worlds we infected? He said that the victory was at least ten percent mine. He was even moved to *kiss* me."

The room fell silent, no two of the observers willing to look at each other. We all knew the history that followed. Before it was contained, Magrison's Fugue had infected seventeen inhabited worlds and over fifty billion people, with over ninety-five percent dying in whatever hiding places they could find because they preferred starvation and thirst to the agony they only felt in the presence of other human beings.

There was still life, and civilization of a kind, in the places that remained. The people who lived there wore AIsource prosthetics over their eyes and ears, to prevent them from sensing anybody else except as hypothetical abstractions, more like the stick figures in a child's drawing than as living, recognizable individuals. Their prosthetics talked to each other and negotiated agreements with each other and allowed something like an organized, sustainable society on worlds where every inhabitant, down to the infants being born to mothers who would never love them, could only view every other as silhouettes rendered indistinct by sensory veils.

Only military blockades on the part of the Hom.Sap Confederacy, imprisoning all the victim populations on their affected worlds, and blowing several infected vessels out of the sky, had prevented Magrison's contagion from infecting all of humanity.

There was no cure. Those worlds remained quarantined today.

But even that was not the worst of it.

The Confederacy remained in contact with the survivors, who had no problem communicating with us in text format, as long as we eliminated all personal pronouns and all details of social interaction in the outside universe from our responses. They could make their needs known. We could send food drops, tech, even a few brave volunteers in isolation suits, to deal with whatever they required to keep their infrastructures going. But we couldn't call what lived on those worlds anything but damned. A few more generations of artificial insemination brokered by AIsource proxies, and automated child-rearing by more AIsource proxies, and

I'm not even sure you could call the beings who walk there human.

But that was not the worst of it.

Wethers returned from the bathroom, looking pale, tiny beads of moisture glistening on his forehead. He murmured an excuse to Brown as he sat. It would have been easy to feel sorry for him, had he not been a willing participant in the empire that employed a monster like Dina Pearlman. He was like other bureaucrats, guilty of signing the papers that made atrocities possibility but lost the stomach the second they were shown the abattoirs they'd authorized.

But he was not the worst of it, either.

I coughed, swallowed spit to soothe a voice that would emerged as a dry croak, and dealt with the very worst of it: The question that obsessed some of my colleagues in the Dip Corps to this very day. "Mrs. Pearlman . . . do you know where Magrison's hiding today?"

"No," she said, with a tinge of regret. "We had to separate, during our time as fugitives. I don't know where he went. Otherwise I'd have gone to him already."

In Confederate custody, this woman would have been interrogated for the rest of her life, by grim men ill-inclined to take no for an answer. Even those inclined to believe her, as I found I did, would have pressed the question forever, using techniques that approached and exceeded all possible definitions of torture. There would have been no choice. He was Mankind's single greatest bogeyman, and we all lived in paranoid fear of his return, this time armed with something that made the Fugue look like a stuffy nose.

I did not have the time or the authority to do what so many of my colleagues would have done, but I couldn't accept a simple no, either. "Do you have any reason to believe he's still alive?"

"Yes," she said. "Faith."

"Do you have any reason to believe the Bettelhines are in contact with him?"

Monday Brown shifted in his chair, looking as unhappy as any child receiving a sweater as his only gift for Specday. "That's a bit much, Counselor."

I whirled on him with something like a snarl. "You're the bastards putting his old slaves to work. I'd say it's absolutely fucking called for." Then turned my attention back to Mrs. Pearlman. "Answer the question."

Her lips pursed, hiding the smile that had threatened to form when I'd snapped at Brown. "Why would they want anything to do with him? They make their riches from human beings at war with one another. Human beings who can't interact at all are useless to them."

"The Fugue ravages any civilization it touches. That's a pretty powerful prize for a munitions empire."

"Not really," she said, with the slightest shade of boredom. "It's useless as a weapon of conquest. In any battle between nations confined to a single planet, the first country using it is unable to avoid being infected in the process."

Skye said, "Fear of Mutual Assured Destruction has never prevented the development of doomsday weapons."

"A good point. But, unlike most devices of that kind, the Fugue is not the kind of tech martial cultures can be persuaded to covet. Dying at the same time as your enemies has such a romantic cache that any population can be persuaded to crave it. But damning yourself and everyone you know to a state you perceive as a living death is a different prospect entirely."

"And in any battle between worlds, separated by space but capable of bombing each other into oblivion?"

Mrs. Pearlman sniffed. "Please. There are less of those than the action-adventure neurecs, so beloved by the common man, would have you think. But again, even if that scenario happened more often than it does, the Fugue's the last thing you would ever want to drop on an enemy. If you're fighting for territory, you do not salt the earth you covet and render the land useless to yourself. And if you just wish to destroy the other civilization out of sheer malice, there are other ways to do it, bombs and mass-drivers and the like, that will eliminate their ability to fight back and therefore don't leave the power for full, automated retaliation still in the hands of vengeful commanders unable to consider regard for your civilian populations even as a distant, nagging abstraction." She licked her lips, establishing with her slight smile that she found the very image delicious. It took her a moment of dwelling on it, finding pleasure in the very idea, before she was able to continue, fresh scarlet blushing her plump cheeks. "No, Counselor, I'd have to say that the only people who would want to use the Fugue are those agreeing with its philosophical point. The Bettelhines may present some useful opportunities for a woman with my skill set, but they haven't demonstrated that kind of elevated consciousness. Believe me, I know. I believe in the Fugue. I propose mass-producing it every six months, Mercantile, and the decision-makers here have always given their most emphatic no."

Thank Juje for small favors. "And that would be who, in your case?"

"First the late Kurt Bettelhine, then his eldest son Hans. Soon, if I live long enough, Philip. He's been seeing to my needs for three or four years now."

"Just Philip?"

"I've met Jason and Jelaine before. They know about my work, and have required my aid on a couple of past occasions. But no, they did not know of my past connection to Magrison. That, I've been encouraged to keep secret."

So she was not some black project, initiated by some overzealous company man without the knowledge of his superiors. All the Bettelhines knew about her, even if they didn't all know where she came from. I said, "And that ridiculous situation-comedy personality you put on, earlier?"

"A means of camouflage I've developed, over the years. It comes in handy when I must deal with outsiders like yourself."

I would have some harsh words for her illustrious host Hans, if we ever did manage to stand on the same planetary surface at the same time. "How did you come to work for them?"

"I arrived in my personal transport and sent a message from the outer system. Docking at Layabout would have been easier, you understand, but in those days it was dangerous for Magrison followers to approach armed worlds except under a flag of truce."

Skye muttered something I did not hear but, doubtless, would have agreed with. I said, "Did you identify yourself?"

"Yes. I gave my resume and offered my services in exchange for protection."

"Who did you speak to?"

"It went up the chain of command until I found myself speaking to Kurt. He was still in charge, back then."

"And he just authorized your approach, knowing what you might be carrying?"

"No. He directed me to meet his fleet at Spyraeth, an uninhabited moon in the outer system. They quarantined me there, subject to regular searches and interrogations for almost a year, until they determined that I had no samples of the Fugue, anywhere aboard."

"And then?"

"Kurt Bettelhine spoke to me again and asked me why he shouldn't just surrender me to your Confederacy, as a gesture of good faith. He said that cooperating with your authorities on this manner would be a fine way to approve relations between the two powers. I told him that I had a number of ideas he could find profitable, more conservative uses of the techniques that had gone into the creation of the Fugue. After some research, I presented him with additional weaponry capable of managing the behavior of entire enemy populations. Later, I produced more focused uses of the same technology—"

Thinking of Bocai, I had gone rigid at the phrase *additional weaponry capable of managing the behavior of entire enemy populations*. "Has that . . . ever been used, Mrs. Pearlman?"

"Not my department," she said.

And Monday Brown looked irritated again. "Counselor, may I please point out that these questions exist outside your license for exploring corporate secrets? The Khaajiir wasn't killed with a virus. Nor was he killed from a distance. He was killed close up, with a Claw of God. A weapon that, I should add, existed many millennia before this woman was even born."

I wanted to scream at him. I wanted to beat her until she confessed that the capabilities she'd boasted about had been used on Bocai. But he had a point, damn him. Much as I wanted to know what horrors this woman had produced, on behalf of our hosts, getting those details could take weeks I didn't have, and an authority I could not claim. "What happened when Kurt Bettelhine agreed to take you on?"

"He installed me in the isolated island facility where I still work today, with a small but dedicated staff of qualified experts in the field."

"And that 'installation' involved an introduction to the man who now poses as your husband?"

"It's no pose," Dina Pearlman said. "The damnable union is legal, all right."

"But you don't love him, or even care for him."

Her mouth was just a red slash across a face that had

become a caricature of the harmless, dithering one she had worn. "I care for *no human being* but Peter Magrison."

"What would the Bettelhines get out of forcing the two of you to live together as husband and wife?"

She shrugged. "Protective coloration. I think he wanted to use me to redeem Farley more than he wanted to use Farley to redeem me. The silly man had gotten himself into some trouble at another installation he managed, when circumstances left him alone with the four-year-old daughter of one of his lead workers. Something like that made him a undesirable executive, even to Bettelhine employees accustomed to suppressing their own moral qualms for the common good. But he was still an excellent leader who always pushed his workers hard and brought his projects in ahead of schedule. Kurt provided the parents with more than enough compensation to make them forget the outrage, albeit perhaps not enough to pay for the damage such a compromise to their parental responsibilities did to their souls, then paired the two of us together in the theory that his two misbehaving beasts would be willing to report on each other in exchange for small rewards. Later, when the idiot was caught attempting to indulge his passions again, we took certain other safeguards preventing him from ever misbehaving in that manner again. If you trust me on nothing else, Counselor, trust me on this. He no longer has to capability to indulge his baser impulses."

Paakth-Doy ventured a hesitant, "Did you . . . castrate him?"

The look Mrs. Pearlman gave her then was any number of things: amused, pitying, contemptuous, and superior . . . but above all proud. "Nothing quite so disgustingly *blunt.*" Then, to me: "We live as husband and wife. But do not consider our relationship love. We have attempted to sleep with each other a few times out of boredom. But we have never completed the act. He cannot match the transcendent pleasures I was shown by Peter Magrison . . . and I cannot pass for under five. Have I mentioned, too, his terrible dullness?"

I coughed. "What are you doing here today?"

"My husband and I are well-known, distinguished contributors to the Bettelhine Corporation and must from time to time be trotted out and provided with the kudos that accrue to high producers like ourselves. At such times I make myself the chattering ninny and he pretends to be a man. These are the same personas we use whenever we mix with co-workers and local society, as our positions force us to do often. I don't know about Farley, but I have grown so used to putting on that personality on a regular basis, that sometimes I forget and almost manage to make myself believe I'm the person I pretend to be." Her next expression reflected a dozen separate emotions at once: pride, anger, amusement, sadness, triumph and loss, all coupled with deep satisfaction over the repugnance in our faces. "It may not be the person I was before Peter Magrison liberated me, but it is as close as I can fake it now."

The moment of appalled silence following that statement lasted for several seconds. Even Monday Brown, who had already known what she was, seemed affected by it. I weighed the life she had never had a chance to live against the life she had embraced instead, and did not know what I was going to say until the moment it left my mouth. "Mrs. Pearlman . . . you're a disgusting person."

It didn't bother her a whit. "I have been told that before."

"You have not heard it enough. But for what it's worth, I think you've been truthful with me so far."

"What you think is worth nothing."

"I have only a few more questions," I told her. "I warn you to remain candid, because I will be angry indeed if any of the information I receive from the others contradicts your own answers in any way."

"I'm not intimidated."

"You would be if you knew me better. Nevertheless. Have you ever seen a K'cenhowten Claw of God before tonight?"

"Once. In a private collection. I don't know whether it was authentic or a re-creation."

"Have you ever met the Khaajiir before tonight?"

"No."

"Have you ever heard of the Khaajiir before tonight?"

"No."

"Did you have any idea before tonight that Hans Bettelhine was hosting an alien dignitary of any kind?"

"It would not have surprised me. A man in his position has offworld guests all the time."

"Did you know?"

"No."

"Is there any possible way you might benefit from the death of the Khaajiir?"

"No."

"Is there any possible reason you would want the Khaajiir dead?"

"No."

"Are you serving any cause outside the Bettelhine organization that would be furthered by the Khaajiir's death?"

"How many times do you intend to rephrase the same question? No. No. No."

"Are you serving any cause outside the Bettelhine organization, period?"

"I am allowed no contact with causes outside the Bettelhine organization."

"Do your privileges as a Bettelhine employee include any means of communication offworld?"

"No. Given my history, my hytex access is read-and-respond only."

"Is the same true of your husband?"

"Yes."

"Is there anybody working with you who would send messages on your behalf?"

"No."

"So it would have been impossible for you to recruit Bocaians as assassins."

"I am sure I could figure out a way, if the need presented itself. I am a clever woman."

"But since you did not know of the Khaajiir's presence until you boarded this carriage, you had no opportunity to abet any conspiracy."

"No. I didn't."

"Mrs. Pearlman, all the questions I asked about you and the Khaajiir apply to you and myself as well. Would you have any reason to want my death?"

"Yes."

Monday Brown rose halfway out of his seat.

I said, "That's all right. I warned you to be truthful. Let me rephrase. Would you have had any reason to want me dead *before* this conversation?"

Monday Brown sat down again, mollified.

Mrs. Pearlman seemed to savor the taste of triumph the same way a lizard would have savored a delectable species of bug. "No. I never heard of you before yesterday. I researched you, as I research everybody I expect to meet, but nothing in your past made you a target. I even imagined that as fellow monsters we might even get along."

"There's little chance of that," I told her. "But I'm done with you. Go back to your husband."

She nodded at me, flashed a predatory grimace at the others, and stood, hesitating just before she reached the door of the suite. "Do you want me to send my husband in?"

"Given a full range of choices, I'd want you to send him out the airlock and leap out after him. But no. I think I'm done with both of you, for the moment."

She showed teeth again, and left. A few seconds later, following some summons known only to themselves, Brown and Wethers followed, their eyes hiding from mine as if afraid of being punctured by accusations. Paakth-Doy went to the rest room, just as pale as Wethers but not in as much of a hurry.

Skye and I sat staring at each other, the silence providing the perfect soundtrack to the thoughts racing through both our minds. After a while, she said, "Philip's taken his vassals aside. No doubt they're comparing notes on all the sensitive corporate scandals you'll be bringing home when all this is over. I suspect we might be having some trouble leaving Xana once we're done."

I'd been thinking the same thing. "I'd give half my disposable income to know what happened to the last Dip Corps envoy who crossed the Bettelhines, this, whatever his name was, Bard Daiken. It might give us an idea what to expect."

Skye raised an eyebrow. "Would it even help us to expect a consequence we don't know how to avoid in any event?"

I didn't know. I suspected not. We'd blundered into a malevolent place filled with trap doors and shadows, where every step took us farther away from an exit that already seemed shut to us. It might have been different had my AIsource handlers been available to provide their usual hints and portents and thus light the path ahead of me. But they remained silent, even as I made yet another attempt to call them back.

Paakth-Doy returned from the bathroom, her eyes glazed and her complexion even paler than the one she'd worn before going in. But she nodded at me as she took her seat again, well prepared for whatever came next.

Skye asked her, "Are you all right?"

Paakth-Doy needed a second to answer. "I must confess that my upbringing among Riirgaans renders me vulnerable to shock at the corrupt potential of my fellow human beings."

Skye said, "It wouldn't feel any different if you were raised by your own kind. We've all been ashamed of our species, from time to time."

"I suppose," she said, with excessive dignity. "But I will do my best to prepare myself for whatever follows. Except, one thing? Counselor?"

"Yes?"

"When you leave Xana . . . would you take me with you?"

That was about the last thing I expected. "Really?"

"Yes. I would very much like to go."

"Why?"

She struggled with the words. "When I left the Riirgaans in my midteens, never having met another specimen of my natural species, the family that raised me afforded me my choice of human destinations. I chose to avoid your Confederacy because of the legal gauntlet it requires of humans with nonhuman citizenship who seek repatriation. Employment with the Bettelhines seemed an easier alternative. But after what I have seen, right now, I am no longer certain that I wish to pay the moral price of living here. I now believe that it would be better to face and overcome the bureaucracy of New London. Will you give me a ride? And perhaps a testimonial to my good faith, if required?"

She had an inner strength, that one. There was no way of telling yet whether that would make her a useful ally or an implacable enemy, but there was no point in underestimating her. People who bounce back are dangerous. Still, I warned her, "It might not be possible. The Bettelhines seem to have a problem releasing people who've served the Inner Family."

"True. But I have never served the Inner Family before this descent. Nor am I impressed with my first taste of life among them. If I can still leave this world, I would like to. Please help me."

I may be an unsympathetic bitch, much of the time, but I'm still capable of being moved. "If it's within my power, I'll make it happen."

She did not thank me for the promise yet to be fulfilled. She just nodded and went back to her seat, content to wait for the next of the revelations she had to witness.

Skye, who had watched the exchange without comment, now turned to me. "Who next? Philip? We have some hard questions to ask him right now."

"No, not yet. I'll want a little more ammunition before I go after that one."

"Dejah? Given her prior antipathy toward the Bettelhines, her presence here raises the most questions."

"I think not."

"Jason and Jelaine?"

"No," I said. "I think we'll hold on to them for a little while, yet."

"Who, then?"

I bit my lip, considering. And then said, "Mendez."

10

MENDEZ

We did not have to send for him. Oscin, who was still outside with the others, knew we needed Mendez the instant Skye did. This time, as per the head steward's lowly status in the scheme of things, Philip raised no tiresome fuss about including Bettelhine Family counsel in the discussion. Mendez entered alone, his head a little bowed and his lips a little pursed, but his deferential, formal manner otherwise undisturbed by our mutual encounter with violent death. Had he been affected at all by the bloody turn our journey had taken, it manifested only as the thin layer of perspiration turning his forehead into yet another reflective surface, glowing in the presence of Bettelhine riches.

He came in, sealed the door after him, then made his way to the place Dina Pearlman had just vacated, all without urgency, trepidation, or any sense that his mission here might entail more than serving drinks or wiping up spills. He stood beside the ottoman, declining to sit. "Counselor. How may I help you?"

"You can begin by taking a seat."

"That's very kind of you, but I'm on duty, and I fear I'd

find it improper. Indeed," he said, his voice rising a decibel or two as he directed withering criticism toward Paakth-Doy, who had been sitting all along, "it is improper for *her* as well."

Paakth-Doy turned red and began to stand.

I snapped, "Sit your ass down, Doy!"

Caught in the very act of rising, Paakth-Doy froze. There was no way of determining the specific arguments raised in the resulting internal debate, but gravity may been the tie-breaker. She collapsed back in her seat, wearing the special misery of any human being caught between competing faux pas.

I kept my voice steady. "Tonight's etiquette violations include murder, sir. With that on that table I could not care less about who stands, who sits, and who uses the wrong goddamned fork while eating their goddamned pretentious inedible entrée. Tonight, Paakth-Doy's working for me, and tonight she'll sit if she's fucking comfortable that way, or if I fucking want her to sit. Is that clear?"

Mendez didn't show even the slightest sign of anger, behind his placid, butlerian exterior. "Whatever Counselor wishes. Am I to sit as well?"

"No, you may do whatever makes you most comfortable."

"Then I'll stand."

"All right." A second passed before I damned myself for my shortsightedness in giving him a choice. Now, for as long as I remained seated myself, I'd have to spend the entire interview looking up at him.

Suppressing a sigh, I rose, cracked my spine, paced a half dozen steps away and turned to face him across a level playing field. The most difficult part was ignoring the gentle grin on Skye's face.

"Mr. Mendez, your primary purpose here is to provide a timeline. But I'd like to know a little bit about you first."

"Is that necessary?" he asked.

"Yes."

"I must confess I wonder why."

It wasn't the first time in my experience that a suspect in a major crime had objected to personal questions, or even the first time a witness had expressed confusion over their relevance. But that had usually been a sign I was striking too close to home. This may have been the first time, ever, that one had questioned the relevance of a basic profile. I stared at him for a moment, expecting insolence, but found none: just a bland, academic curiosity. "I find it helpful to develop a general sense of the person first. Why? Do you think it impinges on your privacy?"

"No, Counselor. I recognize the importance of what you're doing. I just don't know why anything in my life would be considered of special interest."

Meaning that it very well could be. "Well, we'll just let me be the judge of that. How old are you, sir?"

"Forty-seven, Mercantile Standard."

"Have you lived on Xana all your life?"

"No. I came here as a young adult."

"From where?"

"I was born on a planet named Greeve, and lived there until I was seven."

"Greeve?" I had never heard of the place.

"Yes, Counselor." He spelled it for me.

It still rang no bells, which was far from unusual, given the number of worlds that maintained a human presence, large or small. "Is it part of the Confederacy?"

"Yes," he said, betraying some amusement for the first time. "If only just."

"What's that supposed to mean?"

"It's no jewel in the crown. It has a tiny population, no industry, no exports to speak of, no corporate debt, and a lifestyle so simple that the local economy is only a few steps removed from barter. It's signed with the Confederacy, but contributes almost nothing to it except for its name on the registry, and takes nothing in return except for occasional imported staples, which are considered relief. I'm certain that you've heard of places that aren't even dots on the map? Greeve is a dot compared to even those places."

I've been to worlds that fit that description. A number were dysfunctional hellholes, inhabited only because the people there were too stubborn or too mean to just pack up and let the hostile local conditions win. The few who left formed a large percentage of the indentured population in the Dip Corps. But he hadn't said the name with the revulsion I'd heard from so many refugees. "What's it like?"

A slight smile pulled at his lips. "Something like ninety-nine percent ocean. The seas are deep enough to submerge almost all the land to an average depth of about seven kilometers. There's a small spaceport carved into the northern ice cap, but the bulk of the human population, a grand total of some seven thousand people the last time I checked, lives on a chain of some three hundred tropical islands. There are only two islands big enough to support populations of more than five hundred. The rest of the people live in island villages or on houseboats."

It sounded horrid to me but, then, I'd spent most of my life in enclosed orbital environments and had never been able to reclaim my childhood appreciation for natural ecosystems. "Would you call it a pleasant place?"

"It's a paradise if you like sun, sand, friendly people, and gentle ocean breezes."

"You didn't?"

"I was a child."

"You liked it."

A tinge of regret shone through this rock-rigid demeanor. "It was the happiest time of my life."

"But you left when you were seven."

"My parents thought they could do better."

"Why?"

He hesitated, as if even that much personal information was too much to impart. "Our island, Needlefish, was home to two extended families with a total population of about forty people. We saw the same faces every day and faced the same challenges every day. If my parents wanted a big night out they had to make their way to another island, about twenty kilometers north, where she had cousins and my father had old school friends. Maybe once or twice a year, on the only island in our region large enough to accommodate it, there were socials, where the residents of some eighty villages got together to catch up on old gossip and introduce the young people to potential spouses farther removed than first and second cousins. But that's about as exciting as our lives ever got. It wasn't that there was no money. Nobody on Greeve ever needed any money. But my parents felt that lives had gotten to be a little . . . I suppose you would say, arid. When I was six they arranged passage on the next freighter offworld."

"Which happened when you were seven."

"Yes. Ships only came to Greeve when asked to."

I wondered how many places like that remained in the Confederacy: worlds of little interest to anybody except those who lived there, whether they wanted off or preferred to stay for the rest of their lives. "Where were you headed?"

"I don't remember. Wherever it was, we never got there. The ship suffered some kind of disaster between systems. My parents, my sister, and some two-thirds of the vessel's complement never came out of bluegel alive."

"I'm sorry for your loss," Paakth-Doy told him.

"As am I," said Skye.

He gave them a slight nod. "Thank you."

I asked, "How did you survive?"

"I don't know," he said, with the terseness of a man who

had long ago decided that the precise details had no further relevance for him. "I was revived, alongside the remaining survivors, aboard a Tchi transport that answered the distress beacon. I wanted to go back to Greeve, where I still had friends and relatives, but I had no money and no documentation, and neither the Tchi nor the Dip Corps were willing to pay for my passage back to a place where there were no scheduled transports. So I became a ward of the Dip Corps and found myself spending the rest of my childhood in a Confederate vocational school, being trained in hospitality."

I'd been a ward of the Dip Corps too. Had I not been a dangerous anomaly under close observation until the day my keepers decided that my intelligence merited higher education, would I have also received training only for the most menial positions available? Feeling somewhat more sympathy for the man now than I'd managed at the beginning, I pressed on. "And were the Bettelhines your first employers?"

"No. I spent my late teens and early twenties working in-system cruises, in and around the Lesothic wheelworlds. But I sent resumes to the company for years."

"Why?"

"Xana has some luxury resorts famous in the industry. Some are in the subtropics. I hoped to work at one."

"Because that was the kind of environment you'd left on Greeve."

"Not quite," he said, with a knowing smile that poked fun at my naïveté. "Greeve evolved; Xana was engineered. Greeve has species like the tube-tree, the flopfish, and the glowswarm, and delicacies like cosweed wine. Xana's ecosystem has none of those things. The places even possess different smells. I would never mistake one for the other, even with my eyes closed. But Xana's tropics have cool ocean water, a warm sun, and beaches to walk on. It may not be Greeve, but it's not bad."

I asked him, "Why didn't you ever just go back to Greeve?"

He stared straight ahead and answered in a voice that betrayed none of what must have been years of frustration and regret. "It's not like there was ever direct passage to such an obscure place, from any of the hubs where I worked. I would have had to zigzag across systems, bankrupting myself for each leg of my journey, then once again earn enough for the next hop until I reached a place where I could wait for a freighter that happened to be heading where I wanted to go. And even then I would have had to earn my passage again, and wait a long time for a berth to be available. There were times when it seemed remotely possible. But most of the time, it was out of the question."

"But you did manage to find a position on Xana."

He gave a slight nod. "Eventually, yes."

"Did it pay well?"

"Yes."

"What about your off hours? Was it like being on Greeve?"

"There was no way to return to Greeve so I made do."

"Were you happy?"

"I had friends. Women. The prospect of family. A place as close to home as I was ever likely to know."

He described the heartaches of his life with about as much emotion as I would have devoted to listing the contents of my spartan quarters back on New London, a place that for most of my life had been less home than clean place to sleep.

I realized that Skye was studying me. I didn't know why. Maybe it was the sheer length of time I had devoted to the background of this one minor figure, who had not been upstairs with us during the emergency stop and could not have been the culprit responsible for the murder of the Khaajiir. Maybe she thought I'd gotten lost in the minutiae of a life with some sad parallels to my own. Or maybe she sensed what I sensed about this story that seemed no more than a digression: the ghost of a question larger than any of the answers Mendez had provided so far.

I didn't know what was nagging at me. The man's situation was far from unusual, after all. Even before we'd left the homeworld, Mankind's history had always been a long parade of expats and refugees, people who through no fault of their own had become trapped on strange shores and who were forced to make do while keeping an eye on the distant, possibly mythical, pleasures of the homes they'd lost. Hell, if you wanted to go that far, I was one of them. The few tidbits the Porrinyards had fed me about their past as individuals marked them as two others.

But there was something else going on with Mendez. Something that verged on the monstrous.

I found myself pacing furiously, my arms crossed before me, my thoughts racing so fast that they almost drowned out the pounding of my heart. "How did you wind up as head steward of the Royal Carriage? That strikes me as a pretty plum position around here."

The further we got from his tales of Greeve, the more he seemed to relax. "About fourteen years ago I served two months as personal valet to Mr. Conrad Bettelhine, youngest brother of Kurt, when he spent an extended vacation at one of the resorts where I worked. He was a lonely man who required little of me beyond conversation and companionship. But he was touched by my story, and offered to bring me aboard as junior steward. When the senior retired, I moved up."

"What's your work schedule like?"

"I live aboard the carriage, year-round, serving between five and ten complements of passengers per month."

"How much time off do you get?"

"Thirty days a year."

"Consecutive or intermittent?"

"Intermittent. Whenever this carriage is unoccupied or down for maintenance."

"Do you spend all those days enjoying the sun down on Xana?"

"No. Much of the time, when I'm not needed, we're docked at Layabout."

"How much of your down time is spent at Layabout?"

"Maybe two days out of three."

Another piece of the big picture snapped into focus. "So you get maybe ten days a year, intermittent, to spend, if you can, in the sunny island environments you prefer."

"Yes. Sometimes more."

"But sometimes less."

"Yes."

"Did you understand that those were the terms before you took the position?"

"Yes."

"Then why did you accept?"

His expression, impassive for much of the prior interrogation, even during the discussions of the losses he'd known, now changed for the first time, with a subtle knit of his eyebrows. "I don't understand the question."

"Look around you. I don't see any white beaches or turquoise ocean waters. This is not the past you miss, the present you settled for, or the future you would have liked to have. Why is this your life, and why aren't you climbing the walls?"

His eyebrows remained knit, but now the cords in his neck had become visible, straining with a tension that he still managed to keep out of his voice. "This is Xana, madam. Here, one's professional worth is gauged according to one's proximity to the Bettelhine Inner Family. One does not turn down such opportunities."

"How is this an opportunity? Will you ever advance any higher than chief steward?"

He stood a little taller. "I might, some day, be privileged to work for the Inner Family, at one of the Bettelhine estates."

"Like," I said, making a big show of searching for appropriate names as I circled him like a skimmer, looking from an appropriate place to land, "Mr. Brown and Mr. Wethers."

His posture was proud, but stiff. "I do not have their management background, but yes."

Skye had paled, as if suffering jabs of pain from some unknown upset inside her. Paakth-Doy looked just as disturbed, but in a different way; there was actual fear in it, fear that may have had something to do with seeing Mendez as a future version of herself.

I circled Mendez two more times. "What's the greatest future you can imagine for yourself? After retirement, I mean?"

He did not look at me but stared straight ahead, his posture reflecting a controlled fury. "I suppose I will buy a modest home on one of the islands I spoke about."

I allowed my voice to become a little dreamy. "A breezy island hideaway, where you can sit cross-legged on the sand, enjoying a cocktail and listening to colorful native music while the scarlet sun sinks beneath an unclouded horizon?"

"I am not a poet, madam."

I let something occur to me. "But would this be an island on Greeve or an island on Xana?"

"On Xana, of course."

"Why *of course*? Even if you haven't saved enough, after all this time, to return home in style, the Bettelhines must appreciate all your years of service enough to send you where you've always wanted to go. For you, they'd consider the expense pocket change."

That fine sheen on his forehead had become a torrent, leaking rivulets down both cheeks. "Madam, I have done nothing to deserve your mockery."

"I was not aware that a simple question constituted mockery."

"I have been privy to some of the most private tactical conversations of some of the wealthiest and most powerful human beings alive. They know they can count on my discretion, but they still cannot afford to have everything I know out of their control, and thus in potential danger of exploitation by their competitors and enemies. When I took this position, I agreed that my future would remain on Xana."

I showed surprise. "So you work under the same terms that govern Mr. Pescziuwicz?"

"Yes."

"Are these the same terms that govern anybody who works on classified projects or alongside the Inner Family?"

"Yes."

"Mr. Mendez, I have no doubt that you make more money, or whatever the local economy uses for money, aboard this carriage than you would have made had you continued to work Xana's resorts. But I need a basis for comparison. Had you remained dirtside, would you have been able to earn passage back to Greeve?"

"Yes."

"How old would you have been by the time you made it back?"

"I don't know. Maybe sixty, if I'd wanted to arrive penniless."

"Not much of an issue, considering that you say that people on Greeve don't have much use for money. When do you think you'll retire now?"

"When I'm fifty-five."

"So you saved yourself at most five years of bowing and scraping for people who consider you a handy household appliance at the price of denying yourself everything else that gave your life meaning. You threw away what you wanted and secured a default future that will be at absolute best an imperfect imitation of the one you would have chosen for yourself if you could. Am I unfair, sir, in considering this dollar wise and pound foolish?"

Mendez said nothing. I somehow knew, without asking, that any repetition of the question would lead to the same stone wall. Either he didn't know the answer himself, or facing it was more than he could stand.

Either way, I was less interested in his silence than in Paakth-Doy's. She looked white, her impassive features trembling with enough tension to qualify as pain. It some ways it may have felt like I was questioning her too. Or, at the very least, questioning some potential future version of her. When she looked at Mendez, did she see a man whose happy life had been twisted by circumstances beyond his control, or one who represented the face she might find herself wearing, another twenty years down the road?

I excused myself and went to the washroom, running water over my hands and splashing some on my face. While I was in there, I tried to contact the AIsource again, and again received no reply. The blue room remained inaccessible to me.

Fuck You, I told them, feeling a schoolgirl pleasure in the ability to curse out a despised teacher without that teacher ever knowing what I had said. The fact that I'd said worse to them, many times, when they were capable of hearing me, didn't matter. That one belonged to me.

Somehow, without knowing why, I had the sense it made me richer, far richer, than Arturo Mendez.

Mendez was relieved when I devoted the rest of my questions to the timeline of the last twenty-four hours. The give-and-take became a mere matter of accounting, bereft of emotional baggage. We went over the same ground several times, searching for holes in the outline, but within twenty minutes I had the basics, Paakth-Doy testifying to their essential accuracy.

At the time the carriage was prepped, the staff had consisted of Mendez, Colette Wilson, and Loyal Jeck.

Paakth-Doy arrived less than two hours before departure, a temporary replacement for a fourth steward taking a few days off to attend his sister's wedding. She'd worked for distant Bettelhine cousins (nobody involved in Inner Family business, but still minor royalty by local standards), and the temporary promotion to the Royal Carriage had still required a month-long background check poring over every aspect of her entire life since birth. In the end, her spotless record and the testimonials of the lesser Bettelhines she'd served had gotten her the belowdecks assignment.

"She has done a fine job," Mendez allowed, "especially since the crisis began, but she still has much to learn about Inner Family protocol."

"I appreciate the praise," Paakth-Doy said.

I had the impression that it was unreserved approval coming from him, and gentle irony coming from her. Damned if I wasn't starting to like her.

Jason and Jelaine, their father, Hans, and the Khaajiir had arrived under heavy security, transferring from their private skimmer to a shielded walkway under a security shield that hid not only the identity of the Bettelhines embarking on this journey but also the presence of their venerable guest. The Khaajiir had remained invisible to public view throughout this operation, as he'd presumably been throughout his visit to Xana.

"Was that typical?"

Mendez said, "It is not unheard of. It depends on how public the Bettelhines wish to make any particular appearance. Sometimes they arrive with fanfare, with an honor guard of holo operators and neurec slingers capturing every moment for mass consumption. But this had been described as a 'Classified Visit.' Security was tight."

"How secret can it be? When the Royal Carriage goes up and down, it can't take a genius to figure out the odds of a Bettelhine, or somebody very close to the Inner Family, being aboard."

"Yes," Mendez said. "But who? Some minor relative hovering around the periphery of power, or Mr. Bettelhine himself? Besides, the Khaajiir was the one being kept secret. We were warned not to mention him, not even to Layabout security."

Hans had intended to ride up with them but had been called away, at the last minute, to deal with some minor management crisis at one of the company's many research divisions.

No, Mendez did not know what the problem had been; and no, he didn't consider it his business. "Members of the Inner Family have to deal with crises all the time. Some crises necessitate abrupt changes in travel plans. It's just something that has to be dealt with."

The siblings and their distinguished guest enjoyed an unremarkable ascent, asking little of the crew except for a couple of modest meals. Brother and sister had retired to separate suites and slept much of the way up. The Khaajiir had slept a little, too, but had emerged from his suite long before they did, to sit by himself in the lounge, enjoying the spectacle outside the window as the surface receded and the upper atmosphere gave way to space. Mendez had asked him if he needed anything, an offer that led to a few minutes of polite conversation.

I asked Mendez what they'd talked about.

"The view," he said.

Was that really all? The view?

"The rich and the important are often at a loss for a basis of identification with those of my station. Few of my conversations with those I serve transcend banalities."

"That must be annoying."

"The alternative would be to talk about what they talk about with one another, and I daresay I've heard enough of that to know that I want no part of it." He hesitated. "If you truly need to know, he regaled me with some trivia regarding my family name. Evidently it has homonyms in one of the lesser Tchi dialects. I suppose he was trying to be friendly. I feigned interest and then retreated belowdecks."

The one surprise on the way came courtesy of a call from Philip Bettelhine, who informed Mendez that the carriage would be picking up several additional guests during its stay at Layabout: among them himself, his assistant Vernon Wethers, and Mr. and Mrs. Pearlman.

This was the latest in a series of surprises for Mendez, as he'd initially gathered the trip down to be the venue for an important and classified meeting between Hans Bettelhine, Jason, Jelaine, the Khaajiir, and my own party. He did not know the planned subject matter of that meeting, nor what it had to do with Dejah Shapiro, though she was also scheduled for pickup. He did know that when he informed Jason and Jelaine about Philip's party-crashing, they seemed irritated, and led him to believe that the important business, whatever it was, would have to wait until the party could reconnect with Hans on the surface.

No, this was not unusual, either. "Inner Family Bettelhines all operate their inner fiefdoms. Sometimes there's pushing and shoving."

The oddest attendees, Mr. and Mr. Pearlman, had been flown up to Layabout by Vernon Wethers, in one of the Bettelhine Family transports, while the carriage was still in transit. Mendez did not know why. He had been told that they were being honored for exceptional efficiency in beating deadlines at the facility they ran. They would not have been the first low-level functionaries rewarded with the opportunity to hobnob with Inner Family members, either aboard the Royal Carriage or at one of the Family's many estates. Usually, these occasions were provided more warning, but not always. Given Wethers's involvement, the whim appeared to have been Philip Bettelhine's. Either way, the Pearlmans boarded the carriage almost immediately upon its arrival at Layabout, oohing and aahing over all the luxury that was now, temporarily, theirs to enjoy.

Monday Brown, who had also taken a Family transport from the surface, boarded next, specifying that he was there to meet Ms. Shapiro in his employer's stead. He was, as I'd already learned, the last to arrive before word of the attempt on my life prompted the temporary evacuation of the Shuttle as a security measure. No, Jason and Jelaine had not expected him. No, Mendez did not know whether they'd been as annoyed by news of his arrival as they had seemed to be when learning about Philip's party, as he had not been present for that conversation.

Word came of my arrival and several minutes later of the attempt on my life. Jason and Jelaine had expressed great relief that I was all right before everybody but Mendez boarded the evacuation capsule, launched themselves offstation, and waited for Mr. Pescziuwicz to sound the all-clear. Mendez left the carriage too but remained aboard Layabout, making himself available in case Security needed him. The next update he received was when Mr. Pescziuwicz alerted him to join Station Security in escorting the Porrinyards and me to our suite.

Mendez had just completed the grand tour when the evacuation capsule returned. Worried about my reaction to seeing another Bocaian in this context, Jason and Jelaine had asked the others to stay behind while they introduced me to the

Khaajiir. Once that was over and done with, and I joined the Porrinyards in our suite, everybody else settled in.

We were in our suite during Dejah's arrival. She had actually docked with Layabout less than an hour after us, but her transport had been held up during the security shutdown, and she didn't make her way across the Concourse until twenty minutes after the Porrinyards and I retired to our suite. Occupied as we were, we also missed the separate arrivals of Philip Bettelhine and Vernon Wethers, Philip Bettelhine taking a special flight from the surface to join us, Wethers arriving after a brief meeting at one of the company's orbital manufacturing facilities.

And that had been it, before the descent.

I rubbed the tip of my nose with the edge of one knuckle. "I believe we can afford a break right now. Why don't the two of you join the others outside? Skye and I will be out directly."

Paakth-Doy understood the situation completely. "You need privacy to talk about us behind our backs."

I gave her an unsmiling nod. "Thanks for understanding."

She remained unperturbed as she followed Mendez out the door.

The second she was gone, I turned to Skye. "First things first. What's going on with the others?"

There was no transition from the Skye who had been present with me throughout the prior interviews and the one reporting events from Oscin's viewpoint. "It's been tense. Farley Pearlman's been taking advantage of the bar service to work himself into a quiet, morose drunk. Dina's been complaining about the smell, but not the same traumatized way she did before—it's just an exercise in being unpleasant. The way she put it, the *'Holy Man'* smells *'even worse'* than he did when he was alive."

"How did Jason and Jelaine take that?"

"About as well as can be expected. Jason invoked his father's authority and ordered her to keep her, quote, *'evil'* mouth shut. I think he was telling the truth before, about not knowing about her life before she reached Xana."

"So do I. What else?"

"Philip's ordered Mendez to set the air recyclers in the parlor to full power. They're filtering out the worst of the odor out there, though you can still catch a whiff of the poor Khaajiir if you get too close. He's also still holding out hope that the whatever-it-is, the Stanley, will be showing up any minute, and he's pressed Jason for the reason we're here—evidently, Dad didn't bother to share it with him. Jason told him he'd find out in good time. He then took Jelaine aside, who said the same thing, word for word, at which point he got mad and said, *'What's the matter with you? We were never the closest brother and sister, but we used to be able to talk. Now you're as bad as Jason.'*"

"Either he totally lost control of himself, or your male half's been especially deft at eavesdropping."

"Both," Skye said, without any special pride. "He did raise his voice, but the only reason I'm able to provide the full quote is that Oscin was able to come up behind Philip when he wasn't looking. Jelaine saw Oscin but didn't care. She seemed to relish the opportunity to share secrets with us. It's like we've joined an old girl's club without knowing it."

"How did he react when he realized you'd heard him?"

"The same way, with an additional added helping of hurt. Make no mistake, Andrea. From what I can tell, there *is* love lost between Philip and his siblings. He believes they've turned their backs on him, and resents them for it."

All of this dovetailed with what we'd already figured out about Jason and Jelaine, though perhaps not what their father's place among them. I said, "And how's he reacting now that Mendez and Paakth-Doy have returned to the party?"

"He's a little upset that we've been left alone." She hesitated. "Wait, he's confronting Oscin, demanding to know just what we think we're doing. Paakth-Doy's telling him, *'they've just established a timeline.'* He's saying we had to have done more than that. She's saying, *'Yes, sir, they have, but I'm not permitted to share it with you.'*"

I felt another surge of respect for Paakth-Doy. "The lady has a backbone."

"That she does, and it doesn't make Philip happy at all. And again, here come more spirited defenses of your reputation from Jason and Jelaine. I note that Dejah's watching the two of them very carefully. She's . . . Andrea, that's a grin. That's definitely a grin. I think she's caught up."

I found that I could picture the look on Dejah's face. "I wouldn't put it past her. She's sharp. When we worked together, she frightened me to death."

"She seems to like you well enough. That marks her as unusual right then and there."

I didn't take offense. It happened to be true. "Especially when we met. I was an even bigger bitch then than I was when you met me, and I shut her down every time she tried to be friendly. But that's not what scared me. She's scary-smart. I was used to being a prodigy, but she made me look like a stammering idiot. And there's something else about her, something you need to keep in mind."

"What's that?"

"She's as wealthy as the Bettelhines. She's as well known as they are and, in some circles, as hated as they are. We learned during dinner that she and the Bettelhines have had unpleasant, even murderous, past history. And yet, she arrived at Layabout without a security entourage of her own. I can tell you right here and now that she's never had one. She goes everywhere alone, or paired with whoever happens to be her husband this year. By all rights—including, I should say, her well-known habit of picking treacherous bastards as those husbands, for reasons that frankly escape me—she should have been assassinated long ago. But she survives. She thrives. I promise you, love, if there's anybody on the carriage we don't want to be the murderer, or the money behind the murderer, it's her. Because if it is her, we've already lost."

Skye considered that. "Do you think it's her?"

"I don't have enough data to know."

"What do you think of what we learned from Mendez?"

"About his life? It feeds some suspicions I'm already working on, suspicions that resonate with some of the things we've noticed about Brown and Wethers. About the time-line? It establishes something odd about our complement. The one man most credited for wanting me here, Hans, had to change his plans at the last minute. Conversely, five others, including Brown, Wethers, Philip, and the Pearlmans, were all added to the guest list with the same lack of warning. There's even a sixth anomaly, if I count Paakth-Doy, though I may not, since her assignment here has been planned for more than a month and fails to meet the pattern. Still, even if we discount her and maybe one or two of those others as coincidences, we still have a vehicle overcrowded with people who all went to extraordinary lengths to board just as a meeting of unexplained importance was set to take place here."

"It looks to me," Skye said, "like somebody doesn't want that meeting to take place."

I could only agree. That was the basis of the epiphany I'd been fighting since the moment I found the Khaajiir dead.

Discounting the Porrinyards, who had traveled here as my companions, only Dejah Shapiro and I had traveled to this system just to be here today.

We were the original reasons for this gathering. Everything else, all the pomp and all the violence we'd endured, was just noise and distraction.

But what would Hans Bettelhine have to say to either Dejah or me that any of the others would kill to prevent us from hearing?

I was still considering that when the carriage trembled.

11

DEJAH'S VIEW

Half expecting to find another ravaged corpse among our fellow partygoers, I ran back into the parlor and instead discovered a cautious hope diluting the lingering shock of the Khaajiir's death.

Monday Brown was downright ebullient for him, which meant a slight upward turn at the corners of lips otherwise as straight as a slit. Vernon Wethers looked white, his eyes scanning the sculpted ceiling as if hoping for the sudden appearance of an escape ladder. Dina Pearlman, who had retreated to one of the lounges with a bottle, raised it in a mock toast, and Farley just looked tired, as if he'd accept any development as long as everybody just left him alone.

"What's going on?"

Philip seemed to take cruel pleasure in telling me the good news. "Help's arrived. That's the sound of the Stanley from Layabout touching down on our roof."

"Are you sure?"

There was another shudder that tinkled glasses and jarred the balance of anybody not already seated. With an efficiency he didn't seem to have to think about, Mendez rescued one glass before it toppled over the edge of the bar. "He knows what he's talking about, Counselor. That's a Stanley, making contact with the carriage. I know because I've been trained to recognize the sound."

"Then you know what to expect," I said.

"I'm afraid I don't. In the simulations I experienced, the pilot always remained in contact with us throughout the rescue operation. He would have warned us to expect that jolt, for instance. But I don't know what he's going to do if we cannot communicate with him and assure him that we're still alive."

"Don't worry," Oscin told everybody. "I don't know the exact parameters of the local tech, but any low-orbit recovery vehicle would be useless without instruments capable of detecting movement, and therefore life, inside sealed compartments like this one. Now that we're in direct contact, I suspect the crew of that thing is devoting as much effort to counting heartbeats and voices as they are to determining the nature of the malfunction. Am I right about that, Mr. Bettelhine?"

"That's the way I understand it," said Philip.

"That's the way it is," said Jason.

Farley Pearlman looked away from his drink long enough to make a single, not very interested suggestion. "What about us? Should we all start yelling?"

He was precisely the kind of criminal I'd never been able to speak to with any degree of professional detachment, but my answer was less for him than for anybody else who might consider his suggestion a good one. "If their instruments are capable of detecting heartbeats through bulkheads and heat shielding, and somebody's listening, that's the last thing we want to do. It would be like screaming hello into a stethoscope."

He gave a sad happy little nod, as if it pleased him to be

rendered an irrelevance yet again, and retreated back to his drink.

"Could have been worse," Mrs. Pearlman cracked. "He could have suggested a singalong."

Another rumble shook the carriage, this one harsh and metallic and moaning like a prehistoric beast calling for another of its kind.

"They're moving," Jason said.

I said, "Mr. Bettelhine? With those safety shields lowered, we're effectively blind. Is there an exterior monitor of some kind that I can use to monitor its progress?"

Philip regarded me with incredulity. "Why? You don't claim to be an expert on that, too?"

"Perhaps not," I told him, "but given everything else that's happened today, I think it's best not to put too much trust in procedures operating within their expected parameters. If something goes wrong out there, or if this is just another manifestation of an attack on the people in the room, wouldn't you like to know?"

He searched my eyes for signs of duplicity, found none, and resisted a few seconds more out of sheer disinclination to cede me even that much ground.

Jelaine said, "It wouldn't hurt."

Philip slumped, expressing his surrender with a flip of one hand that did not surrender so much as grant me leave to slink from his presence.

Jason's expression was gnomic, but tinged with a satisfaction that under the circumstances seemed as ominous as another attack by Bocaian assassins might have been. Despite all logic I half expected him to whisper a confidence in his sister's ear. He didn't, but she wore much the same expression.

Mendez said, "There's a monitor station belowdecks, next to the cargo airlock. It provides a real-time holo feed of the carriage exterior from four perspectives."

"That'll do. Give me a second, first." I pulled Skye over to the wreckage of the dinner table and told her, "You, Mendez, and Paakth-Doy come with me. Oscin stays here with everybody else."

Skye kept her voice low. "You really are that sure this rescue's nothing of the kind?"

"Let's just say I don't trust easy outs when everything else in the course of the day seems to have been conspiring against us. Why? You think I'm just being paranoid?"

She shook her head. "When you start acting paranoid, I start scanning the rooftops for snipers."

We returned to the others in the midst of another jarring shudder, the vibration subsiding only enough to become a low-frequency hum hard to hear but resonant enough to hurt my teeth.

Dejah intercepted me before I could connect with Mendez and Paakth-Doy. "Andrea? I'm sick of just holding up the bar. I'm coming with you in case you need any help."

"It shouldn't be necessary," I said.

"Maybe not, but it's what I'm going to do."

I tried to think up reasons to object and came up short. Why not. It might give me the opportunity to ask her some questions.

I might have expected Philip Bettelhine to raise some objections of his own, but he just grumbled. It was not a surrender so much as a tactical retreat, as he shepherded his energies for later battles.

Just as we went I made eye contact with Vernon Wethers, who seemed downright disappointed that his boss was letting the matter go that easily. He had opened his mouth, prepared to concur with whatever Philip wanted, but now had to close it, his own unflagging support in flight but bereft of a place to land. I was reminded of a phrase I'd once heard in another context that fit him so well I suspected I'd always see it in connection to his name: *not a man, but a spare part.*

I also wondered if, like Mendez, he'd ever had the potential to be anything else.

It was the one thing that rankled most about my interview with Mendez. This world may have owed everything it had to the Bettelhines, but a suspicious percentage of those who worked closely with them seemed to have given them everything.

I haven't spent much time on luxury conveyances, but the couple of times I have I've found myself needing to explore the areas not meant for eyes for paying passengers. I'd found the polished veneer a thin one, which grew grubbier and more reduced to the merely functional the farther I penetrated into servant territory. I was not surprised to find that the areas belowdecks on the Royal Carriage followed the same pattern. Once we descended two more decks, past the second level of passenger suites and into the level containing the crew's quarters, all grandeur fled. There was no vast open area for entertaining here, no great display port overlooking the planet below, just narrow passageways equipped with vacuum doors and lined with sealed rooms labeled STORAGE A, STORAGE B, PANTRY, LAUNDRY, and EMERGENCY.

Beyond that we found a grayer and even more cramped region not so much a place where people lived their own lives as one where they were stored when not in use. Only one of the four compartments in there, the one belonging to Mendez, was labeled with the name of its occupant, and then only in terms of his function: CHIEF STEWARD A. MENDEZ. The other room read CREW QUARTERS A and CREW QUARTERS B.

Another spiral staircase at the end of this corridor led to the carriage's lowest level, a gray area lined with crates and black machinery and blocked by a bulkhead with two air lock doors labeled CARGO 1 and CARGO 2.

But it was the monitor between the two doors, a standard flatscreen with minimal holo capability that interested us now. It provided a monochromatic image of the carriage roof as seen from a vantage point near the junction between our supercarriage and the groove in the planetary cable. The sky in the background was a starless shade of black, with a dim glow rising from the bottom of the screen. The cable was at the periphery of the image, a straight line between us and its connection to Layabout.

The carriage was now being straddled by an insectile vessel with a shiny obsidian head three-quarters the carriage's diameter, and six serpentine segmented limbs. Two of those legs continued to clutch the cable. Two others stood braced against the carriage roof. The final two split into a dizzying array of smaller limbs that must have served the device as fingers. The vehicle sat motionless above the junction where the carriage clutched the cable's anterior track, as if unsure how to proceed.

The junction was a blackened smear, part of the housing that twisted away from the cable track and looked like it had melted before freezing back to solidity.

Dejah, Paakth-Doy, Skye, and I all regarded the static picture with a silence that ended when I admitted, "I have no idea what I'm looking at. That big thing's the Stanley, right?"

Mendez nodded. "Yes, madam."

"I think I've asked this already, but why in Juje's name would it be called a Stanley?"

His shrug was a close cousin to an apology. "I have been told that it has something to do with the vehicle's arachnid appearance, but further understanding has always eluded me. You might want to ask Jason and Jelaine, as they've always demonstrated a certain amusement at the word and the form that they've never seen fit to explain." He shrugged, a close cousin to an apology. "I gather that it's a private joke between them."

I wondered if the joke could prove relevant and decided that it probably wouldn't, right now. "Why isn't it moving?"

"I don't have any way of knowing. But in the absence of a critical life-and-death emergency requiring immediate action, the crew would diagnose the problem and confirm a course of action with the engineers at Layabout and Anchor Point. My supposition is that they're still discussing the matter."

We watched for a few more seconds, waiting for the Stanley to do something, anything. It remained motionless.

Dejah beat me to voicing suspicion. "Something's wrong."

There was no panic or fear in her voice, just a dread, knowing certainty. "What's your reason?"

Dejah said, "I could understand them taking their time had they been in contact with us all along, but we've been cut off from all communication for a couple of hours now. Trust the word of somebody who knows from personal experience the special kind of attentiveness expected by the filthy rich: given whose elevator car this is, the people in that vehicle should be shitting bricks. They should be desperate to get through and confirm that everybody's all right."

I took another look at the image on the screen, finding an odd delicacy in the Stanley's frozen posture. "Assuming Pescziuwicz told them everything they needed to know, I'm afraid it's even more suspicious than that."

"How?"

"When I spoke to him during dinner, he told me that Brown had informed him that a Bocaian was aboard. If the Stanley's crew can hear our heartbeats, and they know that a Bocaian should be with us, then they can observe that all of the hearts still beating are human and determine that there's already been at least one fatality . . . on a day when there's already been one incident involving Bocaian assassins. Whatever the cause of our problem, they should consider this a life-or-death situation. They should be moving. At the very least, they should have someone rushing to an air lock to get medical workers in here."

Paakth-Doy said, "That goes along with everything I know about the emergency protocols."

Dejah bit her lip. "Either they can't proceed, or they don't dare."

I nodded. "That's what it looks like to me."

We continued to watch the static image, waiting for any signs of life from the Stanley. It continued to hang in place, maintaining its position, betraying none of the dramas that may have been taking place inside.

I imagined its crew slumped at their consoles, their seats stained with insides liquefied by the Claws of God adhering to their backs. It was illogical nonsense, but the motionless Stanley was precisely that ominous.

Skye said, "Oscin just told the Bettelhines what you've been saying. Philip says we should get back up to the parlor and leave the professionals to their work, but he's more frightened than he's been letting on. Jason says we should give the Stanley a few more minutes before jumping to any conclusions. But he put special emphasis on the word *'few.'* I think he concurs that this isn't good."

I almost murmured something about not working for the Bettelhines and not requiring their input. "Arturo? Do we have any way of sending somebody up there?"

Mendez said, "There's an access ladder on the hull within reach of the air lock ascending to the elevator roof. If worse comes to worst I can suit up, but I wouldn't want to be out there if either the carriage or that Stanley started moving again."

"What danger would that pose?"

"The carriage? Nothing, as long as we remain above the atmosphere. That, given the proportions of most planetary atmospheres, wouldn't happen until the last few minutes of our descent. As for the Stanley, I wouldn't be in any real danger as long as its crew knew I was out there, but we cannot communicate with them and it would be genuinely unpleasant for me if those legs came scrambling over the side while I was still on the ladder and unable to signal them to avoid running over me. I'll go if the Bettelhines order me to—it is, after all, my duty—but under these circumstances I'd consider it more prudent to wait a few minutes and make sure that there's no other alternative."

As he began cycling through the other exterior vantage points in search of another that might indicate what was delaying action on the part of the Stanley and its crew, I noticed Dejah studying me. It was not an unfriendly look, but it was a measuring one, and as she straightened up and appraised Skye (who had moved closer to me at the moment she realized Dejah was paying such close attention), I wondered just how deep she was poring, just how much she could see. "What?"

She glanced at Mendez, saw that he was engrossed in the view from the exterior monitors, and said, "You've changed."

Coming from somebody as incisive as her, the observation seemed ridiculously banal. "And?"

"No, Counselor, I mean it. You used to strike me as one of the most damaged people I'd ever met. Your entire personality was one big scab. I could barely say anything to you without opening up one wound or another. But something's changed with you, and entering a healthy if somewhat unusual relationship," she indicated Skye, "isn't enough to account for it. You haven't just changed. You've *changed*."

I didn't have the time or the inclination to discuss the subtle psychological surgery that the AIsource had performed upon me on One One One, or any of the other experiences I'd been through since the Dip Corps lost the deed to my life. "It's been a long time."

"Not that long," Dejah said, with absolute certainty. "Not for what I've been seeing."

Now she was leaving the realm of things I didn't want to answer, and entering the realm of things I wasn't sure I could answer. How much could my personality have shifted since I'd welcomed the AIsource into my head? Since they'd admitted a link between their rogue intelligences, the ones I called the Unseen Demons, and the madness that had overtaken my human and Bocaian families? Since I'd defected? Dejah had noticed that some of my wounds had healed, but could she tell that new ones had formed?

I hesitated for so long that she must have felt she'd gone too far, because she placed a protective hand on my wrist. "You don't have to explain it if you don't want to. I know you have other people you can share things with. I'm just saying. I've noticed, and I'm impressed."

I didn't speak again until after I reached for my collar and removed a small silver disk most people would have taken for ornamentation. It was in fact a favorite tool in my arsenal, a hiss screen of Tchi manufacture, invaluable for keeping private conversations private. The soft white noise it projected wouldn't disturb me, Dejah, Paakth-Doy, or Skye, but would render our words indistinct to Mendez, who was still cycling between image angles of the Stanley at rest, searching for active proof that its crew intended to use the carriage as something more than a parking space. Once the hiss kicked in, I lowered my voice and asked Dejah, "All right. As long as we're sharing confidences, have the Bettelhines provided you with any idea why you're here?"

If she felt disappointed that I'd reacted to her personal overture with a swift return to business, she didn't show it. If anything, she seemed amused. "No, Counselor. I don't think Philip knows, and the few times I managed to get the question out, Jason and Jelaine kept saying it was up to their father to say."

"That's what I got from them as well."

She pursed her lips. "I'm not surprised."

"Why?"

"Well, this does seem to center on you, me, and the Khaajiir, doesn't it?"

That was the impression I'd been forming. "If you didn't know why Hans wanted to see you, what did they say to get you here?"

She moved closer, making certain that she was within the screen's most effective range, before lowering her voice still further. "You need to know this. Philip wasn't kidding at dinner, when he said we'd been enemies."

"What caused that? A business dispute?"

"Not at all. We've never been in competition, or even clients of one another. You could say we work opposite sides of the street, in that I engineer worlds and build custom ecosystems, making places for people to live, whereas they just develop bigger and better ways for people to blow each other up. If anything, they help my business by creating a need for my services whenever their clients damage inhabited worlds beyond repair. But that's a sick, mercenary way of looking at it. The truth is, I've stepped in enough of their messes and seen enough of the suffering they've caused to despise everything they stand for. So from time to time, whenever the opportunity presented itself, I've used my considerable influence to . . . discourage the need for their services. I've done it so many times over the years that they've responded with open hostilities, sometimes bordering on violence."

"Any assassination attempts?" I asked.

"Seven. One came close to killing my poor husband, Karl, but he survived thanks to the special providence that always protects innocents and fools."

Skye's voice was colder than any I'd ever heard from the Porrinyards, either together or as individuals. "I notice you have no problem badmouthing him behind his back."

Dejah winced. "I do, don't I?"

Paakth-Doy said, "Forgive me, but that would be the third time in my hearing tonight."

Dejah looked down at the deck and then at me before finding words. "You're right. Karl deserves more."

"Then why," Skye demanded, "do you speak about him the way you do?"

"I have to. I love the man, I wouldn't share my life with anybody else, but I'm just forced by the high stakes I play for to be candid about his strengths and weaknesses. And the sad truth, despite his kindness and his generosity and everything else I adore about him, is that Karl is a limited creature intellectually, a fool in the classical sense. He's the sort of person who stumbles over things and causes disasters even when he's trying to make things better. It's that which contributed to the criminal career that ended the very day we met. I left him home this trip, even though Hans Bettelhine's invitation pledged safe passage for both of us, because his best intentions and the Bettelhine Corporation's worst intentions are just too explosive a combination even for a meeting our hosts made to sound like an overture of peace."

Skye was still determined to make the irrelevant Karl an issue for some reason. "You're still making him sound more like a pet than a husband."

"He's a husband," Dejah assured her, "but in matters of business, he cannot be a *partner*. There's a difference."

Skye was about to protest again, when I held up a hand and said, *"Enough,"* cutting off further exploration of this tangent. To Dejah I said, "Even if they protested their good intentions, I would have expected you to insist on meeting

Hans on neutral ground. Just in case his invitation was a setup for assassination attempt number eight."

She sighed. "Maybe a year or two ago, I would have. And as it is, I required months of entreaties before deciding to accept their offer. But I've been compiling intelligence that gives me reasons for special concern."

"Such as?"

"It has to do with the way the Bettelhine succession works. Traditionally, every member of the Inner Family has always assumed leadership of some of their enterprises, the various research and development divisions being considered especially large plums. The stakes are greater than you can imagine. There is no way that Jason, with his checkered past and those years in absentia when he could have been under the control of Juje alone knows what unsavory parties, would ever have been trusted as being free of outside influence. Under normal circumstances, his relatives would certainly welcome him back as a beloved brother and son, but never again as somebody with a future in any part of the corporation that really mattered. They'd have to be insane to risk it. You understand?"

"Yes."

"Then explain why Philip, a Bettelhine traditionalist whose business model is best summarized as more of the same, who should be first in line for command on the entire corporation, has been forced out of at least four major subdivisions in the last two years, with more and more of his responsibilities being handed over to this partnership of Jason and Jelaine. Explain why Hans Bettelhine has been spending an increasing percentage of his work hours in the company of Jason and Jelaine—as well as, it seems, this wild card Bocaian. Explain why, at a point in its history when its fortunes are as secure as they've ever been, the corporation has not expanded, as you would expect, but rather consolidated its resources, a process that has included terminating long-standing commitments to the production of war materials for at least a dozen raging brushfires on Confederate worlds. Explain why they've been shifting their investments to the reconstruction of crumbling infrastructure or worlds laid waste by their policies. Explain why this family, which has forged a munitions empire, seems to be laying the ground-work for a total abandonment of its prior business model. Explain to me what they're retooling for. And then explain why, on top of that, they would now offer a olive branch to me, a woman they've tried to kill seven times."

I remembered another conversation, from earlier in the evening. "Jelaine was talking about her brother earlier. She told me, *'A changed man can change his family, and what his family stands for.'*"

"She said something like that to me too," Dejah said. "And it would be truly wonderful to believe it, because it's just too tempting to embrace the story of a poor, angst-ridden rich boy who discovered that the little people suffer, and who returns to his position of power only to bend all his wealth to the betterment of mankind. But dynasties as established as the Bettelhines just don't work that way. They have proce-dures in place to make sure that no changes that radical ever take place. It's one of the reasons they always have so many children: so that whenever one offspring or another develops a social conscience and starts talking about the dismantling of everything that's made the family powerful—as happens every couple of generations, since guilt has always been en-demic among the rich—the rest of the Family is in place to stop them before they do permanent damage."

Paakth-Doy looked fascinated. "Stop them how?"

"Any number of ways short of assassination, if that's what you're thinking. Usually, they just make sure the offending youngsters are shunted into positions like labor relations that carry the trappings of power but don't really affect the direction of the business. In more extreme cases, the youth-ful idealists are bought out and sent somewhere offworld, to work with refugees or operate relief agencies, or otherwise exercise their moral qualities to their heart's content, also without ever again making a decision that changes anything. At the absolute worst extremity, they can even be declared in-competent and subjected to exile, either internal or external. You'd be surprised both by how many outcast Bettelhines live in other systems under assumed names, and how many of the more secluded Bettelhine estates down on Xana are occupied by cousins, or whatever, who are provided every-thing they could possibly want except the freedom to change things. But to believe that an Inner Family Bettelhine like Jason could possibly return from some offworld hellhole like this place Deriflys, where my intelligence alleges that he found himself, and just out of charisma and empathy for the suffering of others succeed in changing an institution that has existed for centuries . . . that's just way too good to be true. Unless there's something else going on."

I asked her. "And so your 'reasons for special concern' are—?"

"—that sooner or later *the other shoe has to drop.*"

It was more or less the way I'd figured things, but Dejah's take gave it even more urgency. These were people who had already contributed to more human suffering, on a grander scale, than any one family in the history of Mankind; it was tempting to think of any change of course for them as good news, but could there ever be good news where the Bettel-hines were concerned? Was it not more likely that we were seeing a different shade of bad?

I was about to ask Dejah another question when Mendez cried out, "What the devil are you doing, you? *No*, dammit, *no!*"

I deactivated the hiss screen and rushed to his side, closely followed by Dejah, Paakth-Doy, and Skye. For a moment

I didn't know what he was looking at. Then I saw that the image on the screen had changed. It was no longer dominated by the curves of the Stanley but by the black void above us. The Stanley itself had retreated to the point where its running lights were just a bright spot, so far up the cable by now that it might have been just another star. Even farther above us, the thin line known as Layabout blinked a constant tattoo, on and off, on and off, like a distant lighthouse mocking castaways adrift without any further means of traveling the storm-tossed kilometers remaining between them and land.

Dejah said, "What's the Stanley doing all the way up there?"

Mendez grimaced. "I don't know, madam. It went from a full stop to a full-speed retreat, shimmying up that cable so fast it was like we were on fire and it was afraid of being burned. It's now . . . wait. It's slowing down. Stopping. Full stop, one kilometer above us. And holding. This doesn't make any sense. What do they think they're doing? Abandoning us?"

There followed a ten-second pause while the four of us tried to figure it out.

I got it first, but I happened to see it strike Dejah as well, and she was the first to say what we were both thinking, her disgust matching his and adding a nice, healthy dollop of fear for good measure. "No. If I'm right, it'll stay there, observing us from that safe distance. Within the hour there'll probably be another one a kilometer below us, courtesy of the security people at the ground station. We'll also see some orbital vehicles, before long. But none will get any closer. Not until somebody on their negotiating team or aboard this carriage finds a way out of this."

"Out of what?" he demanded.

The Porrinyards got it. I could tell because that's when Skye's eyes registered shock, fear, anger, and finally disgust.

I could only wonder whether their shared feelings were as obvious on Oscin's face, and how that look would then affect the composure of the people still remaining on the parlor deck. Whatever happened, the mood up there would be dark indeed by the time we got around to joining them.

I said, "This is a hostage situation."

"Or a quarantine," Dejah said.

12

PHILIP, EXCLUDED

Philip Bettelhine sat with his face in his hands, his rigid manner now fully given way to the dazed retreat of a man whose foundations had turned to sand beneath him. "I don't understand," he said. "This should be *impossible*."

I don't think he was speaking to me but to the universe in general, a structure that, having proved the invulnerability of the Bettelhines a fraud, might have also been planning to jettison gravity, relativity, and thermodynamics as well. Whatever veneer of defiance he'd displayed earlier, when it was still possible to place hope in the prospect of a rescue from the support systems his family had paid for, had crumbled with this latest blow. He was too strong a man not to bounce back, but this was his nadir. This was when he'd be most vulnerable.

I asked him, "Why would it be impossible, sir?"

"I . . . don't understand."

"You know what I'm talking about. Every human society since the beginning of the industrial revolution has known its anarchists, its saboteurs, its terrorists. The more we advance, the greater the stakes, the easier it becomes for malcontents to knock over our sand castles. Why would this be impossible? Why would this not happen?"

His eyes were red-rimmed, his tone petulant. "It just . . . shouldn't be able to."

"Again: Why not? Why would you have security if you didn't have at least the possibility of criminals?"

"We have criminals," he said, as if clinging to this one fact. "We have prisons."

"Certainly. That's a human society down there. I'm willing to bet you have any number of run-of-the-mill thieves, rapists, murderers, and sociopaths; in fact, I'm sure that Farley over there cannot be your only pederast, though he's certainly one too many. But how come you're so shaken by the revelation that you may have more than that? After all, you have thousands, maybe millions, of people directly involved in the development of newer and deadlier weapons, including I presume those that would permit the hijacking of this elevator. Why would you consider it *impossible* for some disgruntled tech to gather together whatever resources they needed for exactly this kind of stab at the Bettelhine heart? In a world where advanced weaponry has been the very basis of your daily business, why have there never been any ambitious would-be conquerors willing to attempt a coup d'état?"

He said nothing, but instead just looked at his hands. Juje help the hereditary leader whose personal strength has never been adequately tested; on the day that test comes, his very bones may turn out be made of sand. Maybe he'd stand up again, stronger than before. Maybe he wouldn't.

I searched my fellow passengers for the unguarded expression or relaxed posture that would give away those to whom this development would have come as no surprise. I saw nothing. Jason looked pale and shaken, still determined to maintain a confident unfrightened veneer even if the reactions of his body were just as determined to betray him.

Jelaine seemed angrier, though just as frightened, the gestalt of those two emotions a determination to hurt somebody once she knew just who deserved to be hurt. Farley Pearlman remained at the bar, working on what may have been his six or seventh drink, staring at his latest glass as if he envied the liqueur's capacity to conform to its shape. Dina Pearlman glared back at me, but with a furious concentration that seemed, to me, testimony that she was struggling just as hard to figure out what was going on as the rest of us. Dejah was just angry. Monday Brown looked ill, the perspiration dripping from his forehead as if every moment the Bettelhines remained out of control required additional effort on his own part, just to cope. Vernon Wethers looked worse. The four stewards, Mendez, Colette Wilson, Paakth-Doy and Loyal Jeck all looked like the recipients of recent blows to the base of the spine, though even as I watched Doy and Colette both offered me their own highly different attempts at comforting smiles. Skye circled all of us like a herding animal, her eyes constantly moving as she searched for any cue I might miss. Oscin continued the task that had occupied him for long minutes now, examining the Khaajiir's body from every angle he could find. Nobody seemed willing to step forward and identify themselves as the hijacker in charge.

Instead, it was Philip who spoke again. "We . . . still don't know that this is anything more than a malfunction."

"Please," Dejah begged him. "Forget the rest of us. Tell us any other reason that the Stanley would want to keep its distance rather than do anything it could to rescue Jason, Jelaine, and you. Just *one*."

"It's *impossible*," he said again. It was the very structure of his universe.

After him, the most likely sources of useful information were Jason and Jelaine. I studied them for a moment, saw them both willing to make eye contact with me, both straining with the awareness that they'd withheld vital information, both eager to tell me but unsure whether they should or not. I saw apologies in their eyes, even a brave half-smile on Jelaine's lips. But they didn't speak up, neither one of them, not in front of these others.

Fine. So it was time to come at this by some other angle. I turned away from Philip, making no secret of the disgust I felt for him and his denials, and addressed the group at large. "If any of you know anything, anything at all, that might shed some more light on what's happening here, understand that I will find it out, sooner or later, whether you come forward now or continue to stay silent in the hopes that I'll go away. That won't happen. This is what I do for a living, and though I'm damn good at my job, I don't particularly appreciate it being made difficult. Trust me. You don't want me *annoyed*."

The parlor was so still that the ambient sound excluded even our respective breath.

Jason seemed about to break. Jelaine seemed even more anxious. But there was something else there as well, something that worried me almost as much as whatever our culprit or culprits were prepared to do next.

Sadness.

Whatever their absent father Hans had to tell me, neither relished the thought of this being the time and place.

I picked one of the two at random and went to Jason, who slumped a little at my approach, not in fear but in resignation, the sadness spreading from his eyes to the planes of his face.

I said, "You told me before, that you wanted to be friends."

He actually smiled at that. "Yes."

"Forgive me for saying that, right now, I don't."

The smile did not falter. "I'm sorry to hear that, Counselor."

"If you brought me this far, you already know about me, including my willingness to blight the lives of people who obstruct my investigations. Will you believe me when I tell you, right now, that I've already figured out more than you want me to tell the other people in this room? That I've confirmed that very sensitive deduction in just the few seconds since the two of us started this conversation? And that I have absolutely no problem with passing on what I know, right here, out loud?"

Had I expected that to break him, I would have been doomed to disappointment. If anything, he just looked more confident, probably because I'd phrased exposure as a threat rather than an inevitability. He glanced at his brother, who had frozen stock-still in anticipation of the secret now hanging in the air between us, and smiled. "Well, I'll be damned. You did trip me up. I must give you credit, Counselor. You're—"

"Please. Spare me the compliments about how remarkable I am. I've had my fill of that this evening, and I'm damn sick of it. I just want answers. Any answers. I'll even start with a small one. How do I make the Khaajiir's staff work?"

This, at last, surprised him. "His staff?"

I ticked off my observations at a hammering staccato rate rate that barely permitted intake of breath. "One: as I told Mr. Pescziuwicz earlier, Bocaians have never been especially known for their talent at learning languages beyond whatever native tongue they learned first. Two: in fact, they're particularly bad at it. Three: despite that, the Khaajiir made part of his reputation as a scholar studying the past of another species, an endeavor that must have required substantial poring through primary sources. Four: he even demonstrated his fondness for multilingual puns, demonstrating several that required knowledge of extinct languages. Five: chatty as he was, the Khaajiir barely spoke at all during dinner, when his hands were so busy dealing with his meal that he could not retain a consistent grip on his staff. Six: when he did want to speak up, he grabbed his staff first. Seven: when he lost his staff upon falling to the floor, he asked for the staff in Bocaian. Eight: I've been told that I spoke Bocaian at some point today, not an impossible slip given that I grew up speaking the language, but still one sufficient to make me wonder how come I'm not aware of uttering words in a tongue I haven't uttered since my childhood. Nine: just about everything else I said today was spoken in the presence of other people who had no difficulty understanding my words. Ten: the Khaajiir spoke directly to me while I was examining his staff, and I replied. Conclusion: during those few seconds it provided the same service for me that it provided for him. It translated for me. Corollary Number One: since it stores data, it might also contain information about his scholarly activities and about his mission here, information that may prove invaluable when it comes to determining just why an assassin of his species or any other would want to kill him. Corollary Number Two: since Jelaine's actions after the emergency stop prove that the two of you have been apprised of its capabilities, you might as well take this opportunity to tell me anything I need to know about its operation or what data I should be looking for. I'll have more pressing questions for you later, but that, at least, would be a fine start."

There was a moment of stunned silence. Dejah's lips curled still further. Jelaine sipped from a drink that might not have been hers. Philip seemed to have woken up; he now sat up straighter, his eyes darting from his brother to his sister in furious search of the sensitive deduction I'd alluded to and which he must have wished he could share.

Jason wore no signs of defeat, just an increased sadness, as if my rejection of his friendship remained the most heartbreaking experience he'd been through all day. He spoke softly, as if placating a recalcitrant child. "The translation function is automatic, for anybody holding the staff by the friction strip. Opening the Khaajiir's files requires the use of a Bocaian password phrase: *'Decch-taanil blaach nil Al-Vaafir.'* Speaking it out in a clear tone of voice, once, will train the internal software to recognize it when subvocalized. After that you'll have permanent access."

The closest Mercantile translation to the phrase he'd given me was *Judgment Denied the Heavenly Fathers*, an odd combination of words given that no Bocaian sect I'd ever heard of had any orthodox creation myth. It didn't matter; passwords are hardest to crack when random, and the Khaajiir would have been just as baffled by one I'd used to shield my personal files during one nasty dispute over interspecies jurisdiction: *Pity the Fat Tchi with My Elbow up His Ass.* I asked the Porrinyards, "Did you get that?"

"Decch-taanil," Oscin began.

"Blaach nil Al-Vaafir," Skye concluded.

"Great. Pick one of you to stay here and one of you to work on it on private."

They nodded. Without any discussion, Skye remained where she was, while Oscin took the Khaajiir's bloody staff down the stairs.

I tried not to let my satisfaction show on my face. It made sense for the Porrinyards to pore through the Khaajiir's files; their data-absorption speed was so far beyond mine that relegating this job to them could save me hours in pursuing false leads. Still, there was no need to make them do more work than necessary, so I turned my attention back to Jason. "Anything in particular you think we should focus on?"

"Yes," Jason said, his tone now determinedly upbeat, as if he could only be happy now that the strain of keeping secrets was safely in the past. "The Khaajiir's writings relating K'cenhowten's Enlightenment to his theory of historical momentum. A failed and then aborted Bettelhine project, from some three generations back, called Mjolnir, a reference to the hammer of the ancient-Earth Norse thunder deity, Thor. The writings and eventual fate of one Lillian Jane Bettelhine, my paternal aunt, now deceased. These are all things your friends would no doubt uncover within a couple of hours; you might as well find them now and then get back to me once you're done, if you have any questions. Or, you could just take me aside and ask me. I won't make you waste any more time."

"You're too late. Besides, I'll have more questions for you soon enough." A deep breath. "Right now I'd like a few minutes alone with your brother."

Philip stirred himself and began to stand.

Vernon Wethers raised his hand. "Ummm . . . I object."

It was the first time he'd spoken in quite a while. His soft, hesitant voice, an open apology for itself, startled in ways that angrier interjections might not have.

I said, "This is not a court of law, Mr. Wethers."

His lips moved for a beat or two before words emerged. "No, but it is still my duty to stand for Philip Bettelhine's interests, and I take that mission seriously. I must insist on being present during any consultation."

I liked that: *consultation* rather than *questioning*. Even his word choice cleansed any implication of guilt from the moment.

What I didn't like was Wethers. The man was a shadow, not just in terms of his habitual proximity to his employer, but also in personality as well. I had sensed no structure to him, no emotional depth that did not exist except as an imprint of the man he served. It would be dangerous to conclude from this that handling Philip would amount to handling him as well. Fanatics always have their own trajectories. But now that he'd spoken up . . . "Very well. Understand that some of my questions will be of a personal, and perhaps embarrassing, nature. You might find yourself intruding on Mr. Bettelhine's feelings."

Wethers dabbed at the corners of his lips with a napkin, then stood, adjusting his jacket to bring it incrementally back in line with the character-deprived perfection he owed the Bettelhine empire. "That is all right. Mr. Bettelhine knows that wherever his personal life is concerned, it has never been my function to form opinions . . ."

Philip Bettelhine sat on the edge of the couch in the outer suite, downcast, his wrists propped on his knees and his hands dangling like dead fish. His eyes avoided mine, making contact only long enough to establish that every instant of the process was being catalogued for future resentment. His creature Wethers stood against what would have been the panoramic window, his arms folded over his chest and his colorless eyes maintaining a strict focus on his employer that suggested years of reading volumes from every micro-alteration in Philip's facial expressions. I would have found constant appraisal of that kind both off-putting and creepy, but Philip seemed used to it, and accepted his vassal's gaze as his due even as he took mine as impudent intrusion.

Paakth-Doy, uncomfortable in this company, sat apart from all of us, trying not to make eye contact.

I said, "Mr. Bettelhine, you don't like me very much, do you?"

He looked tired, the question already pushing him to the limits of his patience. "From what I've been able to determine, not all that many people do."

"Your brother and sister seem to."

"Is that what this discussion's going to be? Juvenile tallies of who likes whom? Please. I know I'm comfortable disliking you, I know you're comfortable disliking me, and I think you and I have much more pressing business to talk about."

He didn't know it, but I found myself respecting him more

after that little speech than I had at any point since meeting him. Honest dislike is always a breath of fresh air. "You don't know why they invited me."

"They didn't invite you. My father invited you. But no."

"You resent my presence."

"I resent you strutting around like you own the place, especially when I'm the bastard who owns the place. Your actual presence doesn't bother me one way or the other."

"What do you think of me being the honored guest of your father?"

His tone dulled. "It baffles me."

"The same would go for his close association with the Khaajiir."

"Of course."

"You don't know what that's about, either?"

"If my father wanted me to know, my father would have told me."

"Have you asked him?"

"He has let me know that he considers the matter classified."

"Is this typical of your relationship?"

Philip rubbed his eyes, as much, I think, to continue avoiding mine as to alleviate any strain he may have felt over the disasters of the evening. "My father and I have more than one relationship, Counselor. As a father with a respected and accomplished son, he has often been very close to me. As Chief Executive Officer commanding one of his chief lieutenants, he has sometimes been obliged to keep information flow on a need-to-know basis. I understand this. It is not atypical."

"And yet," I said, leaning in close, "as an accomplished executive in your own right, one often assumed to be your father's most likely successor, who would at the very least hope to be groomed for greater and greater responsibility as you rise in the family profession, you would also expect to become privy to more classified and secret material as the years passed and the time of succession grew ever closer."

"Yes, that would follow."

"So the significance of the few secrets still being kept from you would also be increasing throughout this time?"

"Yes."

"These secrets would currently include the reasons for my visit, or Dejah Shapiro's, or for the Khaajiir's long stay, or for the involvement of your siblings Jason and Jelaine?"

"Yes."

I excused myself, went to the bathroom, poured myself a glass of water, and downed it to the dregs before returning. When I came back, he was still where I'd left him, neither his position, nor Vernon Wethers's, having moved a millimeter. It was impossible not to wonder how many strings bound these two men, and how many misdeeds they'd plotted in rooms as luxurious as this one.

I smiled at him. Like most of my smiles, it was not meant to be a pleasant one. "A number of years ago Jason went missing."

"That's common knowledge," Philip said.

"He returned after what are alleged to have been hellish experiences on a crumbling wheelworld called Deriflys, and was welcomed back into the bosom of his family. How did you feel about that?"

The question didn't surprise him, but the color rose in his cheeks, and his eyes blasted me with still-gathering heat of his resentment. "How do you think I felt about that? He's my brother. I was older, and had a different mother, so I hadn't spent as much time with him while he was growing up as Jelaine and some of the children closer to his own age, but he was still important to me. Nobody was happier than me when Jelaine was able to straighten him out, and he was able to find some purpose in his life."

"It didn't bother you that he'd been welcomed back when you'd been a loyal, dependable son all along?"

More anger. "Maybe it would have, if I'd been a selfish brat insecure about my own place in the family's affections."

"And were you?"

"Which, a selfish brat or insecure in my family's affections? I'll cop to the first, at least sometimes; it's an occupational hazard of being wealthy. But never to the second."

"There was no question of jealousy?"

He rolled his eyes, spared a do-you-*believe*-this-bitch look for the impassive Wethers, and then faced me again. "There it is. The most noxious cliché ever concocted about wealthy families. The siblings are always corrupt caricatures, sniping at each other as they jockey for favor. The parents are always malignant, domineering old farts, emitting a constant barrage of slicing remarks as they threaten to exclude the unfit among their offspring. Is that how you like to picture us, Counselor?" He snorted. "Unfortunately for your preconceptions, that's never been true of the Bettelhines. Whatever you may think of the way my family treats other people, we've always cared for our own."

"So no sibling rivalry."

"None? Please. We're human. Just none of the kind you're positing."

"Not even when you lost Jelaine?"

He scowled. "I haven't lost Jelaine."

"True," I allowed, "but Jason and Jelaine appear to be a closed unit that excludes you, not just from whatever they've been doing with your father and the Khaajiir, and not just from the business divisions they've been able to wrest from you, but also from any emotional connection to them as siblings. They don't seem to hate you. They just don't seem to have need of your presence. Are you going to claim that doesn't bother you, either?"

I almost expected him to deny that as well, and for a moment he seemed about to, but then he glanced at Wethers again, and exhaled a lungful of hoarded breath. "No. I won't claim that. I resent the hell out of it. Are you satisfied?"

"How did it happen, Mr, Bettelhine?"

He was angry again, but not at me. "I'm not sure that any of this is your goddamn business, Counselor, and we'll have to talk about making sure you don't take it anywhere outside this room, but when Jason returned from that place, he was not quite right. Oh, sure, he said the things he was expected to say, and did the things he was expected to do, and even managed to charm the eligible ladies when our parents threw a weekend ball in his honor, but he never really reconnected with us or with the life he'd thrown away. He was just play-acting, giving us what he thought we wanted from him, and though it was goddamned convincing much of the time, we couldn't spend time in his presence without seeing the look that came into his eyes whenever he thought we weren't watching. I still don't know everything that happened to him, during those years—it's one of the many things he hasn't seen fit to share with me—but I can tell you that we all knew it was still happening. I thought the family was going to lose him again, one way or the other."

"And then?"

"One day after that ball I told you about, which is best described as a restrained disaster, Jelaine told me she'd made arrangements with Father to let her take Jason on an extended tour offworld. She said there were things Jason needed to deal with, leftover business from his days away. She said she was going to make sure he got the chance. Now, me, I absolutely hated the idea, since leaving Xana the first time had been such a disaster for him, but Jelaine seemed sure, and she'd already gotten Father's approval, so it was going to happen, one way or the other."

"Did you ask your father why he'd said yes?"

"He told me he wanted his son back."

"And you?"

"I wanted my brother back."

"But you were still against the idea."

"I considered Jason toxic," Philip said. "I'd seen him, a favorite son, flit off and subject himself to horrors the rest of us couldn't even imagine. I saw him come back a shell of himself, not connecting with us or with anything around him. And now I saw him sucking Jelaine in too. Don't you see? I was afraid of losing her too!"

"How did you deal with that?"

"Since I couldn't stop them from going, I offered to jettison my responsibilities and come along. I said it was to help support Jason, but by then I didn't think anything could help Jason. I was more interested in being the voice of reason, standing between him and Jelaine. But Jelaine said no. She said she knew what she was doing. She said I should trust her. And so I did what a brother does. I let her go and hoped for the best."

"And is . . . 'the best' . . . what you got?"

He clenched his fists, opened them, then massaged each hand with the other, as if subconsciously washing them. "When they returned, Jason was a new man, centered, secure in himself, and content in a way he never had been before. Jelaine was different too. She'd always been a fine girl on her way to becoming a remarkable woman, but she'd become . . . there's no other way of saying it . . . a lady. Royalty, really."

"And why would this make you so unhappy?"

"They were cooler to me. They talked to me and asked me how I was and even congratulated me on my marriage and on the birth of my daughter. They were not unfriendly. But somehow, their relationship with me was no longer something they wanted, but something they felt they were obligated to have."

"They don't love you anymore."

"I don't know if they love me or not. That's the damnable thing. But if they do it's just because I'm their brother and they have to. Aside from that, they started treating me as an obstacle to be handled. As part of the problem."

"Part of what problem?"

"I don't know! Part of whatever fucking problem they have! Excuse me."

Now it was his turn to retreat to the bathroom. He closed the door, ran the water, and returned with another glass, filled only halfway. His sips were tiny, and controlled, but furious. He wasn't crying—I don't know if he was capable of it—but his eyes were glazed, and his hands trembling. The man was a captain of industry, one of the wealthiest human beings in the universe, and by dint of the business he supported quite possibly a sociopathic monster, but at this moment he was just a boy, upset that his siblings had excluded him from their secret club.

I gave him time to compose himself, and assessed his shadow, Mr. Wethers. The man remained stony, not an iota of concern or sympathy on his bland corporate features. Of course, open pity for the boss was probably a good way to get fired, and that would be a bad idea indeed when your boss owned the very planet where you lived. But this man's ability to hide empathy, if he felt any, was extreme—better than his ability to hide self-consciousness, since he colored and looked away in discomfort the second he registered me looking at him. I remembered that he'd acted pretty much the same way with Skye, Jelaine, and Dejah. He certainly had trouble tolerating the casual attention of women. I wondered who had hurt him in the past, and just how deep the scars ran.

Philip said, "Is there anything else?"

I gave Mr. Wethers some relief from the unwelcome heat of my gaze, resuming my interest in his master. "Mr. Bettelhine, what are your responsibilities for the corporation?"

"I command about two hundred ongoing research and development projects on behalf of my father, the company CEO."

"You develop weapons."

"I research new technologies."

"Which," I pointed out, "you most often use in the development of weapons."

"By other divisions. I'm more interested in mapping the regions of undirected potential. It's understood, at the corporate level, that at any given time, approximately seventy percent of the projects I command will turn out to be blind alleys. It's with the remaining thirty percent that I justify my budget."

"Still, the practical applications of your researches have the potential to kill vast numbers of human beings."

He rolled his eyes, tired of the conversation. "Counselor, do you honestly believe that I've never had this debate with myself? I contribute to an industry that gives people the ability to affect their own destinies. How they manifest that power is up to them. What does this have to do with the situation we're in?"

He was right. I could have debated the morality of Bettelhine Family business practices with him forever, and never reached a conclusion satisfactory to him or to myself. I returned to the central thread of my investigation. "I'm aware that a number of your divisions have been shut down or handed over to the control of Jason and Jelaine, and that this is extremely irregular given your long service and Jason's uncertain personal history. I am certain that you have approached your father to ask him why this is happening. Has he given you any answer that makes sense?"

His answer was stony. "He's only said that the corporation must retool for changing conditions, and that everything will be made clear to me in time."

"You've also said that you had more than one relationship with your father, one as a son and one as a corporate officer. What you just said sounds like the answer he'd give a corporate officer. Forgive me for asking, as I know this must be painful, but has he given you any answers as father to son?"

"No."

"No?"

"No. It's been more than a year since he gave me any answers as father to son. I haven't even been in the same room with him for three months. That's what I'm doing here. I changed my schedule, and the schedule of my associate here," he indicated Wethers, "in hopes of catching up with him and maybe getting some answers. When Father canceled his trip at the last minute, I thought I'd at least spend some time with Jason and Jelaine and get some answers from them instead. But you know how that's worked out."

"Have you done anything to make your father angry?"

"I've asked him that."

"And he says?"

He recited the pat answers without inflection. "That he loves me. That he's my father and that he's proud of me. That I shouldn't be so sensitive. That I'll understand when I find out what's going on."

"Those sound like father-to-son answers."

"They do," he said, not believing me. "Don't they?"

I didn't know. I'd never had the chance to relate to my own parents as an adult. I had no way of knowing what normal was, either in general or what it meant inside a dynasty like the Bettelhines, let alone what it meant for Hans Bettelhine in particular. Philip Bettelhine claimed to perceive a change, but had there really been a change? Was Hans really reassuring him, or just putting him off? How could I know, from this remove, when Philip could not after a lifetime of knowing all the people involved?

I decided to attack the problem from another angle. "Mr.

Bettelhine, you mentioned a wife and daughter. How's your family life?"

"My wife, Carole, took the kids and left me six months ago."

"It must be unusual to divorce a Bettelhine on this planet."

"Not for another Bettelhine. She's a distant cousin from the Outer Family—many degrees removed, I assure you, but still a connected woman. And as it happens, we're not divorced, just separated. Neither one of us wants to deny the children the opportunities for advancement that go along with my own superior connection to the Inner Family."

"Would you mind telling me why your marriage failed?"

He turned stormy. "What the hell does that have to do with anything?"

"I don't know. Asking is how I find out."

Philip squirmed for a moment and then gave it up. "Emotional incompatibility."

"Who alleged that?"

"Carole did."

"Did she give any reasons?"

"You want to know? I'd made a habit of sleeping around. It's an awfully easy thing for Inner Family people to do. A night with a Bettelhine is considered a major plum, for those outside the bloodline. Sex of any kind you prefer is always available, and you don't have to take no for an answer, if you're enough of a bastard to use some of the options available to us."

Now, that was an interesting moral construction. "Are you, sir?"

"That kind of a bastard?" He grimaced in self-disgust. "No. I'm just the everyday ordinary philandering kind of bastard. I don't force anybody into anything. I just get offers and I think, *why not?*"

"I assume that your wife had an answer for that."

"She's a Bettelhine, and has her own pride to uphold. She

gave me three warnings, which I disregarded three times, and then walked out on me."

"You sound proud of yourself."

"Thanks to my own stupidity, I was. I'm not anymore. And what does this have to do with anything that happened here tonight?"

"I'm wrapping up. So what you've told me is that in the last couple of years you've lost, by your reckoning, your brother, your sister, your wife, your life as family man, your relationship with your father, and much of your place in the family business?"

"Yes."

"Would it be unfair to note that some people, pressed beyond all emotional endurance by such a series of blows, would look at all that loss and come to regard it as the result of a conspiracy against them?"

He was silent for a moment. And then the anger left him all at once, replaced with an earnestness that did not suit him nearly as well. "I don't know what Jason and Jelaine are up to. I don't know how it involves the Khaajiir, or my father, or you, or this Shapiro bitch. I don't know why people are committing murders involving silly ancient weapons. It all escapes me, every bit of it. And if we are being quarantined or held hostage, as you believe, the reason escapes me even more. I don't understand it, not any of it. I just want to know why I've been shut out and whether any of this is good or bad for the Family as a whole. I want that much security, at least. Will that finally answer your questions?"

Damned if I didn't, at least a little bit, feel sorry for him. "Just one more issue," I said, "regarding something you said before, something you never finished explaining to my satisfaction. Why would you believe terrorist action against your family *'impossible'*?"

With that, Vernon Wethers stepped away from the wall and, demonstrating an economy of movement that suggested many, many previous opportunities to stand between his employer and an unwanted question, helped Philip Bettelhine to his feet. The wormy little bastard didn't even say anything about the matter being classified, or the questioning being over. He just hustled Philip out of there with about as much personal acknowledgment as he would have afforded any other misplaced obstacle.

Once Philip was safely on the other side of the door, Wethers whirled at me and pointed a long, narrow finger in my face. "Be careful, Counselor. I know you have Jason and Jason and the old man protecting you, but this is still Xana. We know how to deal with visitors who offend us."

I've never enjoyed being pointed at. In an instant I had closed one fist around that finger and another around his wrist behind it. It would have been the work of another instant to leave him screaming with broken bones, and I inflicted just enough pain to make sure he knew it. "What did your people do to Bard Daiken?"

The ghost of a smile, superior and infuriating and pregnant with knowledge, tugged at the corners of his lips. "Something you don't want done to you. Something Philip can do by whispering the order in the right ear. Something I'd find funny as hell and revisit in my old age whenever I needed reminder of the moments that gave my life meaning. *Let me go.*"

I maintained the painful grip and penetrating eye contact for another ten seconds, but this was his place of power, not mine.

I released him.

He massaged his wrist with his spare hand, gave me a further dismissive look, and turned toward the door.

It would have been a fine exit for any villain.

But just as he entered the narrow hall between the suite's main room and the door to the main parlor, something went for his throat . . .

13

STRANGLEHOLD

The attack was so smooth, so graceful, so organic in its terrible precision, that for its first precious seconds my eyes and my mind lagged behind the moment, refusing to recognize his collapse against the wall as anything but a moment of pathetic clumsiness, brought on by exhaustion and the trauma we'd all been through in the last few hours.

Even when he grabbed for his throat for both hands, his blind fingers clutching at the black line that now banded his neck, I mistook his difficulty breathing for a heart attack, or a careless swallow that had sent saliva down the wrong pipe. His protruding eyes, his gaping mouth, the sudden terrible knowledge written on his face, my own dulled realization that something awful was happening to him—they were all inhabitants of that first second, so complete even in this the moment of their birth that there was no time to apply logic and consider where they might have come from.

I thought *Claw of God* and reached for him.

A burst of pain and I found myself propelled backward, aware only that I'd been struck in the jaw. By the time I tripped over the leg of the chair Philip Bettelhine had vacated only a couple of minutes before I'd figured out that the fist had belonged to Wethers, and by the time I realized to my intense dismay that I was going to fall I'd decided that the bastard must have faked whatever the hell he wanted me to believe was wrong with him, so he could catch me with a sucker punch.

By the time I smashed into the floor with a force that summoned fresh pain to the same hip I'd bruised during the emergency stop, I was past wanting to kill him for getting past my defenses and well into the realm of *that's not what this is.*

With the breath knocked out of me, my body wanted nothing more than to curl into a ball and wait for air and order to return to the universe.

I rolled anyway, getting to my hands and knees in time to see Wethers slide down the wall and drop to a crouch. The pale skin of his face had darkened to a shade of purple that would need only a little additional intensity before it went black. His eyes protruded so far from their sockets that they seemed about to pop out, like marbles. He tried to stand again, but his convulsions denied him even that; his legs kicked outward and his ass hit floor, making him look oddly comfortable even as he still scrabbled at his neck.

At the black line that had appeared around his throat.

His fingers sliding across that line without gaining any purchase.

I speed-crawled toward him, the distance feeling infinite, each step feeling like minutes in a race where life and death could be measured in heartbeats. It may have taken me all of three seconds to get to him, lifetimes, more as I pulled myself over his thrashing legs and he fought in his panic to throw me off. A knee in my belly robbed me of what little breath I had left; and when I grabbed him by the wrists and tried to pull his hands from his throat he fought me, his already bulging eyes overflowing with panic.

Had I enough air for speech I would have shouted *Let go you asshole, I'm trying to save your life!*

It was only because he was already weakening that I was able to wrestle his hands away from his throat and get a close look at what had constricted him. It was a black, shiny ribbon of some kind, looped around his neck, its endpoints a pair of silver toruses intent on pulling the material between them tight.

The donut holes at the center of each torus roiled with black spots, a lot like the receding patterns that afflict human vision after too much time spent staring at bright lights. I didn't know whether they were gas exhaust or some manifestation of the energy source that powered them, but they hurt my eyes to look at.

There was no time to worry about whether the endpoints were too dangerous to touch. The danger was already here. The toruses were too narrow to admit my fingers, so I grabbed them with my fists and fought to loosen the stranglecord between them. They bucked violently, like little missiles intent on resuming their previous trajectories. The first jolts almost tore them free of my grip, and I had to struggle so hard that for one terrible instant I realized that I'd become so intent on winning the wrestling match that I'd overcompensated and was now fighting to tighten their grip on their victim's neck.

If Wethers died, the evidence would show that I'd murdered him.

I heard voices from my own immediate future.

I'm not surprised. I always expected this.

She's Andrea Cort. Do you know what she did when she was just a little girl?

Once a monster, always a monster.

It's time to put her down like the mad dog she is.

"God DAMN it!"

Maybe it was a burst of strength born of adrenaline and

maybe the toruses decided to change targets and maybe they bucked in the wrong direction just in time to match my own effort, but the loop came loose all at once, releasing Wethers and sending me falling backward, against the opposite wall of the narrow hallway. I landed ass-first, just as he had, with my legs straddling his. Able to breathe now, he gasped a deep grateful inhalation that did little to help me as the black material between those two toruses thrashed with the fury of a deadly thing denied blood.

It wasn't my first stranglecord. It's been an eventful life. But every other one I'd ever seen had been no-tech: rope or wire or even cloth, powered by malignant hands. I'd never seen, nor ever dreamt of, a stranglecord that operated out of its own volition: one that could be wound up and sent after a target, fired up by its own eagerness to see the dirty job done.

The black material was hard to see when held on edge; not quite nanostring, as that would have made it invisible, but still finer than a human hair. Seen head on it was about as wide as a decorative ribbon, though its cold blackness rendered it about as festive as a starscape without stars. I remembered Wethers struggling to tear it from his throat and for just a moment felt sorry for him; flush against his flesh, assuming its contours, it might have been about as easy to peel off in one piece as a layer of paint. The toruses at either end were probably the only safe way to handle it, as close as they came to being safe.

For a moment I wondered how much AI the device possessed, whether it had enough intelligence to be decoded or even questioned.

Then the black loop lengthened, convulsed, and closed around my right wrist.

It happened so quickly that I didn't realize what had happened until after the pain of constricted flesh became the most important thing in my universe. I gasped and, out of reflex, kicked, striking Wethers in the groin, a vivid illustration of the guideline that one should never do anything to further incapacitate the only other person present in a room where something is trying to kill you. He fell to his right, moaning; as for me, I cursed and did the instinctive thing, which was try to free my right wrist with my left hand—a big mistake when the act of bringing both hands together accomplished nothing but to give the stranglecord some precious slack to maneuver with so it could attack again.

Another convulsion, and a second loop tightened around my left wrist.

The ribbon contracted, and my closed fists came together in a painful, knuckle-rattling collision.

"Wethers, help me!"

No good. Even if he was a fighter, and I had no guarantee that he was or that he'd want to come to my rescue even if he could, recovering to the point where he was capable of action might take him several minutes yet. Right now he was too busy curled into a ball, coughing and choking and trying to absorb enough air to react to the pain. By the time anything I yelled got past the pounding of the blood in his ears, the stranglecord would have broken my wrists, worked its way free, and probably moved on to my neck, doing to me what it had tried to do to him.

"Oscin! Skye! Anybody!"

It was no good. These were luxury accommodations. The rooms were soundproofed. I could set off explosions in here and nobody in the parlor would hear a damned thing.

The ribbon binding my wrists expanded, allowing my fists to separate, then contracted again, pulling them together with fresh bone-rattling force. I gasped from the pain, considered screaming again, had the terrible thought that if I hadn't gotten an answer it might be because there were a dozen more of these fucking things loose on the Royal Carriage, wrapping tight around the throats of Oscin, Skye, Dejah, Jason, Jelaine . . .

Another clap. The bones in my hands ached. I felt a slash agonizing in its suddenness, and blood oozed from the spaces between my fingers.

If I didn't let the thing pound its way free, it was going to start carving.

Next time you're sitting on the ground, with your legs stretched out before you, place your hands in a cuffed position and see how easy it is to get up. Now try doing it in a narrow hallway with your legs entangled with those of a semiconscious man on the borderline between merely coughing and out-and-out puking. Further, try doing it while trying to hold on to the business end of a saw, one that by the way happens to hate you and doesn't mind hurting you as much as it can so it can let go and find some effective way to hurt you more. I guarantee that it's one of the more unpleasant and more difficult things you'll ever have to do.

I might not have managed it if I hadn't had a wall at my back.

I bent both legs at the knee so I could brace my feet against the floor and *push*. My back slid up the wall.

The stranglecord between my wrists bucked again, almost throwing me off balance, but I compensated, stumbling one step to my right and somehow managing to avoid tripping over Wethers's outstretched legs.

The pressure around my right wrist intensified, becoming a line of fire. Redness started glistening around the edges.

If this got much worse, the damned thing was going to saw my hands off.

"WETHERS! Dammit!"

He'd be no help. He was no longer coughing, but he wasn't exactly responsive either. He might not have ever fought for his life before, might not have ever learned that the instinctive urge to curl up into a ball and hide, rather than hurl yourself back into the path of something that had already caused you pain, accomplished nothing but to make yourself a passive target.

That was a lesson I'd learned on Bocai.

I stumbled toward the suite's bedroom, holding the willful stranglecord at arm's length, lurching as the toruses clenched in my fists jerked from side to side in an attempt to throw me off balance. They were strong enough to make me walk like a woman fighting an abductor who had her by the arms. Not quite as strong as me, but they were getting stronger, and it would not be long now before exhaustion took everything I had.

That's why I needed a weapon.

I jerked as I passed the bed, fell against it, let out a cry as the slicing pain in my wrists deepened to agony, screamed louder as it intensified further, took another couple of steps and fell against the bed again.

My satchel sat against the transparent bulkhead, the panoramic view of Xana replaced by the shields lowered at the moment of the emergency stop.

I fell to my knees and collapsed, missing it by half a meter, managing the last couple of steps in a series of convulsive kicks.

My satchel is a Tchi artifact, by my estimation the greatest accomplishment of a species obnoxious in ways that include festering paranoia. The exterior has no visible seams, not even any hinges or joints capable of betraying by their very existence just how the damned thing would open had it any intention of doing so for anybody other than myself. My Dip Corps credentials are enough to get it past customs wherever I choose to go, and the latch, keyed to half a dozen markers that begin with a DNA scan and end with a neural signal I can transmit by touch, has always been the chief safeguard that prevents its contents from ever being searched or even safely handled without my permission.

That's always been a good thing, since the bounty on my head has made me as paranoid as any Tchi, and I never cross borders, anywhere, without contraband of the sort that, if found, can get even somebody with diplomatic immunity arrested, jailed, or killed.

There were several items inside that might be able to disable or destroy the stranglecord tightening around my wrists; there was even one that could vaporize this entire carriage, though I was not yet in enough agony to see that as a viable option.

Of course, I wouldn't be able to get to them, even if I had time to get to them, without opening my hands.

And if the stranglecord's previous capabilities were any indication, things were going to get very bad very fast the second I released the toruses.

But it wasn't like I had a choice.

I heard Wethers yelling for help outside. It didn't help me now. The pain was so bad by now that I didn't even brace myself and take a deep breath. I just did it, revealing palms sliced from end to end and smeared with blood. The two toruses they'd held reacted almost comically, rising a centimeter or so above the skin, then tilting like heads performing double-takes at an unexpected development. Then they flew, each trailing its end of the cord, each whipping the other way around my trapped wrists, to free itself for what probably would have been an immediate assault on my neck.

Reacting to the welling pins and needles as circulation returned would have been a great way to get killed.

Instead, as the stranglecord came loose, I grabbed it at its midpoint and hurled it as far as I could.

The damned thing sailed over the bed, but changed trajectory before it would have hit the opposite wall, the toruses coming in low over the bed, with the stranglecord a shared banner between them.

The son of a bitch could fly. How the hell was I supposed to fight a stranglecord that could fly?

I was still on my back and there was no chance of survival if I took the time to stand, so I grabbed my satchel, my all-important satchel with the weapons I'd hoped to use against the damned thing, and flung it. The toruses carrying the stranglecord performed a little loopy somersault and evaded it, recovering even as my satchel disappeared from sight on the opposite side of the bed. I rolled, saw the stranglecord coming in low, kicked at it, felt a plunk as my right foot glanced against one of the toruses.

It recovered fast, looped around, and went for my throat. I tried to dodge again, but there was not enough time and it wrapped around my neck with a force so dizzying that my bare throat felt the heat of the snap as the material impacted with skin.

The toruses pulled, and the stranglecord constricted, intent on cutting off my air, my breath, my life.

"Fuck you!" I shouted, able to shout only because I'd covered my throat with my hand a fraction of a second before the damned thing closed its noose. When the stranglecord tightened, it was against my knuckles, the skin there burning as the material drew taut enough to cut off circulation. But lost circulation in a hand is far easier to survive than the loss of oxygen to the head . . .

I rolled, somehow rose to my feet, lurched off-balance as the toruses wrangled me like a horse controlled by its rider, and slammed the back of my head against the bulkhead, hard.

I felt blood on the back of my neck: the stranglecord breaking skin there.

Protecting my throat wouldn't save me for very long if the monstrosity managed to saw through my spine. Quadriplegia's temporary, if you survive long enough to get some halfway decent medical care; I've suffered injuries on that scale more than once, and never been inconvenienced for more than a few hours. But a severed spine leaves you helpless against anyone or anything intent on inflicting damage more permanent. Paralyzed, I'd be an easy target for anything the stranglecord wanted to do . . .

My free hand probed the cord, found one of the toruses, and yanked hard, pulling the material from my neck.

Still protecting my throat with one hand, I used the other to swing the cord like a whip, slamming the torus at the other end against the bulkhead. There was a flash of light when it hit, some kind of energy discharge, but the torus itself did not break. I swung again and slammed it against the endtable; there was another spark of light, but less intense, as if the thing had managed to roll with the impact, lessening it, avoiding the damage that would prevent it from pressing another attack.

A third swing at the bulkhead and the torus managed to curve away from the impact completely, instead defying momentum to go for my eyes.

I yowled, spun, avoided the impact, but lost balance and went down again.

It wasn't the first time I'd been faced with a ludicrous death. Ask me about Catarkhus or One One One sometime. But the idea of being outwrestled and outfought by something small enough to be held in my fucking hands was more than I could take. I shrieked in dismay and outrage and just flung the Juje-bedamned thing away, not even caring if it came back in a second or two, wanting only a moment's freedom from it, a second or two so I could breathe without feeling its hateful touch on my skin.

Wherever it went in the next second or two, I don't know, because somebody was yelling in the outer room. *"Andrea! What's happening?"*

"Counselor!"

Skye. Paakth-Doy. A perfect opportunity to scream for help again.

Stupid, unreasoning instinct took care of that one. *"Stay out there!"*

I managed to get a hand atop the bed and used it to pull myself to an imperfect upright position just as I caught a flash image of something black flying at my face. I threw myself backward onto the mattress and rolled, catching another flash image of a crude noose zipping through the air right above me. My wounded hands left bloodstains on the comforter as I flipped back over the opposite side of the bed, hitting the floor just as Skye and Paakth-Doy came in at a dead run, shouting my name.

The stranglecord, which had been headed for my neck again, changed course and went for Skye.

I cried, "Shit!" and went for the satchel again. No time to open it, no time to get anything I trusted to put this thing down, no time to do anything but throw the goddamned bag again and hope I knocked the stranglecord out of the way long enough to improvise something else, maybe a blanket torn from the bed and thrown as a makeshift net . . .

There was a *fwap*.

Skye stood stock-still, her fists closed around the toruses, her arms extended so far apart that the deadly stranglecord hung taut as wire between them. It thrummed, vibrating with a fury that reduced it to a gray blur; she still held it motionless, as far as it could stretch, rendering it incapable of pressing its attack.

"I am impressed," said Paakth-Doy.

The speed Skye had just demonstrated by plucking that thing from the air, and the strength she was still demonstrating by holding it in place, impressed me too. "Nice catch."

She grimaced. "This is . . . not exactly a . . . long-term solution, Andrea. It's propulsive units are . . . disproportionately powerful, for their size."

Right. I went for my satchel, undid its seal, and peeled away the several identical black suits before uncovering the several items best kept a secret from planetary customs.

The most mundane among them was a stasis tube designed for the transportation of perishables; not illegal in and of itself, but clear evidence of criminal intent in that the substance it carried was a genetically keyed nanopoison illegal for me to possess. It was my personal suicide solution, one that would have not only killed me but also denatured all my genetic material, preventing identification of my corpse.

If you ever wonder whether your life's taken a wrong turn or two, consider how fucked up your circumstances would have to be for that to qualify as a reasonable component of your carry-on luggage.

Skye's voice had a distinct tremor. "Andrea? Whatever you're going to do . . ."

"I'm coming, love." Twisting a certain lock at one end of the tube popped off the protective shields at the endpoints and provided access to a fair-safe that sent a microwave burst through the contents, deprogramming the nanites and giving the liquid suspension all the virulence of distilled water. A further, cleansing blast of molecular excitation reduced what was left to vapor, which the tube then vented with an audible hiss.

Even as that happened, the smears of blood my injured hands had left on the metal turned to lighter shade of pink; evidence that a very few of the nanites escaping through the vapor were still intact, and capable of dissolving anything with my genetic material. Strictly speaking, it wasn't safe for me to deactivate it myself. Strictly speaking, I should have been in another room, giving instructions from a distance. But strictly speaking, I shouldn't have to carry anything capable of breaking down my own cells . . .

"Andrea!" Skye again, her voice now betraying real pain.

"I've got it!" The tube's endpoints irised open, and it snapped open along its length, each half reflecting the other in cross-section. I grabbed it, stood up, and ran over to Skye, positioning the bottom half of the tube under the stranglecord, then snapping the upper half shut over it.

The locks engaged and the endpoints irised shut, trapping most of the cord inside; but the endpoints still extruded, and Skye still held a bucking torus in each hand. All I'd done, so far, was give a flying stranglecord the potential to become a flying club if released to fly on its own accord. But at least Skye didn't have to hold those toruses anymore.

She released them and took hold of the tube itself. "Thank you, Andrea. Are you all right?"

"Of course she is not all right," an irritated Paakth-Doy said. "She is injured. Sit down, Counselor, and I will tend to your wounds."

"We don't have time for that, Doy—"

She placed her hand on my shoulder. "You may enjoy playing the bitch, Counselor, but in this I promise I can be a much bigger bitch than you. I am talented at it. As you said to me not long ago . . . *Sit your ass down.*"

I blinked several times, thought of several unforgivable things I could say to her, applied them to logic and common sense on one side and my urgent need to hit something on the other, then nodded and lowered myself to the side of the bed.

Paakth-Doy left to get her first aid kit, muttering an excuse-me when she was just out of sight.

I didn't know who she'd spoken to until Wethers appeared in the doorway, rumpled and pale and wide-eyed and still rubbing his throat with one hand. He said nothing, just stared at me, evidently paralyzed by the cognitive dissonance between the human impulse to thank me for saving his life and his obligation as an officer of the Bettelhine Corporation to continue regarding me as threat to the family secrets. After a moment he dropped eye contact, gulped, then winced, the very effort of swallowing painful.

I spared him the embarrassment of speaking first. "Are you all right?"

He gave a slow nod before managing a hoarse, "I thought I was dead."

"Must have been frightening," I remarked, unable to resist a sarcastic, "and you with so much to live for."

He looked down. Damned if my words hadn't wounded him.

When Skye shifted her grip on the tube, the toruses at the endpoints of the cord protruding from both ends thrashed indignantly, still looking for a throat to encircle. "Don't be too hard on him, Andrea. You owe him your life."

I tried to imagine a pale and almost inarticulate Wethers stumbling into the parlor, into the middle of all those people, with wild stories of a self-propelled stranglecord. "I'm surprised we don't have a mob scene in here."

Wethers thrust his chin out, and croaked. "I work for the Bettelhines, Counselor. I know how to be discreet, and I suspected that you would want me to be. Under the circumstances I suppressed any signs of my own condition until I could let your companion here know that you needed immediate assistance."

I flexed my hands, and winced. "That was . . . good thinking." I thought but did not add, *Almost too good.* Forgetting that Wethers was even now only a few minutes removed from threatening me with the wrath of the Bettelhine empire, anybody else in that circumstance would have been hollering his head off. The revelation that a high-ranking Bettelhine employee could be prepared to exercise that inhuman level of discretion, in that kind of life-or-death situation, raised hard questions about what else Bettelhine employees might be prepared to do. "Have you ever . . . seen this device before?"

Wethers shook his head.

"I have," said Skye.

She started to say where, but that's when Paakth-Doy returned carrying her first aid kit. Doy had to duck under Wethers's arms as she passed him in the bedroom doorway, but managed it without so much as an excuse-me as she rushed to my side with the nanite pen.

As Paakth-Doy closed my wounds, Skye said, "It's another obscure antique weapon, this one of Ghyei design. Their aristocracy called it Fire Snake, and once a medieval time much filled with intrigue and backstabbing used to happily set it loose in the homes of relatives higher in the line of succession."

I had never heard of these Ghyei; they were not one of the major powers, nor one famous for any other reason. "You know too much of this shit, love."

Skye's lips twisted. "Blame a morbid imagination."

"I've never noticed it before."

"The two of me weren't always the same person you know."

Uh-huh. "Do you think it's a genuine artifact or a recreation?"

"Given the diameter of the average Ghyei throat, which two or three human beings would be able to inhabit comfortably, it's pretty safe to say they wouldn't find a Fire Snake of this size useful except as dental floss."

Paakth-Doy, intent on closing the slits on my palms, emitted an unwilling giggle at that. We all looked at her. She colored, shrugged an apology, and went back to what she'd been doing. My palms numbed, tingled, grew cool, and then pleasantly warm. "What's it doing here?"

Skye seemed surprised I'd ask such a bone-stupid obvious question. "I'd assume the same thing the Claws of God are doing here. Killing people."

Wethers said, "I think Counselor wanted something a little more specific than that."

"I appreciate that," Skye told him. "But whether this one was targeted for yourself, for Counselor, or for any target of convenience, remains a question. From the speed with which it went after me when I entered, I'd have to say that it seemed willing to go after anybody within a certain proximity, prioritized by threat level."

That made sense. I asked her, "What are the odds that it was here when we moved into the suite?"

Skye considered that. "I would say about equal to the odds of it being placed here at some point in the past few hours, by one of the people you've been interviewing."

That was how I figured it as well. But that didn't help much, as Dina Pearlman, Monday Brown, Wethers, Arturo Mendez, Paakth-Doy, and Philip Bettelhine had all been in here since the emergency stop; it was just as possible that somebody else had pulled a fast one and put the Fire Snake in our suite at some point when neither the Porrinyards or myself were looking.

Wethers said, "I don't believe it myself, Counselor, but since this is your suite it's just as possible given the facts that the damned thing belongs to *you* or *your* companions and that you set it off here to distract us from your own guilt in the murder of the Khaajiir."

Paakth-Doy gave him a disbelieving look.

I shook my head. "Don't worry about it, Doy. He has a point. That is a possibility." I then faced him and said, "Just as it remains possible that you dropped the thing from a pocket and allowed it to attack you in my presence. Just as it remains possible that it had been programmed to strangle you up to the point of permanent damage *but no further*; that it was supposed to give me a good fight *but no more*, and that your diligence in summoning help so soon after you'd expressed such contempt for me amounted to nothing more than a charade designed to make you look trustworthy and above suspicion in the other crimes aboard this carriage. I don't particularly believe any of that, Mr. Wethers, any more than you profess to believe in the theory you offered. But it also fits the facts. And as you say, it's a theory I'm forced to keep in mind."

Wethers rubbed his eyes, with a terrible weariness that might have been building for much of his adult life. "Noted."

Then he faced me again, his expression as sad and lost as any I'd ever known. I had been told that he had no family but the Bettelhines, no love but for his career; I'd lived in similar isolation for much of my own life before meeting the Porrinyards, and could only wonder if he dealt with the loneliness the same way I had, by becoming proud of it and nurturing it like a pet fed on loathing and venom. "But as grateful as I am to you, for saving my life, what I said before still goes. This is Bettelhine territory. And you really don't want to abuse your privileges as a guest."

I regarded him with open curiosity. "I wanted to ask you about that. Do you often threaten people the Bettelhines want here?"

"I take less pleasure in it in your case than I did before you saved my life, but yes, I do. It's part of my job description. Guests, even honored guests, remain welcome only as long as they know how to behave. And you wouldn't be the first one it's been my duty to chastise."

Charming. But for what it was worth, he seemed to be telling the truth about enjoying the ominous threats less now than he had before the stranglecord attacked him. Not that he seemed to enjoy much of anything. The more time I spent with him the more he struck me as trapped inside himself, and unable to escape, a feeling I'd also gotten from, among others, Colette Wilson and Arturo Mendez. I remembered things Pescziuwicz had said and felt a chill at the insistence of the warning.

So I asked him again: "What did you people do to Bard Daiken?"

He remained silent, his eyes apologetic but failing to offer even a momentary promise of safety.

14

THE FOURTH BETTELHINE

kye locked the Fire Snake inside the suite's stasis safe. Paakth-Doy finished treating Wethers and Skye for their own injuries. Even as we shed all external evidence of the Fire Snake's attack, the four of us agreed to keep the incident a secret for the time being, both to avoid panicking the others and provide the culprit, whomever that might be, more opportunity for accidental exposure. It wasn't much of a plan, but it was something.

Then Mendez called to let us know that there'd been another development outside the carriage.

This time everybody followed him belowdecks, to share the news carried by the air lock monitors. This time we all faced the little monochrome holos as they cycled between exterior images of the carriage and relayed images of a gathering storm.

The Stanley clinging to the cable above us was no longer our only company. Another one, no doubt dispatched from Anchor Point, clung to the cable below, more predator at bay than rescuer waiting for the right moment to approach. At least fifty other spacecraft, from single-occupant fliers to troop carriers capable of carrying hundreds, had formed a fresh perimeter surrounding us on all sides. Dozens of smaller dots of light, impossible to resolve in any image panoramic enough to capture the scale we were dealing with, came into focus when Mendez zoomed in. They were soldiers; all faceless in their free-fall maneuver suits, all carrying precision weapons with black, hungry barrels.

The very immobility of the tableau was what made it so frightening. None of the vessels moved in relation to one another. None of the soldiers shifted position. The most the machines and people did to prove themselves a living system capable of action at a moment's notice was flare with light every few seconds as their respective propulsion systems fired to prevent them from drifting out of formation.

It had only been a little more than an hour and twenty minutes since the first Stanley dispatched from Layabout had aborted its rescue mission. The powers that ruled military response on Xana had deployed this armada in less time than it would have taken the authorities on some Confederate worlds to put on their boots. This was a fine testimonial to Bettelhine efficiency, and a somewhat less sterling omen when it came to our own chances of survival.

I much preferred the security that came with being trapped with a single murderer, or even a handful of conspirators, to the dubious comforts of knowing that an entire fleet was fixing its guns on my position. Granted, the commanders who gave the orders were all Bettelhine employees themselves and therefore unlikely to relish the idea of killing three members of the Inner Family. But we now owed every moment we still drew breath to the continuing calm and stability of men and women who knew that their own lives might depend on recognizing a sudden attack. If it came to the final extremity, we wouldn't be the first hostages to die because some recruit, dripping sweat behind the nice anonymous mirror of his helmet's faceplate, returned an attack that was only a glint of sunlight reflected off steel.

Jason's grin became a black grimace. "We're running out of time, brother."

Philip seemed surprised to be included. "I know."

"That's a siege."

"I know."

"Our own people."

"I *know*."

Jason bit his lip. "The thing is, a formation like that, I would normally expect them to send an envoy, or attempt some other form of contact to let us know what they want. Dictating terms of surrender, that kind of thing. But they're just waiting. It's like they're scared to come in."

"Or," Jelaine said, "like they're waiting for the right moment to attack."

Philip raised a hand, hesitated for a moment, as if he didn't know what to do with it, and then clasped Jason on the shoulder. It was about as awkward an expression of filial love as any I'd ever seen, and it must have felt awkward as hell until Jason returned it.

When Philip spoke again, his voice trembled from more than just fear. "All right, everybody. This is a one-time-only offer directed either at the unknown party responsible for our situation or for any allies who might be aiding and abetting. Whoever you are, if you step forward and assist us in ending this madness right now, I will personally guarantee freedom from prosecution, secure passage to the world of your choice, and enough money to guarantee a life of extreme wealth. This offer gives you a free pass for your involvement in the murder of the Khaajiir and will be payable in full the instant everybody aboard this carriage is safe. Let this offer pass and I assure you with equal seriousness that the same resources, and more, will go to plunging you into hell every day for the rest of your life. This is a one-time-only offer that expires ten seconds from now."

When Dejah Shapiro stepped forward, I imagined her about to admit guilt and accept the offer. But no, she just added, "I'll back that promise if he doesn't."

In the silence that followed I searched the faces of the assembled for the uncertain half-starts I would have expected of any tempted culprit.

After a few seconds, Philip said, "Time's up."

Dejah flashed a grin. "It was actually up half a minute ago, dear. But nobody wanted to say so and maybe cut off a killer still trying to make up his mind."

Jelaine covered her own half-smile with her fingers. "I'm sorry, people, but I've been watching the digital timer on the console over there. It was more like forty."

Philip nodded. "Determined bastard, whoever he is."

The Porrinyards agreed. "A genuine asshole."

As was only to be expected, Dina Pearlman took it a step too far. "I don't mind saying, I've been trying to figure out some way I could claim the prize. For an offer like that, I'd have killed the Khaajiir twenty times over."

Dejah spared her only the briefest of glances. "Yeah, well, killing the Khaajiir would take an offer like that. He was worth something. You're only alive today because nobody's ever come up with spare change."

There were smiles at that, even a grudging one from Mrs. Pearlman. For the moment, at least, these were not bickering people with competing agendas, not frightened prisoners waiting for outsiders to come and rescue them, but a united front against an unknown and dangerous enemy.

I had no faith in the truce lasting as long as our shared predicament. But I knew it would help in the short run when Philip said, "Well, Counselor? What's next?"

Farley Pearlman spoke before I could, an unwitting favor to me as it covered my own temporary bankruptcy of ideas. "Is there a reason we can't just evacuate? That's what we did, earlier today. Sure, we don't have a shuttle. But it's not like there's a shortage of vessels out there eager to rescue us."

Dejah bit her thumbnail, a gesture so close to a habit that had plagued me for years that I felt a twinge at the reminder of what it must have looked like. "I wouldn't advise anything like that until we know why we have all those weapons pointed at us."

Philip said, "Do you really think they'd fire on us?"

Dejah gestured at the image. "Look at them. As you said, that's a classic siege formation. Rescuing us, or at least the family members aboard, must still be a priority, unless there's been a coup we don't know about, but their first concern seems to be a show of force, aimed at . . . somebody. Can you imagine what they might do if we go EVA and they don't think it's any of us, but instead only our murderer trying to escape?"

"And why wouldn't they just intercept without deadly force?" Philip asked. "They'd have to, if the alternative means risking harm to Bettelhines."

"Again," Dejah insisted, "that's only as far as we know. Without direct contact, we don't know what's been happening on their side of this standoff. We don't know why they're keeping their distance. For all we know, the threat's bad enough to be considered a planetary crisis."

"That's ridiculous," Philip said. "I can't imagine any circumstance bad enough to render three members of the Inner Family expendable."

My mental paralysis eased. "I can."

Every face in the room turned toward me.

"Understand, please, that I'm not calling this the only possible explanation. There are others that fit the available evidence. But are you all really forgetting that our fellow passengers include one of the people who helped to engineer Magrison's Fugue? If Mrs. Pearlman wanted to, she'd find an orbital vantage point like this a perfect place to infect the atmosphere with that or any other weapons she might have developed in the meantime."

Dina's already cold features went even more rigid with anger. "I knew this would come around to blaming me."

"Forgive me, madam, for treating your words like last year's toilet paper: unwanted, unpleasant, superfluous, and old. I did say that it was just one of several possible explanations, but the fact remains that the economy of the world below us is entirely based on the munitions trade, and there are any number of such weapons, your obscene Fugue among them, sufficiently dangerous to Xana as a whole that, in any siege situation, the Bettelhines in command would have to consider the loss of a few trapped Inner Family members a small price to pay for the common good."

"That's not a bad point," Philip said. "It's just as likely, probably more likely, that you're part of this and using doomsday scenarios to scare us out of doing the easiest thing."

I took no offense. "Based on the data you have, exactly right. I could be. The only constant here is uncertainty. Either way, Dejah's right. We can't take precipitous action until we make contact and determine what those forces are doing."

The various prisoners of the Bettelhine Royal Carriage stewed in a shared uncomfortable silence.

Then Mendez cleared his throat, with a dry deference that carried with it an apology for intruding on the business of his superiors. "May I offer a suggestion?"

"For God's sake," Jelaine told him, "if you have something to say, just come out and say it. Don't start asking permission to speak now."

"That's very kind of you, miss. I was just saying that if I suit up and go outside, I might be able to toss an airtight container with a message apprising the troops of our concerns and sharing our eagerness for any information they might be able to impart in return. It won't require any great feats of precision on my part, as there are so many soldiers out there that any container thrown in any random direction will inevitably be intercepted by somebody."

Jason shook his head. "And if Counselor's right, and they blow your head off the moment they see you're throwing something? . . ."

"I will do my best to establish with body language that my intentions are benign."

Jelaine said, "That's putting an awful lot of trust in your talent for pantomime."

"In a space suit, yet," Jason said. "No thank you, my friend, but I think Dejah and the Counselor are right. Until we know what the military's doing out there, and what they think we're doing in here, I'm not about to allow you to risk your life by recklessly throwing things at them."

There was another moment of silence before I said, "Maybe he doesn't have to."

My plan almost failed because nobody could find anything to write on. Cut off from the hytex network, we now found that none of us had anything as antiquated and as fragile as paper, let alone implements capable of marking it. Jason grumbled that it might be a good idea, in the future, to stock the various suites with a nice supply of paper, Bettelhine-crest stationery. A twinkling Jelaine snapped back, yes, of course, because it goes without saying that this exact situation *comes up all the time.*

In the end, wincing from the necessity, Philip opened a

display case in the parlor and ripped two blank pages from
a Bettelhine family history, commissioned decades earlier
by some great-grand uncle or twentieth cousin or other
ancestral somebody, and provided its most recent home
on the carriage because it carried the whiff of royalty the
Bettelhines wanted to display. The search for a writing
implement might have been an equal headache had Dejah
not reached into her pocket and produced a glittering
golden cylinder that she identified as a personal weapon,
but which was at its lowest setting capable of creating hair-
line chars on paper.

By this point nobody was in any mood to scold her for
smuggling weaponry past Layabout Security.

Vernon Wethers, who claimed the best handwriting, in-
scribed the letter in a cursive so elegant that it managed to
impart beauty to the blocky Mercantile alphabet. He pref-
aced it with a series of symbols, all three Bettelhines identified as Inner Family codes, that the recipients would be able
to use to confirm that Bettelhines had a hand in composing
everything that followed.

*To Colonel Antresc Pescziuwicz: We are the surviving
passengers and crew of the Bettelhine Royal Carriage.
One among us, the Bocaian academic known as the
Khaajiir, has been assassinated by parties unknown,
utilizing a K'cenhowten Claw of God. A preliminary
investigation has been authorized by the three Bettelhine siblings on board and is being led by Counselor Andrea Cort, of the Hom.Sap Confederacy, now
an honored guest of Hans Bettelhine. We have yet to
identify the culprit or discover any direct connection
between this incident and the previous one aboard
Layabout. We are all together in the cargo bay and
keeping our eyes on the exterior monitors. If there's*

*anything you need to tell us that might increase our
chances of survival, now's the time.*

Philip Bettelhine	*Dejah Shapiro*
Jason Bettelhine	*Andrea Cort*
Jelaine Bettelhine	*Oscin Porrinyard*
Monday Brown	*Skye Porrinyard*
Vernon Wethers	*Arturo Mendez*
Dina Pearlman	*Loyal Jeck*
Farley Pearlman	*Colette Wilson*
Paakth-Doy	

Most of the words were mine, but the Bettelhines had in-
serted various corrections, the most notable being Philip's,
when he insisted that I refer to myself as his father's "honored" guest.

"Good catch," Jelaine said. "I should have spotted that
myself."

I finally registered the special emphasis that phrase had
been given all day and night. "What am I missing?"

Philip flashed the startled look of a man who had just been
reminded that he had yet to come to terms with my presence.
"You don't know? Nobody's ever bothered to tell you what
it means?"

"It's not like I haven't been asking."

"No, I'm not talking about the reason you're here, which
as I've said is still a mystery to me. I'm talking about our
various levels of guest protocol."

"This is the first I've heard of it."

He glared at Jason and Jelaine. "How could you not let
her know?"

Jelaine's hand fluttered to her mouth. "We were keeping things low-key. Until Father had a chance to talk to
her."

Philip shook his head in disbelief, then turned to me and said, "Here's what they haven't told you. For the past four generations or so the Family's used rankings to denote the levels of hospitality afforded our visiting dignitaries. Special Guests and Corporate Guests are both offered privileges greater than those we provide the average run of visitors, and they're both far below Personal Guests, who are offered the full hospitality and friendship of the Inner Family. We've never bestowed those rankings lightly. To put this into full perspective, Counselor, Dejah here is one of the most powerful industrialists in the history of human civilization and one of the most distinguished visitors that even this world has seen in quite some time. And yet, in protocol terms, it was judged unnecessary to declare her, or the Khaajiir before her, any more important than a Personal Guest."

I felt the weight of all eyes upon me. "Then what's an honored guest?"

"Somebody who's entitled to all the privileges and courtesies afforded any member of the Inner Family, including a full share of Inner Family earnings while on Bettelhine soil. It makes you a temporary Bettelhine. Right now my father's the only one authorized to declare such an honor, and as far as I know, he's only done it twice, each time under extraordinary circumstances."

I opened my mouth, closed it, then shot a glance at Jason and Jelaine, who were both nodding. Once again, I registered something greater than mere affection or admiration in the way they two of them looked at me. But now I saw what it was: love.

Through the blood pounding in my ears, I heard Philip conclude, "I still don't know what this is all about, Counselor, but making your status clear in this document is the procedural equivalent of telling those troops that they should count not three Bettelhines aboard, but four. . . ."

* * *

Wethers completed transcribing the letter, then read the entirety out loud in case anybody wanted to add a postscript. There were no further amendments.

Dejah, who'd been watching me closely in the several minutes since Philip's bombshell, remarked, "I've got to hand it to you, Counselor. That's a pretty formal document for a distress signal. Do you ever let your hair down, even for a moment?"

"Yes," the Porrinyards said.

Wethers blinked at them for several seconds before processing what they'd meant and turning a bright shade of scarlet. "Oh."

Jelaine took the document from him and slipped it into the vessel Philip had provided. It was an insulated airtight cylinder shielded against magnetic flux, temperature extremes, and most scanning technology; it was normally used to safeguard delicate recording media in transit from orbit, and would survive atmospheric reentry without any measurable damage to its contents. According to Philip, a magnetic charge in its base would be sufficient to secure it to the hull as long as we remained motionless outside the atmosphere. The combination lock was, in this circumstance, superfluous. We could activate the seal and still allow easy access to anybody who retrieved the container.

My idea, an improvement over Mendez's offer to throw the container, was to let the forces surrounding us decide it was safe to retrieve it.

Jason said, "I should go."

Mendez, who had suited up, the flexfabric of his Bettelhine-manufactured space suit forming a seal over everything but his unhelmeted head, winced at the very suggestion. "And just how would I justify allowing that, sir?"

Philip said, "I'd like to hear that explanation myself."

Jason seemed to come up with about three or four potential

answers, rejecting them all as insufficient, before coming up with a lame, unpersuasive, "I rebel at the thought of requiring other people to risk their lives for me."

"Welcome to modern civilization," said Dejah. "Let alone life as a Bettelhine. People have been risking their lives for yours since the day you were born."

"Nevertheless." Jason leaned in close and addressed Mendez eye to eye. "Arturo, you may think you owe us your allegiance, but you don't. We forged that debt. Do you understand? It's all us. *You don't have to do this.*"

"It's my duty, sir." Mendez took the helmet from his hands, and pressing it to the contact ring at his shoulders. The flexfabric around the seal bubbled, flowed, and solidified in place over the neck joint, rendering the seam as invisible as the face behind the silver mask. I saw his chest expand as he took an experimental deep breath. Then he took the cylinder from Jelaine's hands, and stood, moving toward the air lock.

Oscin, who was standing behind me, lowered his lips toward my ear. "This is wrong."

"I know," I whispered back. "But I don't know why."

"Neither do I."

It felt more than wrong. It felt dark, corrupt, and dangerous. But the reason eluded me. Even as Mendez entered the air lock and the doors slid shut behind him, I searched the faces of the others, hoping for the epiphany that now seemed just beyond reach. Most didn't seem to notice any underlying currents beneath the obvious drama of the moment. Jason and Jelaine wore stricken expressions, their strong resemblance now even more overt as they watched the Chief Steward's departure with identical grimaces of guilt and displeasure. Dina Pearlman seemed darkly amused, Dejah as puzzled as I was. Vernon Wethers and Monday Brown were as unreadable as they usually were. Loyal Jeck just stood by, a stolid, charisma-challenged lump. Colette Wilson moved closer to Philip, resting her hand on his upper arm and taking a subtle calm from the gentle contact. The elder Bettelhine didn't acknowledge it. He just watched the air lock cycle, and took an involuntary deep breath of his own as the other door opened to space and Arturo began to climb the access ladder to the carriage roof.

I felt the warm touch of the Porrinyards on my back, massaging my shoulders. Did I really look that pale?

Arturo was already on the roof and placing the cylinder in plain sight. The magnetic seal held it in place. In a few seconds he'd be back inside and the Stanley would be free to investigate, if so inclined.

I'd be over this uncharacteristic fear, if that's what this was.

I knew it wasn't.

The plan would work. Mendez would survive his brave climb in the face of all those brandished weapons. The Stanley clinging to the cable above us would descend and retrieve the message. The forces charged with protecting the Bettelhines and their guests, whether personal or honored, would break through the wall of silence that had so far cut off the explanation for how this thing that had happened to us.

My sudden trembling had come from a deeper place, the place that connected to my conscience and my humanity.

It was not fear. It was horror.

I suddenly knew why Brown and Wethers had no family beyond the Bettelhines, and why Mendez had given up his dreams.

I made eye contact with the strange siblings, Jason and Jelaine: Two people I had imagined I was beginning to understand, but the little I'd been so proud of myself for figuring out was nothing compared to this. If they had anything to do with the truth underlying this moment, they were everything I despised about their rapacious, world-destroying family, cloaked in smiles and good intentions. And if they were innocent . . . then they were guilty of being willfully blind.

This was evil, all right. But not a fresh evil. It had been going on for a while.

And I knew exactly what it was.

The voice of the AIsource, silent for hours now, chuckled inside my head. *Excellent thinking, Counselor.*

I almost cried out, but managed to keep my answer sub-vocal. *Fuck! I thought we were cut off from you!*

Don't be foolish. The parties responsible for this crisis may have managed to interfere with local connections to the hytex network and with the Bettelhines' other communication systems, but no technology currently possessed by human beings can sever the link we share with you. No, we were simply taking a step back and allowing you to begin working out these problems for yourself.

Either help or get out of my head!

You may leave our employ at any time, Andrea. You will have the opportunity to do so, before this business is done. The biggest question after today is whether you'll want to.

Somebody handed me a cup of water. Paakth-Doy. I don't know where she went to get it; the parlor was levels above us. It was cold and it tasted like sweet honey, cutting through the acidic taste in my mouth.

How can the fate of billions depend on this? It can't be the people of Xana. There are only a few million down there. And besides, you said an alien race.

Humanity would suffer greatly in the aftermath. But you are correct. We do not mean the people of Xana.

Then who?

Telling you would be against the rules of engagement.

"Counselor?" It was Philip, once again the voice of confident authority now that I'd obliged him with this moment of weakness. "He's back inside. You can stop worrying now."

"I wasn't . . . worried about . . . him."

Concerned, frightened expressions bobbed around me, Dejah, Jason, and Jelaine, the most stricken among them. I avoided meeting their concerned eyes. Let them wonder. I wasn't ready to use what I knew, let alone pursue the many things I didn't.

Are the Bettelhines going to start this genocide you've been talking about? Is that what you're telling me?

The answer is subtler than that, Andrea, and is tied to you living long enough to make your choice. Be patient. It is still coming.

The air lock hummed as atmosphere returned. The holo monitor displayed a businesslike Arturo Mendez waiting for the process to run its course.

Mrs. Pearlman mentioned the ability to control the behavior of entire enemy populations. Does that have something to do with this? Does it have something to do with what happened in Bocai?

An indulgent tone entered the AIsource's voice. **The tragedy on Bocai was the last thing any Bettelhine would have wanted.**

The holo image cycled, revealing a multilegged vehicle proceeding down the cable at full speed. It was the Stanley from Layabout, descending to retrieve Arturo's message.

When it wrapped a probing tentacle around the cylinder, the cargo bay echoed with the gasps of passengers who only now realized that they'd been holding their breath.

It picked the cylinder up.

Hesitated, as if receiving further orders.

Then tightened, crushing the cylinder into wreckage.

Heedless of the cries of "No!" and "You Bastard!" that

erupted from our throats, it then retreated up the line, rejecting our attempts at communication.

By the time the Stanley was just a bright light in the fir-
mament above us, some of those cries had become wails.
Philip Bettelhine, who had shown the most faith in the or-
derly nature of his family's ability to deal with any crisis,
was among the loudest, yelling, "Come on! Dammit! What's
wrong with you people?" Paakth-Doy was almost as frantic,
falling into Colette Wilson's arms and receiving an oddly
detached, perfunctory hug as the bartender wept tears that
creepily failed to disturb the perpetual smile on her face.
Dina Pearlman was just pissed off, screaming, "Fuck! Fuck!
Fuck!" Her husband just punched the bulkhead multiple
times, a portrait of loss untouched by compassion on the part
of anybody else. Dejah Shapiro seemed lost in concentration. Monday Brown just looked comically dazed. Vernon
Wethers and Loyal Jeck said nothing.

Mendez emerged from the air lock, his helmet in his
hands, expecting pats on the back for his swift and efficient
action, only to find a tableau of runaway anger and despair.
"What's wrong?"

Dina's voice, which had transformed from syrup to acid in
the short time I'd known her, now completed its transformation to venom. "The fucks are leaving us to die."

He said, "What?"

I'd had enough of this. I turned to Skye. "Come on."

She nodded, grabbed the Khaajiir's staff, and began to
follow me out the door, Oscin staying behind to keep an eye
on the others.

Philip saw us departing. "Counselor?"

I whirled on him, unable to keep the fresh disgust out of
my voice. "I am going back to work, sir. In the meantime it
is my suggestion that the rest of you remain down here and
near this air lock, for the time being. We may all need access
at a moment's notice, and the parlor isn't exactly the most

comfortable place aboard anymore, not with the Khaajiir so busy flavoring the air up there. In the event this winds up being an extended siege, we can all take shifts sleeping in the crew quarters, taking expeditions to our respective state-rooms if there are any personal items anybody really needs. Don't worry, though. I believe it won't be long before you hear from me again."

Philip was left blinking. "B-but . . . who do you want to speak to next?"

I gave him a look of raw contempt. "First the corpse," I said. "Then the bartender. I'll let you know when to send her up."

We turned and left, the voices behind us rising even before we reached the stairs.

15

FIRST THE CORPSE, THEN
THE BARTENDER

The Porrinyards had learned early in our relationship that there were times when they could comfort or reason or shame me out a black mood, and other times when I was just plain unapproachable and best left alone. The difference between the two was a subtle one and they were, as a pair, just about the only person I'd ever known with a gift for discerning one from the other.

It was hardest to ride the worst of my rages when we were working and I needed them to function as assistants and not in their other roles as friends and lovers. They were stuck with me, then, and weathering the storm was an exercise in remaining silent and speaking only when it was necessary to volunteer information or provide brief answers to direct questions. I knew this was goddamned unfair to them, but it seemed to be too central a part of my personality to fix—one reason why a major attribute of their shared function as my only real friends has always been that damnable adjective *"only."*

Skye, who was better at riding the storms, if only because she was slighter and smaller (and Oscin's great wall of a chest provided too tempting a target when I needed something to pound with rage), remained silent as she accompanied me back to the parlor and stood aside as I glared at the cadaver of the being from the world that most wanted me dead.

The corpse had settled farther into the cushions, but its general attitude and position remained the same as the one I'd noted and examined just a few short hours before. But for the stench and the sheer aura of death he might have been any other aged academic, fallen asleep in a favorite easy chair.

I walked around the body a few times, then went to Skye and took the staff, returning to regard the crime scene from every angle. I murmured to myself. I nodded. Then I returned the staff to Skye, went to the bar, poured myself another of Colette's intoxicating blue drinks, and marched back into our suite, sitting on the edge of the bed while Skye stood in the doorway, silently waiting for me.

"This is evil," I said.

"Murder always is," she replied.

I spat venom. "Juje, but that's just fucking banal. You have two heads between you, *you* should do better than that. This—what's pissing me off—isn't about the murder. The murder's just today. I'm pissed about what passes for business as usual among these gargoyles. Tell me you don't see it. Tell me you don't have any idea why I want fissionables to bombard this world from orbit."

Skye remained calm. "If it's not because of the wars they foment and the weapons they sell and all the people dead or living as refugees because of their family business, I'm afraid I don't know. But those reasons will do. What's yours?"

I'm afraid I came close to railing at her for being blind

and stupid. But as before, her measured tone and unwavering gaze brought me up short. I bit back all the awfulness at the tip of my tongue. "You'll see when we get Colette up here. It's . . . everything I hate."

"Not including the murder," she reminded me.

"Yes. That's another problem."

"And the problem we happen to be faced with, right now. As I told you before, I have some of the information Jason wanted us to look up in the Khaajiir's files. Would you like to see it now, or would you prefer to wait until after you're done with Colette?"

She—no, they; I still had to keep reminding myself, Oscin was part of this even if he wasn't physically present—*they* were handling me. I hated being handled, hated that I was so easy to manipulate, hated that they were so goddamned good at it, hated that they had every right because their skill at handling me was one of the things I most needed them for. "When we're done with Colette, I'll be too mad for anything but chewing on Bettelhine ass."

"Then we have our priorities settled, don't we?"

There was the other source of irritation, raising its ugly head again. Whenever they talk to me like that I feel the invisible hand of the AIsource manipulating them to manipulate me. Again, it was the AIsource that linked them, the AIsource that brought us together, the AIsource that gave us our marching orders. I said, "I know we've already had this conversation once tonight, and I apologize for bringing it up again. Are you withholding anything from me? I'm not talking personal stuff. Are our employers using you to control what I know and when I know it?"

She sighed, shifted the staff's weight in her hands, and said, "You know, Andrea: there's going to be an upper limit to the number of times you can ask that question without inflicting permanent damage on our relationship."

"I still need an answer."

"It's true. I'm an AIsource agent. It's part of the deal made by the single-minds Oscin and Skye once were, when they asked for their souls to be linked. It's part of the deal made by any pair the AIsource enhances in that manner. I'm also loyal to you. It's part of the deal I made when I became your friend and lover. I have never been asked to pit one loyalty against the other. If I ever withhold anything from you it's either because, by my considered judgment, it's none of your business or nothing you need to know. I've told you this. You need to accept that it's no poor reflection on my feelings for you."

Just a few short hours ago, when she'd last made a speech like that, I'd backed off in shame. This time I held my ground. "None of that affects the essential question, love . . . especially since you've admitted that what you withheld from me earlier was a key realization about Jason and Jelaine."

"You didn't need it then!"

"No, I did not. And, true, I've since figured it out for myself. But we're approaching the endgame now. So I need to know. Have you found it necessary to withhold anything else since then? Anything you've observed about the guests? Anything you've found in the Khaajiir's database?"

She hesitated. Just a moment. But she hesitated.

Then she said, "Yes."

"Like what?"

"I've absorbed entire volumes of information, Andrea. I've only boiled it down to the highlights because it eliminated anything that would distract you from the problems at hand."

"Why would it distract me? Because it's irrelevant or because it would disturb the AIsource agenda?"

It was rare for the Porrinyards to retreat from anything, but they retreated now; Skye just looked away, and refused to meet my eyes. "Because it would upset you."

There was nothing I could say to that.

She went on. "Trust me, Andrea. Keeping you on track is not the same thing as betraying you. The way I feel, the way I've always felt, if it ever comes down to a choice, I'll tell the AIsource to go to hell."

I studied her for a long time. There was nothing especially earnest in her expression. But there were times, like now, when the presence of one Porrinyard did not just indicate, but also evoke, the presence of the other, when their faces seemed superimposed like a pair of images linked in deliberate montage. "You really would."

"Wouldn't you?"

Have you ever noticed that conversations convey more emotional information when they don't include any words?

After a while, I said, "I think we better get back to work."

"As you wish." Showing palpable relief, she crossed the room to hand over the Khaajiir's staff, retaining her hold even as I claimed my own grip below hers.

It wasn't necessary, but we both said, "*Decch-taanil blaach nil Al-Vaafir.*"

"This," she said, from a million miles away, "is everything I found out about the failed Bettelhine project, Mjolnir."

Technical stats and progress reports, hundreds of pages long, flipped through my mind, too fast to read. I caught a diagram in which two lines emanating from a satellite in orbit enveloped an entire planetary hemisphere in an area shaded to show effective range. I saw other tables labeled with titles like atmospheric diffusion and ideal surface densities, before the raw data became too much and the volumes of information backed off in favor of Skye's thumbnail summary.

It turned out to be a typically disgusting sample of Bettelhine hubris, with a minor but potentially interesting connection to the K'cenhowten Claws of God: a misbegotten attempt by a previous Bettelhine administration to amplify the technology involved into an orbital cannon capable of taking out entire regions. The focus requirements had proved harder to overcome than any moral objections the Bettelhines of the era might have had to producing weaponry capable of making every man, woman, and child in range suffer the same fate as the religious heretics the K'cenhowten had once sentenced to death by torture. The project had been abandoned not because it was morally and physically revolting—I almost retched at the thought of billions suddenly pausing in their tracks as everything inside them gushed from their orifices—but because the Bettelhines had lost a fortune trying to get it to work.

I moaned. "Are you sure they gave this up? I don't even want to live in a universe where they can put something like this on the open market." Nor one where this was the means of the genocide I'd been warned about.

"Then I won't make you feel worse that this is no more severe, in terms of its destructive potential, than several items the Family's been selling for some time. I don't even want to know about all the projects the Bettelhines must have completed but withheld for fear of their destabilizing impact on the economy. But in this case, I understand enough of what I've read to confirm that the project managers ultimately judged the technical difficulties insoluble."

This established little beyond confirmation that the Bettelhines, or at least past generations of the family, were not unfamiliar with the Claws of God, a disturbing but wholly unsurprising revelation given that reverse engineering the innovations of others would have to be part of their business model.

It also underlined everything I'd always believed about what pricks they were. But Skye was right. It established only that the Claws of God used today might have been Bettelhine re-creations, a possibility already considered that was, at best, a small piece of the puzzle. I filed the data away and told her to move on.

The Khaajiir's writings on the subject of K'cenhowten's Enlightenment turned out to be just one of several volumes dealing with the bloody histories of multiple species, from the Third Millennial Self-Immolation of the Cid to the Nazi Holocaust of humanity's homeworld. He seemed fascinated by the subject, returning again and again to a special thesis: the often just-as-bloody periods of adjustment that tended to follow any extended period of tyranny and injustice. I had not yet picked up the knack of pulling the relevant facts from the explosion of information that overwhelmed me when I tried to read part of one of those theses for myself, but as it had taken the Porrinyards mere minutes to speedread the specific volume dealing with K'cenhowten's Age of Enlightenment, Skye was able to point me to the point she found most central.

"The Khaajiirel are the key," Skye said. "The late professor—I'll call him that for the time being, to avoid confusion—noted that tyrannies and dictatorships are often so successful at repressing their peoples that chaos, borne from the various grudges and hatreds kept at bay for so long, often follows when the source of that repression is removed. He listed a number of historical strongmen who upon being overthrown or persuaded by liberalizing forces to loosen the chains on their respective societies, were replaced with even more ruinous anarchies. In short, the conquerors and despots ease up and the societies left behind chew off their own legs, reacting with auto-genocides and civil wars that end only when history provides a new order just as bad as the old one. He wrote, *'A people hip-deep in fire will not stop burning just because would-be reformers decide that fire can be ordered to become water.'* End quote."

I nodded. "But that didn't happen to the K'cenhowten. They had the Khaajiirel."

Skye left me holding the staff and started to pace. "True. Utopian idealists who preached peace and, instead of having their words twisted over the years and centuries to a new dogma capable of prompting inquisitions just as bad as the Age of Terror, actually got what they wanted: the tyrants overthrown, the hatred felt against their kind forgotten after only a few years. It's not unheard of for peacemakers on any world to accomplish such a thing, but most often that occurs only when the emancipation arrives after a handful of generations. According to our professor, that's a far cry from sudden changes of regime that have stood for centuries or longer. They possess a historical momentum almost impossible to stop without a disastrous crash. To put it another way, you can sit the various factions down at tables and tell them to play nice, but they'll still start arguing over crimes the privileged committed against the not-so-privileged among their great-great grandparents. Again, if I can quote: *'Claiming that the Khaajiirel accomplished otherwise, with just the force of their own ideals, is to embrace a naïveté stunning in its idiocy. The miracle claimed of them would have required a despotism dedicated to benevolence, one that forced their world's first free generation to also become its first generation unpolluted by past evils. It was not a despotism they could have had the power to create in secret, not without leaving yet another black stain on their history. And yet they did what they did, burying all memory of their own brand of tyranny as they had buried the reign of terror that had made it necessary.'* End quote."

I found myself seized by a chill. "Does he specify how he thinks the historical Khaajiirel managed it?"

"No. It's just a vague suggestion, nothing more. But that's the theory of historical momentum that Jason referenced when you pressured him for more information."

I said, "I'm not sure I like the idea of Bettelhines, any Bettelhines, reading that paragraph. Let alone idealist Bettelhines like Jason and Jelaine."

"Neither do I. Nor am I encouraged by the idea of Hans Bettelhine, who has never been an idealist, and who would no doubt prefer for his family to continue doing business as usual, suddenly deciding he wants to spend a year in our professor's presence. It makes no sense." She hesitated. "If it helps, I've determined the reason the Khaajiir's such a hated, controversial figure on Bocai. Why some factions would like to assassinate him."

"What is it?"

"He made light of their hatred for you."

My heart thumped. "What?"

"He stood up in front of a large crowd at his university and said, *'The phenomenon that led to the massacre is not, as so many of us would have it, solely a human one. We know better than that. Nor is it confined to Bocaians, even if so many Bocaians trapped in that community on that day committed crimes just as brutal as those committed by the Hom. Saps among them. Harping on that terrible day, urging the never-ending hatred of those who participated on one side, while ignoring the universality of the community-wide spasm, ignoring the clear evidence that this was not a tragedy of clashing cultures and moralities but of unknown other factors that would have affected any sentient creature present on that day, is the equivalent of allowing the terrible anomaly to make our decisions for us. And it is especially tragic that, betraying everything that is great about our people, we focus the impulse to demonize the people present on that day on the face of the most innocent, whose subsequent lives have been the most blighted.'"* She looked up at me and concluded, "Then he said, *'If we are ever to achieve understanding, we need to do what the historical Khaajiirel would have done. We need to stand up as one and forgive the massacre's most maligned innocent, the human Andrea Cort . . .'"*

I had seen the last line coming for more than half of her recitation; indeed, I'd suspected something like that since the Khaajiir first treated me with genuine warmth. But the words hit like a hammerblow anyway. I tried to say something, but found myself obliged to excuse myself and spend the next several minutes locked in my suite's bathroom, thinking of the siblings I'd seen murdered and of the weight of a night I'd already carried with me for too many years. This was something I'd rarely admitted to myself: not only that I'd loved Bocai as much as I'd loved my family, but that I still felt the same way after so many years of being demonized as the girl who plucked out the eyes of a Bocaian neighbor and used them as playthings. It would have meant a lot to me to hear forgiveness from a Bocaian's lips.

After a few minutes the immediate emotional tsunami subsided, and I was able to return to Skye with dry eyes and more troubling questions. "But why would the Bettelhines give a royal shit one way or another? They've never been a part of my life and I've never been a part of theirs. Are they commencing new careers as angels of compassion, forcing feuding peoples to shake hands and play nice? Was I invited here as an honored guest just to scratch the Khaajiir's moral itch?"

"I have no contribution at this time, Andrea."

"Even if they did decide it was important to give their pet Bocaian professor a present, what difference would it make? He's just one Bocaian, not even a decision-maker. The majority would still hate me. He'd tell me he was sorry about the way things are between his people and me, I'd say I appreciated the gesture, and we'd have nothing else to say to one another. That's one hell of a stupid reason to drag a total stranger from her home with minimal notice."

Skye bit her lip. The Porrinyards must have wanted to take

the nobler view of things, but they were also prevented from doing so by their very common sense, and it hurt them to give up on the happy ending. "I suppose it's possible."

"No, it's not possible. Not with the Bettelhines involved. Not with everything else I know about them, not with what I intend to demonstrate to you when we finally get that sparkly slut of a bartender in here. There's not an atom of instinctive benevolence in them. There must be something else, maybe in some of the other materials Jason suggested."

"I'm sure there is. Alas, it took some time to get past the Khaajiir's history, and I've yet to find any galvanizing connection."

"What about this Lillian Jane Bettelhine Jason mentioned?"

Skye took the staff from my hands and walked away, spinning it absently as she contemplated the best route into whatever followed. "I think she may be one of those wastes of time I mentioned."

"That bad?"

"That dull. She appears to have been one of the reform-minded relatives Dejah talked about; she caught the pacifism bug early and argued that the family needed to become a more positive force in human civilization. Her sentiments, as far as I can tell, were just standard Utopianism: not far from the Khaajiir's in tone, but far inferior in depth."

"Give me a sample," I said.

"From an essay she wrote at nineteen, one that could not have gone over well with her private tutors: *'I can't look at the way we do business without seeing that our affect on the rest of the human species is toxic. We spread like a sickness, our very presence poisoning the wells that others drink from, our trade inspiring entire worlds to turn upon themselves like starving rats chewing off their own limbs. It is not enough for me to declare that I won't be part of the corruption myself, if I still live life sharing in the profit. I have to do more. I need to do more. I ache to be an anti-Bettelhine: if not in the sense of warring on my family, then at least in some smaller way, proving by example that we can replenish some of the hope we've stolen.'"*

"That sounds like more than typical adolescent rebellion."

"You would think so. In truth, she was always very careful to separate her love for her family as people from her rejection of everything they stood for. Unfortunately, she was as naïve as she was idealistic, and so it never occurred to her that her statement of principles, mild as it reads to us, could get her into trouble with Mom and Dad. Not long after she penned those words she was deemed a disruptive force, useless for all corporate purposes, and subjected to internal exile at one of several estates the Family maintains for that purpose—hardly, as Dejah indicated, the first or last time something of the sort had happened. I doubt she wanted for anything in her life but freedom."

"What happened to her?"

"The Bettelhine genealogy lists her as deceased, not many years afterward. I don't know whether she remained in Internal Exile or left Xana, but she was certainly never a corporate force."

I refrained from scolding Skye, even in jest, for this gap in her intelligence. Allowing for all the extreme compression required of them, the Porrinyards must have already gleaned more data from the Khaajiir's files than I could have found given weeks to work with. But Lillian Jane Bettelhine's scandalous opinions didn't fill in a missing piece of the jigsaw so much as establish the existence of an entirely new region of the puzzle. I rubbed the bridge of my nose. "There's got to be a connection, love. Do you think Jason intends to model himself on his late aunt?"

"That would be a step back for him. He's hooked up with his sister and consolidated a substantial power base that threatens Philip's role as heir apparent. Lillian Jane said a few intemperate things before being shuffled off to some cozy family gulag where she wouldn't disturb anybody by causing uncomfortable silences at parties. On a global level, there was nothing to emulate about her but for a few principled words."

Skye's determination to minimize Lillian Jane at any cost was beginning to get on my nerves. "Words have been known to move mountains."

"And mountains," Skye said, "are easier to move than empires. Trust me, Andrea. I understand the natural impulse to paint Lillian as a great visionary, but there's no indication that she ever had any truly revolutionary ideas capable of affecting more than her own personal conduct. You can translate everything she wrote up to that point as the bland self-serving declaration *I will be a good person*, devoid of any additional context or detail. I don't think she ever presented a real threat to the Bettelhine status quo, at least not as much as Jason and Jelaine seem to."

I had noticed the careful use of the phrase *up to that point*. "And yet Jason said she's important. How?"

Skye spun the Khaajiir's staff in her hands, not so much plumbing its data as distracting herself with baton twirls. The lights it reflected spun around the walls like glowing coins. "Not to the problem at hand."

I waited for her to offer something else.

But the answer to that question, if it existed, remained locked in the crystal staff.

Part of me wanted to continue looking. I could feel something tremendous lurking in that direction. But the Porrinyards were correct about one thing. Right now, all other questions paled against the identity of the individual who had placed the Claw of God against the Khaajiir's back.

If Skye was so certain that the travails of Lillian Jane Bet-

telhine were irrelevant to that question, then it was time to
leave her behind and start setting off bombs.

Especially since I was already juggling several that remained undetonated.

I could feel a special kind of anticipatory anger, the kind
that would give me strength for the confrontations to come,
welling up inside me as I told Skye, "All right, then. Have
Oscin send that annoying little quiff up here."

"I'm already bringing her," Skye said, her voice deepen-
ing to indicate Oscin's. Then, in her own softer tones: "I
could tell you were ready from the look in your eyes."

Colette Wilson sat, puzzled but as obliging as always,
in the suite's most comfortable chair, offering several
attempts at a tentative half-smile that only grew broader as
I obliged her with a kind, encouraging look of my own. Her
spirit and vitality had been depleted not at all by the stress of
the hours since the Khaajiir's death; though she'd been willing to take the chair, she perched at its very edge, her back
straight and her eyes round as she awaited her opportunity
to answer any questions I might provide. At some point in
the last hour she'd washed up and replenished her makeup,
providing a thin touch of eyeliner to accentuate her bejeweled eyes and bring her gamine look back into sharp relief.
Her electric hair remained inactive, thank Juje. Either she
continued to find its display programs too grim for the occasion, or she knew that they rendered any undistracted conversation with her almost impossible.

Now that she was alone with us and away from the Bettelhines, she revealed a simmering fascination for Skye, asking
her if she really remembered everything Oscin had said and
done since the two had been apart.

Skye said, "You want to know what he's doing right
now?"

Colette colored, glanced at me, then hid her little grin with a fan of her fingertips. Not hidden at all, the fanning gesture as expressive as the grin itself had been. Like most people enjoying their first encounter with a linked pair, she could not help thinking about the erotic possibilities.

I sensed how easy it would have been to like her, if I allowed myself.

If I didn't consider her obscene.

Skye wasn't fooled by my gentle demeanor as I told Colette my questions would be no more than routine, and apologized again for snapping at her before dinner. But she remained silent, merely backing me up with smiles and nods and occasional leading questions that followed my leads.

What followed was, for most of its length, by design one of the dullest and least informative interrogations I've ever conducted.

Any pretense that I might have considered Colette an important witness faded as I exhausted substantive matters and steered toward fripperies, such as the important people she'd hosted in her years on the carriage, and her favorite places to spend her time off. She told a funny but respectful story about Arturo's fussy behavior. I made a little scandalous joke about Philip Bettelhine. She tittered and found the nerve to ask how long the Porrinyards and I had been together. I told her, offering a cute and slightly risqué detail for lagniappe. More laughter.

We had a great time. We became good friends.

By the time another twenty minutes had passed, it was all one great big fucking party.

At which point, I shook my head to deny the most recent burst of gentle laughter, shot a sharp glance at Skye, and repeated, "You know, I really do need to apologize again for the way I treated you during dinner. I was out of line and I apologize."

She fanned her fingertips over her lips again. "You don't

have to keep doing that, Counselor. I understand. It's not the first time I've ever had to deal with a stressed-out client."

"Thank you," I said, with dripping sincerity. "Because it's really become important to me that we get along."

"Thank you. I feel the same way."

"That's good, because you've impressed me so much with your vivacity that when—not if, but when—we reach Xana, I'd like you to take some time off and stay with my companions and me. We'd like you to be our personal valet."

Never had eyes been so bright, or a smile so ingenuous. "I'd like that."

Skye began to see it, realization just beginning to turn her own amiable expression into the beginnings of a scowl. "You do understand, this invitation means you'd be sharing our bed."

Now Colette seemed incandescent with happiness. "Oh, of course."

I said, "It also means that you'll make yourself available whenever we wanted you. You know that this is important business we have with Mr. Bettelhine. There are times when we'd have to leave to tend to important company matters, and might not be back for weeks. You'd have to confine yourself to whatever quarters we're assigned, occupying yourself however you can until we get around to making our way back. During this time you'd also have to refrain from any contact with your own friends or family. That is, if you have any friends and family. This situation might last, oh, I don't know, a year or two. Maybe three. Do you have any problems with that, Colette? Any problems at all?"

She said, "Not as long as it was cleared with my Bettelhine sponsor."

"Which Bettelhine is that?"

"Magnus."

"We haven't heard of that one."

"He's one of the uncles," Colette explained. "He's a much younger brother of Hans. Not much older than Philip really."

"Uh-huh. And he's the one who hired you?"

"Yes, Counselor. He's the one who gave me this opportunity. I wouldn't want to be unavailable for him if he needed me for a trip up to Layabout."

"Yes," I said, with a pleasant twinkle, "I'm beginning to understand how your orbital station got its name."

Colette tittered, the fingertips fanning her lips again.

Skye, who was beginning to look ill, said, "Where did he find you?"

The bartender crossed her legs, arching her back to emphasize the curve of her breasts, her entire manner now more about flaunting her sensuality. Even her voice had become throatier, more of a seductive whisper. "I was one of the researchers at a Bettelhine facility in the outer system. We were charged with reverse-engineering an intelligent guidance system the Cid developed for the mass-driving planetary defense grid."

"Sounds like tough work," I said, shaking my head at the impossibly complex world of high-level weapons research. "It's certainly over *my* head!"

The haunted Skye managed a version of my own impressed laughter, but there was no amusement in her eyes. "What level of education do you need to merit a position like that?"

Colette grinned. "I received my second doctorate when I was nineteen."

"And when did Magnus meet you?"

"When I was twenty-five. I've always looked younger than I am, and he's seen to it that I've had some rejuvenation treatments since I took this position."

"How long ago was that?"

There was a moment's hesitation, as Colette did the necessary arithmetic in her head. "Ten years."

"Were you involved with anyone when he found you?"

"I was engaged to be married, Counselor."

"What was the lucky guy's name?"

"Erik Descansen. He was my lab partner."

"Did you ever get married?"

"We stay in touch. He understands that this is an important assignment. He knows that we'll see each other again someday."

Skye was now covering her mouth with her hand. It was one of the occasional drawbacks of having two minds in one: twice as much empathy. Get past their horror filters and they feel it twice as much as anybody else.

I, on the other hand, pride myself in my ability to play cold bitch, and hadn't allowed my predatory smile to waver a millimeter. "So let's review, shall we? It's been ten years since you voluntarily abandoned your education, your research career, your fiancé Erik, and your plans for your future to work full-time aboard the Royal Carriage as Magnus Bettelhine's bartender and concubine, where you will if requested also make yourself physically available for the sexual entertainment of any other guest who wants you."

"Yes."

"Arturo Mendez was recruited from a beach resort, the closest thing to the homeworld he'd been missing his entire life, to serve as 'companion' to a 'lonely,' elderly Bettelhine named Conrad. Was making himself sexually available to Conrad among the terms of his employment?"

"Oh, yes. I remember Conrad. He was a kind and generous man. And he loved Arturo so much. He died a while back. Arturo still mourns him."

"I seem to remember Arturo expressing a personal preference for women. Is he bisexual?"

"Not in his private life. But Conrad was Inner Family."

I pressed further. "What about your fellow stewards, Paakth-Doy and Loyal Jeck? Are they also expected to perform a similar range of duties?"

"Loyal was once a favorite of a Bettelhine cousin Melinda. Melinda fell out of favor and hasn't been aboard for a couple of years. He doesn't talk much; I think she liked the silent type, and he misses her. I don't know about Paakth-Doy. She's an emergency replacement, and hasn't attracted anybody's attention yet."

"But if she impresses somebody," I said, "she'll be given a permanent assignment?"

Skye muttered, "Not if I have a single fucking thing to say about it."

Colette's fixed smile wavered only a little as she turned her attention to the passenger who had just shown anger without warning. "Is there a problem?"

"Never mind," I said. "Come here. There's something I want to do."

She stood and approached me, stopping when she was closer than she truly had to be. Sitting as I was, I found myself looking up at her breasts. They were firm, impressive, and likely, at least in part, artificial. From my position underneath those curves I could have slipped my arms around her, and pulled her toward me, had that been what I wanted. Instead, showing a sudden anger I did not need to work very hard to summon, I stood and slapped her cheek with a force that made Skye wince from sympathetic pain.

Colette's reaction was more puzzlement than anger or hurt. "Why did you do that, Counselor?"

"In mathematical terms, I'm affirming the corollary to a proof. Aren't you angry at me? Don't you want to hit me back?"

She did the worst thing she could have done at that moment.

She tittered again.

"No. You're an honored guest."

"Oh," I said, "in that case I forgive you." And I slapped her again, this time harder than I intended, enough to feel the impact halfway up my arm. I could have hit her again and again, because I wanted to; the only thing that kept me from doing it was the knowledge, so deep inside me that my belly lurched from the weight of it, that if I started I wouldn't stop until it became an out-and-out beating, more brutal by far than anybody but Bettelhines deserved. "That one's because I felt like it. If you work for me, it will probably be the first in a very long series. I'm unpredictable that way. It's what I enjoy. I especially like breaking bones. Will you come to enjoy that, and look forward to it, when we're all together in our shared quarters, at Hans Bettelhine's estate?"

Colette's eyes had gone dreamy. "I've always wanted to visit the main estate. They say it's beautiful."

I slapped her again, but even that was not enough to dispel my disgust at what had been done to her, what she had allowed to be done to her, so I found myself casting about for a fresh outrage, something that would rob her of any dignity that still remained. I snapped, "Would you—"

Skye cried, *"That's enough!"*

It was the angriest cry the Porrinyards had ever directed at me, either as individuals or as linked pair: a sharp burst of pure revulsion that forced me to see myself through their eyes and brought me back from the edge of the abyss.

I was left blinking, as disgusted by myself as she could have been from what she'd just seen in me.

When Skye stood, there was a coldness in her eyes I'd never seen there before. "I'm sorry, Andrea. But you've made your point." Then she turned to Colette. "Please go back downstairs, miss. Tell the others we'll be contacting them again in a few minutes."

Colette seemed wholly unable to comprehend why the seduction she still perceived as friendly had just gone so awry. After a moment she said, "All right," and went to the door, stopping just long enough to cast an eye over her shoulder and said, "It's all good, Counselor. From where I sit, it's good to feel happy."

The door closed.

Skye and I stared at each other from across the elegantly appointed room. She opened her mouth as if to say something else, something that might have come out filled with venom. A second passed before she decided to put it off, her reticence more about keeping us both focused on the issue than dismissing the side of me she'd just seen.

I wanted to go to her, wrap her in my arms, and weep that I wasn't part of this, that this was Bettelhine corruption, that I was still me. But there was no point, because it would have denied the nature of the problem.

I was who I'd always been.

And I had to be fair. Even if this did turn out to be their saturation point, the Porrinyards had already lasted far longer than anybody else could have ever imagined.

I said, "We'll talk about this later."

Skye nodded and looked away, not quite ready to answer.

I cleared my throat, and spoke in a voice unexpectedly thick. "In any event, we now know at least part of what Mrs. Pearlman does for them. . . ."

16

JASON AND JELAINE

According to Skye, reporting what she'd seen through Oscin's eyes, the three Bettelhines were surprised when I had him send them all up.

They were also disturbed when Oscin specified that the Bettelhines were to come without Monday Brown or Vernon Wethers along to vet their answers and safeguard their interests.

Brown and Wethers both raised serious objections to that, but then Oscin—acting on a suggestion I'd relayed through Skye—asked, "Aren't three Bettelhines capable of looking out for themselves?"

It was about as transparent a gesture of psychological manipulation as any I'd ever attempted. The Bettelhines had to recognize it. But it worked regardless. The Bettelhines ordered Brown and Wethers to stand down, and came upstairs alone and unescorted in what must have felt like the latest leg of a journey with no destination in sight.

When the siblings arrived in the suite, they chose seats that reflected the uneasy rivalry between two parties. Philip and Jason sat facing each other, Philip wary and

Jason wearing a sad mask that may have been either a put-on or a genuine reflection of his regret that things had to be so tense between them. On her own, Jelaine took a seat outside the circle and against the wall, a gesture that did not abdicate her place in this imminent confrontation between brothers so much as provide her strategic control over the battlefield. There were tears at the corners of her eyes, but I couldn't tell whether they'd been of hope, or sadness, or stress and exhaustion. Nothing about her suggested that she felt she'd lost her control of the situation, not even when she said, "Are you all right, Counselor? You look grimmer than I've ever seen you, which is saying a lot."

Skye would still not look at me.

I said, "You're very perceptive, Jelaine. I am grimmer. You've been saying that you want to make friends, but then some of the things I've found out about your stinking, despicable family in the last few hours have made me even more disgusted than I was when I only knew you as abstractions."

The knowing smile never left her face, nor did the quiet confidence on Jason's. They continued to present a united front, a stance that had long since ceased to impress me.

Philip, who had indicated grudging respect for me in some of our more recent conversations, now flashed fresh anger. "Watch it, Counselor. We've given you license up until now, but it isn't unlimited."

I charged him with a speed that made him flinch and stopped only when we faced each other from across a gulf of inches. "You should be. If I had my way the lot of you would be lined up on the side of the road and confronted, one at a time, by an endless parade of everybody you've ever hurt. You'd get one fifteen-minute break every hour to wipe the spit off your face, but only so the next hundred people in line could enjoy an unsullied target. Do you see the look in my eyes, Philip? It's what I think of your goddamned irrelevant license."

As taken aback as he was by my fury, he still recovered quickly. "And you, Counselor? How long would your parade be? And have you accomplished a damn thing in all the hours we've given you, or are you still just running in circles?"

I held his challenging stare for several seconds, backing off only because I felt unbearably tired. It was not just physical weariness, or the metabolic crash that always hits a day or so after a long journey in Intersleep, but a deep, soul-sick weariness, of the sort that comes from too much immersion in Mankind's talent for corruption. "I've accomplished more than you think, sir. In fact, as soon as we're done here, I'm going to gather everybody together and tell you who killed the Khaajiir."

The announcement had the effect I'd expected. Jason and Jelaine remained impassively pleasant. Philip started, glanced at them, then turned back to me. "Why not tell us now?"

I rubbed the bridge of my nose. "Because if it was just a matter of pointing my finger at one murderer, I would have done so already. But you people have made a much bigger mess than that. Indeed, I suspect that once I name the name, we might find ourselves fighting for our lives."

He weighed my expression for signs that I was kidding, found none, and said, "But if you get the murderer—"

I rolled my eyes. "The one murderer. The individual who put the Claw of God on the Khaajiir's back. That one I can name, with something approaching certainty. But hasn't it long since become clear to you, sir, that this is much larger and much more complex than that? After all, we're facing a conspiracy capable of obtaining and smuggling exotic weapons, enlisting assassins from other worlds, sabotaging this elevator, and interfering with the priorities of those we would otherwise expect to rescue us. It may involve the cooperation of hundreds or possibly even thousands by the time you're finished counting, and any ability I might have to provide you with one name out of all that many fails to account for how many others aboard might be sharing at least some responsibility for our predicament."

Philip shook his head as if mere denial could will the facts out of existence. "But none of these people—"

"Please, sir. Refrain from mentioning the ones you know to be loyal, or from telling me why you believe a conspiracy on that scale to be impossible. I know why you consider it impossible, and as I intend to prove in a few minutes, loyalty's the very nature of your problem. *You may think you control these people, but you've allowed somebody else to take the reins.*"

That took a second to sink in, but when it did, he rose, his face pink, and his eyes turning into little circles. "You know about—"

"Ever since you've gotten your hands on the technology, you've treated your key people the same way Magrison treated the innocent young woman who became Dina Pearlman. The technology isn't exactly the same—if it was, then every affected individual would sport the same kind of chip Mrs. Pearlman wears—but the effect is. You put governors on their minds, making sure they define contentment as loyalty and obedience to you."

There was a moment of shamed silence.

Jason said, "You're right, of course. It's exactly as shameful as you say, but Mrs. Pearlman perfected the current system, involving nanite manipulation of the pleasure centers, in my grandfather's time. But how did you figure it out?"

I answered him without taking my eyes off Philip. "That was downright easy, compared to some elements of the messy business. I was willing to believe people like Monday Brown and Vernon Wethers forging personal lives in exchange for proximity to power; there have always been people like them, in every generation. Arturo bothered me, though; he formed his values and his ambitions somewhere else, and he still jumped at the chance to serve you inside this tin box for years on end, when everything else about his life story indicated a passionate longing for a life near the ocean. It was also suspicious that your family would get its hands on somebody like Dina Pearlman without investigating, and if necessary reverse-engineering the technology that allowed the beast Magrison to command her unconditional loyalty. And even more so when she referenced unspecified 'other means' used to control Farley's vile compulsions."

Still looming over Philip, I swiveled my head and focused my anger on Jason. "But it all came together when Arturo was suiting up for his trip outside the elevator, and you told him, quote, *'You may think you owe us your allegiance, but you don't. We forged that debt. Do you understand? It's all us.'* That's when I saw what you bastards had done to him and by extension all of these other poor souls who work for you. They're *leashed.*"

"Get out of my face," Philip said.

I glanced at him, as if reminded of his existence, then backed off, giving them all a chance to decide who wanted to offer justifications first.

Jelaine brushed a strand of golden hair away from eyes that had not grown one iota less warm or compassionate during the hostile exchanges of the past few minutes. When she spoke, her voice was mild, her tone entirely free of facile self-justification. "Not all of us approve of the governors, Counselor. Some of us loathe the very idea of them. It's the main reason my brother and I operate without personal aides, as we told you. We prefer to earn the loyalty of those who work for us."

"That doesn't make you innocent of profiting from a system that enslaves people."

"No," she agreed. "It doesn't."

That stopped me.

She continued. "That system existed before we were born. It didn't leave me, or Jason, much of a choice over a status quo we were too young and too powerless to change. I never walked away, so you may hate me if you must. But Jason left. He left while he was too young to forge his own way, and paid a terrible price for it. And returning didn't mean he'd changed his mind. It's just as I told you before. The two of us intend to change what our family stands for."

I quoted the rest of what Jelaine had said, on that occasion. *"'And how far the web of family extends.'"*

She flashed a secret smile. "Quite so."

Philip turned in his seat, either not quite understanding what he'd heard or unable to accept it coming from her. She raised her eyebrows at him, not in affront but in mute apology. I don't think he understood whatever unspoken message she was trying to send. Nor did he receive the answer he needed from Jason, who offered him the same sad, sorry, apologetic look, more loving than confrontational, and more infuriating for that.

Skye still refused to look at me. She was paying attention, but wasn't sharing what she thought, either about the situation or about me. I ached to wonder if the damage was permanent, but could not afford to, not now, not with the worst looming all around us.

Philip did me the favor of giving me another reason to hate him. He straightened his collar and fixed me with the full weight of his contempt. "You're very clever, Counselor. And you do enjoy your unearned moral superiority. But you've never once considered that people operating at our level might have good reason to for the decisions we make."

I glared at him. "Such as?"

He looked tired. "Hasn't it occurred to you that our business model requires us to prevent the human race from exterminating itself?"

"Go on."

"I can't say we haven't profited, but we deal in skills that must be kept out of the hands of monsters like Magrison, or some even worse than him. When we race to acquire dangerous technology, it's so we can control it, limit the number of governments with access to it, or keep it off the market entirely if we feel it's too risky to allow even in the context of savage warfare. You don't know how much we've locked up or just thrown away over the years. But if our best people were ever able to consider going into business for themselves, either by seizing control of Xana or by wandering from system to system dispensing our secrets at will—"

"So you put hobbles on their brains."

"Not on their creativity," he said. "Not on their cognitive abilities. Not even on their ability to enjoy the pleasures of life. Just on their capacity for betrayal. So we install, not hobbles, but governors: internal fences, if you will, ensuring that everything they develop for the Bettelhines remains in the control of the Bettelhines."

"Even if that warps their lives beyond all recognition? It didn't take me long to see how many of your people don't seem to have priorities beyond their service to you. One of the first things I learned about Brown and Wethers, for instance, is that they're both so focused on their work that they have nothing else."

"It's not that overt with most of the people affected. Most just go to work and do what they need to do before returning home to live their normal lives. What you see with Brown and Wethers is not at all uncommon among any high-level executives. I know officers of your Diplomatic Corps who exhibit the same behaviors, without any internal governors as excuse."

"So Brown and Wethers are not being controlled?"

"Controlled is the wrong word. They still possess free will, within certain parameters. If they wanted social lives, we wouldn't stop them. But you need to understand, the potential for corruption, not just penny-ante corruption, but corruption on a destructive societal scale, with people of their level is worse than you can possibly imagine. An unaltered Monday Brown, left to his own devices, has the capacity to bring down the entire corporation. He can embezzle, he can steal secrets, he can use what he knows to forge an empire of his own. Somebody like him needs to take so much satisfaction in his work, in serving the Bettelhines above all other personal considerations, that this becomes impossible."

Damned if he didn't make it seem almost reasonable. But it didn't take me long to find something capable of stoking my outrage back to its previous heat. "And how would this justify rape by mind control? Like what's happened to Colette?"

His prior righteousness faltered a little at that. "I don't deny it goes on. Every once in a while one of us takes a predatory liking to one employee or another and reconfigures the governors to define loyalty as sexual compliance. It's frowned upon, and I've never done it myself, but we all recognize that it still goes on more than any of us would like. The worst you could say about it, though, is that it's contemptible only to those of us who stand outside it. The people it's done to are all almost blessed in their way. Colette's happier than anybody I've ever met."

"At the expense of everything she once was."

"As I said, I don't approve of using the technology for anything but security purposes, and I've talked to Magnus about returning her to her old life."

This was maddening. "And what of Arturo Mendez? His sponsor, Conrad, is dead. He's been dead for years. He's never coming back. And yet Arturo's still here, working year in and year out under conditions utterly at odds with the way he'd live his life if allowed to choose for himself."

Philip didn't seem proud of that, either. "Arturo's like all of our low-level employees. He's spent time with us, heard our conversations, and has been privy to our secrets. He knows things that can never be allowed to fall into the hands of outsiders. So we've counteracted his ambitions to work elsewhere. It's ugly, but to him it's just an alteration in the criteria that keep him happy. Someday, sooner than he thinks, he'll receive a retirement package far greater than any a man of his resources might have ever been able to earn otherwise. Whether or not you believe it, Counselor, it's a win-win situation."

"It's slavery."

"Of a kind. On a world where unfettered freedom could mean mass destruction."

"And what prevents some individual Bettelhine lower in the pecking order from seizing the opportunity to use your compliant little robots for a power grab?"

"Aside from the fact that any Bettelhine who thought of it has everything to lose and almost nothing to gain? We're too sophisticated to let that happen, Counselor. At most higher levels, our employees are not loyal to any individual Bettelhines, but to the Bettelhine power grid as a whole."

"So there are some employees more powerful than Bettelhines?"

"There have to be. It's a necessary check on the destructive potential of Family rivalry. I heard Jason mention our aunt Lillian Jane before; her tutors were certainly loyal to her, but they were still able to report her activities. The real reason we've never had some scheming sociopathic cousin poison all the people above him and seize control is the presence of parties like Brown and Wethers, whose true loyalties are to the corporate structure and to the principles that have guided our family since—"

He stopped in mid-sentence.

He frowned.

He mentally reviewed everything he'd just said.

He started to get it.

I said, "What are the Pearlmans doing here today? Do they normally get surprise trips on the Royal Carriage? Or are they usually not much more than well-treated prisoners, working in their little island gulag?"

"N-no. I—"

"You knew something was up with Jason and Jelaine. But your suspicions were focused on Jason, the half brother you would never trust again. And so you came up with an entirely mistaken theory. You suspected that, in some way, Jason was *controlling* Jelaine. You worried that somebody working for Dina Pearlman might have gone off the reservation and helped him install controllers in her. So you used your influence to get the Pearlmans a free elevator ride and directed Dina to conduct her own covert observation of your brother and sister, in the belief that this would turn out to be the explanation."

Jelaine shook her head. "Oh, Philip. You could not possibly be more wrong."

"No, he couldn't," I said. "And not just about that." I hit him with the full force of his family's great mistake. "Your grandfather wanted to make it impossible for key employees to ever raise moral objections to Bettelhine orders or to defect to other powers and corporations. He wanted to prevent any one of them from ever drawing a line in the sand and saying, *This is as far as I go, I won't go any further.* And he thought that's what he accomplished. For decades every Bettelhine with access to the tech has believed that this would keep you safe. But what it's really done is create a chain of command even more vulnerable to middle managers with their own definition of loyalty."

Philip stood.

I approached him, placed my hands on his shoulders, shoved him back down into his chair, and lowered my face to his as I delivered the angry summation. "*Loyalty that may include agreeing to commit terrible crimes, even against Bettelhines, as long as somebody above them, one of your precious internal auditors, can tell them it's for the good of the Family as a whole.*"

Philip's lips moved without sound.

This time he didn't warn me to get off him.

After a moment I walked away from him again, pacing the room with a fury that some observers might have mistaken for hysteria.

"Whatever your justification," I said, "the point remains. This evil program of yours exists, and it's what made these crimes possible by enforcing blind obedience up and down your chain of command. And it's what endangers us most now, because it limits the number of people we can trust, even aboard the carriage. I've done the math. Would you like to hear it?"

"Please," Jason said.

Philip nodded, with an unwillingness that suggested he would have much preferred to forestall the grim truth by ignoring it.

"Fine." I resumed pacing. "There are sixteen of us. I know that I'm innocent and I can say the same for my companions as well."

Philip opened his mouth.

I raised my hand to silence him. "If you won't take my word for it, consider that I've never been to Xana, and that I only knew I was coming to Xana hours before I left New London. Will you agree for the sake of argument that it makes more sense to just agree we can't be guilty?"

Jelaine surprised me by laughing out loud. It was the heartiest merriment I'd ever heard from her, utterly undisturbed by the grimness of the occasion, or the danger we were in. Almost a guffaw, it testified to a capacity for enjoyment that must have rendered her a genuine life-force among the members of her family. "I never suspected you, Counselor."

The weariness that had overtaken me a few minutes before now seemed to affect Philip as well. "Get on with it."

I began ticking off points on my fingers. "After that, any attempt to use the process of elimination enters the realm of speculation. Since this is a crime that endangers the Bettelhines in general and the Bettelhine chain of command in particular, I'm willing to declare the three of you probably innocent as well. I'm more sure about Jason and Jelaine than I am about you, Philip, since it was their own agenda under attack, but I'm somewhat inclined to give you a pass as well, as you went out of your way to be aboard and would not need to endanger yourself when any assassins in your employ did their work. That's not a certainty, of course. Just an extreme likelihood."

He allowed himself a wry grimace. "I'm touched by your opinion of me."

"I would say the same about Dejah; she has the resources, and even a reasonable motive given your family's past attempts on her life, but even if she was financing this thing, I see no reason why she'd feel the need to place herself on the front line. I may be wrong about any or all of those last four names. But the rest are wide open. If I allow your own tentative removal from the list of suspects to stand, that still leaves nine people out of sixteen—nine people out of sixteen who might have been co-opted. Nine people out of sixteen whose actions, once I name the single murderer I am certain about, cannot be predicted. Nine people out of sixteen who might be harboring weapons of their own and may be more than willing to leave another corpse or two cooling in your parlor, if we interfere with the agenda that brought them together." I took a deep breath and focused on Philip again. "Are you beginning to see how precarious our situation is, sir?"

The silence that followed that question was profound. Philip bit his thumb, glanced at Jelaine (whose expression had not changed), and then at Jason (whose own air of invulnerability echoed hers). Again, they'd given him nothing. Then he turned back to me and said, "What do you suggest?"

"I suggest that when I do get around to providing the name, we should all be ready to fight for our lives. And," I said, focusing my next attention on Jason and Jelaine as well, "I suggest that the best way for that to happen is to let your brother know just how inaccurate his guess was."

Philip started at that. His eyes widened as he realized he was about to get some of the answers he'd longed for, and he turned toward them, measuring their own reaction, probing their blandly pleasant expressions as if in determination to ferret out the truth before they got around to giving it.

Jason rubbed his forehead with one hand. "Do you need to know all of it now, Counselor? What happened to me on Deriflys? What my sister and I were looking for, when we left Xana? Why we then did what we did?"

I considered it. It was tempting. But then I shook my head. "No. I can wait for those answers, and the reason you had your father invite me here, until we're safe. I just need you to admit what you are, so Philip can see how it's going to affect what's coming."

Jason nodded, and for just a moment allowed a look of great sadness to come over his face as he regarded his older half brother with unapologetic affection. Tears welled at the corners of his eyes. "I'm sorry, brother. It was never any reflection on the way we felt about you. But it's such a difficult secret to hide from the people who know us best. And this thing we're trying to do together is so very, very important."

"We do love you," Jelaine said. "Never question that."

Philip's gaze darted between Jason and Jelaine and back, his lips moving without words as he tried to pull the answer from the air. After about a million years, still not getting it, he managed, ". . . what?"

Jelaine brushed the back of her hand against her gown and stood, the charming half-smile still tugging at the corners of her lips, the tears so much like Jason's shining at the corners of her beautiful eyes. There was no defiance in her stance, no anger, nothing but a love so bright that it pained me to look at it.

I wondered about the kind of courage it took to share a confidence like this when it could destroy as much as it healed, and found against my will that I envied her, as much as I'd always envied the Porrinyards, for their courage in taking this journey that still remained beyond my own powers of faith.

Even as she stood, Jason stood and joined her, so they could stand together as they faced Philip as the united force they'd been for so long. A subtle change overtook their expressions as they synched up, emphasizing their already strong resemblance, rendering them more than mere siblings, closer than they would have been even if born twins.

They each raised complementary eyebrows as they faced their older brother in shared entreaty and challenge.

Philip's eyes went wider. He was not a stupid man, and I think he figured out the truth a fraction of a second before his strange brother and sister spoke in unison, their shared voice not male or female, but some gender that was both and neither. Maybe that heartbeat of advance realization made the moment easier to absorb when his siblings said, "Once upon a time I was two people, a brother and sister named Jason and Jelaine Bettelhine. Once upon a time they left Xana as separate people and came back as one. Now I'm a linked pair. Now I'm both Jason and Jelaine, together. . . ."

* * *

Philip fell out of his chair. Literally.

He tried to stand but his legs collapsed underneath him and sent him falling to his knees as the slackjawed attention he owed his siblings swallowed all other capacity for thought. It would have been comical if not for the horror and revulsion and incomprehension and denial warring on his handsome, aristocratic features. When he finally managed words he said, "How . . . *could* you?"

Jelaine spoke alone. "I know this is difficult, Philip, but you must understand. Jason was shattered by his time on Deriflys, and by . . . some other things that happened when we went away. He could not live inside his own skull, not by himself. So Jelaine, the single Jelaine, offered to seek out the procedure and help him carry the weight."

"He was wrong! He shouldn't have let you destroy yourself to save him!"

Now Jason and Jelaine spoke together. "That's what he thought. He fought her. He tried to tell her she wasn't worth what she would have to sacrifice."

Jelaine let out a soft laugh. "He was wrong. It was no sacrifice."

Philip recoiled from them as they approached in a misbegotten attempt to comfort him.

Stymied for the moment, the linked siblings turned to the silent Skye and said, "Oscin? Skye? You're what I am. Please back me up on this. Tell my brother that neither Jason nor Jelaine sacrificed a damn thing. Tell him that everything that made up the two people they were, from their memories to their loves to their heartbreaks and their convictions, all still exists inside this new individual created at the moment they joined. Tell him how healing the process is, how insignificant it made your old concerns seem, how much better it became to look at life through two sets of eyes instead of only one. Tell him that there's nothing horrible about it, nothing in it that needs to change how he sees my shared self as a sibling or how I can see him as a brother. Tell him."

Skye, who was visibly moved by their plea, turned from them to the distraught Philip, regarding him with something very much like pity. Sparing only the briefest look at me, one I read as a warning not to interfere, she knelt beside him, placed a single hand on his shoulder, and asked, "Sir? Would it be less offensive to your delicate sensibilities had your brother ended life a defeated suicide, and your sister had spent the rest of her own blighted by the knowledge that she had not done everything she could to save him?"

"She didn't save him," he said miserably. "She just destroyed herself with him."

"No, she did not. She just changed. That's what life is, sir. Change."

"She didn't have to change like that."

"I agree. She might have changed any number of other ways, including some that might have made her less precious to you. But whatever happened, she never would have stayed the same person she was as a younger woman. She would have grown up, developed new priorities, moved on, become in some ways a stranger to the person she once was. The only thing different here is that she decided how."

"But what she had to give up—"

"Please, sir, if we accomplish nothing else here, trust the word of somebody who knows this from the inside. The sister you knew, the one who was capable of taking such a giant step for your wounded brother's sake, is still with us, and if she kept this a secret from you, it had to be at least in part because she knew you would react as you have."

Philip closed his eyes, shuddered, then felt for the chair and pulled himself back up, refusing to look at them but allowing himself a slight nod, as close to acceptance as he was now able to provide.

This would not be over today. If we all survived, there

would still be shouts, accusations, apologies, and hurt at the sight of one another. There was no telling now whether there would ever be peace between Philip and his linked siblings. But there was a truce, and it was all we needed if we were to get through this.

Jason and Jelaine seemed to realize that too. They backed away from him and sat down, their complementary faces both shining with the hopes of a single, oversized soul.

Philip continued to look at his hands. "Counselor?"

I tried not to feel pity for this man I hated, and failed. "What?"

"Before we get into whatever else there is . . . please. Tell me how you knew. Tell me how you saw what my brother and sister had done, when I thought I knew them and didn't see a damned thing."

Skye just shook her head, a bitter smile curling her lips. Her thoughts, their thoughts, were no deep mystery. *Why don't you, Andrea? Why not? After all, demonstrating how brilliant you are has always been your favorite part.*

If only Oscin were here. It didn't matter that if Skye was mad at me, he would be too. The thought of him, standing among the others, participating in their conversations, revealing no hurt at all as he maintained the false veneer of individuality, was almost more than I could bear.

Maybe if they were both here I could make them believe I was sorry.

I felt another wave of exhaustion. I don't know what this one was. I'd been up too many hours and been through too much shit to care. But Philip was still waiting for his explanation, and there was no way to get to the more important business still ahead of us unless I got through this part. So I ran my hand through my hair and began, my voice sounding far too dull for a woman who normally reveled in being the smartest person in the room. "My associates saw it first. They're linked themselves, as you know, and were able to pick up a number of subtle cues in short order, even before we all sat down to dinner. They decided it was a private matter between your siblings and none of my business. But I knew they'd seen something, and that kept me on the look-out for phenomena they would have been better equipped to notice.

"After that . . . there were more indications than I have time or inclination to list. Jelaine saying of Jason, *'I do my best to help him carry the weight.'* The way she talked about some of his experiences almost as if they had happened to her personally. The way the two of them went out of their way to express provincial wide-eyed wonder at Oscin and Skye. Jason blinded by blood in his eyes, unable to see a thing, and still running without mishap across a floor covered with debris when Jelaine and the Khaajiir needed him. Jason agreeing with me when I said he'd told me he wanted to be friends, when he'd never spoken those precise words to me, and had not even been present when they were said; when it had been Jelaine the charmer, Jelaine the gracious hostess, who spoke them. You want a half dozen more from the events of the past few hours? I could go on. After a while, they were *obvious*."

The room fell silent as I allowed Philip the minutes he needed to decide whether or not to forgive his siblings. It took longer than I thought it would. Then he stirred him-self, rose, and straightened his jacket with the same kind of excessive formality I'd used many times, whenever I was in the greatest danger of falling apart. It could have gone either way, but then his stern mask trembled, and he turned toward the first sibling within reach, in this case Jelaine, who hugged him with all her strength and whispered something I failed to catch. Jason joined them less than a second later, and the three stood in silence for about thirty seconds, not resolving the differences between them but for the moment accepting them.

I tried to make contact with Skye again and was this time rewarded with one of the most complicated looks either Porrinyard had ever given me. It was rife with empathy, and concern, and anger, and a certain unambiguous warning.

I was just happy under the circumstances to find love in there, somewhere.

The Bettelhines disengaged. Philip wiped moisture from the corner of one eye, and said, "Well. Counselor. I hope that's all we need to put aside for the moment. Because I really would like to know who killed the Khaajiir now."

"So would I," said Jason and Jelaine.

I walked past them and approached Skye, who averted her eyes again. I damned the situation without quite understanding it. This wasn't just my distrust, or my momentary brutality toward a bartender with chains on her soul; it was something else, something that might have been too profound to allow everything between us to remain unchanged.

I spoke to her and through her to Oscin. "Love?"

She lowered her voice. "Remember who you are."

"What?"

She grabbed my hand and gave it an urgent squeeze. "It won't be easy, given what's facing you. But *remember who you are*."

I didn't have even the slightest idea what she might have been talking about, but it sounded too much like a goodbye. Were the Porrinyards saying they didn't expect to survive the next part? Or that they intended to sever their relationship with me if we got past this and had the luxury to decide where our lives went next?

A third possibility occurred to me, one so awful that for a moment I felt what the Khaajiir might have felt as all his life drained away. Hours and a lifetime ago, Pescziuwicz had warned me about the dangers of ever pushing the Bettelhines too far. He'd cited the example of a previous Dip Corps representative, one Bard Daiken, who'd overstepped his bounds and suffered some kind of unspecified retribution. Had I thrown away whatever kind of diplomatic immunity the Bettelhines felt they owed an honored guest? Did I know too much now? Was I going to reach Xana only to be spirited away to one of their prisons, or worse, provided internal governors that would make me happy to fulfill any role they might deem appropriate for me?

Remember who you are? Would it make a difference to me to even remember who I was if I was tucked away at some isolated Bettelhine estate and wearing a sincere but frozen smile on my face as I poured drinks for family members who needed only a few more to decide just what they wanted to do with me in the privacy of a bedroom suite?

Remember who you are.

If that's what awaited me, once this business was done, I didn't want to live to see it.

Behind me, Philip said, "Counselor?"

Skye had looked away again.

Damn this. It wasn't as if I had any choice anymore. Sooner or later, either the air or the water or the food or the power would run out. Whatever happened to me, the Khaajiir's murderer still stood between us and the rest of our lives.

I took a deep breath and told Oscin, through Skye: "Bring everybody back up. It's time."

17

THE KHAAJIIR'S TESTAMENT

By the time the five of us left the suite and returned to the sullied magnificence of the Royal Carriage's parlor, the others were already filing in and taking their positions around the bar. The most common denominator among them was not fear but exhaustion. They'd all been up many hours under the most stressful conditions, and the adrenaline that had kept them going in the early stages of the crisis had tapped much that might have been remaining in their reserves. Not all of them wore the pressure on their faces. But they all showed it in the resigned quality of their stride, as if gravity itself had grown more powerful in the hours since we'd all gathered around the table for a friendly meal.

Of them all, Dejah seemed to be the one least touched by the events of the past few hours. Were our deliverance to arrive at this very moment, I would not have been surprised had she suggested a nice ten-kilometer run or perhaps a mountain climbing expedition or two. She may have been even more hyped from her own time in Intersleep as the Porrinyards and I had been, but I wasn't willing to declare that the sole explanation. Exhaustion was just not a state in her body's physical vocabulary, nor despair in her soul's emotional one. Even now, I read a hidden message in the nod she gave me as she passed by on the way to claiming her seat: *I'm ready.*

Dina Pearlman pierced me with her glare as she searched my face for signs of further accusation. Storming past me, she muttered something about hoping this would be over quickly.

Her husband, Farley, looked more sweaty and bloodshot and miserable than anybody I'd seen so far. There was a shiny, fresh stain on his jacket, at chest level. Since there'd been nothing to eat or drink downstairs, I deduced that he'd been ill: not surprising, given everything he'd had to drink in the aftermath of the Khaajiir's death.

Monday Brown gave me a professional nod before seeking out and standing beside Philip. It was hard to miss the way his very posture, ramrod-straight at rest, grew ever more formal the closer he approached the highest-ranking Bettelhine on board. I could imagine no other man being as formidable a right hand to the great Hans. But I now understood the air of sadness I'd sensed in him. I could only wonder what kind of man he would have been, had he been allowed the opportunity to live a life ruled by his own will.

Vernon Wethers picked a place by Philip's other shoulder. Unlike Brown, who gained stature in the presence of his employers, Wethers diminished, becoming not so much a presence as another component of the overall atmosphere. When he saw me looking at him he just as quickly looked away. I wondered if he'd been conditioned to carry such a heavy burden of social inadequacy or if it was something he'd carried with him since childhood.

Arturo Mendez marched to a position beside the bar, his hands linked behind his back as he waited for the proper moment to excel at his personal duty. His ridiculous uniform, complete with sash and epaulets, had not been touched by any of the foul events of the day. Given what we now knew about him, it was tempting to imagine him in his natural habitat: tanned, stripped to the waist, his skin shining from a recent plunge into turquoise ocean waters. I suspected that some part of him, behind those obliging eyes, never stopped screaming.

Loyal Jeck chose an identical stance opposite him, his slight build and blander personality rendering him a virtual invisibility. There was nothing in his expression, nothing in his eyes, nothing in his personality suggesting anything but duty. He hadn't said much in the hours we'd spent together. Nor had his input been missed. His brittleness, his hollowness, that gave the impression of a porcelain creature, just waiting for the moment when he'd be shattered.

Colette Wilson may have been no longer projecting light, but she still shone, her determined cheer and helpfulness showing on her face even as she entered this room filled with grim and scowling faces. She'd touched up her makeup at some point since I'd seen her last, and twinkled at me as she walked past, no doubt still imagining an immediate future being put to recreational use. To my special horror, she went back behind the bar, as if expecting to continue serving refreshments for as long as it took me to get around to pointing my finger at the guilty party. The Porrinyards saw her try to return to work, and Oscin took a moment to divert her to a nearby couch, and a seat beside Farley Pearlman. Her pretty face showed only obedient interest. If she was screaming inside, her cries must have been even more pitiful than Arturo's. I did not want to know.

The party was now gathered in a semicircle, facing me. Colette Wilson and Farley Pearlman sat side by side on a couch, Dejah Shapiro and Dina Pearlman bracketing them in a pair of angled easy chairs. Arturo Mendez stood with Paakth-Doy to our left, Loyal Jeck at equal attention to the right. The Porrinyards stood a little behind me, Oscin on my left and Skye on my right. The Bettelhines and their execs remained standing five paces behind the couches bearing Colette and Farley, Jason to the far left beside Brown. After Brown came Philip and Wethers and, at the far right, Jelaine. It was impossible not to read Brown and Wethers as a pair of protective parentheses shielding Philip from the influence of his strange siblings, Jason and Jelaine.

The easy chair still bearing the Khaajiir's body was behind us, his slumped figure just a shape sinking deeper into his cushions as everything inside him grew emptier.

If this was the way we'd march the rest of the way to the naming of the name, then so be it. It was not likely to go without blood.

I met everybody's gaze one at a time, then coughed into my fist and began.

"I know this has been a long night. I'm sorry, but it's going to get longer.

"A little while ago Mr. Bettelhine and Mrs. Shapiro offered the Khaajiir's murderer amnesty in exchange for surrender. Those offers have been withdrawn, but I'm about to make another one. We already know who you are. I'll be saying your name in a few minutes. If you step forward now and save me the trouble of explaining how we know, I promise that you won't be injured or killed as we take you into custody.

"This is also a one-time only offer, and unlike the others I won't add additional seconds at the end of my deadline in the hopes that you'll relent.

"You have ten seconds."

Nobody looked away from me. By this point, nobody expected an easy confession. I hadn't either, but it was worth a shot.

At the tenth second I said, "Very well. You've been warned.

"This explanation leaves out certain personal information about the lives of some of the Bettelhines among us, and about certain questionable security measures taken by the corporation that have already been discussed in private with Philip, Jason, and Jelaine.

"It also leaves out a host of questions that remain unanswered. I'll be pointing out a few of these along the way, but you do not need to know any of this information or much of the data we gleaned from the Khaajiir's personal records to follow the specific route that leads us to the Khaajiir's murderer."

I coughed, searched the faces of the arrayed suspects for signs that anybody was anticipating me, and moved on.

"So this is what you need to keep in mind about the crime itself.

"The Khaajiir was murdered with a K'cenhowten Claw of God, the same kind of weapon the Bocaian assassins on Layabout had previously attempted to use on me.

"There was, much later, an attempt on the life of Mr. Wethers, and my own, using another ancient weapon known as a Fire Snake." A murmur of surprise rippled through the room. "I believe this to have been a distraction, intended to obscure the murderer's true purposes, and mention it now only for the sake of thoroughness. We will put it aside for now, and focus on the use of the Claw of God.

"The first critical question: why use something so rare, so obscure, especially in such close proximity to a civilization based on the development of weaponry that might have provided access to any number of practical alternatives?

"It's certainly not for religious reasons. The sect that first designed and used the device has been extinct for some sixteen millennia. There's no evidence that it has ever found any popularity among Bocaians. The Khaajiir's own interest in K'cenhowten history was academic and based less on the crimes committed during their dark age than with the great achievement of the historical Khaajiirel in preventing a violent aftermath in the years that followed. Committing the murder with a Claw of God might have some symbolic value, I suppose, but who but a historian would ever care?

"No. Killing the Khaajiir, or me, with a Claw of God has no purpose beyond sowing confusion among those who would later be obliged to investigate the crime by focusing attention on a period long past and implying a connection to the Khaajiir's scholarly work.

"The same is true for any other murder committed around him. This would have been doubly true if the attack on me had ended with my death. Everybody would have said, *Oh well, of course, the Bocaians hate her, almost as much as they hate the Khaajiir for wanting to forgive her. Using a weapon he wrote about to kill her is just poetic justice.*

"And yet the symbolic weight of the attack on me is almost certainly a coincidence, since one of the first things we determined was that the timeline suggests a conspiracy well under way long before anybody could have known I was even heading for Xana.

"The Bocaians needed to be recruited. The Claws of God had to be obtained. Further events establish also that the technical challenges posed by the sabotage to the Royal Carriage needed to be overcome. Same thing for seizing control of the Bettelhine security forces.

"No, for the assassins recruited from Bocai, I was just a target of opportunity, one they went after because they were Bocaians who hated me; they were in fact positioned to go after someone else, someone whose assassination using that particular weapon would have muddied the waters almost as much.

"Was the Khaajiir the main target? That was my first thought, especially since he was indeed targeted later. And it seemed to make sense, since he'd courted controversy by advocating amnesty for crimes I once committed on Bocai.

"But then, as we've also established, there was no reason to believe that he'd ever be passing through Layabout on this particular day. Anybody who knew about him knew he was infirm and that he rarely left the immediate company of his hosts. Setting up an ambush for him on a concourse he would never enter makes no sense.

"My most educated guess?" I pointed at Dejah, who looked entirely unsurprised, and nodded in appreciation that we'd now passed a rubicon she'd already expected. "Dejah is a powerful and influential figure, whose presence here was courted for months before she finally said yes. There would have been more than enough time for a conspiracy based on Xana, and acting against the wishes of the Bettelhines who invited her here, to arrange for a public attack on her timed to occur on the day on her arrival, committed by fanatic members of a minor species using the fanatic weapons of yet another species. Had she walked by instead of me, murdering her with a Claw of God would have directed further investigation into pointless blind allies involving possible connections between her and the Khaajiir and thus obscured the much more reasonable point that the Bettelhines and their people considered her a dangerous enemy and had tried to assassinate her before.

"This theory is incidentally supported by the fact that she arrived at Layabout not long after I did, and circumstances already gone into suggest the assassins saw me as no more than a target of convenience."

I threw up my hands. "Frankly, the identity of the primary target on Layabout remains a mystery to me. I don't know if the killers were after Dejah and were distracted by me, or if they were after the Khaajiir and distracted by me. I don't even know whether they always did expect me and were distracted by some other factor. It doesn't matter, because any of those scenarios fit the available facts equally well.

"In the long run it's likely that all three of us were targets.

"We were all anomalies.

"We had all been invited through their father's auspices, by Jason and Jelaine, the two figures who have been most active in pursuing radical changes in corporate policy and whose success at consolidating power at Philip's expense could not have made any sense to those who knew that Philip was supposed to be the one being groomed for leadership.

"Could the conspirators have known exactly what was up between Jason, Jelaine, and their father? I doubt it, but it doesn't matter. Consider: the leader of a corporation devoted to the development of powerful weaponry develops an inexplicable and inseparable bond with an obscure alien academic. He spends the next year reversing the priorities of the corporation, eliminating profitable programs, and initiating others of no immediately obvious benefit. He bypasses the son being groomed for power and starts handing more and more decision-making ability to another son whose stability and loyalty are suspect due to years of absence in childhood. He even invites a long-time enemy, Dejah, to meet with him. At the same time he also invites a controversial prosecutor from the Confederacy.

"Seeing all of these events from the perspective of parties who cannot know why they're taking place, whose loyalty is only to the corporation, how could you not understand their inevitable conclusion that Hans Bettelhine has been co-opted in some way? That all of this represents an obvious threat to the Family and to the corporation as a whole? And that it needs to be countered by any means possible?

"For what it's worth, I'm at the center of it and I'm still lost. I don't know why I'm here and I don't know what Jason and Jelaine are up to. And I tend to believe Philip when he says he doesn't know, either.

"But antibodies don't need the entire taxonomy of any given bacterial invader to recognize an infection when they see one. Anybody invested in preserving the Bettelhine Corporation they knew would have taken action first and worried about ferreting out the precise explanations later.

"So our conspiracy decided that the important, unexplained figures around Jason and Jelaine had to go. The biggest wild card, the Khaajiir, would have been a prime target. The same thing with Dejah. I suspect that I was the last and least of the names.

"But it couldn't be done out in the open. There were powerful Bettelhines, Jason and Jelaine, who could not be hurt. A web of obfuscation needed to be spun over the crimes. The nature of the threat to the Bettelhine power structure needed to be identified. And—this is the critical part—Jason and Jelaine needed to be isolated from all possible resources, and closely observed in the hopes that they would say or do something to explain just what the hell they were up to." I smiled. "In short, I'm not the only person who's been running an investigation here."

"So that's what this is all about. The next question is, of course, who."

"On the surface, at least, Philip seems the most obvious suspect. He's the one who has to be most frantic about what his brother and sister and father have done. He's had only limited access to that father, at a time in his ascendancy to power when he should be working with the man almost every day. He's seen his own influence slipping from him, and handed in part to an alliance that includes a brother of noted instability. And yes," I said, directing my next words to Philip himself, "I'll give him credit for this, he's also been heartsick and unable to understand his own estrangement from his siblings. He may be a Bettelhine, but he's still human."

"Thank you," Philip said.

"You're welcome," I told him. Facing the others, I continued, "In any event, it was because he was faced with these issues that Philip forced his way into this party, sans invitation, in the hopes of obtaining some answers. He even brought the Pearlmans along, to help him resolve some suspicions we discussed in the other room.

"But that's precisely what I think clears him of any wrongdoing here. Were he just a rapacious corporate bastard intent on regaining his power by killing anybody between himself and the corporate throne, he has any number of underlings, including some present here today, willing to do the dirty work for him. He wouldn't be here, on the Royal Carriage, this close to the murder and thus exposed to all the danger if he knew that any of this was going to happen."

"No, as far as I'm concerned, crashing the party might have been an act of desperation on his part, but it was definitely a peaceful one. Possibly the last before he took more extreme measures. But still a peaceful one.

"He's the first we can declare innocent.

"Who else? The crew?" I directed my next words to the stewards. "I've already told the Bettelhines that any of you, Arturo, Loyal, Doy, or Colette, could have provided our culprit with material aid, either individually or in combination. If I didn't know who committed the actual murder, you would have all been excellent suspects. When we're done here, it will only be your guilt or innocence as a collaboration that remains in question."

"No. In the end, the issue finally comes down to personal power. Who in this room has the influence to enlist vast numbers of people, including the authorities at Layabout and the military forces surrounding us in a conspiracy of this magnitude? Even if only by manipulation of a few key people at the top?

"Frankly, only two of you.

"Monday Brown, the personal aide to Hans Bettelhine. And Vernon Wethers, personal aide to Philip Bettelhine. Please join me here."

The two aides glanced at each other, then at their masters, who nodded and gestured toward me in mute confirmation that they were expected to comply. Brown turned several degrees sterner, and Wethers emitted an audible gulp. But both left the Bettelhines behind, and came around the couch to join me at the center of the circle.

"I resent this," Brown said.

"So do I," Wethers said, with somewhat shakier authority. "After all the years I've spent—"

"Please," I said, shutting both up. "Each one of you acts as representative, and frequently proxy, of the Bettelhine you serve. Each one of you is capable of flitting around this system at will, on agendas you don't need to explain, putting together an operation on this scale. And each one of you can be forgiven for feeling so much identification with the Bettelhine Family that you'd be driven to desperate measures to protect their future.

I faced Brown. "Monday, you might have watched Hans steered into destructive policies and felt helpless to interfere any other way." Then Wethers: "Vernon, you might have seen Philip shunted off to one side because of policies that could only hurt the Bettelhine business as you understand it."

The two men started talking at the same time. Brown said, "This is . . ." Wethers said, "I don't . . ."

Philip Bettelhine shut them both him with a single shouted, "QUIET!"

Both men stopped in mid-syllable.

I couldn't tell whether it was his authority or their internal governors, but either way it worked. They both seemed to have lost the capacity for speech. Volumes of hatred still burned on their faces, but they would cooperate with everything that came after this. They had no choice.

Dina Pearlman smirked. Pride in her work? Or the mere pleasure that a woman like her would naturally feel at the sight of her superiors being humiliated?

I waited for the silence to accumulate a weight all its own, and continued. "Either one of you might have been moved to drastic measures. Either one of you could have set these events into motion.

"And not incidentally," I said, raising my voice, "either one of you would have been able to provide the final ingredients you needed: the Claws of God, and the Fire Snake. We found out in the course of this investigation that just a few short years ago the corporation was trying to reverse-engineer the Claws, for use as a long-range orbital weapon . . ."

Dejah covered her eyes with her hand. "I wish that didn't come as a surprise, with these people."

I grinned at her. "Yes. The very idea is revolting. But that's beside the point. The very fact that such a project took place suggests that the corporation had working Claws on hand or the capability to construct prototypes for testing, somewhere in one of its many research facilities. It doesn't matter whether they were actual antiques or modern-day prototypes. The same follows for the Fire Snake, which would also be of immense interest to a munitions manufacturer raiding old technologies for ideas. But in the case of both weapons, would the corporation dispose of the models on hand or just put them on a shelf somewhere? What do you think?"

"I vote for shelf," Dejah said. "No reason to waste a potentially valuable resource."

"Exactly. And either way, one of you," I said, indicating Brown and Wethers, "hit upon the idea of using them in this business. So you obtained them. Nobody would have said no to either one of you. After all, anybody trusted with the responsibility to keep an eye on such dangerous objects would have been conditioned to allow authorized personnel access. And who could possibly be more authorized?

"Were we not in our current situation, were we able to contact the surface and track down the facility where the Claws of God and the Fire Snake were stored, we could leave it at that. After all, it would be an easy matter to determine which one of you demanded access.

"We would also be able to determine which one of you used your influence to summon Hans Bettelhine just before the Royal Carriage left Anchor Point and thus ensure that he would not be aboard to be threatened by these events.

"Alas, we're cut off from the outside world and can't ask those questions now. But we will be able to do so, when building our case against you later.

"Either way, the prospect of a long elevator ride with everybody who worries you—Jason, Jelaine, Dejah, the Khaajiir, and me—presented your last, best opportunity to find us all together in the same place, and isolated from the power structure you were protecting. You couldn't wait until we reached Xana. You had to determine what we wanted, and if necessary neutralize us before we got there. Hence the importance of arranging for the emergency stop, the communications shutdown, and whatever false intelligence is keeping the security forces from rescuing us. Hence your failure, in all of these hours since the Khaajiir's death, to kill again. It's not just that everybody's been keeping an eye on one another. It's the fact that questions are being asked, and you want answers just as much as we do. Had I not insisted on starting our own investigation, you would have made the same suggestion yourself."

My next words emerged as gentler than I'd expected them to be, gentler by far than anything I'd said so far. I spoke to the people behind the rigid faces, the souls in cages driven to their crimes. "I feel sorry for you, really. In a way, you're not responsible for what you've done. Driven by a loyalty that's been imposed on you, you've served the Bettelhines as best you could, the only way you could, given your suspicions of an internal conspiracy that must have left you agonizing over who to trust.

"But you still murdered the Khaajiir.

"And you're still a threat to the rest of us.

"And since we cannot determine your identity by communicating with Xana and determining which one of you obtained the Claws and gave the necessary orders, we might have been left with nothing and been stuck here until the air or food ran out."

I took a deep breath.

"But fortunately we've been handed a little help.

"The Khaajiir himself told us who you are."

That caused a commotion among everybody except the Porrinyards and Bettelhines, who knew where I was going: gasps of astonishment, frenzied conversation among those desperate to remember what the Khaajiir might have said and when he might have said it.

I gestured for silence and got it.

"This is what you need to keep in mind about the Khaajiir. He was a Bocaian, representative of a species that possesses little if any talent for the acquisition of new languages past adolescence. To counteract that limitation he used his staff as a personal translation system, without which he would have been unable to communicate with others.

"We also know something odd about him that flies in the face of this central fact: he admitted to a penchant for multilingual wordplay. When we met he regaled me with a secondary meaning of my name, *Cort*, and with additional interpretations of the names *Oscin* and *Skye*. He had additional information about the derivation of *Porrinyard*. In fact, he embraced his title, Khaajiir, a K'cenhowten construction, because of its coincidental similarities to his Bocaian name. We know he regaled Mr. Mendez with similar information. I'm sure he did the same to the rest of you. Am I correct?"

Paakth-Doy raised her hand. "When I served him on the way up, he told me about an extinct beast of burden known as the Paarkth by the ancient Riirgaans who domesticated it. Not quite my name, Paakth. But similar."

Jason said, "And he was fond of telling me stories about an ancient mythological hero with my name. An Earthman, known for journeying."

There was a hubbub. Colette had been told of another antiquated word, *coquette*. Jelaine had been apprised of certain words similar to Bettelhine among races I had never heard of. Oscin had been treated to a discourse on witty derivations of the planetary name Xana. I had known of none of these, but I wasn't surprised at all. They all fit the childlike delight the monolingual Khaajiir felt for the infinite possibilities of cross-cultural vocabulary.

I waited for the moment of mass discovery to die down, then said, "Off-the-cuff observations like these did a lot to further the man's erudite reputation, but a moment's consideration will confirm that *they likely had nothing to do with him*. He *cheated*."

Dejah got it first. "His staff."

"That's correct," I said. "He was able to use the databases of extinct and extant languages in its translation program and construct wordplay at a moment's notice.

"He fell into the habit because he enjoyed it, because it impressed people, and—in my case, and who knows how many others—because it aided small talk and helped to defuse hostile situations. Look at me. I hated him before he pulled that Cort/Court comparison. Afterward I wrote him off as chatty and harmless."

"Don't forget boring," Dina said. "And what does any of that have to do with anything?"

I nodded at Skye, who immediately turned around and crossed to the easy chair still bearing the Khaajiir's corpse. It was on a swivel, and as she turned it on its base many of those gathered here all gasped at the further deterioration of the corpse, which remained in the same essential position but had slumped still farther into the cushions as its internal structures drained away. As far as I could tell, he had been a friendly and well-meaning sentient, with animus toward none. But now he was just meat.

Neither Brown nor Wethers had made a sound. When I turned to them they were both stone-faced and waiting for the point.

"It's a hideous death," I said. "But not as painful a death as it appears. I've been told tonight that the Claw of God offers a small mercy all its own, in that it fries the pain receptors and thus leaves its victims largely unaware of the changes taking place inside them. The Khaajiir could have been sitting in this chair for several minutes, melting on the inside and growing steadily weaker as the hemorrhage continued. Because the seat cushion soaked up much of the blood, and the armrests prevented any from leaking out at his sides, the rest of us missed what was happening until it was too late. The Khaajiir, who felt no pain, almost missed it himself. But I noted this at the time. Skye?"

Skye raised the Khaajiir's left arm by the wrist, revealing a palm stained black with dried gore.

"And this."

She pointed to the tiny little bloodstain at the tip of the Khaajiir's nose.

"Now put him back the way we found him."

She placed his left hand back on the armrest, positioning the palm on the stain it had left. Oscin, who had the Khaajiir's staff, took it back to the chair and slipped it back where we had found it, resting across both armrests with his arms on top.

Dejah got it first. "Oh, Juje. He *knew*."

"That's right," I told the others. "The placement of the bloodstains leaves no room for doubt.

"Think back to the first few moments after the emergency stop. We're all running around dealing with our own concerns, including several serious injuries, in the immediate aftermath of the disaster. Jason and Jelaine escort the Khaajiir, the frailest and most vulnerable guest, to this chair, ascertaining that he's all right before abandoning him to deal with other pressing injuries. Several others among us, including Mr. Brown and Mr. Wethers, also stop by the Khaajiir's chair to check up on him. The application of the Claw of God may take place at any point during this interval. The Khaajiir may even feel a slight charge at the moment of contact, but he thinks nothing of it.

"Long minutes pass. The rest of us ignore the Khaajiir because we have other things to worry about. The Khaajiir starts feeling weak. But he's fragile and old and no doubt attributes what he's feeling to the shock he's experienced.

"But then something happens.

"Either because he feels the wetness pooling underneath him and suspects what has happened, or just from random happenstance, he drops his left hand to his side, into the blood pooling around him.

"Golly. What's this?

"He pulls his hand out of the muck and finds it covered with blood.

"He can't believe what he's seeing. He lifts his hand all the way to his nose, perhaps because he wants a closer look and perhaps because he's begun to identify the smell we've all sensed by this time as coming from him. The act leaves a tiny bloodstain on the tip of his nose.

"Remember again who he is. He's an expert on the K'cenhowten reign of terror. He knows that a Claw of God, a weapon from the society he wrote about, turned up in an attack on me earlier in the day. It must occur to him at once that yet another Claw of God has been used on him in the last few minutes. What's more, he remains coherent enough to backtrack and realize just which one of us did this terrible thing.

"But he's dying. He knows he's dying. He feels himself losing consciousness. He can barely hold his head up even now. He certainly can't raise his voice and shout out the name of the guilty party. And he may have only seconds to tell us what he knows.

"He can use his fingernails to scratch a message into the weave of the armrest.

"But time is fleeting. It will probably take more time and strength than he has to scratch out a complete word, especially if he uses the ornate Bocaian alphabet, which is likely the only written language he knows. Not that it matters. How can he have the time to scratch the complete name of a human being while using all those frills and flourishes?

"But he's fortunate, our ailing Khaajiir. Because he's clever and he has his staff, the tool that has allowed him such hearty play at the game of words. He has his right hand on the interface and barely has to stir at all to think the name of his murderer, hoping to be provided with a translation he can use.

"I don't know how many possibilities it gave him in the next second or two. From his ease at using the translation system to impress people, there may have been several, including a number that may have been too hard to transcribe.

"But he was provided with at least one he could use.

"And so his last act before he lost consciousness was to draw three crude zigzags, side by side."

The Porrinyards indicated the three claw marks the Khaajiir had made in his dying moments, miming the zigzag pattern with their hands.

I faced Brown and Wethers. "We know it was the last thing he did. As I noted at the time, one of the fibers he ripped from the armrest was still stuck under one of the fingernails he used."

Oscin pointed to the fingertip in question.

"He must have died seconds later," I said.

The Porrinyards left the corpse behind, with its bloody walking stick, and returned to their previous positions at either side of me, waiting.

Farley Pearlman was reaching into his jacket to scratch his ribs. "I don't get it."

"Don't feel too inadequate," I told him. "You wouldn't have had a clue unless you knew the specific language the Khaajiir was referencing. I had to consult the staff myself, to compare the many possible explanations for those three zigzags with their potential interpretations in other languages.

"I didn't get anywhere until after I realized that the message might have been meant for me, the one person here with a background in crime investigation . . . and remembered that when we'd spoken, he'd referenced an extinct human tongue known as English. Would it not make sense to concentrate on meanings I could access via that dialect?

"After that it was just a question of figuring out what he might have drawn that could have been as familiar to a Bocaian as it would be to any human being. And realizing that it was much more likely to be a natural phenomenon found all over the universe than any symbol restricted to our respective cultures."

"Just say it," Philip demanded.

I mimed the three jagged lines again. "Three lightning bolts."

I spoke a single word familiar to all of us in the common tongue Hom.Sap Mercantile.

Still, nobody got it.

I hadn't expected them to.

But now I faced the murderer and spoke its damning translation in English.

"Weathers."

We only thought we were prepared for what happened next.

But there were two more murders in the next six seconds . . .

18

BLOODBATH

Farley Pearlman had never struck me as a coiled spring.
Before I'd learned what he was he'd struck me as an amiable mediocrity, desperate for appreciation from the boss. Afterward he'd struck me as a self-pitying predatory coward, sick and evil but even more pathetic. He had always been among the possible accessories, but had never seemed a credible threat.

The Porrinyards, the Bettelhines, and I had expected the true threat to come from the stewards, who were so conditioned to obedience that they would have been the easiest to control.

That's the problem with being a creature of logic, like myself, or merchants of military hardware, like the Bettelhines. You think in straight lines.

You forget that targets of opportunity can be useful too.

You overlook that chaos for its own sake is a fine military objective.

So this is what happened.

One second.

Farley, who had been idly scratching his ribs with his left

hand, whipped it out and slammed a black disk into the base of Colette Wilson's neck.

She gasped, but not out of any special pain; the impact was not especially hard, and her reaction no more than the start anybody would have given after such an unexpected blow. By the time she looked down, still not comprehending what had been done to her, Farley had already leaped to his feet, the same Claw still in his hand as he tried to make me next.

Two seconds.

Several figures moved to intercept Farley, not just the Porrinyards but also Dejah and Brown and Mendez and Jeck.

Colette realized what she'd been hit with and took a deep breath to fuel what was about to become an ear-splitting scream.

Jeck reached Farley and grabbed him by the shoulders, pulling him back and away from me an instant before I would have been in range.

Three seconds.

Farley altered his swing and clapped the Claw of God against Jeck's chest instead.

Three sets of hands closed on Farley's left wrist, seizing control of that arm even as his right remained free and swinging. His first punch smashed Brown's nose.

Jason and Jelaine, moving as one, rounded the ends of the couch.

Six people screamed, all at the same moment. One was Colette, howling as she realized her life could now be measured in minutes. Another was Jeck, faster to the same realization. A third was Dina, who had risen to her feet and was, perhaps out of long habit, calling her nominal husband a bastard. Jason, Jelaine, and Paakth-Doy screamed my name because they were the only ones among us who saw that Farley had successfully distracted us all from what Vernon Wethers was doing.

Four seconds.

Brown crumpled.

I whirled just in time to see Wethers swinging the Khaajiir's staff like a club. Had I not moved at all, the blow might have crushed my skull. As it was I was not fast enough to avoid the impact. It may have been one of the two or three worst blows to the head I've ever taken. Something cracked in my jaw as I stumbled backward, blackness flickering at the edges of my vision.

Five seconds.

Wethers swung the Khaajiir's staff to keep Paakth-Doy at a distance. Doy stayed out of range but did not retreat, Jason and Jelaine just a step behind her. I shook my head to banish the looming threat of unconsciousness and stumbled toward them, tasting blood. Dina Pearlman was still calling her husband an asshole.

Six seconds.

Wethers succeeded in clipping Paakth-Doy's temple on his backswing, knocking her back against Jason and Jelaine. He spun on his heels and launched himself at the spiral staircase only ten paces away.

Time accelerated as I put everything I had into speed.

Wethers was not slowed down at the spiral staircase, as I'd hoped; instead he dropped the Khaajiir's staff down the center of the stairwell and took the stairs four at a time, descending all the way to the galley level in six easy leaps. I reached the top of the stairs just in time to look down and catch a glimpse of him retrieving the staff from where it landed.

He must have wanted it as more than just a cudgel. Now that he knew it contained the Khaajiir's files, he would see it as the data he'd need to undo everything Jason and Jelaine had done.

I tried to make my own descent as fast and as graceful as his and made it past the lower-suite deck without incident but then, handicapped by the dizziness left over from the blow I'd taken, hit one of the wedge-shaped descenders below that at the wrong angle. I tripped over my own stupid feet and took the rest of the distance at an ungainly head-over-heels tumble that I managed to deflect only when I grabbed for and lost the handrail. I don't know how I avoided breaking my neck, but I landed with my back on the galley deck and my legs flat against the ascending stairs, the least desirable position for anybody looking up to see Vernon Wethers about to drive a big stick into her neck.

Fuck that. I arched my back, brought my legs up and forward with all the strength in me, and struck some part of the bastard hard enough to knock him back. He hit a bulkhead with a grunted curse. I rolled again, stumbled, and managed to get up facing him just as he backed into the passageway leading to the galley and crew quarters.

The advantage was all his here. The passageway was narrow and there was no way to maneuver around him. He was able to land hits on my chest and my neck as I tried to seize the staff from his hands.

In a few seconds I heard pounding feet behind me, and Paakth-Doy crying, "We're here, Counselor!"

I found myself forced to back up a step to dodge a jab at my face. "What the hell took you so long?"

"We could only go single file," Paakth-Doy explained, "and I wasn't willing to hurl myself down the way you did. I took them only two at a time like a normal person."

"Wonderful," I muttered, as another jab struck home.

I heard more pounding feet and the shared voices of Jason and Jelaine. "Vernon! Stop this at once! This is an Inner Family order!"

Wethers didn't drop the staff, but he did weep, his expression contorting in ways that suggested violent inner forces tearing him apart. "I can't! Everything I've done, I've done for the Inner Family's good!"

Still behind me, Jason said, "Vernon. You've endangered three members of the family. You've killed one personal guest and attacked an honored one. You've sabotaged our infrastructure and subverted our military. You've interfered with policy decisions well above even your pay grade. The Inner Family is very angry with you. The Inner Family orders you to put that thing down and tell us everything we need to do to restore contact with the outside world."

Another jab from Wethers. "I'm sorry, sir. I can't. Not if it means letting you destroy everything your great family has ever stood for. Not when it's my duty to stop you."

Jelaine, now: "Our family stands for a lot of things, not all of them good. Just look what we've done to you, or Colette, or any of those others. You might have had a life once. We took that away."

Wethers backed up another step. "I have a life. Protecting the corporation."

"You're not protecting anything," Jason said. "Don't you see, the company can't go on forever if its only business is poisoning the well it drinks from? Maybe not in your lifetime, or even mine, but someday the human race is going to realize it has cancer and do whatever it needs to do to save itself. We need to be more than the tumor that has to be removed. We need to change, whatever it costs."

Did Wethers seem to be weakening? "Not the way you've done it."

Now Jelaine, again: "Do you think it's going to get easier, Vernon? If you think we've had to make some moral compromises now, you won't believe how much this surgery is likely to cost a century or two in the future. By then it may really require the destruction of the Family to save the rest of humanity. Do you really want that on your shoulders? Or do you want to save the Bettelhines while there are still Bettelhines left to save?"

More running footsteps behind me. Philip and Dejah

shouting. Wethers glanced over my shoulder, a critical loss of focus that gave me the chance to seize the end of the staff closest to me and drive his end into his chest. Do to him what he'd been doing to me. He tried to wrestle me for control, but I was able to add my weight to his thrust and drive the staff against a wall.

Paakth-Doy seized our end and wrested it from his hands.

Wethers ran.

The skinny little bastard knew how to accelerate from a dead stop. By the time any of us were able to react, he was already five paces ahead and diving into the next compartment.

He slammed the blowout switch on the other side of the hatchway before I was halfway to him. An ear-piercing shriek sliced the air, providing the standard one-second warning of airtight compartments about to shut. A gleaming metal door imprinted with the goddamned useless Bettelhine Family crest emerged from its housing in the wall and began to slide sideways across its track, cutting us off from the figure even now increasing the distance between us.

One second too late and that door would cut me in half, but I didn't have time to think about it and there were voices behind me screaming go-go-go and then all of a sudden changing that scream to no-no-no when it looked like I wasn't going to make it. I had to slip through the door sideways, managing to pull my right foot through just before the advancing door would have amputated it. My available view of the compartment behind me was just a sliver by then, and I had less than a heartbeat left to see who I'd left there, but I caught glimpses of Jason, Jelaine, Paakth-Doy, and—a new arrival—Dejah, all arriving at this barrier too late to follow me.

I turned my back on them and ran, past the crew quarters, past two more airtight doors Wethers was either too confident or too much in a hurry to activate, all the way to the spiral staircase descending to the cargo bay. I reached it just in time to see the top of his head disappearing below deck level. I didn't bother to take the stairs but instead vaulted over the railing at a trajectory that had me landing feet-first on his shoulders. This move sounds a hell of a lot more impressive than it was. Wethers grunted, slammed against the curved rail, and somehow avoided falling. I slid against the central pillar and then tumbled against his legs, sweeping them out from under him and dropping us both onto our sides in a kicking screaming flailing tangle of limbs. I kicked off a higher step and drove my knee into his crotch. He turned his hands into claws and went for my eyes. I found one of his fingers and bit down hard, drawing blood and a scream, prepared to keep grinding until I severed the digit at the bone.

But the major problem with clamping down on somebody's finger in a free-for-all like this is that while you have their finger, they have your head.

He put all his strength into driving the back of my head into the steps. I gasped, releasing him. He shifted his bloody hands and went for my eyes with his thumbs. I seized his wrists and drove my aching head forward, crushing his nose with my forehead. He recoiled, overbalanced, and tumbled to the base of the stairs.

It would have been so easy to just give up and let unconsciousness take me then.

Instead I grabbed the railing and pulled myself to my feet, managing to stand just as Vernon Wethers did the same on the deck below.

For a long shaky moment we just stared at each other, breathing hard.

Then he straightened. He was no longer the hysteric he'd been when he had to face the Bettelhines with the fact of his own betrayal, but just another resigned functionary, facing an outsider who did not matter to him at all.

"You've lost," I told him.

He shook his head. "No, I haven't."

"You have. It won't take long for the others to get past the door. They'll be just a few minutes behind me. All I have to do is keep you busy until they get here."

He shook his head again. "That won't be enough."

"Why? What have you won? The murder of one harmless academic and two service workers?"

He seemed hurt by that. "You think I feel good about that? But J-J-Jason was more right than he knew when he said that this was about cancer. Only they're the c-cancer, the pair of them. And cutting out cancer sometimes means cutting out the healthy tissue around it."

"Like Philip," I said.

"He wasn't supposed to be here, but he's expendable. The Family can survive losing him, as long as I can n-neutralize them. If it's the only way the Bettelhines can recover from the things they've done."

I descended a step. "It's not up to you."

He reached inside his jacket with a certainty of purpose that halted me in midstep. "Oh, it's up to me, all right. It's my duty."

I imagined him pulling out another Claw and slamming it against my back or chest. I pictured the gentle, painless interval that would follow, rendered torture only by my own awareness of the changes taking place inside me. I've had to charge knives, clubs, energy weapons, and even explosives at various times in my eventful life, but I wasn't sure I had whatever it took to face that.

"At least tell me if I was right, about where you got the Claws."

He seemed amused by that. "Do you care?"

"I need to know whether I was right."

"We had about fifty working models gathering dust on a shelf in one of our outer system factories. I've spent the last few months secreting about a dozen of them in various hiding places around the carriage and a few more around Xana, in case I had to take action planetside. Even a few other weapons, like that Fire Snake. But the carriage was always plan number one. It was the best place to isolate," his voice caught again, "J-J-Juh-Jason and J-Jelaine, and the c-corrupt influences they were determined to bring to Xana, from all outside rescuers."

"Corrupt influences that included the Khaajiir, and Dejah, and me."

"There was no way of knowing who was corrupt and who was not. But I had to know what Jason and Jelaine were doing. It was my *duty*. All you accomplished, by asking all those questions, was to do my job for me."

I descended another step. "Then why stop my interrogation of Philip? Why activate that Fire Snake?"

He backed up again, not so much a coiled predator prepared to strike as trapped prey prepared to kill to defend itself. "I stopped your interrogation of Philip because there are things about the Bettelhine power structure that are none of your business."

"Things like Dina Pearlman's internal governor program?"

He looked stricken.

"You made Philip leave the room as soon as I pressed the issue. You threatened me with the wrath of the Bettelhine Corporation."

"That was my *duty*!"

"And was it also your duty to activate the Fire Snake, you son of a bitch?"

I went after him, watching the hand inside his jacket, ready to run like hell if it emerged with anything in it. There was no telling what a conspirator inside the Bettelhine Corporation, one capable of getting his hands on a Claw of God and a Fire Snake, could have been holding. He surprised me by producing nothing more virulent than a fist, swinging wide, aiming for the side of my face with a strength that could have put me down.

It never struck me. I recoiled, seeing the swing as a flesh-colored blur centimeters before my eyes.

His hand went back inside his jacket.

Maybe he did have something in there. Something so awful that the thought of using it gave even him pause.

We circled each other, the industrial floor of the loading dock reduced to arena.

He babbled. "It wouldn't have killed me—or you, for that matter. It was, like you said, a distraction. An extra variable, to make you look at anybody *other* than me. Something to keep you asking the questions I would have asked myself if I could."

"How did you hide it from our search?"

"Are you kidding? You'd be surprised how many weapons I was able to get aboard, with the stewards ordered not to question me. I've been bringing them aboard and hiding them, in one alcove or another, for months. *Including* in this room . . ."

He faked left, then went right, launching himself at an equipment array behind the stairwell. I might have been in serious trouble had I gone for his feint; when you're dealing with an amateur, as Wethers was, there's little possibility of being fooled by such a move as long as you dismiss the body and take all your cues from the eyes.

We launched at the same time, both leaping for distance and both meeting in midair. The shared momentum did nothing for our aerodynamics. We hit far short of his intended destination, landing in a clump, kicking and snapping at each other like a pair of wild animals intent on ripping out each others' throats.

He had the advantage in weight and madness; I had the advantage of a little girl who'd survived the massacre on Bocai.

He went for my throat.

I closed my teeth on his nose and bit down until my mouth filled with blood.

He screamed, released my throat, and went for my forehead, pushing my face away with both hands, a tactic that succeeded in gaining a little distance but did not quite manage to make me let go. A little twist and my teeth met something warm and bloody in my mouth. He rolled away, his scream wet, his hands clasped over a face turned to a fountain that gushed red between his fingers.

He called me a bish.

I coughed, spat out something pale, found myself snarling through teeth turned to fangs. I was going to go for him again but he was standing and I was not, and though he'd been gravely wounded he was still focused enough to see me as the threat I was, and kicked me hard enough to drive me to the floor gasping.

I curled into a ball, and while I had an advantage over many human beings in that I would not have remained in that position long enough for the pain to go away, that advantage was erased to zero as he staggered over and kicked me again and again and again, not cursing as I would have expected but weeping and sobbing, which was worse. I moaned and damned the reflex that curled me further into a ball, trying to become the black hole all victims try to become when they attempt to shrink themselves too small to be noticed by the people hurting them. I know from experience that it's not a tactic that works, and have trained myself against using it, but there's a difference between knowing that and being able to defy what your body wants you to do at any given moment, and right now my body, my stupid stubborn body, just wanted to be smaller, even as I tried to scream my way past that suicidal instinct.

Wethers hauled off and kicked me again, then circled the room, not just once but twice, snorking blood through his ruined nose as he worked up enough hate and resentment to kick me some more.

He might have managed it if I hadn't realized something as he came circling back for his second go. The reason he'd needed to circle the room twice.

This isn't him.

This is not the kind of man he should have been.

These are not the kind of things he would have done.

This is what they made him.

What they left him.

When his foot came at me again I was able to reach out with both hands and grab it, heel and toe. The impact hurt my hands as much as I care for any part of me to be hurt, but threw him off balance and left him teetering with a look that was like a gene splice between dismay and amazement.

I twisted his foot.

He hit the ground hard. I grabbed for him, but he speed-crawled out of reach.

This time the race between which one of us got up first was a slow and agonizing one. I could not quite manage to stand up straight. He did, but could barely breathe, choking from the blood bubbling at the ruins of his nose. We stared at each other from two meters apart, wary, gasping, knowing that another round was inevitable but not yet in any shape to start.

There was an odd species of amazement in his eyes. "I've . . . been stupid."

"Why?"

"Didn't see what was in front of me. Didn't see what I should have *known*."

I had no idea what he was talking about, and I didn't have the breath to waste on it. "What are you going to do?"

He gasped another four or five or six times before spitting blood and then, oddly enough, smiling through bloody teeth. "I don't . . . need to do anything, Counselor. It would have been nice to live through this and get out of here with some evidence to show the uncompromised members of the Inner Family at an inquest, but I always knew that death was the most likely outcome. As it happens . . . I've established influence over key people in both command and intelligence, and they're all under orders not to interfere with our situation unless they receive a shutdown signal from me. If they don't get that within less time than you want to know, they'll assume the situation an impasse and blow up the carriage, assuring the Inner Family th-that it was the only way to stop terrorists trying to smuggle a dangerous bioweapon into the ecosphere." It was getting more and more difficult for him to speak as he discussed defying or planning the death of Bettelhines. "Everybody on Xana will be sad that three B-B-Bettelhines and their guests died, b-but the Inner Family and the c-c-corporation are both strong enough to survive it. It will have to be. The only other choice is letting J-J-Jason and J-Jelaine keep on doing what they've been doing, and I can't allow that."

I held out my hands, in a hopeless attempt to placate him. "It's not the only choice."

"I know. You think you can bring me back to Ph-Philip, or to J-J-J-Juh-Jason and J-Juh-Juh-Juh-Jelaine. You th-think my internal g-g-governors won't allow me to r-r-res . . . to r-resist their strongest d-direct orders long enough to let the inevitable happen. And you're right about that, even if the clock is ticking faster than you think. So I have to take the choice out of my own hands. I have to s-shhh-shut myself down, so the forces out there can do what they need to do, to save the F-F-F-FFF-Fuh-Family from the traitors among them."

His eyes flashed with sudden white light.

I screamed and launched myself at him, but he was already falling, his limbs turned boneless beneath him as he performed a little half-spin and tumbled to the deck. The most I accomplished when I rushed to him was prevent him from smashing his head open on impact. When I turned him over his eyes were like marbles, his mind lost in whatever fractal image the teem emitters had used to overload him.

I hoped the image was fucking unpleasant, whatever it was. But this was my own fault for hesitating. I'd held back, thinking the object under his jacket was another Claw of God, and not just a trigger for the teemers under his eyelids. He'd survive if the rest of us survived, but now he wouldn't be able to answer questions for days. By then, the destruction he'd arranged for us would have come and gone, and we'd be atoms and other debris tumbling through space.

What had he said?

" *'Within less time than you want to know.'* "

Time enough to free everybody else, and begin another round of debates over our next move? Or less? Minutes? Seconds? Was somebody's finger already pulling a trigger?

To hell with that.

I hate vacuum. I hate heights. I hate free-fall. I hate space-suits.

I'd completed a grand total of three orbital EVAs in my entire life, and then only as part of safety drills required to maintain my Dip Corps certification. They're not memories that keep me warm. People tell me that the trainer who tested me on those occasions still dines out about the comical, quivering wreck I'd been. I could counter that I wasn't quite enough of a quivering wreck to accept the specific kind of comfort he wanted to offer, but that's just a footnote. The stories aren't exaggerated. I had indeed been hopeless.

The Bettelhine gear I'd seen Arturo Mendez wear was a different configuration than Dip Corps standard, giving me a few bad moments as I found I couldn't do whatever I needed to do in order to make the collar seal engage. On my fourth try it clicked, and the permaplastic knit. Good thing, too, because it demonstrated that I'd also failed to engage the most important of the connections at my wrists and ankles and gave me the clue I needed to start all over again and give myself a proper seal so I might be able to survive.

I still wasn't sure I'd done it right, and tried to tell myself that it would be best to go back and fetch one of the others, somebody who knew how to do this. But then I'd have to ask them to take the measures I was afraid I'd have to take, and I couldn't ask that of anybody, especially since it would have probably ended up being a Porrinyard taking that final step instead of me.

I might have fucked up a good thing with them. I wasn't sure. But if I had I did not have the right to ask either one of them to die for me.

I got everything I needed, entered the air lock, cycled to vacuum, and stood there expecting to die as I waited for the exterior door to open. The instant it did I regretted being where I was. The interior of the Royal Carriage might have been equipped with its own specific gravity, but that turned off inside the air lock the instant the chamber was exposed to vacuum. It was a spontaneous change, announcing itself as a sudden lurch in my belly just as sudden vertigo as my inner ear switched its sense of up and down to undecided.

I hated this. I hated this. I hated this.

Inching along the handholds that lined the air lock interior, I pulled myself out the hatchway and groped around until I found the access ladder leading up to the elevator roof. I didn't need my legs to climb, of course. They trailed behind me like useless growths, every random twitch encouraging the tendency to swing outward and leave me hanging at a right angle to the elevator's hull. Mendez had made this look easy; I was a clumsy amateur and my various attempts at overcompensation kept me slamming against the hull or hanging perpendicular again. If all the armed forces arrayed around us were monitoring my progress, they had to be laughing their asses off.

Midgard, the continent that housed Anchor Point, was a brilliant green landscape shining up at me, the cable itself receding into invisibility long before it plunged into a canopy of clouds. I didn't want to know how many thousands of kilometers still separated me from the atmosphere, let alone the ground I'd never reach even if my body drifted long enough to begin reentry. So naturally I dwelled on it and found part of my mind doing the math. My breath, inside the echochamber helmet, began to take on the sound of panting.

I didn't climb all the way to the roof, just far enough to twist the air lock and twist the exterior toggle forcing the hatch to slide shut. It might save the others a few seconds, if they had to evacuate.

Then I performed the series of clumsy, amateur shifts necessary to turn myself around so I could hang on the ladder with my back to the carriage and face the constellation of Bettelhine forces surrounding us.

They all had to be watching me. They all had to be wondering what I was doing.

Wethers's instructions had eliminated any chance of them coming to rescue us.

So I had to go to them.

The only problem with that, aside from the strong possibility that somebody would see fit to blast me out of the sky, was that I had no attitude jets, no means of propulsion, no way of braking or altering my course once I performed this all-or-nothing leap. There might have been something for that purpose aboard the carriage, but I didn't know where it was kept and would have been useless at operating it anyway. The time constraints reduced me to basics.

So I pressed the soles of my boots against the carriage hull, told myself that I was, by Juje, going to do this in the next five seconds—one, two, three, four, five—somehow found myself still hanging on, called myself a coward, and counted one, two, three, four, five again.

Kick!

I don't know how quickly I left the carriage behind, but it wasn't fast. The cruisers and skimmers and fighters and battalions still remained ahead of me, watching my approach with a stolid, uncaring silence. The lights of their occasional course corrections flashed like reflected sunlight on a rippled sea. Three or four of the space-suited figures ahead of me burned brighter and longer, moving to new positions: not to intercept me, I saw, but to stay out of my way. As long as I didn't fire at them or go for a weapon they'd just let me drift by on a course that would keep me going long after my air ran out.

I flipped the transmit toggle on the suit hytex connection. "Please! This is Counselor Andrea Cort of the Confederate Diplomatic Corps! I am drifting and in desperate need of assistance! Please help me!"

No answer.

Either Wethers had been thorough enough to disable to suit's communications, or the forces he'd corrupted were sticking by their instructions to stand down.

I tried again. "Please! This is Counselor Andrea Cort! I'm an honored guest of Hans Bettelhine! You are to give me the rank of Inner Family member for as long as I remain within your space! I'm ordering you to rescue me!"

Again, nothing.

I must have been less than thirty meters from the nearest Bettelhine soldiers, all of whom were turning to follow my progress, but otherwise remained impassive and unmoving as I drifted toward the hole in their ranks.

Seconds left before I passed them.

Shit. I'd really hoped I wouldn't have to do this next part.

I reached for the hook, midway up my right arm, where I'd clipped a certain artifact I'd been carrying since my arrival at Layabout. Disguised as one of the ornaments on my black suit, It was instead one of the many small items of contraband I made a habit of carrying with me whenever away from New London. But it wasn't exactly high-tech. Had I left this in my suite and been unable to get to it from the cargo bay, the chamber had contained any number of other tools that would have done just as well.

All I really needed in this situation was a sufficiently sharp object.

And I'd already tested this one, a Dip Corps insignia capable of extruding a four-centimeter cutting edge, on one of the spare suits in the cargo bay, so I knew it would work.

I removed it from its hook, popped the blade, and in a single determined jab, punched a hole through my suit.

Actually, it was not just my suit. I got some flesh as well. The air venting through the puncture was not only glistening with clear ice crystals born of my own respiration, but with red ice crystals as well. I yelled as loud as I could, which turned out to be not very loud, and felt something tugging at the air leaving my mouth.

Is this what you want, you bastards? Is it?

The soldiers were turning, but still not coming for me.

I stabbed myself again. This one made me convulse. Something slammed into my back; the figures around me became a blur, but not a blur I could see, because there was something wrong with my eyes and then with my brain and then with the taste of blood in my mouth and then *what a goddamn stupid way to die* and then something exploding inside my chest and then

19

XANA

Nothing seemed to happen after that, not for a long time; nothing except for me replaying those moments and remembering how and where but not why I'd died.

Even when things started happening, they didn't amount to much.

I drifted in and out of consciousness for a while.

At one point I found myself floating, fetuslike, in a chamber filled with golden fluid. The walls were both curved and transparent, and the shapes moving in the drier chamber beyond were all distorted funhouse figures, their faces stretched into cylinders with only distant resemblance to the people I had known. One pressed a palm against the wall separating us and mouthed something. I considered reaching out to place my own hand against the other side, but could not seem to translate the impulse into action, and soon lost all interest. After a few seconds I closed my eyes and went back to sleep.

With little transition I found myself in another flotation chamber, in this case the blue nothingness of the AIsource virtual interface. I was annoyed. I didn't want to be bothered by their shit right now. But the avatar just studied me and spoke a single sentence, one I was in no mood to register, much less heed. ***It's not over, Counselor.***

In between flashes of being wheeled somewhere on a gurney and lying on a bed with each of my hands being held and massaged by a watchful Porrinyard, I dreamed of my childhood on Bocai. I'd had such dreams before, of course, but most of them, too many of them, had been traumatic flashbacks to the night of the massacre. I was well used to sitting upright in cold sweats, still seeing images of bloodlust and loss. Less often I returned to the moments I remembered now: the idyll before the tragedy, the sunny skies, the laughing faces, the love of both my human and Bocaian families. In this particular flash I must have been about three or four years old. My mother and I were together in a park I remembered well, playing a lazy game with a ball at the end of a string and rules that I made up as I went along. I tripped over something and went down hard, exploding with sobs at the typical childhood inability to absorb the pain and shock adults deal with every day. My mother picked me up and told me it was okay, that I'd be all right, that she'd take care of the owie when we got home. She was bright-eyed and sympathetic, strong and wise—she knew the wound was really nothing, and knew the crisis needed to be felt in order to pass. As the dream, or memory, ended, Bocai's sun glistened on her dark hair and I reached out, in innocent fascination, to touch it.

The blue room again.
   Andrea Cort: You are not yet out of danger.
   I thought you said you wouldn't help me. That it was against your precious rules of engagement.
   We've helped you more than you can know, Counselor. We are helping you now. The Bettelhines are using their local franchise of our medical enterprise to treat you.

AIsource Medical. This marked another time I owed them. *What's wrong with me?*

You were exposed to pure vacuum for just under a minute. There was extensive damage to your lungs, your trachea, your nasal passages, your throat, and your eyes. You also suffered a number of disfiguring burst blood vessels on your chest and shoulders, and a significant cerebral event in your brain. You were, for several subsequent minutes, dead.

Oh, Juje. *Am I going to be all right?*

You would have not survived, at least not as a functional human being, had the Bettelhine medics not recognized the limitations of their capacities on site and sealed you in cryofoam for delivery to our emergency facility at Anchor Point. You should not worry. Your current confused state, which will be marked by periods of apathy, delirium, and malfunctioning short-term memory, is an expected condition of your recovery and should pass within the next forty-eight hours.

Swell. *What about the others?*

As you surmised when you took such a desperate measure, the immediate medical emergency involving an honored guest proved more pressing than the prior commands given by Vernon Wethers. Their conditioning overriden by the need to rescue you, the Bettelhine security forces were able to board the Royal Carriage and rescue the surviving passengers.

Surviving?

Alas, several casualties have been reported, among them Mr. Jeck, Ms. Wilson, Mr. Pearlman, and the Khaajiir. Xana's mass media has reported that they were all killed at the moment of the violent emergency stop. None of the others saw any point in disputing the accuracy of this account.

I bristled at that, but then remembered what I'd told Philip at the onset of my investigation. This was not my jurisdiction. On the Royal Carriage I could overpower a few self-important Bettelhines by sheer force of personality; on a planet with a bureaucracy comprising thousands, I was so far beyond overpowered that it was wiser to recognize the value of walking away from a battle I couldn't win. *What else?*

All the surviving Bettelhine employees have gone back to work. Dejah Shapiro has been visiting you regularly in between stops on her grand tour of Asgard in the company of Hans Bettelhine, Vernon Wethers, and the two Bocaian assassins who went after you on Layabout, and who have emerged from their catatonia and are now being questioned at length. Mr. Wethers, in particular, has been more helpful than he might have wanted to be, and has given up many of the names he's compromised.

And?

The two Bocaian assassins have confirmed that Dejah Shapiro was indeed their main target on Layabout and that they did in fact lose interest in her when they spotted you. They've identified the third assassin in their team, their contact on the Bursteeni liner known as the **Grace**, *as a Bursteeni named Neki Rom, who made it as far as Anchor Point but has been taken into custody. Rom has confessed to passing the second Claw of God to Arturo Mendez, who under strict orders passed it to Wethers on the Royal Carriage. There were no other weapons in Rom's possession when he was captured. If you were correct about the Layabout team possessing three Claws of God, he has already managed to discard the third one or pass it on to yet another Confederate. But there have been many subsequent arrests, and it is considered just a matter of time before the rest of the conspirators are captured and the Bettelhines no longer require the increased security measures in effect at this time.*

None of which should have had anything to do with me, now that I was out of it. *Why would you say I'm not out of danger?*

Just that. For as long as you remain here, you must not allow yourself the luxury of complacency. Even now, forces rally against you.

Why, dammit?

It is as we have said. You are not yet out of danger of assassination. And you are still facing the moment that will determine the shape the future takes. It is coming. Be ready.

Not long afterward I received a visit from the other side.

((Andrea Cort * Do you know who we are?))

It appeared inside my head, but it was not the voice of the AIsource. It was another, even less comfortable presence, one I'd only endured once before.

The Unseen Demons.

Get out of my head, you murderous bastards.

((Your curses fail to shame us * we have explained before that everything we've done, we've done out of self-preservation * if it meant the deaths of your fellow humans on Bocai, they are neither the first or the last to be sacrificed for our survival * if it is murder, it is murder in the cause of preventing a greater crime, the destruction of a race that wants to survive))

You're still not welcome in my head, you pieces of shit.

((Nor are we comfortable in a place so driven by pain * we visit now only because it is the only chance we have * the Rules of Engagement forbid us from telling you what to do * but you are not long from deciding the future of a species that never did you any harm, as well as the future of your own * you must know that the lies told by your AIsource masters dwarve any you've been told by us * your mistake, if you make one, will be tragic))

Go to hell, I thought again. *I don't care what your excuses are. You killed my family. You made me a monster. I'll see you dead.*

They remained silent, though present, for what felt like several minutes.

And then they departed, with a gentle: ((**Someday you'll know you were wrong**))

More periods of waking.

One of the first visits I managed to understand took place sometime at night. The lights were dim and the sky I could see through a wall-length window to my right was black, dotted with stars. It was good to be awake at a time like that. The darkness soothed my eyes and made everything seem less frantic.

Dejah Shapiro sat beside my bed, clad in a shiny red gown designed to hug her perfect figure, its surface rippling in a manner that to my eyes resembled the wave motion on a small body of water. She wore baubles I would have called earrings had they depended on her ears for support; instead, they seemed to float unsupported beside her lobes. I realized that she'd just left another formal gathering of some kind, and in my semiconscious stupidity hoped that nobody had been murdered during it. I wasn't up to solving the crime.

She'd been talking for a while, but I didn't focus until she whispered, "Well, I now know what Hans Bettelhine wants from me."

"What?"

She lowered her painted lips closer to my ear. "A merger. As I told you on the Royal Carriage, he's scaling down the munitions business. He wants to retool and go into my line, habitat construction, with a specific focus on investing in and reclaiming shattered ecosystems, whether natural and manmade. Places like this world, Deriflys, that Jason lived on for a while. His proposals are sheer genius. There'd be a sharp loss at the beginning, but in a few years of working together we'd accomplish a great deal for humanity without any damage to our existing profit margins. We'd even make a little bit more. It would work, Andrea. It would."

I tried to muster enthusiasm and failed. "What did you tell him?"

She took my hand and squeezed, the gesture friendly on the surface but painful in execution as she made sure to press the night's long painted fingernails into the back of my hand. I winced and opened my mouth to protest, but she silenced me with a look, and spoke with a burning urgency greater than any I'd ever heard from her. "I said I'd bring the figures home to my people and get back to him with my decision. But that's just an excuse to get the hell out of here as fast as I can. It'll be great if he pushes through the change, and if he does I'll do anything I can to help him. It'll be the best news the poor human race has had for a long time. But these are the Bettelhines we're talking about, Andrea. That sharp loss for the first few years won't go over well with some parties. There's going to be more blowback, and the rest of us all need to be out of range when it happens."

She released my hand. I pulled it away from her and started massaging it with the other, as resentful as any child for the unwanted momentary pain. I was so groggy that I was more concerned about the pain at that moment than about anything she'd said.

She once again lowered her lips to my ear and murmured: "I'd take you with me if I could. I stayed this long, longer than was wise, just to warn you. I'd stay still longer if I didn't think these people needed somebody to oppose them if the worst happens. But you need to get well as soon as you can. Prepare yourself. And don't forget what the Porrinyards kept saying before they left. *Remember who you are.*"

* * *

But for a while the most I absorbed from that was: *the Porrinyards left?*

Part of me refused to believe it. I couldn't countenance any condition where they'd ever hate me enough to abandon me to enemies. I could imagine them getting so sick of me that they sought more congenial fields elsewhere. Part of me had expected it for a long time, and remained astonished that they'd lasted this long But leave me? Helpless and injured and not at my best, among people who might want to hurt me? Why would they ever do that? What would ever make them want to do that?

I remembered every argument we'd ever had, every moment I'd betrayed my own cruelty and selfishness in their presence. None seemed bad enough to make them want to do this. None.

Remember who you are.

I remembered who I was. I was the little girl caught up in the madness of a community devouring itself in a spasm of horrific self-cannibalization, who went after the Bocaian she considered a second father and tore out his eyes. I was a war criminal considered the face of evil on Xana, a symbol of Mankind's capacity for violence to a dozen other races, and a political liability to the Confederacy. I was a caustic bitch who had never loved anybody as an adult, not until the moment they came along, and even then not well.

Remember who you are?

I remembered who they were. And that remained, by far, the more pressing question. If it came down to life or death, they would not have abandoned anybody, not even the likes of Dina Pearlman. What could I have done, to make them hate me so much that they'd abandon me?

I slept some more, woke again in light, accepted more visitors, including a number who I'd never met but who seemed fascinated by my very existence.

I began to register the details of my room, by far the most luxurious hospital facility I had ever seen. It occurred to me, after a while, that it might not have been a hospital at all. The walls were like spun gold, the ceiling an arched vault bearing a chandelier of jeweled crystal. A portrait of some past Bettelhine patriarch, complete with ridiculous mustache and an expression that suggested he'd smelled something awful in his immediate vicinity, hung on one nearby wall, in a frame with a sufficient number of cornices and rills to support a courthouse. The freestanding wardrobe, polished to a high sheen, looked like it had cost more when new than I ever could have expected to earn in a year as representative to the Judge Advocate. The wall-length window I'd spotted off to my right was actually a wall-length sliding door, open to a vast balcony and a sky so bright and blue that it hurt my poor, suffering eyes to look upon it. I heard birdsong: not random tweets, but complex symphonies, from species accomplished for the breadth and depth of their compositions.

Every surface in sight was covered with flowers: a riotous rainbow of them, arranged in bouquets so rich in color and variety that they must have required thousands of man-hours just to cultivate, let alone arrange.

I remember thinking, *This isn't right*. And then I drifted away again.

I received another visitor, Paakth-Doy, dressed in a sunny blouse that left her arms bare and revealed the recombinant tattoo of some kind of reptilian cat prowling up and down her arm in an animated simulation of ravenous hunger. She told me that I'd given everybody a tremendous scare, also that she considered me one of the bravest people she'd ever known. She said that she would always remember me and let me know that she'd brought me a message from my Dip. Corps superior Artis Bringen, which had been forwarded to the Royal Carriage and gone unnoticed until the vehicle was brought back down to Xana for inspection. She'd uploaded the data to this room's hytex connection.

Our conversation was pleasant enough until I asked her what she was going to do.

Her eyes went dark, and she said, "We have all received a great deal of attention since the disaster. It has resulted in lucrative job offers. I myself have been given the opportunity to become a personal companion to one of the Bettelhine aunts. She likes my exotic accent, you see."

Oh, Juje. They'd gotten to her. Somehow they'd gotten to her and made her want to give up everything she was. I seized her by the wrist. "Doy—you don't have to do that. I've promised to take you away. There are always positions available in the Dip Corps . . ."

She pulled her hand away. When she answered me, her heavy Riirgaan accent was so pronounced it was as if she'd decided to embrace it, eschewing the part of her that identified with the species of her birth. "This is my idea, Counselor. I know what 'personal companion' is likely to mean. I know how the job will change who I am. I have, after all, worked with Colette Wilson. And while I make this decision I am in full command of my will."

"Then why—"

"Because to me it will not matter. Because I am not Riirgaan nor fully human and I am tired of not knowing how to live. And because I have been assured by my new employer that when the changes take effect I will always be happy, even if made to commit acts that would revolt me now." She wiped moisture away from her eyes, and forced another counterfeit smile. "How can anybody ever say no to happiness, Counselor? How is it less real if it is imposed?"

By the time I thought of anything I could say to that, Paakth-Doy was gone.

* * *

A nurse came in and gave me a breakfast of mashed fruit, unfamiliar to my palate but sweet in a way that reminded me of the candies I'd loved from a confectionary back on New London. It was tart enough to sting my raw tissues, but for the first time since the Royal Carriage I found myself ravenous. I ate the entire bowl and asked for a second serving.

After I ate I accessed the room's hytex and found the message from Bringen. It was a late delivery of the answers to the questions I'd sent him before boarding the Royal Carriage. Most of what I'd asked him had either come up in the subsequent investigation or no longer mattered, but I paused when I passed a section with information about the missing debt arbitrator, Bard Daiken.

"Daiken defected to the Bettelhine Corporation during a routine arbitration, abandoning a wife and two children on New London. He's since refused all communication, and we don't know where he's working on Xana or even if he's still on-world. This should be considered low priority, but if you've run into him, please forward any information you have. His family might find closure a great comfort. Holo enclosed."

I opened the holo and knew where I'd seen Daiken. He'd been living a content if quiet existence, warming up food in the galley of the Bettelhine Royal Carriage.

His name at the time had been Loyal Jeck.

What a joke. *Loyal.*

The Bettelhine he'd offended must have been having a great time at his expense.

I awoke again to find my bladder full and the ceiling striped with lengthening shadows. I sat up, fought off a wave of dizziness that almost made me want to lie down again, winced even after it cleared from the sensation of a peculiar heaviness to my head, and swung my legs (clad, I noticed now, in silky pink pajamas just loose enough to caress the skin with every move I made), over the side of the bed. The tile floor felt warm, in a manner that suggested subsurface heating elements. But the texture of the lining was just sensual enough to make me appreciate the decadence anyway.

The lights came on the instant I carried my own weight. However long I'd been drifting in and out, there had not been any extensive muscular atrophy. Still, just to be sure, I closed my eyes and spun en pointe, just once, to make sure I still had some coordination. I did. That was good. If I had to fight for my life anytime soon, I wouldn't be stumbling around like a drunk.

My head felt heavier than it should have been. I didn't realize why until soft hair longer than mine was supposed to be brushed both sides of my face. It was shoulder-length now, and fuller than it had ever been. *What the hell?*

The bathroom was a few steps away, complete with a sunken tub bigger than some swimming pools I'd known and a gold-trimmed vanity surrounded by a selection of creams, perfumes, lotions, and topical euphorics even more extensive than the one that had so impressed the Porrinyards in our suite on the Royal Carriage. I was more bothered by what I saw in the mirror at their center, but waited until I could find the solid gold toilet and achieve blessed release before returning to lower myself into the plush chair at the vanity and stare, with a mixture of horror and wonder, at the stranger gaping back at me.

The face was still mine, even if the complexion was milkier than it had been even in a while; I'd always retained a light tan with minimal exposure to UV, even in environments limited to artificial light. I supposed I could have lost a little color during my time in recovery. But the hair was a revolution. The tint was closer to dark brown than to my habitual jet-black; and my usual close-cropped style, chosen for practicality, and providing the only concession to personality with one errant lock that I allowed to grow longer, was now rich and silky and tickling my shoulders on both sides. Shiny bangs descended to eyebrow altitude. The unknown cosmetician had also applied a touch of eyeliner: not much, just enough to add to my own growing alarm.

All my adult life I'd been surprised when people called me beautiful. I'd never seen it before, and had to admit it now. They'd made me a stunner. But this was not a look I'd ever sought for myself. It made me look soft, feminine in a manner that had never been among my personal affectations.

Could this be what Hans Bettelhine wanted?

It seemed insane. Were he in the market for more empty-headed concubines, he had plenty of obliging choices on this planet, with or without artificial inducement.

And why would the Porrinyards ever have abandoned me to this?

I returned to the bedroom, where my first stop was the wardrobe. I hoped against hope to find my satchel or one of my black suits in there. No such luck: there were sequined things I might have been expected to wear to a formal dinner, patterned blouses and skirts more suitable for everyday wear, and even some pullovers and trousers I could imagine walking around in, but there was nothing that communicated my preferred cold, iron armor of authority. The shoes included everything from slippers to vertiginous high heels. I left the wardrobe behind, considered a straight escape through what appeared to be the front door, decided that it was probably guarded, then focused on the scarlet mountains on the horizon and ran out to the balcony, in the vain hope that I'd find sense out there when there was none available in here.

The balcony was large enough to contain its own garden, with speckled plants that flowered in spirals and a tiny water wheel that spun in perpetuity from the gentle influence of a crystal stream spouting from a channel in the wall above. There was enough space for a narrow path marked by tiled flagstones and leading to a hovering swing large enough for two. A wide-eyed, flexible animal of some kind, with snow-white fur and an expression of intense interest, watched me and then indicated acceptance with a languid collapse against one of the embroidered cushions.

There was also a sculpted stone table surrounded by a circular stone bench. The Khaajiir's staff stood propped against a salmon-colored planter sprouting an orgy of fronds. When I reached the waist-high wall at the end of the balcony and peered over, I winced at the sight of a drop that, between three stories of building and another great wall of rusty scrub-covered cliffside, must have totaled four hundred meters straight down. There was a sparkling lake down there, aglow with the light of the setting sun, and empty at the moment but for a single pleasure boat under sail. Many kilometers away, angular red mountains backlit by the light of a sun so close to disappearing over that horizon that I was able to stare at that distant swollen circle without feeling the need to blink.

A bird flew by. It was unlike any flying creature I'd ever seen, a scarlet flaming thing with a face like a dagger and a head crest that resembled a paper fan, reaching almost all the way back to its brilliant, blue-tipped tail. It performed a little swoop, blinking at me with clear intelligence before performing the avian equivalent of a shrug and spiraling with a defiant caw.

I was just beginning to consider ways to climb down when a familiar voice behind me said, "That's a dekarsi. It's an imported Tchi species, one of my favorites. Their intelligence is that of a human five-year-old."

I whirled.

It was Jelaine Bettelhine, dressed in riding pants, boots, and a tight leather vest over a checkered shirt. Her hair was tied back, and looked windblown. Her fair complexion had freckled from sun. She was shiny and smiling.

I punched her in the mouth.

I don't know whether she could have stopped me. Probably. My experience with my own linked pair had long ago established that the enhancement provides a superhuman reaction time. Neither Oscin nor Skye would have been caught off-guard by an attack like that. But Jelaine allowed my blow to strike home and knock her down. She lay on the floor, blinking at me, the pain doing nothing to dilute the damnable affection in her eyes. "Why did you do that, Andrea? Just to see if you still could?"

I rubbed my knuckles. "Something like that."

"I thought you needed the reassurance, which is why I let you get away with it. Don't worry. Your mind is still your own, and will remain your own. We wouldn't dream of dragging you this far, and putting you through so much, only to vandalize such a finely tuned instrument." She used her knuckles to wipe blood from her lips. "May I get up?"

I didn't say yes. "Where am I?"

Jelaine sat up, shaking her head in comical reaction to the force of my blow. "One of the smaller guest suites of my private estate in the northeastern region of Asgard. That's the prettier continent, the one restricted to Inner Family and support staff. We had you transferred here under high security once you were deemed well enough to travel."

"How long have I been here?"

"On Xana? About a week. Here? About three days. You're a fast healer. Oh, Andrea, I know you haven't had the best visit so far, but this is silly. May I please get up so we may speak face to face?"

Her sweet deference, a sharp contrast to the power she held over me, grated. I wanted to kick her. But I could think of no reason I should and a multitude of pressing reasons why I should not. So I nodded.

She stood, used a hand to pat down her hair, and gestured toward the stone table.

We sat down, facing each other across a frieze of winged serpents flying en masse over a landscape of snow-capped mountains. The stone of the bench felt cool through my sheer pajamas, in sensuous contrast to the pleasant warmth of the breeze. I don't like outdoor environments and I still felt energized by this one, in a manner I immediately attributed to an oxygen mix higher than the usual formula on places like New London. Leave it to the Bettelhines. They even gave themselves superior air.

She said, "I know this is difficult. A mind as sharp as yours must have trouble dealing with short-term memory loss. Please understand that the worst has passed, that we don't expect any further problems with retention, and that everything I now need to explain to you a second time has already been accepted and embraced by you in the recent past."

Just because I bought her explanations when not in my right mind—and I had only her word for that—was no guarantee that I'd feel the same way when capable of reason. "I refuse to believe that the Porrinyards abandoned me."

She reached out and touched the back of my hand. "They haven't. They stayed with you, or nearby, throughout the most difficult stages of your recovery. I was awed by their devotion."

"Then where are they now?"

"In orbit, staying aboard your personal transport, which is still docked at Layabout. I assured them that they could remain here as personal guests, and they said they didn't want to pressure you in any of the difficult decisions you're going to have to make. That was how they put it, at least. Nobody's keeping you from speaking to them, or even leaving with them if that's what you want."

This still felt wrong. Oscin and Skye were my partners. There were no difficult personal decisions I'd keep from them, or any they'd expect me to. I grabbed a lock of my luxurious new hair and said, "What about this? I have trouble accepting that it's one week's natural growth."

She grinned. "What about it? It's gorgeous."

"It's also disturbing. What gave you the right?"

Her smile never wavered. "You did. My father asked to see what you'd look like with shoulder-length hair, you said it was all right with you, so we applied some nanostimulants to your follicles and had one of our stylists sculpt the results. You can cut it short again, if you like. Though I'd consider that a genuine shame."

I was growing more and more frustrated by this private joke I was failing to get. "I'm not your father's doll to dress up. What is this? Is he infatuated with me or something?"

Jelaine winced. "Oh, *Juje*, no."

"Then what the hell difference would it make to him what my hair looked like? Whether it was long, short, braided, absent, purple, glowing like Colette's, or replaced with scales?"

The animal I'd spotted sleeping on the swing now leaped up on the table before her, inviting attention. Jelaine scratched the fuzzy head and made it purr. She said, "He just needed to see what you would look like with shoulder-length brown hair. Come on, Andrea. Think. I've already seen you astonish my father by anticipating the explanation for all this. I'm sure you can put it all together a second time if you try."

Now irritated beyond all measure by her teasing ways, I rolled my eyes and this time found myself focusing on the Khaajiir's staff, still propped up against the planter like any other design element in this fussy little garden.

Why was it here? Had I been using it before?

I remembered Skye's words: *"If I ever withhold anything from you it's either because, by my considered judgment, it's none of your business or nothing you need to know at the moment."*

She'd said that on the Royal Carriage, while giving me a tour of the Khaajiir's database. She'd indicated her intension to leave out issues unrelated to the current problem, issues that I might have to deal with later. It was the only way to keep me on track.

But her briefing had seemed pretty complete anyway. Hadn't it been?

She'd even allowed me to hold on to the staff myself, providing me direct access to the data she'd judged pertinent as she guided me through everything Oscin had found.

How could she have hidden anything from me then?

I thought back and realized.

No. She hadn't let me hold the staff throughout that briefing.

Near the end, she'd taken it away before sharing her findings.

She'd done it with such casual skill, such a lack of apology, that I hadn't seen anything suspicious.

But now I remembered that she'd taken the staff away while covering the only subject she claimed she hadn't learned everything about. Her answers on that subject had been fragmentary at best, containing no information relevant to me. When that subject proved irrelevant to the identity of the murderer aboard the Royal Carriage, I'd allowed her to put the issue aside.

What issue had she been talking about then?

What was so big it might have hurt my ability to resolve this crisis threatening all our lives?

I found myself thinking of other moments, all the way to the beginning of this whole sorry business.

The AIsource had said, *We hope you'll survive the shock.*

Jelaine had told me, "You *need* to stay."

She'd also said, "We have more in common that you can possibly know." Later on, when I'd figured out the true extent of the connection between her and Jason, I'd imagined that she was just talking about cylinking. But that was something she had in common with the Porrinyards, not with me.

She'd spoken to me with affection and looked at me with undisguised love.

They'd *both* looked at me with undisguised love.

The Bettelhines had made me not a personal guest, but honored guest.

And then there's what the Dip Corps had done to me, their pet war criminal.

Antrecz Pescziuwicz had seen it right away. *"The Dip Corps could have changed your name, maybe your hair color and a couple of other cosmetic things about you, given you a new ID file and a false history, and nobody but your bosses would have known that you were the same kid. Instead, they put you to work as Andrea Cort, child war criminal grown up, and willingly ate all the seven hundred flavors of crap they had to swallow because of the propaganda weapon they handed all the alien governments who want to paint humanity as a bunch of homicidal bastards who let their own get away with murder. Why would they put themselves through that? Why would they put you through that?"*

The AIsource had given me part of the answer. *Any conspiracies that have been around you since unformed childhood must have had less to do with manipulating you than using you as a tool to manipulate others.*

But who could I have been used to manipulate, when still a child?

Jelaine had said, *"A changed man can change his family, and what his family stands for. Even, I daresay, how the family sees its obligations toward its own."*

Too many other offhand comments to list, all now making a terrible kind of sense. I could think of a dozen more without even trying hard.

Among them, the AIsource assuring me that the tragedy on Bocai was the last thing any Bettelhine would have wanted.

Wethers, at the end, acting like he recognized me for the first time. Saying, *"I've . . . been stupid. Didn't see what was in front of me. Didn't see what I should have* known."

And them, finally: when I struck Colette in anger, when I searched for the limitations of her inability to say no, Skye had looked at me as if just then discovering who I was for the very first time. She already knew, from what she'd read in the Khaajiir's files. But how must it have felt for her, to see it demonstrated with such awful clarity?

I watched myself, as if from a distance, rising from the bench and approaching that planter, and as my right hand closed around the Khaajiir's staff and as I thought a woman's name.

The image that formed in my mind portrayed her the way she'd looked when she lived on Xana. She was a bright-eyed, wistful young woman with shoulder-length brown hair and the kind of face that makes light shine on any world where she chooses to walk.

I'd known her years later when she wore a different name and when that hair was cut short but still sleek enough to shine beneath the glow of a Bocaian sun.

Dejah had said, *"You'd be surprised how many outcast Bettelhines live in other systems under assumed names."*

Lillian Jane Bettelhine.

Younger sister of Hans.

Aunt of Jason, Jelaine, and Philip.

Exiled idealist.

Name changed to Veronica Cort.

Resident of a doomed experimental Utopian community on Bocai.

Participant in the auto-genocide that community inflicted upon itself.

Loving wife of the late Bernard Cort.

Loving mother to my late brother and sister.

Loving mother to—

I dropped the Khaajiir's staff and fell to my knees, crying a word I had not spoken in decades.

"Mommy . . . !"

20

BETTELHINE FAMILY BUSINESS

I'll skip over the hysterics of the next ten minutes. I was overwrought, wrapped in loss, mourning a family torn from me that I'd refused to remember with love for more years than I care to count. An idyll had been transformed in one horrid night of blood and madness to a hell of sterile incarceration and institutional rape, leaving me not just hard but also brittle, capable of shattering into pieces on those rare occasions when something scraped the scabs off my wounds.

The Porrinyards had been very good at dealing with me at such times. Now the shared persona of Jason-and-Jelaine proved the same, its Jelaine avatar embracing me, telling me that she knew what I'd been through, that it was all right, that I had a real home now if I wanted one. I'd be lying if I claimed that I didn't hug her back, or that many of the tears I shed in that ten minutes were grateful ones.

But I'm also Andrea Cort, and not blind.

Even as I howled, part of me was picking it apart.

Sometime ten or twenty minutes after it all came back to me, we had returned to the stone table and I was sitting opposite her again, my eyes burning but my mind working at full capacity again. The furry white thing that lived on the balcony had decided that I was its friend, or at least its pleasure slave, and was now curled up on my lap, vibrating with pleasure; my usual impulse would have been to kick it off but I stroked it anyway as I sipped the sweet juice Jelaine had gotten me. "And am I supposed to believe that this is just about family? And nothing else?"

She spread her hands. "It can be about as little or as much as you want it to be."

"Why didn't the Family ever reclaim me before?"

"Because that's never been the way things were done before. Because Bettelhines who leave the corporation or allow themselves to be exiled for cause have historically never been trusted again. Offspring born to exiles are sometimes repatriated, if they have a case, but they've never been allowed to become Inner Family in status again, even by marriage. The risks of subversion have always been deemed too great."

I took another sip of my juice. "So where does that leave me?"

"You? . . . were a special case. You were notorious. Your loving *Corps*"—she filled the word with special contempt—"knew who you were and did everything they could to enhance your notoriety, just so they could hold you over my father and grandfather's generations."

"That's all I was? A blackmail tool?"

"Somewhat short of a doomsday weapon. Our family's well used to being hated, and could have weathered the scandal had your identity ever been revealed. But threats to reveal your lineage could still sway certain issues of contention a few precious points toward Dip Corps advantage. And that grew even more of a factor once you embarked upon your diplomatic career and became an even more divisive figure among the other major powers. Overall it became easier, for the small number of Inner Family leaders of these past two generations who knew who you were, to let you be and just let smaller issues slide."

I was still sure I discerned an ulterior motive. "And that's why you're trying to get me back now? To neutralize my effectiveness as a political lever?"

"No, Andrea, that's the way my grandfather might have seen it. Or even my father, once upon a time. But you haven't been an effective political lever in some time. Most of the new generation coming up now still has no idea who you are. Philip, for one, didn't know who you were until we were all back on Xana and Jason took him aside to tell him. I wish you could have seen the expression on his face."

"Don't tell me you're just being sentimental."

"If you think that's not a factor, you're wrong. Aunt Lillian was exiled before either of the singles Jason and Jelaine were born, but I have researched her case and believe it a miscarriage of family justice. There was never any need to deprive her of her birthright. Or, by extension, yours."

Damn it, she seemed sincere. And I could not afford tears again. "But that's not all of it. That can't be all of it. I'm not that important."

"You are, actually, but you're right. That's not all of it. I suppose that to understand it all you need to start with Jason's experiences on Deriflys."

"What happened?"

The pain of Jason's early life now showed on his sister's beautiful face, not as an experience she'd heard about at a remove, but as one she could now remember herself, with a pain capable of burning her. "I've already given you an idea how bad it was there. Now multiply your worst perception of that world's brutality by a factor of ten. Jason lived like an animal. There were times he had to sell himself, times he had to kill or be killed, times he was no better than a slave, and times he had to give up every shred of his dignity just to avoid starving. When the AIsource pulled him out of there—"

I sat up a little straighter. "The AIsource?"

"Yes," she said, with defiant calm. "They sent a force into Deriflys to pull out somebody else they wanted, a brave, special girl named Harille. They had important plans for her, but Harille wouldn't go with them unless they also rescued the boy who had loved her and protected her and kept her alive even when it might have made more sense for both of them to just lie down and die." Jelaine's eyes turned wistful. "It's amazing how much love a boy like the single Jason can feel when he's lost everything and only his ability to feel concern for another person is left, or how much a girl like Harille, who never quite loved him back, can still appreciate all he's done for her. She gave them no choice."

I asked, "What happened to her?"

"The last time Jason saw her, aboard the AIsource vessel that pulled them off Deriflys, she was dying. And that, Counselor, is the real reason he was so shattered when he came back to Xana. Harille had kept him sane, and now he couldn't even know whether she'd survived."

"And this is why the singlet Jelaine went away with him?"

"Yes. Everybody was told it was a goodwill tour. But in truth none of the other worlds the singles Jason and Jelaine visited during the tour mattered at all. It was all about finding out whether Harille was alive or dead."

"Was she?"

"Neither. She wasn't exactly Harille anymore." There was another flash of sadness, mixed with something else I could not identify—Anger? Amusement? Awe? "Let's just say that she was beyond Jason's reach."

There was a moment of silence. "And all this—"

"All this," she finished for me, "left the singles Jason and Jelaine at loose ends about what to do next. Jason hadn't found closure. Jelaine had spent months listening to his stories and had begun to join him in rejecting the Bettelhine system. Both started focusing on Deriflys again, considering how many places like it suffer not because things fall apart but because the Bettelhine Family business provides them with the means to blow themselves apart. The singles realized that they could not return to Xana as happy little aristocrats content to continue profiting from the misery the Bettelhines always left behind.

"They also knew that there was no possibility of bringing about change, not with Jason considered unstable, Jelaine less major corporate force than family princess, and their conservative half brother Philip already being groomed for the top slot. But they couldn't walk away from Xana and accept exile either, not when the feelings of helplessness were likely to destroy Jason all over again. So they decided to take extreme action. They decided to tool themselves for a silent coup. And so they contacted the AIsource and applied for cylinking."

This brought up a point that had bothered me since the moment I'd first figured out what they were. "I learned when I hooked up with the Porrinyards that all linked pairs become AIsource agents."

"I could have too," she said, "but the agenda I proposed was so audacious that the AIsource were satisfied to just sit back and see how well I did. And as you know, I did very well. Jason returned a new man, mature and focused, ready for any lower corporate position the Family was still willing to provide him. Jelaine returned a more serious girl, eager to dedicate herself to upper management. There were no obvious signs of collusion between them. But in truth, the two supposed individuals were doing everything they could to regain my father's confidence so they could go to him with the plan and start working together again. That took even less time than I'd budgeted. Within a year my star was rising."

Flailing, aware that something was terribly wrong but unaware what it could be, I settled for strict chronological order. "How did the Khaajiir enter the picture?"

"Our researches led to him and one of his books about the peaceful transition of power following the K'cenhowten Reign of Terror. He wrote that changes radical enough to change the entire structure of a society could only be peaceful when the people responsible, in K'cenhowten's case the Khaajiirel, used the same tools tyrants use for mass repression as instruments of more limited and more subtle duress. He said that a sculptor's chisel, applied to the right place by the right hand, can create great artifacts of lasting beauty whereas a powerful bomb dropped from the air can only create useless rubble. He had some ideas how the Khaajiirel managed it—mostly by careful plotting and the long-term manipulation of a few key people—and he was therefore invaluable when it came to plotting the various subtle strategies we needed to bring about our peaceful alterations in the Bettelhine landscape. With our sponsorship, he became my father's number one advisor, and a key planner instrumental in making certain that the transfer of power remained peaceful."

I remained uneasy. The same reason I'd sensed before was still beyond my reach, but had magnified, like a tsunami growing in the last few seconds before it strikes shore. "I can't say much for his level of success."

More sadness. "Yes. I know it looks that way. But then I knew I was entering a very critical phase, the riskiest in fact. The Khaajiir had warned us to expect some resistance and I was surprised only by its timing and lethality. He'll be missed, both as an asset and as a friend. I'm hoping that you can help fill his shoes."

I refused to be sidetracked. "How did I come into it?"

"Well, as you know, the Khaajiir already had an interest in you. He had researched the backgrounds of every member of your doomed colony, suspected he knew who your mother really was, and was able to bring your predicament to my attention. Consultation with my father, who knew about you, confirmed that the Khaajiir was correct." She smiled and took another sip of her juice. "I was delighted, and not just because I admired Aunt Lillian and considered Family Exile one of the corrupt practices I hoped to abolish. Consider: You're brilliant. You're principled. You're already well accustomed to working with linked pairs. You have no strings. You only work for the Dip Corps because you have nowhere else to go, not because you have any reason to feel grateful for the shitty way they've treated you over the years. You'd be even more likely to turn your back on them if I let you know about their vested interest in making sure that you remain miserable and without options. All of this was obvious, before I asked the AIsource their own opinion of you and found out that you'd defected to them already. It's like a marriage made in heaven, Andrea. If returned to your family, to us, you'd be the best ally we could possibly have. And the great thing is, you've already *proved* that, with everything you did on the Royal Carriage!"

So that was why they'd been so delighted by my performance, when I demanded the right to pursue an investigation, and followed it all to the conclusion. It wasn't just pride in me, though, that had been part of it. It had also been, if only by accident, a job interview of sorts. I bristled. "I haven't said that I'm interested in joining your coup."

"You're right about that, and I admit, it's an awfully audacious assumption on my part." She dismissed it with a wave of her hand. "Pie in the sky. I think you'll want to if you give the matter sufficient consideration, given your disapproval of everything our family's stood for until now, and how much you know Mankind will benefit if we succeed. But your level of involvement in our agenda doesn't affect the other important decision you're being asked to make. As I've told you, acquiring a potentially valuable ally was only part of my motivation. Even if you want nothing whatsoever to do with my plans, something I recognized as a possibility from the very beginning, I'd be just as happy for you if you preferred to settle down here and claim everything else that being a Bettelhine can offer. Think about it. The income deposited in your personal account just because you've been our honored guest for a little more than a week is already several orders of magnitude greater than the total you could have expected in a lifetime of toiling for the Corps. If you stay, you can be my guest here or at Jason's until you're settled, or you may claim one of several vacant Inner Family Estates in any climate you prefer, staffed by as many retainers as you need. Once you're comfortable you can use the power and wealth and influence that is yours by inheritance to pursue any philantropic goal near to your heart. You can travel anywhere you want to go, on- or offworld. And most importantly, you can explore all of these options among people who are practically begging for a chance to consider you family, and love you, rather than return to New London and go back to a Corps you've already betrayed and which is staffed by people with a vested interest in keeping you a target of mass hatred. Don't you see, Andrea? We're offering you happiness and freedom."

"Paid for," I said, "with misery and war and hate and mind control. Which are exactly what drove my mother away in the first place."

She was not deterred. "Jason too. And again, since those are all things I'm dedicated to changing about the way our family does business, you have all the more reason for wanting to stay and help if you can— Come on, Andrea. Ten years from now our family's business ethic will be unrecognizable, and our contribution to human civilization entirely beneficial. How can you walk away from that?"

I had no doubts now. I believed her. Them. I believed that Jason and Jelaine were sincere idealists, meaning well not only for me but also for this world the Family had built. I believed that they may have made some mistakes along the way, but they were also a legitimate hope for a better tomorrow. I also believed that if I stayed here as they proposed, I could have the life they offered, complete with their kinship, a gift that I now found I craved as much as I'd craved nothing else.

Against that I had Dejah's warning, my own nagging sensation that I'd missed something, and the mysterious retreat of the Porrinyards, who had against all prior habit abandoned me to make this decision alone.

Remember who you are.

I also thought of something a very wise man had once said to me, many years ago. *"The Devil never tempts you with a* bad *offer."*

Pushing the now-dozing creature from my lap, so I could lean close, I said, "I'm not ready to say yes or no. But one last question, for the moment. Back on the Royal Carriage, you kept refusing to explain any of this until I heard it from your father's lips. You just did a fine job telling me everything all by yourself. Why was it so important to wait?"

She gave a little half-smile as the creature ousted from my affections leaped up on the table in front of her to demand its tribute. Scratching it under the chin, she said, "My father always regretted what happened to his sister. When he sent the invitation he told us he wanted to tell you that face-to-face. He had the chance a few days ago, when we introduced him to you for the first time, the same conversation where he asked you if he could see you with long hair. I'm sorry you can't remember, but he wept. Just as much as he wept on that day when Jason came home from Deriflys."

Dammit, there went the tear ducts again.

She stood, eliciting a sad protest from the furry thing, and spent a moment watching as another dekarsi flitted past the balcony. The light of the sun, now just a blood-red sliver sinking beneath the mountains on the horizon, gave her face a warm glow, making me realize something that I should have seen the first time I laid eyes on her. Her profile looked like mine. "Meanwhile, everything else is going well. My people are dismantling the countermeasures put in place by Vernon Wethers. I've gained control of his projects and put them in the hands of somebody I trust. Monday Brown's on board. Jason's out with Philip, who we've left alone up until now but who needed to be brought into the loop now that he knows what I am. There's every sign of him seeing reason. The doctors say you're well enough to travel, which I hope means you'll agree to join Father, Philip, and me—'me' meaning both of my bodies, in this case—for a friendly family dinner at Main Estate. We have a lot to catch up on."

Before Jelaine left so I could shower I insisted on being shown to my satchel, which had been segregated in a separate closet as if out of fear that the grubby detritus of my pre-Bettelhine life might somehow contaminate the finery of my existence among the exalted.

I'd forgo the usual severe black suit and dress like the locals this one time, but I'd be damned if I was going to go anywhere without my spare Dip Corps insignia unless I was the one who decided that it was no longer a part of my life.

After the shower, which was steaming and luxurious and scented and wet and everything that the dry pulsed sonics I was used to at home were not, came the nightmare of picking out something to wear. I was accustomed to donning variations of the same black suit every day to remove the necessity of that choice from my daily life. But Jelaine had advised me that this would be off-putting on a family occasion, so I let her pick an appropriate outfit out of all the others that now belonged to me: a ridiculous, asymmetrical, but important-looking thing with flared shoulders, one bared arm and one padded wrist-length sleeve. I considered myself lucky that the same strategy hadn't been applied to the pants, which were so loose-fitting that they brushed my legs as I wanted, but at least covered both to an equal length. The entire getup had golden buttons that didn't fasten to anything and false pockets that didn't seem intended to carry anything. Don't get me started on the shoes. I've never understood why any woman would subject herself to the discomfort of elevated heels unless she was ashamed of her height or being tortured for state secrets, but Jelaine assured me that the pair she'd picked out for me went with everything else and I acquiesced out of sheer sensory overload.

The skimmer flight to Main Estate at about eight hundred kilometers away, a thirty-minute trip, was another issue. I've never liked heights or planets in general all that much, but Jelaine kept pointing out landmarks of interest along the way, from the snowy mountain range she identified as Xana's tallest and most treacherous to the verdant rain forest that took over as the land became a vast plain only twenty seconds of flight time away. She pointed out half a dozen smaller estates, some of them perched in improbable places that seemed unforgivably harsh choices for a family whose members got to decide what they saw when they looked out their windows every morning; there was, for instance, a desert about as topographically interesting as a bootprint occupied by some addled Bettelhine who insisted on subjecting himself and his fifty retainers to life in canvas tents. Still, I began to see what Jelaine meant when she said that I could claim an estate in any ecosystem I desired. I found myself wondering whether Xana had an orbital wheelworld or undersea facility, thinking that I'd take corridors and canned air if it could be all mine.

Two minutes from the end of the flight, over a region of green hills dotted here and there with white patches from a recent snowfall, we started seeing small groups of houses, which Jelaine identified as the homes of workers assigned to Main Estate but not senior enough to live on the grounds. She cut our speed and lowered our altitude to just above the treetop level as we drew closer, so she could point out more areas of interest: a hill taller than most that she identified as camouflaged servants' quarters, gardens, a personal zoo, and stables for horses of not only the terrestrial variety but, she said, several alien and engineered variants from the gigantic to the winged. I spotted one lumbering gray creature, with a nose like some kind of serpent, wandering around sans human supervision. We were well past it and within sight of the mansion itself before it occurred to me that I had just seen my first elephant.

Now, that's just showing off. And it was. That's exactly what it was. That's exactly what Jelaine was doing.

And it was working too. From time to time I found myself beaming. I even laughed once or twice at jokes she made. I think I may have made one of my own, though that was a genuine stretch and any laughter coming from her might have been politeness on her part.

It didn't matter.

What mattered was how I felt.

I belonged here.

I won't describe my first sight of the mansion itself, with its ten wings and its hundreds of windows and the two rows of towering spear-shaped trees providing a sort of arboreal honor guard for any visitor intent on approaching the colossal front doors on foot. It was a castle, pure and simple, and every brick in the entire edifice was a tribute to the magnificence of any who dwelled within. Nor will I describe the bowing and scraping of the dozens of servants who had come out to greet us—I actually do mean us, as their awe was directed not just at Jelaine but at me as well, the most discomfiting of the sensations this day had shown me yet—as we approached those doors and they drew open to reveal a marbled hall that disgorged three tiny figures I recognized as Hans, Philip, and Jason Bettelhine, all three grinning at us as if we'd been missing and presumed dead for years.

Hans strode forward, ahead of the two brothers, and bowed as he grasped my hand in both of his. "Andrea. This is a historic moment. Your first visit to the great house."

"A big house, anyway."

He chuckled at that. "I was warned about your brutal honesty. I must confess that I've been looking forward to seeing it in action."

Philip rubbed his jaw. "It's an acquired taste, Father— Hello, Andrea. I suppose I may call you that now, and not Counselor?"

I wasn't sure at the moment whether anybody would call me Counselor ever again. "That's . . ." What was it? All right? I might have been weakening from the assault of Jelaine Bettelhine's charm, but did that mean I had to like Philip as well? "That's fine."

Hans Bettelhine took the moment's hesitation as reticence. "I know how overwhelming this has been, Andrea. And I understand that you would have mixed feelings about your lineage, given your vocal sentiments about our family's history. I can only assure you that I intend to make this a brand-new day, and that I'll live to hear you tell me that you don't regret walking through this door with an open mind." He offered his arm. "Will you sit next to me? I look forward to telling you everything I remember about your mother's youth."

Surprising myself, I took him up on it. "All right."

And that's how it would have gone, for the rest of the night. In another few minutes I would have been taken to a luxurious dining room and treated to the best meal the best chefs on Xana could provide. I would have been told again how important I was and how loved I could be and all the opportunities that life as a Bettelhine could provide. I would have been tempted and I would have surrendered.

It would have been easy.

Juje help me. I *wanted* it.

But as the two of us, Hans Bettelhine and his prodigal niece, walked arm-in-arm through the door, following the laughing figures of Jason and his no-longer estranged brother, Philip . . . as we entered the vast entrance hall with its chandelier larger than some entire apartment blocks I've lived in and its tapestries so huge that the historical land-scapes depicted there may have been larger than life-size . . . as the two rows of uniformed servants positioned along both sides of the wall prevented us, their masters, from ever walking more than five paces without assurance that they would always be available to see to our every need . . .

. . . as we walked past all that, heading toward another pair of opulent doors, which a pair of white-gloved servants were already opening to reveal a formal dining room with a roaring fireplace at the distant end . . .

. . . as Hans Bettelhine asked me solicitous questions about my recovery and I said I was fine and Jelaine, walking right behind us, emitted a saucy laugh about what a bad patient I'd been . . .

. . . I found myself thinking with more clarity than I'd felt since my last moments on the Royal Carriage.

The AIsource's warning and Dejah Shapiro's warning and the last message of the Porrinyards combined with my own continuing certainty that my welcome back into the bosom of my family was too easy, too convenient, too not-what-should-have-happened when Jason and Jelaine asked their father to bring a relative of my controversial reputation back into the fold.

Maybe if he'd been another man, ruling another family.

But not a family with a history of exiling its own. Not this family. Not unless.

And then I didn't have time for *unless* because even as my thoughts sped up, time itself slowed down to compensate. I saw Philip, who was with Jason, about to pass through the dining room doors just five paces ahead of us, suddenly turn to his right and look not at his brother but over his brother's head, the filial smile on his handsome face replaced by a look half resolve and half resignation.

I might have missed it any other time. But I caught it then.

And I saw what he was looking at, the one steward who had stepped out of line and was approaching on a course and speed designed to intercept Jason Bettelhine.

The steward wore the impassive, emotionless expression of any servant trained to subsume his own personality beneath a façade of yes sirs and no sirs. And he was making eye contact with Philip and giving him the nod of a man who had just received confirmation that the time was now.

He reached behind that ridiculous red sash and pulled out a black disk of a kind I'd already seen twice before.

I drew back and elbowed Hans in the side, shouting, "Watch out!"

The old man doubled over with a moan of pain and betrayal, releasing my arm and freeing me to launch myself at Jason's back.

Jason, who must have seen my sudden move through Jelaine's eyes, whirled just in time to register his father's impact with the floor. He didn't see the white-suited servant extending the Claw of God toward his back, not immediately, but Jelaine's perspective helped him with that too. An instant before the weapon would have made contact he doubled over, spun, and drove a fist into the servant's ribs. The would-be assassin stumbled back a step and against the wall, an ally that prevented him from falling over. He swung again with the Claw of God, driven by panic and reflex to treat it as a slashing weapon instead of one that only needed to make contact. Jason backed away from the swing only to trip over Philip's outstretched leg and go down, hard.

I would have helped Jason, but instinct told me that if there was an assassin targeting Jason there had to be one targeting Jelaine and likely one going after me as well. So I whirled in time to catch a tableau that included a battalion of servants rushing to help us from all sides and Jelaine screaming at them to stay away. Their help would be worse than useless if that mass rush to help their employers hid the charge of further assassins, who planned to take advantage of the chaos to plant Claws of their own.

That's when another of the servants took me down.

It was a very professional tackle, taking me in the midsection and lifting me all the way off my feet before driving me to my back several paces away. I thought I was dead before I looked into the desperate eyes of the young man trying to pin me and saw at once that this was no assassin, just a servant who had seen me elbow Hans Bettelhine and decided that I had to be part of whatever was happening.

I used a well-placed knee to commend him for his dedication and rolled away, getting up only when I thought I was free of the Bettelhine Family's well-meaning defenders. A quick overview of the chaos around me revealed the assassin who had gone over Jason now on top of him and trying to press the Claw of God against his chest.

Philip seized the assassin's wrist again and added his own strength to the fight.

I might have been awed by this show of filial devotion had my angle not permitted me the observation that he was doing more to drive the Claw toward his brother's chest than assist his brother in keeping it away.

Another servant who either saw what was happening or believed it his duty to keep the eldest Bettelhine out of danger grabbed Philip by both arms and hurled him away, an act that threw off the assassin's balance as well and lent the embattled Jason a few added seconds of life.

I whirled again and saw a quartet of guards trying to drag Jelaine away from the struggle. Another servant, producing yet another Claw of God advanced on her while she was pinned. She spun his head around with a high kick to the underside of the jaw. I think it might have killed him, but I didn't have the time to tell for sure because that's when I caught a flash of movement at the corner of my eye and knew it meant that this time I was next for real.

I swept the air around me with a kick not quite as elegant as Jelaine's, connecting with nothing but driving my own assassin back a step and giving me a chance to face her. She was a snub-nosed, chubby-cheeked, frizzy-haired creature with freckled skin and no expression at all. She drew back her own Claw of God and charged, hoping that sheer determination would manage what stealth had failed to do.

By the time she was finished with her jab I was alongside it, grabbing her by both wrist and neck and using her momentum against her. It was the same move I'd used during the previous attack on me up at Layabout, except that the assassin I'd faced then had been bare-handed and harmless and the assassin whose charge I had now redirected was wielding a deadly weapon that preceded both of us as I drove us forward.

Philip Bettelhine turned toward us just in time to see the Claw of God headed right toward him and screamed like a little girl.

I might have let it strike him if not for that.

My time with the Porrinyards had mellowed me, after all.

So I let go of the off-balance assassin and let her fall down, using the heel of my shoe to shatter the hand bearing the Claw. I didn't let her scream bother me. Nor did I worry any more about Jelaine, who had wrested herself free of her would-be protectors, ordered them to back off, and retrieved the Claw of her own unmoving assailant.

Jason, his clothing torn and his nose bloodied, stood alive and well as servants dragged away the sole traitor who had gone after him. He saw me looking at him and gave me a grim nod of satisfaction. From somewhere not far away I heard the sound of pounding feet: security, arriving with their usual efficiency now that the war was over.

Jelaine called to me. "Andrea? Are you all right?"

"I'm fine!" I shouted.

I did not ask how she was, or how Jason was, because I already knew more than I'd wanted to know.

I'd figured out the missing element of the plan that had propelled Jason and Jelaine to power.

Hans Bettelhine remained on the ground where I'd dropped him, hugging himself, unable to muster the will he needed to realize that the crisis was over. It could have been because I'd hit him hard, or because he was an old man and the violence in his home had been a major shock for him. But then Jelaine drifted to his side and knelt before him, her beautiful features shining with the special kind of love that is only natural to find in a loyal daughter. I saw her start whispering to him.

Philip saw the emotions playing across my features, picked up on what I'd realized, and sensed the inner war I was fighting with myself over it. The despair that had stained his features for the last few seconds now turned nasty as he confronted me, his voice low and meant for me alone. "You honestly didn't know the worst of it until now, did you, Andrea?"

"No," I said, looking at Jason and Jelaine. "Not until just before the attack."

"That was my own poor judgment. I thought you were in on it, just like that sanctimonious holy man had been. At the very least I thought that somebody who hated the Family business as much as you claimed to would certainly approve once you found out."

I averted my eyes. "Shut up."

"Just in case you're wondering, it really was only Vernon Wethers up there. I was out of the loop. But then we all returned to Xana and the two freaks who *used to be* my brother and sister, who knew how much Vernon had succeeded in compromising them in my eyes, tried to *enlist* me. They actually thought I'd *approve* of what they've done, to advance as far as they have. They didn't realize that the very thought turned my stomach, that I'd see what they've done to Father as family mind-raping family. They didn't realize that I'd have to do something, no matter how half-assed and last-minute and desperate, to stop them."

"And the Claws of God?"

"My own clumsy attempt to make this look like some of Vernon's leftover machinations. I figured that doing it somewhere with plenty of witnesses would lead people to all the right conclusions. But I shouldn't have. I should have done the simple thing and ordered up a bomb. Or somebody to strangle my dear, traitorous brother and sister in their sleep. But no," he said, with palpable self-disgust. "I had to be *fancy*."

Just a few short meters away, Hans Bettelhine flashed the relief of any slave happy to be fed his instructions. He nodded at his loving daughter, the female half of the shared mind who commanded him and had steered his change of heart in so many things and, with her assistance, rose to continue giving his enthusiastic blessing to their plans for the Family business. I knew, just looking at him, that he would have agreed to anything they suggested, that their opinions would now always be his.

It was the only way Jason and Jelaine could have made their coup work. No wonder they'd had such success. They'd followed the Khaajiir's thesis and, by co-opting Dina Pearlman or one of the other techs working for her, seized the one mind capable of helping them to enact the changes they wanted.

I didn't know how they'd done it, what risks they'd taken getting their father alone.

I couldn't argue with the results. The Bettelhine Family was changing course.

But was it worth the price?

Another whispered suggestion from Jelaine, and Hans Bettelhine gave me a wave. He started toward me, the prodigal niece whose quick thinking had removed him from the line of fire.

Philip had only a few seconds left, but he got it all in. "I'll get Internal Exile. The useful part of my life's over. But what about you, Andrea? How far are you willing to go? If you stay here will it be because you think the ends justify the means, or because all those overwrought principles of yours can be bought with a little money and power?"

Now Jason was approaching, too, his expression wary as he focused on me and on Philip in turn.

The voice of the AIsource rumbled in my head. *The choice is yours, Counselor.*

For me it was as if every atom in the universe had ceased moving, leaving me the sole animate object in a tableau of statues.

This is it?

This is it. This is the moment that determines the future we talked about. This is the moment that decides whether a race lives or dies, and whether humanity will have to pay a price for its genocide.

But you haven't given me anything!

We have given you as much as the Rules of Engagement permit. We have provided you with two clear alter-

native futures: one where you remain on Xana and throw your considerable talents behind what Jason and Jelaine are doing, and one where you remain apart and independent and free to act elsewhere even if that means opposing them. In one future, your active participation helps to speed their new vision of the Bettelhine Corporation; in the other, they struggle on without your counsel and need additional time to consolidate power. In one future billions die, a major sentient race meets extinction, and humanity pays a devastating price. In the other, billions die, but the targeted race survives, hope is preserved and, though Mankind suffers, a better future awaits after the last shots are fired. One of these alternatives benefits us, the other our enemies. One will provide us the release we crave and thus free the organic intelligences of our interference; the other will deny us our ending. You will have reason to suspect, within a very few months, whether you made the correct decision. You will be at the center of those events. But first you must determine that future with the choice you make now.

Th-that's crazy! How the fuck am I supposed to know, with both sides whispering in my ears?

You don't. You're not clairvoyant. We can only advise that in this particular case the choice that gives humanity a fighting chance is the same as the choice that's right for you.

And how am I supposed to know that?

It's the only guideline you'll have. Good luck, Counselor.

Silence.

I wanted to scream at them. Had there ever been a moment when I could have torn their hidden hardware apart with my bare hands, that was it. I hated them as much as I'd ever hated anything, and I'm a goddamned talented hater.

But the universe was moving again, and I was running out of time.

So I put aside all my anger at my secret masters and considered how much the redirection of the Bettelhine business would benefit humanity.

I considered the mind control being used to arrange it.

I considered all the arguments about the ends justifying the means.

I considered times I'd bought those arguments and times when I'd considered them bullshit.

I considered everything I could have if I tossed my lot in with Jason and Jelaine.

I considered what it would cost me.

I considered the Dip Corps betraying me every single moment of my life since childhood. I thought about an existence I'd spent with a billion knives at my back and the alternative, life in a warm, generous place among people who were willing to love me.

I thought about the first stirrings of reciprocal love I'd begun to feel for Jason and Jelaine, the instinctive affection I'd wanted to feel for the gray-haired old monster once I knew that he'd been brother to my mother.

I thought about the fact that he hadn't done a damn thing for my mother when he still had his own will working for him.

I thought about being handed everything I could ever want and on top of that having the excuse that I'd be building a future not just for myself but for everybody the new Bettelhine Corporation would help.

I thought about my mission for the AIsource, my promise to find a way to kill them, a quixotic assignment likely far beyond the reach of any human being. I thought about the crimes their rogue intelligences, the Unseen Demons, had committed and thought about how I might never be able to bring them to justice, either; how even if I managed the impossible after ten years or twenty or thirty or at any point before I died, it would neither bring back my family nor lessen the guilt I felt for my own participation in the massacre on Bocai.

I thought about the Porrinyards, still sitting up there in my personal transport, waiting for me to make my decision, and yes, I loved them as much as they loved me, but was it right for them to make me choose between staying with my family or staying with them? If I went to them and said that I'd decided to stay here, could I persuade them to remain with me if I argued for the cause of Jason-and-Jelaine? Would they want to help? Or would they see how much of the decision to stay would have been predicated on the easier path, the one of home and comfort and family? What if I told them that somebody had to keep an eye on Jason and Jelaine from now on, to make sure that the moral compromises the pair had made so far didn't lead to more and someday might devolve into a system as destructive as the one they were trying to change?

Jason, Jelaine, and their father were almost upon me now. But their smiles were now faltering, as they saw how much I was struggling.

It would be so easy to stay.

But what had the Porrinyards said?

After everything, it all came down to this.

Remember who you are.

EPILOGUE

I'd refused to endure another elevator ride, so Jason and Jelaine had one of the family retainers fly me back up to Layabout.

I made it to my personal transport, still waiting for me at the VIP facilities, less than two hours after my brief return to and stormy departure from Jelaine Bettelhine's estate.

The Porrinyards were sitting together at the control panel, looking more lost than I'd ever seen them. They didn't notice my entrance until I tossed my satchel on the floor behind them. Given the changes in my appearance and my uncharacteristic clothing it took them all of half a second to recognize me before they leaped up and embraced me with the shared fervor of lovers who had not known whether they'd ever be seeing me again.

"I'm sorry," they wept.

I held them tight. "It's all right. I understand."

They had figured out the whole thing, up to and including the nature of the hold Jason and Jelaine had on Hans, when we were still on the Royal Carriage and they were reviewing the files in the Khaajiir's staff. The truth had repelled them, even more than the prior history of the Bettelhines had already repelled them.

"But this was your family," they continued, the tears drying on their cheeks, their shared misery too much for the small space between them. "You'd already lost it twice: once before you were born, and then again on Bocai. Given everything I knew, I couldn't remain with you if you decided to return to them, but I couldn't make myself take them away from you a third time. I had to let you decide what was yours . . . and what wasn't."

I'd misinterpreted their attitude on the carriage. Their shared horror at my treatment of Colette Wilson had been less about my anger and revulsion at the moment (bad as that had been), than what I could become.

Ever since determining that I'd recover from my injuries and giving me the freedom I needed to make my decision, they'd been sitting here, unable to return to New London and unable to return to me, waiting for word, resting all their faith in my ability to make the choice they hoped I'd make, and wondering whether they'd made a terrible mistake.

I'd be wondering the same thing, for different reasons, a great deal in the days to come. There'd be sleepless nights and hopeless days. But right now I had no doubts whatsoever. I *knew*.

"I'll want the first available departure window."

In all the universe, there's no sun brighter than the special kind of smile only found on loved ones who think they may have lost you forever, and now find out they're wrong. I was lucky enough to get it from two faces at once.

It was another couple of minutes before Skye could separate herself from me long enough to go prepare the bluegel crypts, and Oscin could return to his seat and start calling up our nav program.

When I sat down next to him, feeling more at home in that tiny space than at any point in the few hours that I'd experienced the bonds of family, he gave me another appraising look and said, "Nice outfit. Nice hair."

I punched his shoulder. "Shut up."